NATIONAL RAVES
FOR THE SENSATIONAL NEW
POLITICAL THRILLER BY
WASHINGTON'S TOP REPORTER

"What Ian Fleming did for secret agents . . . Les Whitten has done for journalists in *Conflict of Interest* . . . the book is a delight to read."
—*Washington Post*

"I loved it. It has come-alive characters and the swift pace of a Washington rumor."
—Dan Rather, CBS News, author of *The Palace Guard*

"This is a dramatic insider's story that contains more truth than fiction. It's dynamite."
—Senator J. Abourezk, Dem., South Dakota

"A RAUNCHY, RACY NOVEL WITH A REALISTIC RING."
—Clark Mollenhoff, Pulitzer Prize-winning reporter

"More enthralling, more exciting and racier than Watergate."
—Arthur Hailey, author of *The Moneychangers*

WHO IS LES WHITTEN?

Les Whitten joined Jack Anderson in 1969 and now shares the by-line of the Washington Merry-Go-Round, the most widely syndicated news column in the world, appearing in nearly 1,000 newspapers in the U.S. and abroad. Les came up with scoops on Billie Sol Estes, the Nuclear Test Ban Treaty, the Kennedy assassination, Bobby Baker, congressional scandals (one of which helped convict a congressman for kickbacks), stories on the intelligence community, the Mafia, consumer frauds, and maltreatment of minorities, primarily the Indians. As a result of Whitten's investigations of Indian affairs, he was arrested in 1973 by the FBI and charged with a felony count that carried a ten-year jail sentence; the Justice Department finally dropped the case. Because Les refused to reveal his sources while under pressure from the FBI and the Justice Department, he received the American Civil Liberty Union's Edgerton Award, December 1974. This is his fourth novel.

Les Whitten

CONFLICT
OF
INTEREST

*This low-priced Bantam Book
has been completely reset in a type face
designed for easy reading, and was printed
from new plates. It contains the complete
text of the original hard-cover edition.*
NOT ONE WORD HAS BEEN OMITTED.

CONFLICT OF INTEREST
*A Bantam Book / published by arrangement with
Doubleday & Company, Inc.*

PRINTING HISTORY
Doubleday edition published in June 1976
1st printing . . . . January 1976
2nd printing . . . . . April 1976
Bantam edition / August 1977

ISBN 0-553-10360-1

Published simultaneously in the United States and Canada

PRINTED IN THE UNITED STATES OF AMERICA

TO LINNORA

Contents

Ragpicker . . .

Often by the red glow of some forlorn street light,
Flame guttering and thick globe rattled by windy night,
In the labyrinthine heart of this foul, old *quartier*
Where mankind pustulates in stormy, close decay,

One sees a ragpicker who comes with bobbling head,
Knocking it like a poet against a fence. Instead
Of heeding gendarmes' spies, who follow him like ants,
He feels his heart burst with mad pipedreams of romance.

He preaches sermons and dictates Augustan laws,
Flings down the wicked strong, upholds the paupers' cause.
Beneath skies draped like canopies over earth,
He waxes drunken on the splendors of his worth.

Such men are rubbed raw by their families' hostile tears,
Men cracked by overwork, tormented by their years,
Crushed and bent down beneath the curds of vile debris
Which Paris vomits in gutwash variety.

These ragmen come perfumed like dirty tuns of wine,
Followed by stumbling pals, blanched by life's firing line,
Mustaches hanging down like flags from ancient days.
Triumphal arches, bright war pennants, and bouquets

Give to their staggered ranks a stately, mystic tinge!
Out of this deafening and luminescent binge
Of bugles, cheers, and drums, the hot sun straight above,
They translate glory to the people, drunk on love! . . .

—*Charles Baudelaire*
(lhw translation)

CONFLICT OF INTEREST

1

The Speaker's Wife

To one whose eyes were flawed in dark, large rooms, the Speaker's wife appeared at a distance an unstylish, soft little woman. She seemed one of those appendages of the mighty who would have been fine for a politician in Fresno or Duluth or even Minneapolis. But, unlike her mate, for whom, after all, it was so much easier, she did not look the sort who would ever adjust to Washington.

She stood, talking to some other legislators' or lobbyists' wives, the drink in her hand not often resorted to, munching a canapé that her hips did not need. That was how she first struck me.

The reception was given by the milk producers, once the center of such scandal in our city that you would think a Speaker of the House and his wife would never again be their guests. But in our compromised capital, all things can be forgiven except for certain overt types of disloyalty and persistent rudeness.

I was at the reception because I had recently written a minor exposé on imported cheeses that had been discovered, in part, to be homogenized Swiss garbage. The milk producers' public relations man had invited me, and since I was not asked to very many swank affairs, I had come.

Predatory, I stared at Speaker Pommery Edwards' wife. There were prettier women at the reception, and

1

many of them would have been far more available. She, I doubted, was available to anyone but her once-brilliant sot of a husband.

Yet in her there resided knowledge of things I wanted to know. That latent, untapped information was for me a special aphrodisiac.

Why should I not be drawn to someone like the Speaker's wife who carried within her stories I could not even imagine? In her fathoms, perhaps, were revelations about her husband's betrayal of a public trust, or a bit of gossip about some other notable that I could use as a tip for chasing down facts about the self-important, the self-righteous.

Now that my wife was dead, and—why lie—before, too, I had courted women, with an eye toward those who could tell me things. I was no reportorial Don Juan. None fell on her back, warbling state secrets. But if there were a chance, I would pick one who, over drinks, or at a good restaurant far enough away from town so we would not be recognized, might make some newsworthy disclosure. Sometimes, it was in bed. They were minor lodes for news, but they were pleasurable ones.

The Washington *Eagle* willingly (not really wanting to know about it) picked up all such expense account charges, even when they did not result in a story.

And I scrupulously—all of us have certain codes—never charged off a meal, a motel room, or (as miscellaneous supplies) a pack of Trojans unless it was in quest of news. For an abortion once, years ago, I had even paid a third out of my own pocket as private punishment for my unprofessional carelessness. I had billed the other two thirds to the *Eagle* as air fare.

That fertile source had been an FBI secretary in a job so sensitive that her handbag was searched each day as she left work. In my meetings with her, I sharpened and exploited her decent outrage over the bureau's passivity toward the corrupt senior Senator from her own state.

Finally, she had smuggled out, *in utero* beside the

then unsuspected fertilized egg, my minicamera loaded with films she had taken of the Senator's FBI files. The *Eagle* won a Page One Guild Award for the exposure of the Senator's grafting. The Senator did not run again.

The secretary, who had, in fact, hated the FBI more than she liked me anyway, was suspected by the FBI of the leak. But she refused on civil liberties grounds to take a lie detector test, was transferred to the Department of Commerce, and was now a GS 10, a substantial job.

Although I was at the reception as a guest, not a reporter, I could never really forget my job for long. Reporting has an obsessive quality to it for many of us. I fetched a Galliano and soda—how could a hotel with such overrated restaurants have such fine canapés and so many choices of liquor at a reception?—and watched Mrs. Edwards for a moment.

The secrets she must know were like musk for me, an aura. I thought of her: a walking week of front page stories. Though short, she had well-calved legs over thin ankles. Her handsome hips were belted in at the waist. Beneath the chaste throat of her scalloped print dress I saw a dark shadow of cleavage. I popped on my horn-rimmed glasses. Her features focused clearer. What would she be? Forty? Forty-five? I walked to where she stood beside a taller, but deferential, companion, the wife of an ex-Congressman named Rennet.

"Mrs. Edwards?" I introduced myself, with a small, courteous bow. "I'm Aubrey Warder from the *Eagle*." Before she could answer I pronounced an excuse for my intrusion. "Has our good Speaker had any more to say about not running again?" He had grumbled about it a week before, but no one had taken him seriously. The perfect question, I congratulated myself: apt, slightly ingratiating, wide open to answers, and putting her a bit on the defensive.

I kept my eyes on hers. Wary, wary they were, hidden as you'd expect in a woman married to a man like Pom Edwards, who was betraying her with his Danish legislative aide. But it wasn't a bitter face, rather a pretty, optimistic one, still with the bloom of some Kansas farm town in it. Her eyes were green, and the age—I saw now it was going to be in the early forties— only really showed in the wrinkles at their corners.

She smiled, to give herself a little time, her thin mouth bowing on top of small good teeth. Then she bought some more time by introducing the other woman.

"You put me on the spot either way, Mr. Warder, don't you?" she said agreeably. "If I tell you, 'He didn't mean it,' you write a story that says 'Edwards to Run Again,' and if I say he did mean it, you write 'Edwards Still Ponders Stepping Down.'" Then, some of the wariness went out of the eyes and she gave a snort of humor. "Why don't you leave questions like that to the political reporters anyway?"

I was flattered she knew my byline well enough to know my speciality, if you can describe it as that, and was surprised at her quick mockery.

"In an election year, the paper calls in even the second string to write politics," I said. The taller woman, Mrs. Rennet, giggled nervously. A year before, I had done a junket story on her lame-duck husband. I had suggested unsuccessfully to the desk that its headline read, "Rennet Junkets for Dessert."

"Well, you'd better ask the Speaker about that," Mrs. Edwards said, investing the title with the familiarity of a personal pronoun.

"The Speaker would give me an equally evasive answer, only a little less diplomatically," I said lightly, glancing over at him. His long head poked up over the broad backs and shaped hair of the special pleaders.

"They never leave him alone, do they?" I risked.

"No," she said. "They don't." Then she closed up.

"They never get anything out of him, though," I said. Both of us knew it was a lie. Damnit, I thought, there's the real story: that the man second in line for the presidency was a corrupt lush, unable to function if some emergency summoned him after seven or eight.

"No," she said, a bit coldly now. I was losing her. The hook, if it ever was in, was coming out. Move fast,

I thought. "Look, could I just ask you something very quickly?" I took her arm gently. It was rude as hell to lead her away from the Junket lady. But what did it cost me? She withdrew her arm carefully, but went with me a step or two.

"That's wretched manners," she said testily.

"The *Times* is working on a story about his drinking," I lied to her. "I could beat them to it and give him a break on it, a kinder slant. Will he talk to me, could you . . . ?"

She looked as if she were going to slap me, then gasped, "I don't even know you. How dare you ask a question like that?" It had broken through, but it had spooked her. She turned away, straight-backed, and marched into the protective crowd.

I was abashed, humiliated. I had pulled a shoddy trick, and it hadn't worked. I tried to mend my self-esteem. I told myself that if she were really so scrappy, why did she put up with the skinny bastard's guzzling and running around.

That didn't work either. I had blown the question, misjudged her, really, for I had hoped the shock would help me enlist her. Even by my standards, I had cheapened myself.

I drank the flat, sweet liquid, ate a deviled egg, and moved away from the table, my stomach churning with self-distaste.

The crowd around Edwards broke briefly as his lackey and administrative assistant, Georgie Hedaris, left with an empty glass in his hand to replenish it for the Speaker. Edwards drank Cutty Sark on the rocks, watered slightly. I glimpsed his still handsome equine face above the smaller men before he turned and they closed in around him again.

As casually as I could, I edged up to him. Already his speech was so slurred that he was hard to understand. The simplest introduction was more than he could manage. I looked at the slightly protuberant eyes, straining through the alcohol to see what the moving lips around him were saying. One more drink and he

would be all but dumb. By the time he reached his next
party he would be a stalagmite, voiceless, unable to
hear. Second behind the President!

The press corps did not write about his drinking (as
we did not write about sex unless it involved the "X"
factor of politics). Instead, we sickly and hypocritically
joked about him. He would make his first state visit
after inauguration to Scotland; he pissed on a windy
day and was arrested for dispensing alcohol without a
license; he was the Scotch-and-Watergate scandal.

Although he was six-three, his admirers humorously
called him the "Little Major." When a columnist had
written about his drinking once, the columnist's syndicate lost three papers in Edwards' home state, loyal
Kansas. Kansans did not want their myths tampered
with.

He had been one of those young World War II aces.
Now pushing sixty, he still had a casual swagger in his
manner and walk. During the day, he was able, even
ruthless, in his control of the House. From the press
gallery, I had seen him time and time again corral his
party to block a bill, or ease one through on a narrow
vote.

But on the issues themselves, the poisons eating at his
system had gotten to his will. Or did that romanticize
it? Perhaps even without the booze he would have
favored oil, the natural gas transmission companies, the
pharmaceuticals, the banks, the great buccaneer industries that were killing the small businessman. Yet,
sheeplike, the small entrepreneurs returned him to his
office biennium after biennium these two and a half
decades, even as he slit their throats.

Edwards was a Republican who moved with the
times in organizing the House, and the times were now
liberal. Some good liberals got strong committee ap-
pointments under him. And when his leadership was
threatened from within, he yielded enough to preserve
it. This gave him the shape, if not the substance, of a
friend of the poor on medical aid, minimum wages, and
education, and of a conservationist and even judicial
reformer.

It was widely assumed that he was no personal thief, being rich enough not to have to steal for himself. When Edwards made shady concessions to the rich, it was purportedly only for his district, his state, and his party, in about that order.

He was powerful enough for his deals to be implicit. Others, before they granted favors, might have to exact at least a clear verbal agreement for a new plant or a campaign contribution. Those lesser Congressmen were caught and indicted when the prosecutorial screws were put on the businessman-briber. Not Edwards. His deals were sealed with a smile or even less, by a sort of "Washington osmosis" as one columnist described it: a voiceless seepage of understandings.

As I stared at him, all my instincts told me, he *is* a crook. They *are* paying him off. The group around him was breaking up now. A Kansan transplanted to California, an oilman, was tapping him on the shoulder, smiling. The Speaker's balding head was bowed toward his smaller comrade. I smelled money, certain and unprovable as a silent fart. The stuporous Little Major was leaving, as always, with pint-sized Hedaris at his arm: George and Lenny.

Mrs. Edwards was drifting toward the two of them. She walked with grace for a short woman. Those calves had come from some long-ago volleyball court where she, too, had excelled. I had first seen her as almost dowdy. Now she, and the sting of my stupid behavior with her, corroded me, and I wanted her, not dangerously, but sufficiently.

Damnit, I mused. She would have such a neat little tutti. Such a finely boned and fleshed body. Surely, it longed to be pressed against a gut not awash with Cutty Sark, a mouth smelling of something besides stale whiskey working rot on duodenal tissues. Better my faulted body, I thought, and began to get an erection.

That night I ate in the Detroit Bar with a copy-desk man. We bitched about the copy boys. You couldn't shout "Boy!" at them because half of them were black and snotty and some were girls. When I needed one to run my copy to the desk, I said, "Hey." When I wanted one to get me some coffee, I said, "Hey, you, please." The copy-boy section of the Newspaper Guild had talked about making a grievance of my demands for coffee at my desk. But that chicken-shit case was dead. After all, I had been Guild Chairman at the *Eagle* twelve years before. And quitting the Guild entirely after we found out they were taking CIA money had more or less endeared me to most of our union membership. Besides, I went on paying my dues, contributing to strikers at other papers, and walking the picket line, albeit with my own antimanagement sign. Fuck the Guild, I thought.

"D'ja ever read *The Undefeated*," the copy-desk man, two martinis into his late supper, was asking me over the Formica table top. He had a literary bent and I didn't mind his getting, as I knew he was, into the let's-abuse-Warder stage of the conversation. It was a form of respect.

"Yeah, you're going to tell me I remind you of the matador," I sneered. If I were going to be compared to a literary hero, it would naturally be to some failed Hemingway wreck like that bullfighter, only played by a graying Van Heflin or Spencer Tracy—in their late forties. I knew that. The trend among investigative reporters was young "with-its" like Woodward and Bernstein. I resented them in my bad moments. I knew I was a sort of dinosaur.

"Why don't you compare me to Our Lady of the Flowers?" I said to the copy-desk man. "Show a little class."

He laughed and drank his martini.

"Whatcha up to?" he asked.

The Speaker had stuck in my mind. I thought of his wife moving toward him. Hedaris and she were his tugboats, bumping his ocean liner body toward the port of his next party.

"Somebody ought to rip up the Speaker," I said.

"On the hootch? On the Swedish chick?"

"She's Danish. No, on the hootch. Or on the fact that it's rotting him out as the leader of the House, when the House needs all the leadership it can get. Also, you

know, in these big powwows on the Middle East and
war and et cetera, he's supposed to be down there at the
White House representing the people, the House. The
country could get creamed because of his boozing.
That's an exaggeration, a slight one."

"He won't change. Why do it?"

"Aw, come on. He's second in line for the presidency
and we sit around on our hands, pretending it's not
news that his boozing leaves a Goddamn scary gap like
that."

"You want to fuck his wife," stated the copy-desk
man. I always wondered how desk people, so different
from reporters, really, got so perceptive. They're like
private eyes.

"Not just her," I dodged.

"You're a disgrace, Warder," he smiled.

"I don't screw my way into many stories; I do my
time in the files," I said, surprised at my defensiveness.
I tried to recover. "Look, you remember when women
like Vivian Maccabeas . . ." I started to defame a
woman reporter who had gotten stories on her back
during the Kennedy days. But why? She was older now
and a fine reporter. "I'm a product of sexually liberated
times," I said.

But the copy man had made his point.

"Okay, somebody ought to do the Speaker," he said,
satisfied now that he had surmised my thoughts. "He's
an old friend of Mr. March." Everybody's an old friend
of our publisher, I thought. "Besides," the copy-desk
man was going on, "Edwards is a viperous bastard.
Everybody knows that. You fool around with him and
he'll find a way of doing you in. Sic the FBI on you,
or get your tax forms leaked out, or undermine you
with March. Look what he did to—"

"Yeah," I said. Decades as a manipulator of people,
as a dispenser of favors had given the Speaker that kind
of power. He had all those sober daylight hours to do
in his enemies with the skill of a Florentine. I tried to
think what he could get me for. What the hell. "I think
I'll ask," I said.

"It's good to see that the celebrated investigator still

asks." We were back in the old Front Page tough-guy shit.

"Be honored that the celebrated investigator still eats with you cityside turkeys in this trash bin instead of frequenting the Cantina or Sans Souci with his national staff colleagues."

The truth was, as both of us knew, that my colleagues on the national staff—the prestigious side of the paper —by and large wished me ill. I had pissed all over their cozy sources at the State Department, the Capitol, the White House, and the Pentagon. Every time I wrote a story about how one of these people in high places had dipped in the till or otherwise screwed the country, my colleagues on the national side lost an easy source.

Fuck 'em, I thought, a little lonesomely. Mr. March liked to think of such intrahate as "creative tension." What he and his various editor-henchmen meant was that it kept the rest of us sufficiently marinated in our acute mutual dislike so that we did not turn on him and the senior editors.

"Pirsfell is going," the copy man was saying. That would be the new assistant national editor. Mr. March went through low-level editors like Catherine the Great went through lovers. Come to think of it, that was the way he went through mistresses, too.

"Maybe we can blame the fire-bomb threat on Pirsfell," I said. The copy man permitted himself a bark of glum laughter. We had been getting a rash of arson threats on the paper, and death threats on Mr. March, and neither I nor the police had come up with any suspects.

Around the bar, the nightside reporters were bundling up to cross the cold street and go back to work. I looked around guardedly, wondering if any of the young girl reporters I had made it with—or, to be altogether accurate, tried to make it with—were working tonight. But there was none.

Mr. March's daughter, Connie, a skinny, quick little feature writer, came in with the black urban affairs reporter she was living with. Mr. March wanted the girl to learn the paper from the ground up. She was doing so. She'd been on night police at headquarters for a few months and had gotten mixed up with a married detective. Now she was doing night feature stories. I nodded to the black, an overpaid Harvard type, and said, "Hello, Connie," to the girl.

She said, "Hello, Aubrey" back with a precociously direct look. She knows what I want, I thought, but somebody else is going to get it tonight.

I went home in a cab. My driving had been suspended for the second time, for ignoring a red light, and I dared not use my car this time until our police reporter could angle my license back. My errant thoughts relaxed. Why not see if I could get the desk—Cubbins, the managing editor in this case—to let me do a take-out on Edwards' boozing? It was bitter winter and a little slack. Oh yes, I knew part of it was meanness on my part: to exorcise the humiliation I felt from my botching up what could have been a promising talk with Mrs. Edwards. But it was a legitimate story, despite that. Edwards' drinking was a national hazard. If the *Eagle*, with its hair shirt about tough stories, didn't do them, nobody would. Besides, I rationalized, it might shame him into leaving the stuff alone. And, as I investigated, I might even catch him on the take, something really big that would blow him out of the water. It was a reasonable idea.

The next morning, I went into the managing editor's office, bypassing the bullshit chain of command he was trying to set up.

"Did you talk with Speedy?" he asked, referring to his assistant, the national editor. They were like a bunch of Paraguayan generals with their titles and ranks.

"No," I said. I could see him wanting to say, "Why not?" But we had disliked each other too long to fight over niggling things.

"Why pick on Edwards now?"

"His drinking hurts his work. He's a peril. We should have done it two years ago, when he became Speaker. You know that."

"How hurts his work?"

"At a party last night. He was there an hour and they damned near had to splash him out. Suppose we get a missile crisis, or another Israeli-Arab thing between 7 P.M. and morning? He'd have to be funneled into the Situation Room. Besides, he's overdue for a general look-over."

"Mr. March likes him."

"I know. How big a problem is that?"

"Some. Means you have to make a very good case, a very specific case, a big issue. Maybe several big issues. And you can't harass him. Don't get Mr. March calling me up and saying, 'Who told Warder to harass the Speaker?' "

Fair enough except about the harassment. I could tell he was warming up to the story. So long as it did not get his ass in too big a jam. In other words, he was willing to take a bit of heat on it.

"As I go along, do you want me to let you know what I'm up to?" He would know I was being conciliatory. Of course I mustn't go too far with any editor. Before Chaim Leyte, a very fine reporter, became editor of the editorial page, he had once said, "All editors are idiots. There are no exceptions."

"Do you mind?" Cubbins said. He had good antennae and my words had put him on guard. "What have you got in mind that I ought to know? Red wig? Voice modulator? Bugs?" I grudged him a chuckle.

"Nothing special. I'll just try to get to parties where he is. Maybe find his friendly local neighborhood bar and liquor store. Talk to his political enemies . . ."

"He doesn't have any." That was almost true.

"Maybe he's got a disgruntled employee somewhere."

"Maybe."

"That sort of thing."

"None of your usual bullshit, okay?"

The managing editor was a prude.

"What do you mean, bullshit?"

"You know what I mean: Mrs. Edwards."

"Oh," I said.

"Goddamnit, I mean it."

"Oh, for Christsakes," I said and got up to go.

"Ticker okay?"

Three years ago, on one of those endless political hops with the last President, there had been a heavy clutching in my chest. Back home I had gone to a doctor. It was a heart infarction that had kept me away from work for three months, and left me, forty-five then, thinking of myself as older than I was or felt.

"Yeah, I hope." Cubbins and I had been good friends a long, long time ago when we were both young reporters on the *Eagle*. But we had gone different ways.

The *Eagle*'s morgue was the envy of the East Coast. I had a librarian pull Edwards' clips and microfilms going back to the first ones, twenty-five years ago.

Into the ugly, air-cooled projector, I slipped the strips of microfilm that had replaced some of the old, finger-worn clips. To get a copy, you pushed a button. Such technology in a newspaper made me feel old and a little useless. But I dug in. There was plenty of useful stuff in the forty packets of clips and microfilm. They followed him, relentlessly, if kindly, up the House seniority ladder.

Most of the political stuff was unneeded, since I was making what we call "black book," the sum of bad things I could find out about Edwards from the public record. It is the week-long *sine qua non* of every major investigation. And I would have to make twice the case on the Little Major that I would ordinarily make, things being what they were with Mr. March.

Only rarely did I find any personal stuff in his file. A traffic accident eight years ago. I'd get the Accident Investigation Unit form on it to see whether it showed drinking, assuming the form had not been deep-sixed.

Lately in his elections, he had run almost uncontested. But the contributions had been ample, according to one wire-service piece. The biggest money, $1,000s and $1,500s, came from Oil and the farm lobbies. But that wasn't unusual. To buy even a cheap New York assemblyman cost ten or fifteen thousand. And Big Oil

could afford to give $1,500s to even its harshest ene-
mies, just to keep the machinery greased, as it were.

I put aside for duplication a few stories about his
races. People who get beaten in politics have long
memories. I would want to talk with them.

Here was a snippet from Pearson about an argument
fifteen years ago in the Metropolitan Club with feisty
old Maurice Chlorstand, the right-wing lawyer. Maurice
was eighty now. But he also never forgot.

There was not a word on hootch. Not one. And yet,
he'd been an alcoholic for five, ten years. We all knew
it. While he was a ranking member of Ways and Means,
and then minority whip, and for the last two years
Speaker. But out there, they didn't know. Didn't "they"
have a right to know this? Why didn't we write it?

The material on Edwards' wife was lumped into *his*
file, amusing when you thought about how strong our
paper was on women's rights. Here, in its bowels, was
the newspaper's real view of women.

The former Betty Page Rawlinson of Bailey River,
Kansas, had married Edwards twenty-two years ago
when she was twenty-two. That would make her forty-
four. She had gone to Smith—how about that?—and
come home to teach English. The Little Major was
fourteen years older. He met her when she was a campaign worker on his first try at the House, so one clip
said. I looked at her young face in the society page
wedding picture. Soft hair falling down around the
cheeks, a modified Veronica Lake. The lineaments were
still all there.

She had been the good Congressional wife. Among
other items, there were shorts on speeches to women's
clubs, and a line on her as organizer of a "Wives for
Boys Abroad" breakfast during the late 1950s.

My first surprise in his file was a review of a book. It
was poetry, translated by her, *Pantoums and Rondeaus*.

"Better stick to chain letters on behalf of her husband,
and let French chain verse translations be forged by
more skilled Smithies," it said. Jesus, I thought, what

a smart-ass review. Some lousy French teacher, probably. The poor woman.

There were other items about the family. His oldest son had been busted for pot. (I put that aside for Xeroxing.) I probably would not use it, but things like that came in handy for bargaining with both the paper and the target. If the libel question came up, you could always claim that there was much you could have written but didn't. It was a good defense.

There were pictures of Edwards, his wife, and the two sons when he was named head of some parliamentary delegation. The accompanying feature had the frilly Bodoni inserts of that *Eagle* era and mentioned her translations, saying they'd been well-received. By whom? I wondered. By friends at Christmas?

The Edwardses had gone around the world with a Secretary of Commerce, attended a trade fair in Teheran as the Shah's guest, inaugurated a Kansas Korn Kween, gone to parties, parties, parties. Her face peered from behind his back at rallies, officiated above cups at a Congressional Coffee, bloomed over microphones at women's clubs.

As the clips and microfilms got fresher, her face grew older, fuller, but it retained a peppy look, something of that milk-fed air, upbeat, American. Here was no trace of the intellectuality that must, in some pain and love, have produced her translations.

I looked up "Pantoum": a Malaysian verse form adapted by the French. Her poems made her sexy by surprise, like finding that an available woman in a second-rate bar was a Ph.D.

After I finished the clips, I first tried the easy way to do a backgrounder, knowing that like a ten-to-one shot at the races it wasn't likely to win but would pay a bundle if it did.

I called up Brent Melz, an old contact at the Washington Field Office of the FBI. The bureau has a marvelous computer system that they don't talk much about. You punch a couple of buttons and get a printout on almost anybody important. It is the ultimate dossier.

Unfortunately, clerks keep tabs of which FBI agent does the punching. So when I reached my FBI source on the phone, talked him into going to a pay phone and then put it to him, he was not enthusiastic.

"You know they keep a record of who asks for printouts, Aubrey," he said. "What the hell would I be punching up the Speaker for?"

I'd already thought of that. "It's simple, Brent. Say you're checking out a third-rate assassination threat on him or a bombing threat on his office. You know damned well you run the file for past enemies on threat cases. Come on, Goddamnit."

"There hasn't been any threat."

I paused a moment. Some things were dangerous: deep, sinister waters that I had risked from time to time, but hated to. If you got caught it could wash you out as a reporter, even bring an indictment, like stealing government documents and some other occupational hazards. Contriving an assassination threat was just such a thing.

"Suppose there was. When you punched him up could I get the printout, the whole printout?" I could feel him thinking: about the lead I'd given him on a cop kidnaping three years ago; about the civil rights case at this city's jail where he'd come out a big liberal at a time when the FBI needed a liberal hero; about the Soviet embassy press attaché I'd helped him finger as a KGB agent. I had a lot of blue chips with him.

"How soon after you got the printout would your story be coming out?"

"A month? I could wait a month. Or else I wouldn't use the printout stuff for a month and do my other stuff earlier."

"Aubrey," he complained, "that's itchy. Can't you get it from somebody else?"

"No," I said, "not this."

"Let me think, okay?"

"Think hard, Brent," I said. "I'll call you Wednesday night."

Meanwhile, I would have to ponder faking that bomb

threat against the Speaker. In the final analysis, I didn't
think I would. I wanted the story, but I did not want
a criminal charge. Maybe Brent would think of another
way.

I left the clips and microfilms that needed duplicating
with the copy boy.

Outside, away from the warmth, the cold bit at me.
I longed for spring, yet did not, for it meant that time
would have passed. Except for that, it would be nice to
dream of the old Chez François on a hot day, and a
bottle of Gewürztraminer on the terrace with Connie
March, or with Mrs. Edwards, or with some other
woman. But, even with the slush freezing on the curb-
stones, it was good, as it always was, to be out on a
single worthy story, removed from the everyday
drudgery.

I took a cab to the Library of Congress. The Capitol
dome, as we approached it, glinted dully in the heatless
sunlight.

At the Library, I put in a request for Betty Page
Rawlinson's book, while I looked for Edwards' name
in the guides to periodical literature and the index cards.
Our morgue had reciprocity with the Library, but it
was faster to do it myself, and besides I liked it. Files
were the quiet places where no one, no editors, no telephones, could get to me, sanctuaries like the cool
closets where I had hidden as a child.

The Library had everything from a piece he'd written (more likely had someone write for him) on international taxes, to a *Good Housekeeping* article by
sundry Congressional wives called, "Congress Is What
It Eats." Of the dozen recipes in it, one, for Kansas
Korn Pie, was contributed by Betty Page Rawlinson
Edwards.

I skipped both articles, but read a *Playboy* interview
with him, a story on their family in *Parade*, an ambi-
tious *Redbook* piece called "Congress's 50 Best-looking
Wives"; and, in *Town and Country*, "The House Is
Not Their Home," about the residences of powerful
Congressmen.

This miscellany included a few new facts: The Little Major had been an all-county high school first baseman (batting .358); he had once opposed federal laws against county options on prohibition; his most embarrassing moment was when he addressed New York's fulminic baritone feminist Cosima Anstecht as "the esteemed *Gentleman* from New York." On Betty Page, the files showed that she liked Chopin and Scriabin; had once miscarried; got the "Madame Policewoman of the Year" award after Edwards rushed through a federal subsidy for cop salaries.

When her translations came down from the stacks, I leafed through them, feeling a little guilty, as if I were improperly touching her in some way.

What the hell was she doing up here, I wondered as I read—fixing her face in the Congressional Wives' Smile for twenty years while she had stuff like this inside her.

Now has that season come, when shuddering as they blow,
The roses seem as censers filled for evening prayer
Whose perfumes and soft sounds turn in the dusky air
Like melancholy waltzers in languorous vertigo.

The roses seem as censers filled for evening prayer.
Violins shiver now like troubled souls in woe,
Or melancholy waltzers in languorous vertigo.
The sky is perfect, sad—an altar made of air.

"Altar made of air?" With Edwards? What was there of her in the intricate rhymes? Of him? The poem might not have much depth to it, but it was a hell of a lot better than I could ever do.

Next day, I started in on Edwards at the court complex. Small Claims Court: a couple of eight-year-old debt suits, both dismissed. He must have paid up. Criminal misdemeanor and criminal felony: both negative except for the kid's pot bust. I took the cops' names off the son's court paper (the case had been dismissed) for checking later with police records.

D.C. tax lien: negative. Ditto, Federal tax lien.

Domestic Relations: nothing. Traffic: negative. The accident would be over in police files, not here. It had undoubtedly been washed out before it got to court. Lunacy proceedings: fat chance, still negative. Wills: negative, must be filed somewhere in Kansas, if he had one. Federal civil equity: two cases filed against Congress naming him as a defendant. I looked them up. One was a civil liberties case, ex officio thing; the other was a nut case by some guy wanting to decaffeinate Coca-Cola. Neither touched him personally.

I ate alone in the court cafeteria, then went shivering across the sheet-iced patio, following the gritty sanded path to police headquarters where I had begun for the *Eagle* so many years ago. Most of my old sources, old friends, were gone now, retired. The chief had been a corporal when I left. Now he was leaving, too. I felt old, still beating my soles on the cold pavement around headquarters. Most of the guys I'd come up with in the newspaper business were editors or publishers going to fancy conventions. Or they were making big money in public relations or advertising. One was an ITT vice-president.

I avoided the police pressroom. There was no use alerting that incestuous little shop that I was at headquarters.

In police records, I found Willy Pascado, a lieutenant now. I had known him while I was still on cityside; I could ask him a favor every now and then.

"No talk on it. Okay, Willy?" I prefaced.

"Who is it, Aubrey?" he asked cautiously.

"Three people." I saw in his eyes he wanted money for it. But that way lay disaster. They'd locked up a reporter in New Jersey years ago for much less. I'd rather blast it out of the chief than pay, I thought. "For old times, Willy. I need it bad."

"Give me the names," he said, irritated.

When I gave him the names, he read them, and shook his head, saying "Fuck" loud enough so I could see he wasn't going to do this for me again for a long time, at least not for free.

He gave me the write-up sheet on the kid's marijuana bust, entries on two moving violation tickets Betty Page had gotten and three moving tickets, one with bodily injury, against the Little Major.

Both her moving tickets were for speeding and had been honestly paid. All three of his had been quashed without charges. Seems they had a different code on paying moving violation tickets. There was also a batch of parking tickets, about half were paid, the rest *nollied*.

"They all do it," Willy said, talking about the fixed tickets.

"Yeah, I know. Where's the accident report on the bodily injury?" It could be the only real police evidence of his drinking.

"They've moved the files on those down to the accident unit, except the DWDs and revocations and the Negs"—negligent homicides. "All the chicken-shit stuff is down there now."

"Okay," I said. "Look, Willy, if I paid you on this it could fry us both; you know what I mean. It's not smart anymore, that kind of stuff." He smiled with no warmth.

"Yeah. But I'm off the street now. And I'm hungry." I shrugged.

"There's worse things than getting hungry," I said.

As I feared it would be, the accident report was out of the file. Neither of the cops listed on the ticket itself was still with the accident unit. One was retired in Florida, the guy at the desk told me. The other had gone to Montgomery County, in Maryland, a Washington suburb. Unless I could find one of them and he had kept his records, or unless I could find the name of the victim or his lawyer, the Little Major was safe on that one.

I went downstairs to Motor Vehicles and ran off a copy of both his and her license applications. Then I checked out their cars. He got free use of one through the House. It was owned by Cadillac Leasing Corporation. I wondered what the House paid Cadillac for that? One dollar? One thousand dollars? He owned a Mercury Marquis. No lien. She drove a new little Olds. No lien. They weren't hurting for money.

The older kid had a Mustang convertible with a big lien, financed by Ford. That meant about 20 per cent by the time all the extras were added on. In other words, the parents were making him finance it himself. I imagined the family argument over whether the kid would buy a used Chevy II or the Mustang. Edwards would have said, "Okay, Goddamnit, buy it yourself. Finance it yourself if you're so Goddamned bullheaded." So the kid did. Well, that said something for all of them.

Out again in the steely sunlight, I walked up to the Recorder of Deed's office. God, how many times had I made this circuit? And on how many people? My ears tingled with the sudden warmth as I entered.

No chattels, mechanics' liens, no small-fry loans. On his house, though, he had a big mortgage. The tax stamps showed he'd paid $125,000 for the house with $100,000 of it financed at only 5 per cent. Bam! Here was my first story. He'd gotten a 5 per cent loan five years ago when everybody else was paying eight. There it was, on paper.

The Washington Consolidated Bank was, in effect, giving him $3,000 a year. Looked at the true way, that 3 per cent was as much a gift as $3,000 in new hundred-dollar bills. Maybe not illegal, but a tawdry payoff. I ran off the lien and deed.

On the back of the Xerox, I wrote a reminder to check the officers of Consolidated to see whether they also contributed to his election campaign, to check his voting record on banking legislation, and to see whether other bankers kicked in to him.

Dumb bastard, I thought, so secure in his power he doesn't even worry about filing a lien record like this.

So now I had the Little Major's ass in a small crack already, FBI help or no FBI help. I began to whistle. No matter what, I had some kind of a story. Mustn't tell the paper, or they'd want me to settle for this.

Slogging from office to office, I checked the corporation records for names of the directors and officers of

Consolidated during the last seven years. On Capitol Hill, I ran his voting record on the banking bills of the last decade. I checked the House data for his employees during the last seven years. Then I ran off copies of the contribution records. On the House records request form, where they make you sign your name, I faked it slightly by dropping my last name so they wouldn't know the *Eagle* was looking into Edwards. The fink who ran the office always informed the member when a paper checked out his records.

Back at the office, bone-tired now, but warm, I ran through the two lists of names, the contributors and the bank people, checking them out in Who's Who and our own morgue, and against each other. Through its directors, the bank had been kicking in to his campaign for years, even when he faced only token opposition.

I ran the contribution lists for Oil and hit a few of the same contributors I'd seen in the clips and some new ones. But it was still nickel-and-dime money.

On the odd chance, I called up the octogenarian right-winger, Chlorstand, who remembered the fracas at the Metropolitan Club.

"Oh, I buried that thing years ago," he said cautiously, but his garrulity got the better of him. "God, man, I haven't worried about Pom Edwards for years. Still eating at that liberal trough," he went on sarcastically.

"Contributions from—?" I asked.

"Now, Goddamnit, how would I know?" he interrupted me irascibly. "Not from me. Used to be . . ." he paused a moment, aware that nowadays his sharp old mind sometimes lost control over his sharp old tongue. Then, he must have thought, what-the-hell, I'm old enough to be forgiven anything, as years ago he had thought, what-the-hell, I'm powerful enough to be forgiven anything, and said:

"He made a lot of money in real estate once. He knows the field a little. But I think he sold it out, years ago. And Oil . . . God, the oil companies used to force-feed him booze and money and Christ knows what, but that's all rumor."

I jumped at the Oil thing.

"Anything definite on Oil?"

"No," said the old man. "No, I can't think there ever was. The old Taft people might know, maybe." But then he paused. "Except they're all dead now. Taft's policymakers are still around, a few of them, but his bagmen, the ones that would know . . ." He coughed at the joke he was about to make and cleared his throat. "Good bagmen die young," he said.

I turned back to my sweetheart loan story. The Little Major might someday come to think that his most embarrassing moment was when he failed to arrange that 5 per cent loan through a third party.

Using such a "straw" was the next best thing to anonymity. It would have looked like a personal loan, at worst. Or it could have been arranged so it wasn't filed at all.

I looked at Edwards' outside holdings to see whether he voted his interests and whether there might be some clue to an Oil payoff. He owned nice chunks of Bethlehem Steel, Union Carbide, and Union Pacific, but there was no sign of the big oil companies. There were also some little firms: Tidewater Land and Guaranty, Boles-Panjunk Corp., Pacific-Century Industries. I didn't know who they were, but he was getting handsome dividends from some of them.

For safety, I'd check out their boards of directors to see whether any of his pals showed up there, and then see at Securities and Exchange whether he held any major options. That was a long shot: even Edwards would be cautious enough to put stock options in some lawyer's name.

I packed up the papers in a manila portfolio and caught a taxi home.

I laid out all the papers on the bed, and jumped in.

"This is your life, Speaker Edwards," I said to myself. I leafed through the House disbursement records. There might be employees who didn't work for him in Washington, but were paid by the taxpayers to do political work for him in Kansas.

The name of the Danish girl, Laura Axelsen, "legislative assistant," popped out. She made a handsome $27,500 a year. If he laid her once a week, that was about $530 a screw. Enough to dress well on. But that was unfair. She was a smart, efficient staffer by all accounts.

It was eleven-thirty before I had finished going through the papers. I paper-clipped the data into appropriate sheaves—personal life, banks, financial interests, non-bank contributions, political history, crime stuff, miscl.

Where would I clip Mrs. Edwards' poetry? I looked at the thin hardbound book. Powder-blue cover, a handsome, tasteful job, by Van Nostrand, conglomerated away into Litton or some place years ago.

I held the book in my hands, and it opened to the poem I had been reading. I finished it:

Violins shiver now like troubled souls in woe.
Here is a heart which dreads the void's vast, empty lair.
The sky is perfect, sad—an altar made of air.
The sun drowns in its blood as darkness slays its glow.

Here is a heart which dreads the void's vast, empty lair.
But gathers in the past, that luminous long ago.
The sun drowns in its blood as darkness slays its glow.
Like monstrances of light are memories we share.

Could she have been thinking about Edwards? No, of course not. Even though it was a translation of Baudelaire's sentiments, not hers, she had put the passion into the English. I stacked up my papers neatly and put the book of poems on top of them. With the light off, my thoughts turned and turned on the Little Major. I was a spider and slowly I was webbing him in. And her. Baudelaire? Scriabin? Well, really, who was Mrs. Edwards all these years she'd been sharing a life with the Speaker, with his drinking, with the fact of his girl friends?

Ah, I was tired. How tired I got now. I thought of that soft little woman and the fading corn-fed face. What funny dreams did she build in her head? Where had he been when she miscarried? Why did his kid get himself busted with a stupid stash of marijuana? What was she like? As I slipped off, I loosened the half hitch on my own dreams. At forty-eight, I was a most excellent reporting machine.

2

The Speaker's Bar

Week's end. The reporting machine had virtually finished its black book. Besides much more of the same
trivia about the Edwardses, I had picked up a few good
facts. Brent at the FBI had turned me down, but the
old accident record had been available after all. It had
taken our regular police reporter to get it. I hated to
think what promises he had made to the cops. In the
space "drinking," the cop had written in "unknown"
even though there was no box for that remark, and
there was one for "none." That "unknown" meant that
Edwards *had* been drinking; it was a well-known way
for a cop to cover his ass when he had busted a big
shot full of hootch. But there it stopped. In Montgomery
County, I found the cop who had signed the report, and
he had conveniently forgotten everything. The other
policeman on the report who had retired to Florida had
died in Palatka earlier this year.

The *Eagle*'s House man, a prodigy of a reporter who
had somehow burned out early, but still out-reported
most, had made it a point to approach casually a friend
of the Speaker's. The friend had let drop the magic
words:

"Look, of course I'm glad you guys aren't writing
anything about it. Shows your responsibility. But
damnit, I worry about Pom. He's even hitting it in his
friendly neighborhood bar, you know."

Our man had only nodded sagely. To ask "Which neighborhood bar?" would have raised the alarm.

I had checked the sign-out sheets in the House and found that the Speaker and his Scandinavian mistress had both left at about 10:30 P.M. on Friday. The sign-outs were on different sheets, which meant they had left by different exits from the Capitol complex. That also meant that the Little Major was getting it in his office or a hideaway in the Capitol itself, not a motel.

I imagined that bony giraffe, full of Cutty Sark, huffing and puffing on his sofa into that creamy Nordic flesh, then going home like a drunk turning himself in at a clinic. Poor Betty Page Rawlinson Edwards.

Saturday morning I lay in the tub, luxurious in the steam, in the fact of my good sleep and my paucity of systemic alcohol. I had a vision of the Speaker's wife at the other end of the tub, malleable, full of poetry, innovative. I pushed away the idea. Why build up a letch? That would only initiate the ritual preludes to a piece of tail: a phone call to some old casual lay; or lunch and an afternoon with a nonchalant office romance; an effort to make Connie March, if only as an exercise in cuckolding Black Harvard.

What solidly writable did I have on Edwards so far? The home deal wasn't a bad story. It would go something like this:

"Speaker of the House Pommery Edwards, who plays a key role in all bank legislation, got a low-interest home loan from a major bank at a time when most borrowers were paying 8 per cent or more.

"The $100,000 bank loan was made five years ago, when Edwards was on the powerful Ways and Means Committee, which handles all tax matters, including those relating to banks. The loan was in the form of a first mortgage on Edwards' $125,000 Wesley Heights home. It was granted by the Washington Consolidated Bank.

"In the last ten years, Edwards has voted with the position of the American Bankers' Association"—I'd have to get up a good tally on that—"per cent of the time. He has opposed the ABA position et cetera per cent of the time."

Then there'd be a horseshit paragraph from Edwards saying the low-cost loan had not affected his voting stance, and the bank's statement saying whatever they wanted to say about the propriety of the loan. Then on into the details.

It wasn't the drinking story yet, but it was a fine little story that had just been lying down there in the files waiting for old Aubrey to find it. I hummed to myself as I washed under my arms with the homemade soap one of my would-have-been conquests on the city-side staff had given me. I had confided to her my hatred of male deodorants and she had made the damned soap, using the creosote odor that had distinguished Lifebuoy in a nobler age.

It was her way of letting me know that it didn't matter I had popped off too soon and hadn't been able to get it up again.

I had flopped with so many that I had come to accept it. Only a shrink might discover why. In matters of screwing, I had put myself in the hands of the gods, or, rather, the goddesses.

The paper would pay me no overtime if I worked today. But, once on a story, I hated to let go. Out of the tub, into a soft button down and wool slacks, I called the managing editor and wheedled a car and copy-boy driver out of him.

"Is it that good?" Cubbins asked irritably.

"Yes."

"What'll it say?"

"He got a 5 per cent loan on his house, $100,000."

"Ah?"

"Five years ago when he was on Ways and Means."

"Little old, isn't it?" He was unconvincingly skeptical.

"The House has got some big banking stuff up now."

"Is he into that? You sure? What bank?"

"Washington Consolidated."

"Did they—?"

"Yes, the last two campaigns. I've found about $2,500 so far."

"You get his vote on bank roll calls?"

"Yes," I said.

"It's nice," he said. I began to like him a little. But he went on, "What'dya need the car for?"

"I want to go by his house. Get some description. Feel of the place."

"Why not a taxi?"

"Oh, for Christsakes."

"Suppose the copy boy tells the Guild you're working on your day off. We're not going to pay you for today, you know."

"Goddamnit, Cubbins." He finally had gotten to me. "Don't be such a fucking suck. Shove your overtime up March's ass if you can get your nose far enough out of the way. . . ." He had gotten the reaction he wanted.

"Watch out for that heart," he said mildly.

"I hope when you get yours it kills you, you mother-fucker!"

The Edwards' house was one of those big places built on half-acre lots just before and after World War II. The trees were oak and cherry in front, with a now-bare rose garden on the side. Ivy ran up the brick in front, and the chimney. Inside would be the big step-down living room, and he would have a paneled study full of lawbooks and foreign mementos, with a deep leather chair or two and a liquor cabinet, full.

I'd interviewed enough of these guys, in office and out. I always wondered where their money came from. Sometimes that was why I was interviewing them. The classy ones asked me what I wanted to drink, and when I said brandy and soda, they didn't flinch. They poured out cognac and soda as if they did it every day. The very classy ones gave you ordinary brandy, not cognac. Edwards would flinch, when his time came, and putter around until he found some cognac and it would be Remy Martin and he would ask, "Is this okay?"

"I want to make another pass at it," I told the kid driving. "Take off the shades, okay?" When he looked curious, I added, "Sunglasses in winter make you look like a cop. Cops only come into this block when they're invited."

I took a page of notes about the brickwork, the colored glass in one of the second-floor rooms (hers?), the ivy, a black guy I saw chipping ice off the driveway, and, through the naked hedge, the small kidney-shaped pool in back, the tag numbers of the Olds and Merc to check against my notes at home. . . .

"You want to do me a favor?" I asked the kid as we drove away from the house. "Tonight, get this car again or your own car and park right there." I indicated a section of the street at the juncture of two of the big houses' property. "That way they'll both think you're at the other one, okay? Get me the number of all the cars that visit the Edwardses tonight. Okay? Don't do it if you don't want to. Okay? I mean nobody may ever show up."

He was delighted, a good kid.

"Sure. Where to now?"

I had a service station map of the area.

Wisconsin Avenue would be his nearest general shopping street, where she would shop, and, because it was on his way to work, it would also be where he would naturally go to drink or to buy booze instead of MacArthur or that big sterile stretch of Massachusetts west of Wisconsin.

"Up to Wisconsin Avenue," I said.

We drove up Cathedral to Wisconsin and then I had the choice of turning down toward Georgetown or back north.

"Which way?" the kid asked.

I thought a moment. Not Georgetown. That wasn't his style. That's where he would see the Georgetowny people: the columnists, and the richer reporters, the political lawyers. . . .

"Take a left," I said. "Slowly."

Between the Episcopal Cathedral and Tenley Circle there were five likely bars: Churchill's, the Friendship Tavern, the Zebra, Warren's Alery, West Winds.

As we drove, I also thought of pumping bartenders,

or liquor store clerks on how much he bought for home consumption, but that was tedious business and might alert the Little Major, given the loyalty of bartenders and merchants to their clients and their allergy to unknown reporters.

Finally, I grunted, irritated with myself. The easy solution to the Speaker's bar, or any problem, is always a thought away.

I had the kid stop at a pay phone. In the phone book, I found Blathe, the Reverend Dinan. He was a priest at the Episcopal Cathedral and an alcoholic. Once, long ago, I had lusted for his wife.

"Dinan," I said, my breath frosting, "it's Aubrey." We made some small talk about the last story I had done with him: He'd gotten me an interview with the Canon on the Canon's efforts to mediate in the Middle East. It was a good inside piece.

Then I got around to leveling with him about why I was calling and added, "If Edwards is a parishioner, don't tell me." I knew the Little Major was a Methodist.

"I hate to see you chop him up on hootch," he said.

"Yeah, you would. Any progress?"

"No," he said. "Esther had me try a shrink."

"You mean *you* finally got desperate enough to see a shrink. Don't chalk Esther."

"Okay," he said.

"Your innards were kicking up?"

"Yep. Still are."

"Wish I could help."

He laughed harshly.

"Me, too." He switched back to my question. "Warren's Alery," he said. "I've seen him in there a couple of times. Want me to meet you there some night?"

"No," I said, embarrassed by the sick breath of eagerness in his tone. "I worry about your fucking liver." I thought of him, I liked him, and never saw him.

I pictured myself at his funeral saying consoling words to Esther. It pepped me up slightly. Funny, I thought as we wound up the conversation: Dinan, my friend, and me thinking that about his wife and feeling better about things. I thought of telling him honestly, "The only thing good about your death, you marvelous Yeats-quoting man, is that I might get a piece of your wife."

"Come for supper soon?" he was saying.

"Yeah. I'd like it. If I can bring the wine."

"I'll have Esther call you," he said.

Warren's Alery was the usual Iceman Cometh-White Horse saloon, with booths on both sides of a long room. The long, stool-fenced bar interrupted the booths on one side. In the middle were tables that would be filled only on Saturday night. Its jukebox played moderately low. It was a dark, warm neighborhood bar for serious drinkers and talkers.

I spent the night miserably, slowly, drinking bourbon and soda. Galliano might have attracted attention. I used the soda to dilute the whiskey until it was almost tasteless before I ordered the next. It was lonely and, ultimately, useless.

The copy kid called me at home at seven the next morning, full of excitement.

"The Secret Service was there," he said. "With somebody."

"Hunh?" I said, wobbly, grabbing for a scratch pad.

"Aubrey, there were two cars, about seven guys in all. Maybe the President; somebody, anyway, went in. Was in there for two hours. Then they drove off."

"How do you know they were Secret Service? The plates?"

"I went down to headquarters after they left and looked them up in the registration book. . . . They were 'security' plates."

I started to curse him for doing that without calling me.

"You should have waited," I said. Then I was afraid I sounded harsh. "Look, you did great. But you could spook the thing that way. Could see who went in?"

"No," he said. "The porch light was off. When they

came out I followed them, but I didn't dare leave right after. They got away. So—"

"It might have been the Vice-President?"

"Yeah, maybe. They turned right on Wisconsin. I did see that."

"Security" on a plate could mean any of the investigative agencies: Secret Service, FBI, CIA, State Department Security, Narcotics, even some local cops.

"What kind of cars?"

"Two Pontiacs. Black."

That figured to be Secret Service or CIA, if I remembered right. And even the CIA director would have gone with only a couple of security men, and then in his limousine instead of a security car.

"It had to be Frieden," I said. "Or the Vice-President."

"It *felt* like Frieden," he said.

"Keep this to yourself, okay? Don't tell Cubbins unless he asks you outright. I mean don't lie, but don't volunteer, okay?"

"Okay, Aubrey," he said. I thought, If the kid shuts up they ought to make a reporter out of him. He had good instincts.

"Make notes and keep them someplace, okay?"

"Okay," he said, pleased with himself. "Thanks."

Well, motherfucker. So Harry Frieden, the President, the old master manipulator himself, had been meeting with the Speaker. And gone to Wesley Heights to see him, not calling in the Speaker to the White House. No wonder Edwards wasn't barhopping.

Goddamn, I thought, I wonder what they were talking about. If only I had it all on tape somehow. The Mighty in relaxation. Good story. I fantasized on the dialogue. Betty Page, serving drinks. And the Goddamn President, lusting after those volleyball legs.

Realistically, there was every reason for the President to talk with Edwards. And Frieden had at least a likable unstuffiness to him. He was the sort who, if he got it into his mind, would go for a spin. LBJ had been like that at first, and Kennedy sometimes. Even Nixon had done it, although there had always been that quality about him: the insecure second-rate Latin American dictator.

I'd get our White House guy to find out discreetly on Monday if it had been Harry. Ten to one it was.

I spent another night in the bar with Nabakov's *Ada*, but the print was small and the bar so dark it was tough going.

The next night, about nine, the Little Major came into Warren's Alery. A tall, slightly stooped man in a heavy tweed overcoat, he was as unobtrusive as a clerk.

He sat in a booth up near the bar, out of my line of sight. Still, I could count the drinks as the waitress brought them. After the first two, the bartender came over, stood by the booth, then, apparently at Edwards' bidding, sat down, talked with him for fifteen minutes.

I sort of wished I could join them. A man who was second in line of succession to the presidency couldn't be all bad if he drank with his bartender. The bartender left and another man, perhaps the owner, wearing a big apron, came out of the kitchen with a small pizza. He stood also for a moment beside the booth. Then, after he served the pizza, he sat with the Speaker. I went to the bathroom and glanced back. The two were laughing, the owner drinking a beer as they shared the pizza.

I felt shitty, sitting there gloomily jotting down the time that each fresh drink was served him. It was hard to believe—eleven, in two hours. At an ounce and a half a shot—they'd be bound to give the Speaker a full ounce and a half—that was about 17 ounces. If you figured the hootch at 86 proof, 43 per cent pure alcohol, that was .43 times 17 ounces. In other words he'd drunk better than seven ounces of pure alcohol.

But the exercise depressed me. Here was the seedy side of reporting. True, if I were going to write about how his drinking affected the nation, I had to nail down the squalid details of just what was meant by "drinking," down to the ounces per hour I had personally seen him putting down.

Why do it, though? Why not just write the bank story and be done with it? Let him drink himself to death in peace. And that would leave me in peace. No bullshit from Mr. March about writing a major story on his friend; no vengefulness in God-knows-what way from the crafty and powerful Speaker. I could go back to other scandals, other muck. There was plenty for everybody. Edwards lurched up from the booth.

He went first to the bathroom and then to say good night to the bartender. As he talked, I paid up and left ahead of him. Well, I thought, that's another line in the story:

"In one recent drinking bout at his neighborhood bar, Warren's Alery, the Speaker consumed eleven scotch and waters—scotches and water?—in the two hours between 9 and 11 P.M."

I left the bar. It would be better if I could follow him home. The lack of a license was pinching me. I would watch him get into his car, and then get a cab back to my own place. From across the side street, where I pretended to be looking for a cab, I saw the bar's door open.

The owner, still in his apron, was talking to the Speaker; I knew what he was saying, "You gonna be okay, aren't you, Mr. Speaker?" The Speaker nodded. The bar owner cast a glance over at me, then one at the Speaker as he walked fairly straight down the street to the parking lot.

I moved down the opposite side of the street, parallel to the Little Major. By now, the alcohol had hit him fully and he was staggering. Halfway down the block at the entrance to the lot, I saw him fumble in his jacket pocket for his keys. Finding them, he turned into the dark parking lot. The car's lights would be coming on in a moment, and I could go home out of the cold.

Suddenly, I saw dark shapes moving fast in the lot among the three or four parked cars. Muggers!

Oh, shit, I thought, my first instinct one of fear for

myself, for my unreliable heart. Don't mix in this. You're a reporter. Let it happen. Your job is to write about things. But I couldn't just do that.

Oh, fuck it! I thought.

I ran toward the lot, shouting, "Police! Police!" hoping that would convince the robbers that I was a cop or that they were on the way. I prayed I'd be heard up the street and that someone would rush down to save the situation—and me. God, I hoped the muggers didn't have guns.

Once inside the darkness, I could see a tangle of bodies on the ground, hear the hard breathing, the growl of ghetto voices saying, "You motherfucker," the Speaker's slurred shouts. Incapacitated by the booze, the Little Major was not putting up much of a fight.

I was trying to decide which one to take on, if any, when I felt a jolt of pain across my shoulder and fell heavily against the side of a car.

I had been bushwhacked by the look-out. I covered my head and took a second blow on my arms, as I turned on my attacker. He was a black boy, about fifteen and no higher than my shoulder. He swung a wooden baton—could it be a policeman's club—at me again. I took the blow on my arm, which jarred me with another shock of pain. I grabbed the stick.

Wiry as he was, my vestigial halfback's body had the heft on him. I wrenched at the stick, feeling his body come with it. As he drew toward me, cursing me in a high voice, he kicked at my shins. The hard shoe toe sent a streak of anguish up my leg.

With the adrenalin pumping, I kneed him as hard as I could in the balls, and felt his hands let go of the stick. He shrieked and doubled up and I swung the club at the back of his head. There was a satisfying crack as he splayed out onto the concrete.

I rushed over to the Speaker. Two blacks crouched over him. Edwards whimpered. He was on his stomach, his face in profile. Even in the semidark I could see blood covering his face.

One of the men held the Speaker's arm behind him,

a knee on his back. The other had Edwards' overcoat up and was fumbling in the pants pocket. He saw me and sprang back on his heels, his back against the Speaker's car, a knife glinting in his hand.

Shit, I thought, they're going to stab me. I swung the club wildly at the man with the knife. He dodged and I brought it down full on the other one, catching him on the shoulder.

The knife came at me again. This time, I caught him in the face with the club. Goddamnit, it felt marvelous. The Speaker's attacker jumped off and went for his own pocket. The Speaker rose groggily to his feet. He peered at the black on the ground and shambled around the car like a crippled old hermit crab. The son-of-a-bitch was trying to get away.

My breaths were coming in gasps. I tried to shout "Police!" again, but couldn't. The uninjured man had a gun half out of his pocket and was struggling to bring it out all the way. I hit him on the wrist this time, and the gun came out, skittered across the parking lot. The man howled in pain, then scrabbled after it.

The Little Major had somehow gotten the car started and was leaning on the horn. The lights came on blindingly. I rushed over and swung open the door. The bastard had passed out from the excitement and booze and was draped over the wheel. I clumsily pushed him over to the passenger side, jammed the automatic drive into reverse, and rushed the vehicle rapidly backward.

As I turned the car out of the parking lot, the lights caught my most recent assailant. He had found his gun. His arm was outstretched and I ducked involuntarily, just as the shot burst the windshield. I gunned the car as the second shot hit, but I had pressed the accelerator too hard as I drew into the street. I jammed the brakes on to avoid ramming a parked car and felt one of the muggers bounce off a fender. The sudden stop threw the Speaker's head onto the padded dash, and he sagged against me.

Tough titty, Mr. Speaker, I thought bitterly. Tough titty, black boy. I reversed the car, crouching down, fearing that I would be hit by another shot. I whirled the wheel to escape. The injured black was screaming at me wildly, holding his side. There was no shot, but I saw the lights of another car flash on. Police, I thought. Thank God. But instantly I knew it was not. The thugs were going to follow me, get me for my mayhem. The third shot smacked into our rear window.

There was another "blam," as I roared down the street, honking the horn furiously. The Speaker's seat-belt buzzer was buzzing. Fucking Ralph Nader, I thought. I'll never do another consumer story. Never!

I pushed at Edwards' bloody face as the Mercury leaped forward under my acceleration.

"NIGGERS!" I screamed. What was left of my thin liberalism dissolved in fear. Suppose they hit a tire, sent me into a tree. The Speaker of the House catapulted forward into the dash again. Maybe he broke his neck. I laughed hysterically. Me without even a license.

"NIG-ahs!" I shouted.

Another slug hit the plastic facing of the dash with a crack.

"NIG-ahs! NIG-ahs!" I screamed, then gasped aloud or in my mind, "You fuckers, you can't fight right! You don't even steal right! You can't hold on to a knife! You can't shoot straight! And you are crazy—NIG-NIGNIG-HAHAHS—Failure!" No old orange crate of a car was going to catch the Speaker of the House's Mercury! "ASSHOLES! ASSHOLES!" I screamed.

I sped through stop signs, a certifiable racist now, seeing in the rear-vision mirror the headlights still coming. There was no use running for the cops. The Seventh Precinct House was all the way in Georgetown, and the old Eighth was out Wisconsin the other way.

I kept honking the horn, hurtling past the sedate dwellings. All of a sudden, I saw a traffic light ahead, Massachusetts Avenue. I roared through a red, pressed hard on the Mercury's accelerator. Thank God the Little Major had bought a car with a supermotor in it. The car jumped forward. Surely the police would come now. I could see lights behind me, farther back now.

I wasn't sure it was my pursuers. I roared westward at ninety miles an hour, ripped around Westmoreland Circle and decelerated the car rapidly to whirl onto one of the dark streets off the circle.

I'd lost them.

Now I had to get my thoughts straight. The Speaker had to be taken to a hospital, or we had to run to the police. My own heart was knocking inside my chest and I was deathly afraid; I could feel the beginnings of those pains in my arm and that queasiness and pain in my stomach. This was no Goddamned way to die. I slowed to a normal speed.

We were down there among the woodsy lots and medium-ritzy houses of Westmoreland Hills. I couldn't remember for sure how to get back to one of the big arteries. I glanced at the Speaker and stopped under a street light. His hands were making awkward swipes at his face. I could see the blood caked around his nostrils now, and knew that the blood on his face had come out of his nose.

"You okay?" I asked, buckling his seat belt to stop the buzzing.

"UMmmmm-uh," he groaned noncommittally.

"Where do you hurt?" No answer. I turned the car around to get us back toward Massachusetts. The Speaker didn't look all that bad. I remembered the adage about drunks never getting hurt. With the wolf-pack off, I could think of options.

First, I had a hell of a story. But what was I going to do about it? A "First personer" about how I saved the Speaker? Would I put in that the reason I was so propitiously on hand was to skewer him for being a drunk? Why not? Get everything said at once.

One thing was sure. If I wanted to do that one, I'd sure as hell have to stay clear of the police station. We'd lose it to the *Post*, the *Star*, the wire services, TV, everyone. All one of them would have to do was to make the morning routine police checks and the station clerk at Number Seven would blab the whole thing.

"What do you want to do?" I asked Edwards. If he

were hurt, I'd have to take him to the hospital. Again, that would be good-by story. Nobody can stop nurses, orderlies, clerks from leaking to the press.

"Ummhh," he groaned again. There still wasn't much life in it.

Shit, I thought, I'll take him home. I thought of Betty Page at the party. Snubbing old broken-down Aubrey Reporter. There was something pleasant about the prospect of making her sweat. I felt a guilty twinge: That is a pricky way for a hero to be, it said; you are not so pure you can afford that satisfaction, or so stable.

"You want to go home?" I asked him rhetorically.

"Home," he mindlessly echoed.

I turned on WGMS. They were playing something from *Prince Igor*. I am between two worlds, I thought; I am tired of being Aubrey Reporter. My bruises ached. My right hand throbbed where I had held the baton. I wondered if the kid had been really hurt. Should I feel some compunction about it? I did not. He was fifteen or so and he had tried to rob someone, and maybe I had broken his skull. I looked in my mind: I was glad I'd gotten a good crack at all three of them. If I had killed all three, I would not mind. And if the state killed them, I would not mind. They were, in my view, animals. I wondered aloud what I was doing in the ACLU.

The Speaker mumbled witlessly. Okay, I thought, so what about this guy? Isn't he a sort of criminal, too? Second in line for the presidency and thus maybe the most dangerous lush in the country; a man who was going to run off and leave me after I saved him his ass.

I was getting into Wesley Heights, feeling guilty now about my outcropping of racism. I thought of the filthy white trash I had seen on my first big story: Little Rock, all those years ago. A white man, maybe twenty-four, chanting "NIG-ah, NIG-ah!" at some little black girl, the cords of his red neck standing out like a rooster's. My fury at him must have equalled his at the child.

I, too, had shouted "NIG-ah!" Even so, that man, all

those years ago had not been shot at as I had been tonight.

"Oh?" I asked myself aloud. "Hadn't he?"

My chest was feeling fullish. I was afraid. The sweat popped out in my palms, wetting the wheel. I had had a sensational life, and I wanted it to go on, but I knew how fast death could be, had seen the smile of sweetness on enough corpses come to sudden ends by unexpected gunshots to know that they went damned easily into that good night. It was the climb to the precipice of death that scared me: cancer, mutilations, heart attacks, that drawn-out haul as a cripple toward death.

"It's all your fault, you skinny prick," I said to Edwards. But he had begun to snore, slumped like a long-armed, raffish puppet within the circlet of his seat belt.

I pulled the car into his driveway and up to the front door. When I tried to get out, I was dizzy again and had to lean against the fender. The front door of the house opened, and I saw his wife outlined in the light from behind her. She'd been waiting for him.

Before I could say anything, she crossed out into the driveway and caught a look at his bloody face. She must have heard him snoring, and knew he was alive.

"Pom," she said sharply, still peering at him. Then she looked up at me, not recognizing me. "He's hurt. Badly?"

"No," I said. "I don't think so."

"My God," she said. "You!"

"Yep."

I limped around the car.

"What happened?" she asked. The color was out of her face, and it looked all her forty-four years. She wore a sedate housecoat and Persian-boy slippers.

"Let's get him in," I said.

"My God," she said again, seeing the shattered windows.

"Let's get him in," I repeated, beginning to feel cold.

We dragged him into the house. The dried blood was all over his tweed coat and had dripped down his neck onto his white shirt. In the light of the living room, I saw he was whiskery. I didn't say what I wanted to about "two heartbeats away," and I didn't even look at her. But I felt she knew what I was thinking.

We got him into a big downstairs bathroom and out of his coat, his sport coat, and his shirt. The poor goof had on a long pastel blue undershirt stuffed into what looked from the tops like pastel blue jockey shorts. To impress his Danish girl friend, maybe. It was touching and disgusting.

"You've got yourself quite a story, haven't you?" she said nastily.

"Now, let's not start that shit." I began to get angry. Maybe they deserved each other. Suddenly, I was swept by rage. "I save this shithead's life, me with a bad heart! And catch a load of crap from his snotty wife!"

She had a wet washcloth out now and was about to wipe the blood off his face. His nose had turned a faint blue bruised color already.

"Well, thank you and good-by!" she snapped back. Somehow I got myself under control. My God, I thought, what a snippy little bitch.

"He may have a broken nose," I said. "You'd better get a doctor in tomorrow. I mean later today," I said coldly, getting ready to go.

"Why don't you just tell me what happened?" she demanded.

"Why don't I just call a cab and you can read about it in the *Eagle*, Florence Nightingale. I can maybe get a paragraph or two in the final if I go now, assuming the pressmen aren't on strike." I went to the washbasin. In shoving him around, I'd gotten some of his blood on my hands. I washed them and then washed my face.

She was looking at me curiously now, wary; she realized I could hurt him with a story. It had taken her long enough.

"How did the windows get broken?" she said with a hint of conciliation.

"Shots," I said.

I took my comb out and started to comb my hair, but when I raised my hands, I began to feel dizzy. Shit. I thought, here it comes. I felt myself let go of the comb, ever so slowly, and heard my voice say, "I have to lie down." Then, I was trying to kneel to make sure that when I fell I would not hit the basin or toilet.

I came to, coughing. She was holding something under my nose. It would be one of those little ampules of ammonia broken between thumb and finger. My eyes were opened, looking up directly into hers. There was mostly curiosity in hers.

"I'm sorry," I said, coughing from the sharp odor.

"Are you having a heart attack?" she asked unsympathetically.

"I don't know." I was afraid to move. As I came to, I didn't feel any pain anywhere. "I don't think so. Where's your husband?"

She nodded to the other room and rose. Now I was looking up at the globe of the lamp fixture.

"You got a softer light?"

"What's the matter with you?" she said somewhat more kindly. She leaned over me again and her breasts moved forward in her housecoat. She saw me looking at them. "Hunh," I murmured a faint laugh.

"My God," she said. "This is crazy."

I thought I would try to get up. Very gingerly, I rolled over, came to my knees, and then steadied myself, holding on to the basin.

"It wasn't a heart attack," I said, fairly positively. "I got giddy and I fainted. Thanks for helping." It had gone from the hostile with her to the formal. "Look, I'll put your car up in your garage. I can't make the final deadline anyway."

We walked out of the bathroom. The Speaker was slumped in an easy chair, snoring, his chest thin yet flabby beneath its pale blue covering. What a hell of a life for her, I thought.

"Could we start all over again?" I asked. "Back before I said whatever I said at that party." She looked at me still warily, but I could see her leveling out.

"Let's put up the car," she said, throwing on a heavy wool coat.

I gave her the keys and she drove it into the dip of the driveway, past the photocell that triggered the doors and into the garage, out of sight. I stood on the lawn, my breath pluming in the cold night, feeling almost cleansed by the fainting. I figured it had something to do with exertion. But also I knew it wasn't a heart attack. At least it wasn't like the last time. And it would not kill me.

She came back through a door beside the garage doors and stood for a moment on the frozen lawn with me, silently. Then we both walked in. The Little Major still slept drunkenly.

"Let's get him to bed, and I'll tell you what you want to know," I said.

After we had shoveled him in, clothes and all, we sat in the living room, she drinking a cognac straight and I a Galliano on the rocks. She had provided it with only a slight smile. I felt grubby and I ached all over. It had been a dreadful night.

"First, are you going to write about this?" she asked, now without rancor, but with understandable caution. Clearly whatever the story was, it could hurt him badly. It would not destroy him, because he would make some self-serving pomposity about drying out the better to serve his country. But it could damage him.

I shrugged.

"Why don't I just tell you what happened, okay?"

But that wasn't going to do. She had a firm little face, blond hair pulled back, and no make-up. It was not beautiful. But it was, well, a good face, an uncorrupted face. The green eyes were clear, the nose small. The lips prim and the cheekbones highish. She did not pluck her brows and they were brown, darker than her hair. I could see the aging lines at the neck. She was cranking up again.

"God, it's sickening for you to play cat and mouse with me," she said sharply. "Don't I have enough—"

"Yes," I said. "But what the hell should I be saying?

I don't know what to do with what I've got here, either."
I could see her brighten at that. "Let me just begin at
the bar, okay?"

- I pulled at the strong, sweet liqueur. Then I got the
cognac and poured a nip in to brace up the drink. It
tasted steelier that way.

She listened, interjecting a question here and there,
nodding, looking at me seriously, still without any
warmth, but without any hatred, an honest politician
trimming losses after a bad break.

"Why did you come to the bar anyway?"

I only shrugged. Though she must have guessed it
was to catch him drinking, I did not want to disclose
the full extent of the investigation.

"So you have a good story," she said matter-of-factly.

"Yes."

"How much time do we have?"

"Until tomorrow, rather this evening. The first edition's out at 11 P.M."

She looked at me, assessing.

"Nobody over there is going to kill it, are they?"

"You mean because of Mr. March?"

"Yes."

"No, they'll put on the hair shirt and run it. They'll
play down my role in it and pull a long face. But it'll
go."

"You don't look all that good in this," she said, not
argumentatively, just trying it out. "I mean you were
spying on us when it happened."

I didn't contradict her.

". . . and following him in to his bar. That's a cheap
shot."

"Participatory journalism," I said unkindly. Then I
tried to explain. "I saw him at that party. I thought,
'What the hell is a lush like that doing where he is?' "
She looked struck. "Now wait a minute. Why don't I
just go at it straight, okay?" I got up and poured her
another brandy, this time giving myself the same. "We
—we reporters—don't write about him. We avoid such
stories. But it *is* a story. Suppose—okay, this sounds

unduly pious—suppose there is some crisis about now and he's needed." I again short-cut all the work I had done, the business of the bank loan and so on. "So I dug up what I could and staked out the bar three nights running." Momentarily I wondered what the President had been doing here. I started to ask her, but didn't. "And here I am." It sounded a little flat.

"How much did my snubbing you have to do with it?"

The weariness hit me again.

"Some," I said. "Maybe not much. I didn't even think you would remember it." She was tougher than I imagined. But, she would have to be, married to Edwards all that time.

When I looked up, the tears were streaming down her unmade cheeks. I felt like shit.

"I'm sorry," I said. "I have to go."

She wasn't sobbing, merely weeping. The tears came down and she pulled a Kleenex from her housecoat and blotted them out. When they stopped, she said:

"Is there anything I can do to get you to kill it?"

I suppose if I'd said, yes, let's screw, there might have been some discussion about that, and eventually it might have happened. But that was not what she meant, and we both knew it.

"It's tough being married to that creep," I said. "Why don't you leave him?"

I saw her tightening up her face for a nasty reply. It was a dirty question, but I was curious.

"Why ask that? It's so cheap, so cruel."

"It may be cruel, but it's not cheap. I'm curious." I began to warm to the idea of it. "Goddamnit, I read your poetry. I read your damned recipes"—she looked startled—"I get a feeling about what you are like and what he is like, and then I see him tonight, and frankly I don't see why you stay with him. You're too good for him, to parrot the wily seducer."

"For that, thanks," she said, smiling at last. The even little teeth showed and I began to itch for her for the first time that night. Now that we had gotten past the peelings, it began to go easier. "You didn't exactly see him at his best," she said. "You did quite an investigation of us, didn't you?"

"Why not?" I said. "He deserves quite an investigation. He's the Speaker of the House and he drinks too damned much and he's played ball with some funny special interests."

"He's a politician," she said.

"He's an important one," I said. "The President came to see you two nights ago." She was suddenly wary again.

"You've been watching our house?"

"No, I had a kid doing it."

"But—" She was really upset now.

"I'm sorry I told you. You make me feel like the Gestapo."

"You *are* like the Gestapo."

I had blown it again. Now, I was exhausted.

"I have to go," I said. "It's damn near two. Can you get me a taxi?" She started to go to the phone, then must have thought about a taxi picking me up at this hour with blood all over my shirt at the home of the Speaker of the House.

"God, I'll take you. Let me change."

In a minute she was down again, wearing a heavy sweater and blue jeans. Her hair was pulled back and she had on a little lipstick.

"What a night," she said, the way women do when there's nothing to do but accept the worst and get on with it. I laughed a little and she smiled back.

Driving back, she punched up WGMS on the radio. It was a string quartet, and very soothing and away from all the excitement of the night. I looked at her half-lit face, now intent on the driving.

"It was a fine poem. They were all good," I said.

"How would you know?" she said with a smile. "A gumshoe."

"I was going to be a poet."

"Ah," she said, not believing.

"No, really."

The strain had all gone out of her.

"Me, too."

"You are. You've been published."

"You, a poet?" She gave a little snort, accepting the possibility of even that, of anything.

"Sure," I said. "In college after my junior year, I went to Paris and there was an old guy, Raymond Duncan, the dancer Isadora Duncan's brother, and he had this atelier and he said, 'I've got a press and paper. Print up your poems and sell them in the cafés. If nobody buys, give 'em away.' But I had return fare and I came home." I was surprised at my long-windedness.

"Some poet."

"Well, I didn't marry a politician."

Between us, I felt that little puff of smoke that you see when a rifle is fired far off. You see the smoke, and an instant later you hear the snap of the gunshot. So, I thought, it is going to come out this way after all.

She was cutting toward Southwest along the river, and across it was the flicker of the lights of Rosslyn, high up in the buildings where the cleaning women were now. The light rippled on the black of the river.

"What was the President doing there? What was he talking about?" I asked her. She looked at me sharply.

"I'm looking for a way not to write about tonight," I said.

How dazzlingly open her face was at that moment! I saw her realizing what I had said, her lips parted just so slightly. She was thinking: If I tell him, he will find a means of writing what the President said in a way that will not make it look as if I told him because he wants to see me again. And he will kill the story about Pom, so I will have been justified in telling him.

And lastly, and it stirred me, age, weariness and all, with a breath of lust, I saw she wanted to see me again, and that this was a sort of compromise toward our own conspiracy.

"Will you kill it?" she asked, still only half believing

I was serious. Then she said, "Why, you're as bad as we are."

"Yes, I can kill it," I said, not agreeing with the last part of what she said. "If what you give me in return is good enough."

"Can you write it so it won't sound like it came from us?"

"Maybe. How many people know whatever it was Frieden told you?" Tired as I was, I was getting excited about the story.

"A few at the State Department. Maybe three on Capitol Hill. More at the White House."

"A dozen or so," I said.

"Yes."

"That's easy."

She glanced over seriously now.

"So you'll kill it?"

"If the story's good enough," I repeated. "We kill this part of it, the bar bit and the fight. I give this part of it back to you. I don't promise I won't go after him again, even into the same bar."

I had parlayed stories this way before, in other circumstances, swapping off an embarrassing story about someone for a real scoop. Nobody talked about it, but it was fairly common.

"The story is good enough," she said positively. She did not say (nor did I believe she even asked herself), "Can I trust you?" I found I was thinking of her again, and not about the story.

"Okay," I said. We were back in the real Washington world, of bartered confidences, of compromise and trust, of political-bologna slicing.

"Frieden's going to Cuba, on a state visit," she began. "He's going to try to get the Cubans away from the Russians with a big mutual aid thing."

"That's a lovely story," I marveled. It was. I could see it eight columns across the top of page one. "That's a lovely story, and you're a lovely girl. Did you hear any more?"

"No," she said. "For God's sakes. I ought to feel like a prostitute anyway, trading off something like that. . . ."

"You were smart to," I said with certainty. We both knew it.

"Yes," she said glumly. In a way, she was a very tough lady.

"You saved him a story about him being a drunk. It's worth it for you, a little breach of confidence."

"I put the drunk story off for another day," she said. "That's all."

"Yes," I agreed. "I was thinking the same thing."

"I know," she sighed. "And now——"

"And now," I said, "I'm going to ask you whether you will see me again." My heart felt oddly young. Something had lifted. I thought, She is a beautiful lady who has given me a very, very good story and with whom, not too many hours or days from now, I may, very likely will, be making love to on a large, clean bed.

She smiled, and answered: "Well, that's brash enough."

"You knew I was thinking it. Will you?"

"That's something I'm going to have to think about," she said.

"Why think?" I said, disappointed.

"Because I have enough problems." She laughed, the same little snort of self-satisfaction at knowing how the wind blew. "Don't pout. It's not from any lack of charm in you." The age showed beside her eyes from the wrinkles of her smile. "Celebrated Reporter is still adequately dashing despite his fainting spells."

"Screw you, Mrs. Speaker," I said, in kind, liking her for mocking me, exhilarated by it in a way because the heat was on her from a lot of directions and she was coping gracefully.

She drove on, still smiling, pleased with herself and now with me for liking her and the talk came easy, the tentative things that begin a friendship: where had we gone to school, and what had we taken, and how long had I been married, if I had? And, so, had my wife died? Yes, of cancer, three years ago.

And where did the Edwards' kids go to school? On that confiding note we parted. I left her, oddly, with a handshake. Upstairs, I collapsed into the soft, cool bed.

I felt young, and exhausted.

3

The Reporter

How hard I slept. And waking, I ached, ached with age so that I nearly gasped with the pain in my shoulder, and my right hand and back.

"I am old; I am old," I derided myself. I limped to the bathroom and turned on the tub taps, then to the kitchen for a huge glass of fresh orange juice, one of my few luxuries.

I thought of calling up Betty Page and telling her how old and creaky I felt. I liked her, both for being blackmailed—oh, that is too harsh a word—into giving me the gold nugget of a story, and because she seemed to like me. No, I could not call her yet. Later in the day, maybe. I should have asked her to call me; that would be safer. But would she have? If I had kept the fearful bait of a story about her husband over her, then she would have, using that as the excuse for doing what he wanted to do anyway. No, I would not call her. I would soak in the tub again and then I would call the Secret Service.

That was the way to confirm the Cuba story, and to get some more details on it. Our State Department guy could weasel it out of State and our White House guy could get it out of there, now that I had the first tip. But as an old police reporter, I would get it out of the cops: the Secret Service. Once I had it hard enough to get Cubbins to go with it, it was all mine, nobody could hop it.

I lay in the bathtub, soaking. Luxury: lying in a tub while you imagine an eight-column-across-the-top story.

I reached Knowles Irvin on the telephone. He had been a bright cop, working his way through night school when I first met him. Now he was the chief paper shuffler at Secret Service, the administrative officer.

"Big favor," I said to him when he came on. "Can you talk?"

"Who knows?"

"You got a direct line?"

"Yeah," he said, giving me the number. I hung up and called it.

We talked a little about family and about how nice it was for him to be off the street.

"When is the President going to Cuba?" I asked him at last.

"Oh, fuckers away," he said. "I can't."

"Why not?"

"I don't even know if he's going."

"*I* know he's going."

"Aubrey, I can't talk about it. It's too damned closely held."

"No," I said, "you're safe. State knows and the President is telling the top Hill guys. Listen, it will make me a good front page story, Knowles. If I can't nail it down, then those woussies at State or White House will get my story. Think how good we'll both feel when an old ex-police dog scoops them."

"Think how good you'll feel," he said. "I'll be shitting myself. Everybody knows—"

"Everybody knows nothing," I interrupted him. "I haven't put the arm on you for a story in two, three years."

"Suppose they ask me?"

"Look, Knowles. Let's do this." It was an old newspaper subterfuge. "I'll give you certain statements, okay? But if they're false, you say check with the White House. Then if they ask you if you talked to me and what you said back, then you tell them, 'the son-of-a-bitch called and I didn't say anything and finally I just said go to the White House.' So you're telling them the truth, right? And you're confirming my story, okay?"

"That's an old sick game," he sighed. "Everybody knows it." I resented that. Everybody didn't know it.

"It protects you," I said.

"How are you going to attribute the story?"

"Administration sources," I said.

"Shit," he said. "Shoot."

"He's going to Cuba in a week?"

"Talk to the White House," he said. So that was wrong.

"He's going in a week to three weeks?"

Silence. That much was true, then.

"Two to three weeks?" Silence.

"It will just be Cuba and back, not part of a general tour?"

Silence. That made it a big story. Not just a stopover trip, on the way to somewhere else, but the full-dress thing, a trip just for Cuba.

"Staying one day?"

"Talk to the White House." Not one day.

"Two days?"

Silence. A two-day visit.

"Gonna take Secretary of State?"

Silence. Gonna take him.

"Gonna discuss mutual-aid program to steal them from Russia?"

"Aubrey, how in the fuck would we know what he's going down there for?" Irvin exploded softly. "Now that's enough. Why the hell do I do this?" he whined.

"Love of the game," I told him cheerfully. Old sources, I thought, God bless 'em. As I got dressed, I thought out the story in my head.

"President Harry Frieden is planning a two-day visit to Fidel Castro in hopes of dramatically bettering U.S.-Cuban relations, administration sources said.

"The President is expected to take off in Air Force One for the Communist island in about two weeks, the first visit of an American President to Cuba since (whoever) was there in (whatever date).

"Those with knowledge of the trip said the President will hold out a promise of economic aid to Castro, whose sugar crop fell short of expectations this year.

"With Castro already grumbling about the low levels of Russian and Chinese aid, Frieden's personal diplomacy could be the first step in bringing Cuba home to the Hemisphere, the sources said."

Yummy.

Cubbins was always in the office at nine.

"Why can't you go through channels?" he complained when I got him.

"Every paper needs an Aubrey Warder," I told him, feeling slightly sick of his bureaucratic bullshit and of my trying to put a cute complexion on it. "I have a good, good story and I want you to know that I have it so that nobody hops it on its way to eight columns across the top."

"Yeah?" I felt his excitement. He knew I wouldn't say it unless it were true.

"Frieden's going to see Castro. In about two weeks."

"No shit," he said. He would be thinking now of how he was going to mollify the national editor for my trespass on protocol, how to soothe the White House and State Department reporters who would see it as an invasion by me of their turf, how to keep it secure so it didn't leak out of the vast office to AP or UPI or the afternoon *Star* or morning *Post*. "How secure is it?" he said.

"It ought to hold."

"How hard?"

"Secret Service confirmed, not for attribution."

"That's hard enough," he conceded. "Any other confirmation?"

"Not that I want to talk about."

"You want Bothild"—the White House man—"to get some comment?"

"If he can be discreet about it, yeah."

"I don't guess you want to share the byline with

Cassani"—the State Department man—"if he'll do the background stuff."

"No," I said. "I'll dig it out of the morgue. Let him do a 'think piece' for the jump page," I said, beginning to enjoy it a bit. "You gonna get them to write an editorial on it?"

"Yeah," he said.

"Why don't you get them to mention me in it?"

"Arrgh," he said.

"My mother would like it," I told him, laughing.

"You never had a mother," he said irritably. "You came out of somebody's colon."

"Now," I remonstrated, a little hurt, "that's not nice."

He must have heard the note in my voice.

"Can you come in and put it together so I can take it to the conference?" That would be at 3 P.M. when they began to plan the next morning's paper.

I wrote the thing in the office. Cubbins, and, finally, even Mr. March dropped by, hovering momentarily around the desk as I toyed with the lead. His daughter brushed by, pushing, I felt, a bit close to me.

"That's a nice story, Aubrey," she said, her voice a little high for someone who would soon have all that power and who had all that tennis-hardened, sun-tanned meat in her tailored pants suit.

"Thanks," I said. I looked at her straight in the eyes, wondering how much to risk. I saw there the same hint of curiosity I'd always seen there. But one didn't fool around haphazardly with the publisher's daughter. They didn't call her a young Elizabeth Regina for nothing, and I sure as hell didn't want to be her Essex, even if the black guy did. "You can get your old man to drop a couple of shares of stock into my pension fund, maybe."

She paused a moment, perhaps considering whether I had breached that elaborate, unspoken protocol dividing the Marches from the rest of us.

"I'll get him to put it into a decent wine for your anniversary dinner," she laughed. I was pleased she knew it was coming up. The dinner was a ceremonial thing for hotshots or semihotshots who'd put in twenty-five years. Maybe I should invite Connie March, I thought.

"You mean you're gonna dig out the real McCoy instead of that Mouton Cadet your old man served Cubbins?" I risked, again looking at her. Cubbins was glaring hatefully, but when she turned quickly to him with a light smile, he put on his Petunia Skunk grin.

"Jesus," he said to me. What he meant was, "You shithead." She put her hand lightly on my shoulder.

"You'll have it," she said.

I started to say, "Thank you, mem-sahib," but even a good story carried only so much weight. And in my heart I disliked her for the power that she had not earned over Cubbins and me.

Oh, there is something to this business: The story broke in the "Bulldog" which hits the street about 11 P.M. The wire services couldn't confirm it at the White House that late so they had to carry "according to the Washington *Eagle*," the best kind of flattery.

It was on the morning TV news and all the radio stations. By about 10 A.M., the story was getting confirmation from "White House sources" and an hour and a half later, at the White House briefing, it was somberly confirmed. The *Eagle* got a nasty going over from the schmucky whore who handled Frieden's press.

"The President has apologized to Premier Castro for the unfortunate premature release of the information," said the press spokesman. "The two heads of state had planned to announce the visit simultaneously next week and the President told Premier Castro that he was sure no one in his official family had been responsible for the insensitive breach of security."

When I arrived at the paper, I got the various pats, handshakes, gooses, and insults that made me know my colleagues felt I had a good one.

Full of myself, I called Betty Page Edwards at home.

The maid answered and I gave her the name Mr. Samaritan. Betty Page came to the phone.

"Mr. Samaritan," she said, getting the point, but still wanting to be sure, totally sure, who it was.

"Thank you," I said. "I had found a poem by e. e. cummings about somebody who saves a man found by the roadside—"

She interrupted me, talking low into the phone to keep the maid from hearing it: "I get the point. Anyway, I know the poem. You must be a very nervous man to begin a conversation so defensively. . . ."

Suddenly I saw one reason Edwards drank. It was that recurring tough streak in her. She had set me back on my ass.

"I was afraid if I began any other way you'd say 'no.'" Where had the camaraderie gone? "Are you nervous about the story?"

"My God," she said. "Don't you have any discretion on the phone?"

"No," I said. "Not much. If they're tapping your house, then it's the end of democracy as we know it." I realized I was half-serious. "If you treat the phone like it's tapped all the time, then you've given in to them. I mean the Nazi bastards have succeeded in doing what they set out to do."

"I don't need a discourse on the Fourth Amendment," she said, not all that unkindly.

"Well, are you? Nervous, I mean?" I ignored the slap.

"I suppose so."

"But you suppose we can have lunch tomorrow?"

"No," she said. "Not tomorrow. The next day. He's speaking in Buffalo."

"What is safe for you, for us?" I asked, heart thumping. "How about Angler's?" It was an innlike place upriver from the D.C. line.

"That's a good place," she replied, seeing that I had planned, and feeling better for it. "Are you okay?"

"Yeah," I said. "Just stiff. How's he?"

"He always snaps back."

"Did you take his car in? You've got to be careful about that."

"Tell you when I see you," she said.

My heart leapt up, my old untrustworthy heart.

We agreed to meet at the Fletcher's landing turnoff from Canal road. Because I still didn't have my license back, she had to drive. I knew she was scared to death of us being seen together, so I had chosen that out-of-the-way place to meet, cold as it would be. I got a cab down there and stood by the road, looking at the brisk sunlit river. Years ago, I had covered a story in which a crazy bastard had drunk the blood out of a couple of bimbos and thrown them in the river upstream from here.

I remembered the body of one at the morgue: fat and obscene as a dead turtle, because the gas in the warm river had inflated it. Well, it was too chilly for any "floaters" today.

The bitter cold, however, had broken during the night. The faint smell of effluvium from the river mixed with the fresh exhalations of Fletcher's now-leafless woods. It had country in it. I pulled my coat around me and kicked at the tattered weeds by the roadside. I looked way upriver at the big rocks and the cold spume flashing whitely in the brilliant sun.

Forty-eight, I thought. God, life is sweet.

I saw her small Olds moving slowly toward me and waved. Then she stopped, I walked around, got in the passenger side and leaned over to kiss her on the cheek.

She pulled away tensely.

"Don't do that," she said, her thin lips tight.

She had on sunglasses and a rich, plain blue coat snugged in with a belt at the waist. She looked like any well-to-do housewife, going out to a not-too-important lunch.

"I have nothing to gain by this," she said, "except that you've blackmailed me into it." She was a very nervous lady.

"Oh, that's bullshit." We drove off toward Maryland. "If you want to look at it existentially, the best thing I could do for you is to blow that turd out of the water. Then you'd be free."

She said nothing, her lips still tight.

"Smile," I said.

"I don't want to talk about that," she said, finally. "But you didn't blackmail me. Okay?"

"Yes."

"Does anyone suspect where the story came from?"

"No. I mean, they suspect it came from the Secret Service. I am not exactly the type who gets stories from the Speaker's office."

She smiled for the first time that day.

"Listen to him brag. 'Us tough police reporter types don't lolly it up on Capitol Hill, no sirree.'" There was a hint of the flat Kansas accent in it.

"Well, it's true," I said, pleased at her joshing. "We don't."

"And take a left-handed pride in it. There's a lot of the counterfeit in you. There you are, the tough investigator, and you try to butter me up with your talk of poetry."

"There you are, the distinguished Speaker's wife, but it's not enough. You have to translate obscure French verse forms." I started to jibe her harshly, to say "No wonder he runs around with a passive little Danish pastry." But it was too early for that.

To my astonishment, she had sensed my thought.

"Brother rat," she said, wistfully. Something in her dropping her guard that way caught at me.

"I will be careful not to hurt your feelings," I said cautiously. "I have you at a disadvantage. Lots of them. I know so much about you and him."

"Oh, now that's bull," she said tartly. "I know a good deal about you. You are pretty much on the surface. I may not know what stories you've been covering since the Chicago fire, but you are not hard to read."

Angler's Inn is off the old C & O Canal. In summer it has a patio, and inside there are Edwardian sofas instead of chairs drawn up to the tables. The food is fair and it has cold wines at good prices. No more than a dozen couples ever show up on weekdays for lunch, particularly in winter.

We found a table in a corner. My bruises still ached

as I eased my body down into the red plush of the couch. I got us a half bottle of rosé for openers.

"Ice us up another bottle, a whole bottle, okay? Real cold. Put it in the freezer," I told the waiter.

"I don't know if I want to stay for a bottle and a half," she said. Looking across at her now, I saw how pretty her hands were, delicate, small, deftly slipping the napkin from the table to her lap.

In the dimness, the wrinkles that had stood out so tellingly in the sterile sunlight melded into smoothness. She looked the way she must have all those years ago when Edwards met her.

"I've been meaning to ask you. Did you play volleyball when you were at Smith?"

She laughed softly.

"Yes. . . ." Wondering how I guessed.

"Good legs," I said.

How marvelously young she looked. The wine came and I gulped down a half glass. At first, we talked of things that were immediate, that had pressed us together.

She was going to tell the auto shop that joy riders had taken the car, then left it in the neighborhood where Edwards had spotted it. The story ought to hold water. As to the "rescue," she had told Edwards a real whopper. He remembered being beaten by the black delinquents, but not much else. She fobbed me off as an off-duty policeman, since he remembered nothing of the ride home. I had supposedly withheld my name, not so much out of nobility, as out of fear. I, so her story went, did not want to get in trouble for failing to make a police report. That would necessarily have revealed I was out drinking instead of on sick leave as I had reported to my precinct that day. It was a serviceable lie, mainly because Edwards understood things like that.

"He'll be back someday to get his reward," she quoted Edwards saying.

"Little did he know," I laughed.

She thought I had concealed the source of the Cuban

story well. And yes, she was scared to death. She had never before passed on anything he told her in confidence. In fact, she went on, when he drank, he used her as a confessional, getting rid of any desire to blab by rambling on to her about it.

"I felt guilty about telling you," she mused. "But it was his own fault. I had to save him on the drinking story."

She must have caught my delayed tremor at her monumental confession that she was the repository of the Speaker's secrets.

"Goddamnit," she said. "I am *not* going to be a milch cow for you on news. That *would* be blackmail." But she was not really mad. It was all too comfortable: the cold outside, and us warm inside, with the rosé, and now some paté and bread to munch on.

"I wouldn't do that to you," I said with mild insincerity.

She caught the tinny note.

"Don't think it isn't written all over you," she said. "My God, I'm just getting used to calling you Aubrey, but I already know you. You letch just like the rest. But it's really worse. You want me to talk about him so you can use it."

We sipped the wine. All was peace, no matter what she said. Both of us knew it.

"Mostly, I letch," I said.

"That's ordinary enough. That will resolve itself one way or the other. But the use of people as sources, the way ants carry aphids around, to eat them. . . ."

"Oh God," I sighed. She was blunt without being abrasive.

"I mean, how did you get this way? You know it's like the lobbyists you despise so. They butter up my husband, the big friendship act. And some of them have been his friends for years. But ultimately what they want is his power."

"Okay," I said, lowering my voice. "I have certainly thought a good deal about your sweet ass. But I'd be lying if I denied that I got a shiver when you said that about his telling you everything. That's the way my mind works. And maybe the lobby comparison is fair in a way. They want money, and the feeling of influencing power. I don't care about money, but I get a kick out of a good story, any good story."

"Why?" she said with soft sarcasm. "What's so big about a good story? It's gone, forgotten in a week. It's even more vain in a way than lobbying. They've got a long-term contract or a new law to show for it. That's their scalp." She laughed. "Your scalps are made of old newspapers. So why? Damnit. It would be much more flattering if I thought you just wanted me, you know, liked me for what you found in that absurd investigation you did of us. . . ."

"Liked you for your poetry, you mean . . ." I said. But she had piqued me with her "Why?" At the very bottom, had I ever really thought about *why* I found a good story so thrilling, almost sexual? There on the stem of her glass was that delicate hand and I looked up her forearm to the eyes, dark emerald. How deeply I was interested in that face, so transmogrifiedly young now.

"Well," I said, "I'm not sure I honestly ever thought about why I sort of lust for a good story. Actually, I've thought about quitting newspapering, hundreds of times. But I am not a psychiatric self-studier. I—"

"But, my God, isn't that 'lust for a good story' at the heart of what you've been doing for what, twenty-five years, more? And you don't question why?"

"You are undermining me, Betty Page Rawlinson. That way lies introspection and disaster."

We were finishing the little bottle of rosé, and I was thinking about the iciness of the next bottle and the long afternoon.

"Well, okay, because I've always done it," I said.

Momentarily, I forgot about the anguishes that living with Edwards must have caused her, and the job of raising kids, and the poetry and the things that happen to everyone when they live forty years, and think during a good part of them. She seemed only young now, slightly taunting.

"You should accept that," I said. Lightly, carefully, I went on. "You should love me for the dangers I have passed. And I should love you that you pity me them."

"So," she said. "Poor man. Where did you learn that?"

"Hamilton, a little school up in—"

"I know, you took—"

"English. And went to Paris between my junior and senior years, wanted to be a poet. Raymond Duncan, Isadora's—?"

"Yes," she interrupted. "You already told me that story. Then you came back from Europe."

"Yes, and quickly enlisted for eighteen months while you could still enlist for eighteen months. Besides, I was taking math at Hamilton and I knew I didn't want that."

"That would be?"

"Just before Korea. So I met all these academic types in the Army because I scored well on the tests, and we all got into classification work. Some were reds, and I was very big on the reds for a while. I got *Das Kapital* out of the base library.

"By the time I got out of school—I went back and took English—all I had left of the reds was some of their social consciousness, and I hope the balls. It takes balls to be a Communist here. And you also have to be a jerk."

"And from there to the *Eagle?*"

"No, a little paper in Oneida."

"Then?"

"Then, the *Eagle*. And that's where I've been."

"Then that's been your life." What was she driving at?

"Right, in that sense, it has been."

"So that's where you became what you are."

"Ah." There it was. "Yes," I said. "Aubrey Reporter."

"That's where you got to where you want to go to

bed with a woman, but in part it's to squeeze a story out of her." She paused. The full bottle had come. "Is that unfair?"

I thought of the girl at the FBI whom I had knocked up in those dangerous prelegal-abortion days, smuggling out the film in her woussie.

"No, probably not. In some cases."

"So, what happened at the *Eagle?* You know, don't you agree, that your condition is a little unusual? I mean, it may not be unique that other men visualize sleeping with women to get stories from them, but I don't know that many actually do it."

"It's not what you'd call gallant," I conceded. We both ordered broiled rockfish. The place had filled up somewhat, but our corner was still isolated.

"I'm not judging you, you know," she said.

"I know."

For the first time in a long time, I thought about those long-ago days when I had come to the *Eagle* as a legman at police headquarters. When a big story broke, I rushed down to the garage, where the cops let us park in those days, and drove out to the fire or murder or what-have-you.

"I saw an awful lot of things when I was young," I said. "I've covered an awful lot of things." I was a little giddy at the long look back.

"I've seen a lot of awful things," I modified it. And then, glancing up at her, I thought, well, we both are lonely and have time on our hands, this day. And we are beginning to like each other. And out of the loneliness and that affection for her, it began to come out.

"The worst story. There are some awful stories," I began. "We had a man call on the radio in a fancy section of town. And when I got there, at the same time the cops did, almost, there was this guy. He'd stabbed his mother, an old lady, and there he was . . ." Suddenly, I was terribly upset, wrenched unaccountably by the past. I looked to see if she really did like me, if I could trust her, and wondered why with so little liquor

I was tearing up. ". . . and there he was frying his own cut-off testicles in a frying pan."

She put down her wine, jolted by the story, her face twisting in disbelief. Then, she saw it was true and wondered what to say. But we were into it now, and she just made a little "ahh" and I went on.

"So that was that. It has an effect, maybe, and one summer a woman beneath Taft Bridge in the woods, who'd jumped a week before. And I heard the radio call and there were the kids, two of them, who'd found her, standing away because of the stink. And the cop, an old man, I mean for a cop, put his hand on his nose and went toward her and a rat, big as a little dog, came running out of her, where her vagina had been."

"Please, I don't need any more of those," she said softly. But I did not want to stop, now I was started.

"And some are funny, Betty Page, really, but sexual. They're all sexual that stick with you, most of them anyway, or about death. A plumber in the old First Precinct was cheating on his wife. So one night he came home and flopped on the bed and had an erection and his wife slipped one of his hardened-steel pipe joiners over his . . . you know. He woke up and wanted to go to the bathroom and he couldn't get the damn sleeve off because it was threaded and his penis was swollen. She was worried now, too. So they put butter on it, but it still wouldn't come off because of the threads.

"So they called the rescue squad, and Rescue Squad Number One, the best and the proudest in the city, responded. The firemen got to work with a ring-cutter. The plumber was scared to death, rolling his eyes, afraid the cutter would slip and . . .

"But the steel sleeve was too hard and it got hot so they poured ice water on it. They talked about cleaving it with a cold chisel and the plumber fainted. Well, back at the squad headquarters they were calling around and they located a ring-cutter with a diamond-edged wheel in Baltimore.

"Sirens going, they fetched the jeweler down and by this time they got the guy at the hospital and catheterized, but still the erection wouldn't go down. So the jeweler went to work with the diamond-edged ring-cutter, with everybody taking turns pouring ice water on the joiner to keep it cool. The poor bastard was just lying there praying, half under from sedation. It was horrible in a way, and his wife, who'd done it, was holding his hand.

"Well, they cut through twice, once on top and once on the, well, balls side. And the guy was freed and to this day the two halves of the sleeve are on a beautiful wooden plaque that the plumber made for them and it's hanging in the chief's office at Rescue Squad Number One."

The exhilaration of telling the story had left me dry-throated. I gulped down the icy wine, thinking how that ice water must have felt on the poor guy's cock.

She had begun to laugh, and the curse of confession was off me. I took a bite of the rockfish.

"What happened to him finally?" she said.

"Oh, he was okay. It was mainly shock. You can imagine."

"Not entirely," she said. "No, I mean about his wife?"

"They got back together. So the firemen said."

A calm had settled on us now, of absolution. It was very nice. And I could talk now with none of that stormy passion I had felt.

"And that's the way it's been," she asked, "all these years?"

"Oh, I did the courts after police. And then the *Eagle* sent me to an investigative reporting seminar for two weeks. That was what I always liked. And when I came back I did local investigations. Slum landlords and credit gougers and unsafe construction sites and various miscarriages of justice and crooked auto dealers and a couple of hard pieces on narcotics and gambling and one on police corruption that finished me with the cops, most of the cops."

"And that brought you to my doorstep," she said quietly.

"Yes, because after that they gave me political cor-

ruption and corporations when I could get them to cut
me loose on a corporation."

"And so the *Eagle* loves you, and you love the
Eagle."

"Except that papers really don't want investigative
reporters. You wind up embarrassing the publisher's
friends, like your husband is Mr. March's friend, or
you find things wrong with your own paper like
building-code violations. So I got sent to the Dominican
war and Indochina, on misuse of federal funds, not the
politics of it, and was scared to death in both places."

She had been sipping along, watching me.

"It makes it easier to understand. The way you
gushed."

"Yes," I said. "It's what I know how to do well."

"And that's why it's a sort of lust?"

"Well," I said, thinking about it now that I was into
it. "It may be more that I'm *addicted* to it. At forty-
eight I ought to begin to grow out of it. Most of the
guys I started with are editors or vice-presidents for
public affairs of some big outfit. I got atrophied."

"And prideful. You look on them as sellouts. On
most of us as sellouts."

"Maybe," I said, assessing how much hostility was in
that.

"So you go after my husband." She said it in resignation.

"Yes," I said. "And caught you in the seine. And you?
I've let myself go on, made a baby of myself. How about
you? I know the facts about you, but that's all, really."

"Oh, Aubrey, another day on that, okay? You want
to know about him and me"—it was odd she seldom said
his name—"and while it's tempting, let's just wait, all
right?"

"But you're not happy with him."

She brushed her hair back now, and I saw the round-
ness of her upper arm, the flesh hardly hanging from the
bone and thought, Well, one day soon. She watched me
watching her, and in a gesture as if to say, "If *you* get

drunk and use it to do what you want, here is your excuse," she poured my glass up almost to the brim.

"No," she said. "If I were, I'd hardly be out drinking with the man who's trying to destroy him."

"Why *are* you out with me?" I asked her, touching her small hand now, where it lay on the table. "Is it because I might destroy him, or to try to keep me from it?"

"No," she said. "It really doesn't have anything to do with that."

"Then why?"

"I haven't got it entirely defined, but it was because I thought it might be fun, different, anyway, to be with you."

"And has it been fun?"

"Yes," and she went on, "and I guess I thought it would be easy to talk with you and that you—"

"What?" She was seriously looking for something now, down beneath the surface where she was both open and a bit hard.

"And I thought probably you wouldn't hurt me because it seems you've been banged around a little yourself."

Banged around? I thought about all those years with my wife. How good they had been. Sharply, I felt her absence. Banged around?

"Well, I wouldn't hurt you," I said flustered at this odd admission. "But banged around?" I thought of the heart attack. And all the stories: trying to get photographs out of parents who had just learned their kids were run over by a truck, or drowned.

Or seeing that poor guy in Hue with his four sons all lying dead on the street in front of him while he shakily tried to put a candle at each of their heads and feet; and the time when I had stepped heavily into a story myself to put a tourniquet on a black militant's shotgunned leg and his friend had come up to me and screamed "Get your motherfucking hands off him." The friend had ripped at the adequate tourniquet made of my shirt sleeve and ineptly tried to shut off the bleeding with his thin belt. God. God.

"Oh, shit," I said. "I've been banged around but it isn't any more than what comes with the territory. No, I won't hurt you." I smiled, a little weary and even tipsy now. "I like you. You heard me out."

" 'She gave him for his pains a world of sighs,' " she quoted with a grin that curled one side of her mouth, " 'She swore, in faith, 'twas strange, 'twas passing strange . . . She wished that heaven had made her such a man.' " This time, it was she, her fingers soft as little animals, who reached over and took my hand.

"And I guess because I thought we would be friends," she said.

"And because you can outquote me," I countered.

We picked out the last small bits of flesh from the rockfish, which still tasted ever so slightly of fennel. The wine was almost gone. God, I did not want to leave her.

"I'm not even thinking of you as a story any more," I said.

"Ah," she said. "I know. It will come back when the wine wears off," she added practically.

"I mean I don't want to end lunch."

She caught her breath. I could sense her making up her mind, abruptly.

"What do you have to do?" she asked, sipping the last of her wine, a little nervously.

"Nothing. Just call in. What about you?"

"I could say—I mean I don't have to say anything. I can just tell the maid I'll be having supper out. I would—"

"Have to be in fairly early tonight. . . ."

We were looking now into each other's eyes, and what I saw in hers was some trepidation, even fright.

"Yes," she said.

"Shall we have another bottle of wine?"

"Do you want to? Maybe a half bottle."

"Okay, an old fat burgundy with some cheese. Then we go?"

"Yes," she said, the hawser loosed now, the resolve made. "Yes," she said, "that's a lovely idea."

To prolong our time away from the city, and more practically, out of fear she or her car might be recognized if we went back in town to my apartment, we drove to a big, impersonal motel out Gaithersburg way.

Once inside the room, she swung into my arms and I saw that she was a very hungry Betty Page Rawlinson Edwards. I was slightly unnerved.

We kissed each other a long time and then broke for air.

"He must be nuts," I said. But she was saying "Mmmhh." She was in another space where I was not going to arrive in time.

I lifted her skirt and felt the softness of her buttocks, then slipped my hand for a moment around to her front and she was already damp, even slickish and I thought, My God, how long has it been for her. What's the matter with that clown?

She was breathing very hard now, and so was I. I unbuttoned her down the front. And leaf by leaf we took off each other's clothes, there on the carpet. She was just as pretty as I had thought she would be. I stood back a moment, saw the slopes of her breasts, and a rounding stomach and the wiry patch of her pubis. Then back to the face, and it was a lovable face, open and happy and anticipatory, and I thought, even at that moment, this is going to be complicated because we are going to make it good.

She pulled back the covers on the bed and we fell into it.

I am not sure the way women's minds work, but I know it is different from men's. I think she must have been thinking for some time about how horny she was and specifically about what was going to happen, but not specifically about with whom.

Because we had been kissing only a few minutes when she grabbed at me and thrust me into her, me on top. She was there, ready, and thank the Lord, because with my lifelong record of embarrassing precipitancies, except for my wife where we had worked it so well, I was a very nervous lover.

"Now, now," Betty Page said, just as if I had a choice. And then that was the last little humorous thought I had as I was carried on out of mind with the familiar explosions. And, oh, my God, how good it was to be hugged and sighed over gratefully until she began to drift away from passion and into sleep beside me, both of us warm and filled with wine and good food, and quickly, thickly satisfied in sex.

Shortly, we woke up.

"Did you have any protection?" I asked.

"No. It's okay. It's not time."

"That's what they all say," I sighed, turning to kiss her lips, the thinness poutier from kissing.

"I'll have to start taking the pill," she said. How matter-of-factly she had assumed we would be lovers. And yet, to me, too, it seemed natural, an assumption I did not question.

"How've you been keeping from getting pregnant?"

She snuggled up closer to me. I surmised she was saying she kept from getting pregnant by her husband not screwing her.

"The dumb stick," I murmured, thinking of that mule face staring out of a bill-signing or TV interview.

Still, she said nothing.

"Why not?" I asked, kneeling above her and looking down. Even flat on her back her breasts rounded up nicely. "You're beautiful. I bet you're more beautiful now than you were when he married you. Look at you. Why not?"

"Ah," she sighed. "Just think about it. I mean if you really want to talk about it. You saw the way he was the other night. It's disgusting. And I know about the girl, and he knows I know."

"How?" I wondered momentarily how I could get into print that he was sleeping around.

"How else in Washington? An anonymous call. So the next time I saw her at a party, I listened hard to her when she was talking to me, and when she was talking to him and when he was talking with us together. And I knew." She shrugged.

"Did you put it to him?" I lay back down beside her.

"No. Why?"

"That's a shitty life."

"Well, not entirely," she said, and paused. Then she said, "We've still got one son at home to bring up. I like Washington. And I like being needed."

"You mean the way he confides in you."

"Yes. Without it, he'd become . . . unstructured."

"Jesus," I said. "You make me feel like I've just fucked a confessional booth."

"Ah," she laughed reaching over slowly to caress me. Damned if I was not coming back.

"Hurray," I said. "This is fantastic. I'm generally such a pathetic failure after the first time, I never make it back for a second. One girl felt sorry for me and made me some Lifebuoy soap."

She stopped what she was doing and, elbows down, head in hands, looked at me.

"I wish you would stop talking about anybody else." I was abashed.

"I'm sorry," I said. "Don't you—?"

"No," she said. "Once, three years ago, just a little—"

"Do I know him?"

"God," she laughed. "Don't you have any restraint?"

"Not much." I sensed it would be somebody important. There had been a trace of reserve in her laugh.

"Well," she said, "it didn't work out. It couldn't."

"So for two years?"

"No, we, Pom and I, I didn't mean it has been nothing that long."

"When did you stop, last—"

"Oh, maybe once a month, but—"

"Oh," I said. "And he just uses a—"

"Yes," she laughed with a bitter edge. "It's not enough to take those damn pills for. Anyway, shut up."

She began caressing me again, and suddenly I was hard.

I kneeled again between her legs and slowly and softly rubbed it on the lips of her vagina. "Listen," I said, suddenly overcome with gratefulness to her, "we can be lovers; I won't fool around with anybody else. Okay? I won't press you for stories. I'll just be wherever you can be whenever you get away."

"Oh, now," she said. "It's too soon to talk that way," reaching up to my forearms and holding them gently in those hands, those beautiful little hands. "Oh," she said, and the tears welled up in her eyes, dark green in the shuttered room. "Oh," she said, and pulled me slowly into her.

4

The Betrayer

On the way home, I told her I was going to put together
the story on Edwards and the bank and be done with
the investigation. She shrugged. The bank story was,
after all, something I had researched in the past, before
we had become lovers. For now, for fair, we were
lovers.

I did the piece almost mechanically, calling the
Speaker for comment. I was uncomfortable on the telephone when I heard his voice, but he gave me that old,
sure bullshit that he knew would be carried in full and
high up in the story because the *Eagle* strove to be fair,
whatever that is. After he had lied to me, I felt better.

"I received the loan on a routine basis, with no
favors promised or granted by either party," he said,
his voice—so slurred when last I heard it—crisp and
decisive now. "The banking industry knows well my
stands in favor of tighter bank restrictions, and on
behalf of the small depositor and loan seeker.

"To suggest that any contributions would affect any
decision I have made in my twenty-five years in the
Congress is to suggest that our system of political financ-
ing itself is corrupt and that the thousands of persons
in politics are corrupt. I reject that kind of cynicism.

"I strongly favor now, and have in the past, the right
kind of public campaign-financing law. Until we get it
passed, I and my fellow candidates will function as we

75

have in the past, without fear, and with favor toward none."

With all that space devoted to his statement, the guts of my story were pretty far down in my article, but the paper carried it out front. It caused a good deal of interest in the press gallery and the wire services picked it up.

It would give him some grief in his coming campaign.

Behind-the-scenes, Edwards retaliated predictably. He had the Kansas Republican Party tear into the *Eagle* for "discriminatory muckraking against one of America's finest leaders," which was more or less true, given the quality of our other leaders. Edwards also briefly stopped talking with our House reporter.

Washington Consolidated Bank transferred its advertising from us to the *Post* and the *Star*, but it hadn't amounted to much anyway. Mr. March, in return, pulled one of the accounts for his pulp paper interests out of Washington Consolidated and gave it to Riggs, another big bank. He also sent me a snide little note saying, "If you can't nail people for anything more than that, why bother?" There was something, but not much, in what he said.

When I called Betty Page the afternoon of the day the story broke she promised to meet me for a brief lunch the next day in Palisades Park. She came, cautious in dark glasses, and tense again, but soon we were laughing together, chilly, sitting on a bench watching the bundled-up kids swinging.

"I knew about the note to you from Bertie March," she said. "He told Pom about it, called him at home during supper."

"What'd *he* say? I mean your husband." It was intriguing to get this kind of backstairs chatter firsthand.

"He told Bertie that it was part of the game, not to worry, and then he said that if he trusted anybody at the Federal Communications Commission to keep his mouth shut, he'd have tried to get them to challenge the *Eagle*'s TV subsidiaries."

"He was joking, right?"

"More or less. But last night, he told me that anybody

with no more control over his reporters than Bertie
March has should give up publishing."

"That's what makes March a bearable publisher,"
I said.

"Aubrey, I'm not arguing the case. I'm just telling
you what he said," she replied.

When she had to go, we agreed to meet again that
weekend. The Speaker was off to San Francisco to
address the National Association of Manufacturers.

I justified my desertion of the overall Edwards story
to myself: The only hard news I had turned up was the
bank payoff and the drinking episode, and I had bartered off the bar scene for the Cuban visit of Frieden.
The rest, including the smell of Big Oil money, was
no more than surmise.

At the paper Cubbins alone was disconcerted by the
time I had invested for one story. But he was too busy
to make more of it than a suspicious sniff about "low-
yield reporting." For my part, I felt guilty about aban-
doning the drinking story, but to pursue it while I slept
with his wife would be sick even by my low standards.

I tried with little hope to wheedle myself onto the
President's Cuban trip on the grounds that I had broken
the story. But Bothild, the White House man, quite
properly foiled me. Nevertheless, I took a vicarious
pleasure in the visit's success.

Meanwhile, I worked sedulously every day digging
into the dunghills of corruption in the three branches
of government. To Frieden's credit, his administration
seemed far cleaner than his predecessor's which hadn't
been all that bad.

Or maybe Frieden's credit with the press still had
not run out. During the campaign, he had happily dis-
posed of the a-Jew-can't-be-elected-President myth. He
had faced his Jewishness head-on, tackling at whistle
stop after whistle stop the tough questions on Israel.
The college kids backing him had even minted up
"Harry Frieden, the Golden Jew" buttons.

Liking him, we made no real effort to spear him.
Even muckrakers like to suspend belief in the infinite
corruptibility of politicians when they can.

At night I ached for my next tryst with Betty Page.

By now, we were semidesperate to see each other: "in love," if there were enough explicit left in the little cliché to make it still worth employing. We started meeting in motels outside town on days when Edwards was speaking somewhere away from Washington. But after a little such inconvenience, she began coming to my apartment, parking her car downtown and riding the rest of the way by taxi.

I lived in one of those impersonal towers the federal government helped build when the old Fourth Precinct was cleared of its slums, blacks, waterfront salmonellarias, and blind alleys. Ten years ago, it had been called the New Southwest. Now, rents were lower, along with the expectations for perfect renters.

But I loved my apartment. It looked out over the new freeway and the old tracks. Beyond were the government buildings, the dull red slate of the older roofs, the cool domes of the National Gallery and the Natural History Museum, the old Post Office tower and there, atop its own hill, the failed Michelangelo dome of the Capitol itself.

On my balcony I could see the residences of power from the executive departments to the Capitol from whence cometh our health. My eating table was by the sliding glass balcony doors. Directly off it was the living room, comfortable and eclectic, a chair from my mother's old house when she died those years ago, the furniture my wife and I had gradually bought.

I had kept the king-size bed my wife and I had slept in all those years before she died. I suppose a more sensitive man would have felt he was polluting a memory, lying with one woman or another in that bed, but I did not think so.

It was a good bed, a fine mattress, a bed where my wife and I had made almost the best of a good marriage. There, beneath the semi-abstractions of Venice where we had been happy, and Paris, and Munich on those few long vacations, and a good, funny print by Rossant, I felt I had been able to be me.

Sometimes, Betty Page slipped into the flat before I

went to work. I had fresh ground coffee brewing and had shaved and made the place reasonably neat. She quickly poured herself a cup, and pushed off her shoes.

When we had drunk the coffee, chattering about what we had done since we had last seen each other, we went to the bedroom, often laughing. She left a trail of clothes behind her. She was a very free and beautiful Kansas lady by the time she got to the bed.

Or at lunch, she met me for cold cuts and a bottle of Rhine. As spring came, we ate on the balcony swathed in my old sweaters. We looked out from the Southwest over the freeway at the Capitol now surrounded by patches of blossoms, and gleaming in the noonday sun. I thought of Pom Edwards taking his first Cutty Sark of the day up there. In the past, I had felt a sort of shameful joy in cuckolding him. Now, I thought about Betty Page being at their home when he rolled in full of booze and stinking of another woman and my rage at him was murderous.

"You've got to leave him," I growled at her. "Got to make him go."

My anger caught her as she washed down a bite of pastrami with a sip of the wine.

"My God," she said, startled into talking with her mouth half-full. "What did he do now?" And when I explained, I got the increasingly galling arguments of that first day: It wasn't that bad for her; the Speaker needed her.

And there was, genuinely, the younger son. She could force Pom out of the house. But suppose he contested a divorce. Could she risk the son living with a lush whose life, when it was not drinking and whoring, was in the House with its endless, complex compromises and other subtleties?

These were real enough reasons, but they were also symptoms. She was a woman who had weeded her portfolio long ago. She was not going to give up her pattern of life for a new world that held no great promise.

What would she get? A love affair, and at best (or worst) a marriage to an aging man with a bad heart, a life of having me away on stories, at the paper, involved in the habituating rigmarole of the *Eagle*, a gumshoe reporter's wife instead of the wife of the Speaker of the United States. Was that such a good switch when she could have our love for each other without so drastic a step?

In this context, even what she said of his needing her made sense. Fulfilling his need was part of her bargain with him. Our love for each other, however intense and joyous, was not a practical replacement for her status quo. At least not now.

The spring weather chilled one last time into biting, windy days. Now, we walked more, her quick strides so long accustomed to her husband's long steps, that I sometimes found her hard to keep up with. We gabbed happily and diversely. She first talked vaguely of the secrets Edwards told her at night, then openly, trusting me not to divulge them.

Sometimes I felt my failure to write these secrets made me a tame, housebroken reporter. Loving her, I had to get her permission to pursue anything of value she gave me. There was a dollhouse quality to it: She would reveal a confidence—the Vice-President's son had gotten a GS 13 job for which he was totally unqualified. Then we would figure out how long I had to wait before I could pursue it in order to make sure that Edwards did not marvel that his private words were so soon translated into news stories.

Once, when she told me that the President was going to order an antitrust prosecution of the steel industry which had just co-ordinated a blatant price rise, we agreed I could do the piece quickly. The morning the story broke, Edwards muttered to her over breakfast, "This bastard is coming up with everything." It was enough to spook us away from using anything he told her. And from this I champed more than ever.

The constraint of withholding stories only exacerbated the jealousy I already felt toward the Little Major. Her refusal even to think of leaving him seemed illogical, almost infantile to me. I felt hostile and hurt over her staying with him.

Still, there was that honesty between us. I never betrayed her confidences, never permitted myself the knowing look or hint that would indicate I knew something of the gossip or major stories that she transmitted to me from her conjugal bed.

One morning, she came in and reached for the coffee-pot, nervous and excited.

"Did you come across anything about a company called Boles-Panjunk, when you were snooping into our business?" she asked. I had not seen her for three days and wanted her, had been lying awake for an hour thinking about her. Piss on Boles-Panjunk.

I came to her and began unbuttoning her blouse.

"No, damnit," she said. "Really, Aubrey. Just wait, okay?"

"Boles-Panjunk," I said. "It's a California company. I never heard of it until I saw it on his House stock ownership report. There's a Securities and Exchange filing on it."

"What else?"

"Nothing else. Let's go to bed."

"Now come on," she said, going to the refrigerator for, I thought, some cream for our coffee. She came back to me and kissed me and I felt the hardness coming on and tried to push up against her through my pajamas. Without breaking the kiss, she reached carefully down toward my groin and put the piece of ice she had secretly palmed from the refrigerator under my tightening testicles.

"Holy God!" I shrieked, pushing her away and dancing the ice cube out of my pajama leg. "You could sterilize me, you dumb bitch." She howled with laughter and in a moment I was roaring with her.

"Boles-Panjunk," she said. I threw the piece of ice in the sink.

"I never found out who any of those guys in the company were. I never heard of them. They weren't in Who's Who and Pom didn't show up in the SEC filing."

"What kind of company was it?"

"Who knows—one of those miniconglomerates. They

owned a seed company, I think, and a little factory with
a patent on some drill bits. That's the only thing interesting, the oil bits and—"

"Was there a Webb Renardi—"

"Can't remember. Why, Betty Page?"

We were across the table now, I blowing my black
coffee and she taking little sips with her thin, facile lips.

"He was full of Webb Renardi along with the scotch
last night."

"You've got to leave him," I nagged her. "I'm not
pushing now; I simply want to keep the motion before
the House."

"Look, spare me that. This Renardi, he said he was
going to do him in."

"Who do who in?" For the moment, I forgot about
sex.

"Renardi do Pom in."

"Oh? So you said, 'Who is Renardi,' right?"

"Yes, and he said, 'He's a son-of-a-bitch at Boles-
Panjunk,' and they'd stupidly fired him."

"It's a little two-bit company out in California," I
mused again, wondering why the Speaker of the House
would be worried about a firm I'd scarcely heard of,
and, moreover, one I had almost skipped over in my
investigation. I felt the guilt of the cabinetmaker who
failed to put in a significant joint pin.

"What else did he say about Boles-Panjunk?"

"Nothing," she said, gulping down the rest of her
coffee. "I thought maybe you knew something. You'll
leave it alone, right?"

For once, I said nothing, secreting the knowledge
she had given me. She had possibly put into my hands
the means of really hurting her husband. Edwards had
never talked of anyone "getting him" before. Always
the optimist, his strength in his ability to deal with his
enemies, he would not have mentioned his worry, it
would not have come bursting through the alcohol if
it were not real.

Now, I could perhaps get a clear shot at him. I only
had to betray Betty Page's trust in telling me. Yet,
hadn't I come up with the name of the company myself,

those many weeks ago? Didn't I have a right to go ahead on this one, at least to see where it led, why Renardi had been stupidly fired, for instance? The thrill of having what I knew was a definitive clue, quickened the excitement of being with her.

She stood now beside the bed, naked except for her half slip. Where the morning sun from my windows hit the sheen of her slip, I could see the dark bush. Without kissing her, I looked into those bright green eyes and took her nipples gently in my thumbs and forefingers.

"I wouldn't put ice under your woussie," I said to her, feeling the presto beat of blood in my pulses.

"What would you put there?" she said, catching her breath, savoring the same excitement.

I dropped my hand to the hem of her slip and lifted it up. Then, ever so gently I opened her vagina with my fingers and ran them lightly up and down around the soft hairy curve of their lips. Finally, I slipped my first two fingers into the slickening opening.

"I would put my fingers in there, and then something else," I murmured to her.

It had never been better. And yet when she left, I lay back in the bed and thought of how I would find Webb Renardi and what I would say to him when I did. Only fleetingly did I think that I was betraying a confidence. And again I passed it off with the thought that I had come across the company before she named it to me. She had put me back on the track, and now I was going to follow it where it led.

The SEC files showed Renardi was a vice-president of Boles-Panjunk and that he had a nice chunk of stock. And the bits they had patented were oil drill bits. I thought excitedly of what the old lawyer, Chlorstand, had said about Edwards and the oil industry.

At Boles-Panjunk's headquarters in San Francisco, I got the "He is no longer with us bit," when I asked for Renardi. There was no forwarding address and no phone number and his secretary had left too, and, no, they were not permitted to give out her name.

I located his name in the Mill Valley phone book,

but it was disconnected. That was all about par for something like this.

I sent an air mail special envelope marked "Personal" to him at Boles-Panjunk with a note inside telling him to wire me at a post office box because I had important information about his "case." Even angry companies think twice about failing to forward special delivery mail to fired or disgruntled employees. If anyone in his old office opened it, I didn't want them to know the *Eagle* was looking into the company, so I didn't sign my name.

Sure enough, I got a wire back giving me some times to call a telephone number in Mill Valley. That would probably be a drugstore pay phone near his home. I got him on the first try and he was scared to death, but at the same time bitterly angry at "the screwing I took." He only asked weakly how I'd heard about him.

For all his fears, I knew he was going to be okay, and after a little conning and sympathy, he began to want to meet me, even though he recognized I had gotten to him through a bit of subterfuge. He must suspect I really knew nothing about "his case."

At first he wanted me to fly to California, and I said, all right, I would if I were sure he had the goods. But gradually he came around and agreed that since he had some business in Washington, he'd fly in and see me in the process.

"Bring your papers," I told him. "Everything. Okay?"

"Okay." By now he had that sense of participating in great events that sources often get. It has a hypnotic effect on them.

"And be careful about letting the Speaker know you're in town."

That was the first time I had mentioned the Little Major. It was important that Webb Renardi not panic the Speaker into blackmailing him off, or buying him off. I had not even wanted to mention his name on the telephone. But the warning had to be made.

"Why?" said Renardi cautiously.

"We'll talk about it when you get here," I said. "Bring everything."

So much is implicit and so little explicit in such talks. He sensed, and I knew, that we were going to try to knock out the Speaker of the House of Representatives. But not a word had been said about it and now he was flying across the country to conspire in the act.

Betty Page could not see me for two days. When she did, at my apartment, I faithlessly said nothing to her about Webb Renardi. Somehow, my treachery, for I saw it now as that, made our love-making less good. In that way that women who are not young know things, she must have recognized that some odd infidelity lay behind it.

"You're getting tired of me," she said lightly, in a parody of women who say such things seriously.

"Never," I said. And yet, I could not be totally dishonest with her. I had to signal to her that I was betraying her. "Is he still worried about that company guy?" I said.

"Renardi?"

"Yeah, that was his name, right?"

"He didn't say anything more."

"I took another look at my notes on it," I said.

"And?"

"Renardi did work there. He was a vice-president." Suddenly, she was cautious, sensing what I was up to.

"You aren't doing anything on it?"

"Are you kidding?" I said, backing away from a confession by telling her a misleading truth. "Before I ever sat down to a typewriter on anything like that, I'd have you protected in eight different ways."

"So you aren't doing anything?" she persisted.

"No," I said. "Just those checks." I meant her to think "those checks" were merely my check of my notes. Again, I had not literally lied. But in my dirty heart I knew I might as well have. It would have been cleaner, far cleaner.

Renardi was just as foxy as his name implied. He was short, maybe five-seven, and must have weighed two hundred pounds, but he was well-tailored enough to look lighter, and with his suntan he probably still had no trouble finding women. We met at the bar atop the

Marriott Hotel across Key Bridge where there wasn't much danger of any Congressional types seeing us.

I made small talk with him, looking way down the river where you could see boat lights, and watching the headlights of the cars heading upstream on the George Washington Parkway. It was a hell of a sight. Across the way, the city itself was spread out like the flat-chested bejeweled whore it was.

"They wrecked the work of a lifetime," he had begun to say, working gradually into a good anger. Since he was only about thirty-five, I wondered about the "life-time" bit.

"How, exactly, did they do it?" I asked. "I mean so an old broken-down police reporter can understand it." First, it was important to let him say it, then I would get him to open that three-cylinder-dial briefcase he had with him.

He was rude to the waitress when she arrived with his Heineken. I didn't like him. She was a tall, pretty sailorette in one of those short skirts that showed a lemon-peel moon of ass when she bent to serve a drink across from us. Despite this distraction, I thought mainly about what a good story I was going to get.

As Renardi explained it, the Little Major had been given a huge stock option, using a lawyer named Nicholas Kitticon as the straw. It would be hard to prove Kitticon, whoever he was, didn't own the options himself. But that we could see later.

Renardi said that the options had been promised to him, Renardi, and their value had gone up considerably. Kitticon bought seven thousand options at two dollars a share. The option was to buy at $11. Now the stock was at $85 over the counter. It didn't take long to compute that each share would now cost Kitticon $13, that he could sell at a profit of $72, which, times seven thousand, came to something like a half million. Nice. I remembered I had seen Kitticon's name on the SEC stock offering prospectus as what?

"As consulting counsel?"

"You mean Kitticon, yeah," said Renardi. "But, I'm

telling you, he was a straw for Edwards. Edwards got my stock. He—"

"How can you prove Kitticon was a straw?"

"I can't, but I know. Boles"—that would be the board chairman—"told me."

"Would he swear to it?"

"No. He'd say Kitticon got the options because he gave them advice on how to float the stock."

"Why did Edwards get any stock?"

"He's going to get the drillers to adopt our—Boles-Panjunk's patent." Ah, I thought, there it Goddamn is.

"Is it any good?"

"Yeah, it's a fine drill bit."

But there would be other good competing drill bits. It was clear: Renardi had been promised a killing in the form of the options. But there were only a limited number of options and the Speaker's price for getting the drill bits in general use, which would bring Boles-Panjunk millions, was the seven thousand options. As proof of the fact that the industry knew these drill bits were going to be standard equipment, Boles-Panjunk stock had increased phenomenally.

The Speaker had covered himself neatly. He had bought a few shares of Boles-Panjunk on the open market so that he could record honestly on the House records that he had a holding. To have had nothing on the record would fry his ass with his colleagues if he ever got caught in the greater "investment" of the $14,000 worth of options. If he got caught now, he could claim he had disclosed, while admitting he had perhaps mistakenly disclosed a bit too little. And if the full value of the windfall ever came out, he could say it had succeeded beyond his wildest dreams. As to the quo for that quid, there wouldn't be an oilman alive who would admit that Edwards had forced the Boles-Panjunk on them. Anyway, there would be only three in the country he'd have to speak to for general acceptance of it on a near industry-wide basis.

As to Kitticon, the straw but not the beneficial holder, Edwards could simply say he bought the options in

Kitticon's name because he planned to use Kitticon as lawyer to set up a trust for his kids. That was common enough.

Thus the good Speaker had not only hidden a half-million profit well, he had provided for a cover story if, as I was about to do, anyone caught him. Then why was he so afraid? Obviously because he thought the pressure on the oil companies was provable.

By dessert, pineapple with heavy cream for both of us, Renardi and I were doing fine. I understood the deal well, and I was ready to know how the thing could be proved. Saying we got it from a disgruntled ex-officer would be the least effective way of doing it, and besides Renardi was not that suicidal. His lifetime of work may have been wrecked, but he was already looking into a couple of new hustles.

"What can we show on paper, Webb?" I asked him gently.

With things "Webb" and "Aubrey," he efficiently opened up his locked briefcase and pulled out a sheaf of letterheaded paper, all Xeroxes and carbons. As I feared, most of them involved Boles's promise of the options to Renardi, and the ultimate sale of them to Kitticon. There was no mention of the Speaker in any of the papers. On the other hand, there were also letters to Boles-Panjunk from eight big oil companies, all about the same time, asking for information on the drill bit. That left me with two enormous gaps:

I had to show Kitticon held the stock for Edwards.

I had to show Edwards had intervened with the oil companies.

Something else nagged me and suddenly it hit. "Why'd you bring the carbons?" I asked.

"What do you mean?"

"The carbons, why didn't you Xerox them, too?"

Renardi felt my concern and was frightened.

"No time. I took the carbons when there were carbons and Xeroxed the originals when they were the only copy."

"What was your status when you took the carbons?" It hit home.

"I had already quit. It was when I went in to clean up."

"Shit," I said to myself. We had hot documents on our hands. Interstate theft. A federal offense, even if they were carbons. I had taken chances like this before, but I never liked it. Now, I would be paranoid about being followed until I could get the damned things copied and out of my sight. I didn't want to spook him by telling him my worries, which were real.

"Let's get these copied, these carbons, okay?" I said.

"Any big problem?" he said, worried now himself.

"No, I worry about even the little things." I tried to soothe him. The fucking FBI, I thought. Could this be a setup? Could Edwards have gotten to this guy? A terrible chasm opened up: me busted, the *Eagle* caught with stolen documents. Some of the stuff got technical about the drill bits. They could even make a cheap industrial-espionage case. And for Edwards, they would. Surely, I thought, this is my overactive fantasy life triggered by the cuckoldry and, worst, my treachery toward Betty Page in even crapping around with this story.

But Renardi couldn't read my thoughts. Besides, there was this: If Edwards sicked the FBI on me, his story would be sure to come out. Unless the whole thing were a setup, right from his telling Betty Page about Renardi.

Yet, even if it weren't set up all the way, I might still be in trouble. From the beginning, Edwards must have feared Renardi would "go public." Drunkenly and thus honestly, that was what he was telling Betty Page that night. Since he believed the story was coming out anyway, better for him that it come out tarring simultaneously both me and the *Eagle* for using stolen documents. I began to sweat despite the air conditioning. Still, it was too good a story to let go of, no matter what.

We drove toward the *Eagle* in Renardi's rented car. Across the street from the paper was an all-night drugstore with one of those twenty-five-cent duplication machines. That way I wouldn't have to take the lousy carbons into the paper. If I had been alone, I would have circled the block, gone into an alley, turned around and headed back, just to be on the safe side. But above all, I didn't want to scare Renardi.

He parked outside the drugstore. Inside the almost empty store, I stood before the machine putting in quarters while he handed me the dozen carbons. The copying was lousy but legible. I kept looking over my shoulder. This would be when they'd bust me, I thought. They'd want to get me with the stolen carbons.

We finished the job and were back out on the street, getting ready to part, me for the *Eagle* across the way and him for his hotel. It was then that I saw the yellow unmarked Chevy without any fancy trim and the two young FBI cop types inside, screeching up in front of the *Eagle*'s side exit just across from me. Up the street, another car, a Plymouth, was barreling in. Shit, I thought.

The two Feebs bailed out of the Chevy as I began to run. So long as they don't get a chance to identify themselves, nobody's going to make a resisting arrest case on me, I thought.

I started screaming for the police, knowing that this ruse would come in handy, if it ever came to court, even though nobody would ever mistake these two Neat Nellies for yokers. The Chevy guys were new at it; one came straight at me and the other came around the front of the car.

That was my way out. Two others were already running at me from the second car and another two from God knows where. Renardi had retreated into the store. He had the carbons and he was a goner.

My only way lay behind the Chevy and into the *Eagle* and I took it. One of the FBI men moved to block me and with a lunge I jumped on the hood of the Chevy, rolled across it and fell to the street, hurting all over from the thud.

Blessedly, the guard from the *Eagle* had seen the activity and came out. He recognized me and I him. For a split moment I felt remorse for him, but only for that instant.

"Help, John!" I cried, rising and running for the door as one of the men came at me to tackle me.

The guard, a wonderfully good-natured black man when he greeted us or bid us good-by, darted in front of the tackler. I was one of his.

"Motherfuckers," John screamed going for his holster. "Motherfuckers." I scrambled for the door.

When I looked back, he was crouched in the classic gunslinger pose and had his gun out and aimed at the FBI man. The FBI man was screaming at him. "FBI! FBI!" But he wasn't making any move for badge or gun. Across the street, two of the other well-clad agents were shouting the same thing, like enraged cheerleaders.

Thank God, I thought, as I flung open the door, the FBI were well trained enough not to shoot just because they see a drawn pistol. As I darted inside, I could hear them arguing heatedly with John; I knew it would be only a moment before the badges were produced and had their effect.

As I got to the end of the hall, I looked back and saw the door swing open, and two of the men in suits rush through. I ran down the steps at the end of the hall toward the presses, still clutching my copied documents. Motherfuckers, I thought in echo. They weren't going to take away my Goddamn story without a chase.

The huge Goss presses were spinning their inky skein of paper, smooth and flat, for the second edition. The pressmen looked up as I ran by, first with a shock of outrage, but then, among the old-timers, with a gasp of recognition. I had walked the picket line with enough of them.

Some gave me only a marveling helpless look, but others saw my pursuers with their badges in their hands and knew instantly what was happening.

When I turned back once, I saw that the FBI men were running an obstacle course of stools and rag buckets thrown in their way by the pressmen. Even one half drum of paper had been toppled. The FBI men bumped past it.

My breath came fast and heavy. I thought, for an

instant, of halting. Why not just give it to them? But Goddamnit it was only copies now, my copies, the *Eagle*'s copies. Let them go to court and block it, not snatch it, my story, out of my hand as "stolen goods."

I was exhausted. I lurched and stumbled toward the back door, leading up to the loading dock. One of the pressmen, his eyes jerky, beneath the traditional newspapersquare hat, was holding the door for me. He and two others got me in their arms just as I almost collapsed and half dragged me into the back of one of our trucks.

I flopped down on a stack of bound papers in the rear and the big truck growled away from the dock just as six FBI men ran up to it. One was jabbering into a walkie-talkie. Someone had alerted the newsroom, because there were three cameramen in shirtsleeves flashing at the truck, the FBI men, and at the door behind them out of which a crowd of pressmen and others had burst.

Oddly, I had begun to laugh hysterically. The truck lurched through the lighted alley into Eighteenth Street, rushed through a red light and headed out K.

"Aubrey, Aubrey," the older of the pressmen bellowed, "what the hell is this? Is that the FBI?"

"Yeah, yeah," I roared with laughter. "The FBI."

"The FBI?"

"Yeah."

"It's the FBI," the old man said, and the three of them began to laugh wildly, too.

But it was no go. Although one of our own radio cars had swung in behind us, right behind it was the plain yellow sedan with the siren going. At Seventeenth, a cop rushed out in the street and thinking we were getting an escort held traffic and waved us through, but the Feebs had the next intersection barricaded with two cars, and the driver of the big newspaper truck bumped it up over the curb and into Farragut Square.

I shouted with discomfort as the baled newspapers bounced up and onto my back, then righted myself and clung to the side as the truck yawed up to the subway hole. These boys had seen some FBI TV shows of their own.

As the truck shuddered to a stop, I fell again, but the two younger pressmen grabbed me roughly and half helped, half handed me to the ground. We ran for the tube, down into the glistening new *enceinte* of the stop, past the illuminated route map. The two men had somehow kept on their pressmen's hats and the few late patrons stared incredulously as we rushed past them. All three of us plunged through the out doors, past a tired old woman with spectral skin, and onto the platform.

But now, God, we were trapped. I had wadded up the papers and had them in my coat pocket. I thought of handing them to the pressmen, but I knew the FBI would search them; even now they would be going over the truck. Those bastards could turn out fifty men in fifteen minutes if they had to.

I looked down at the tracks. I didn't want to run anymore. I had already almost killed myself one time for a half-assed story involving that rangy pecker. My heart was bad. Suppose I died trying to save the Goddamn papers? But there was a stubbornness, too. Those young mindless Janissaries who served any master they got. Did I want them taking *my* Goddamn papers? Mine! The *Eagle*'s, and damnit, the First Amendment's!

"Fuck 'em," I gasped to my two friends. "Help me down there." Gently they helped me down to the tracks and I started up into the tunnel. After a minute, I looked back. The FBI men were manhandling the inky printers. Solidarity forever, I thought, disappearing into the dimly lighted hole. I jogged along beside the tracks. Now, I thought, it's just a matter of time. The piss-ants are going to catch me. Age, I thought, remembering a fine poem from somewhere, marks the chink in every armor. The young fuzz were going to catch me.

I thought of hiding the papers under the tracks or in a cranny along the wall. But the FBI was always very good at finding things. Besides, at this stage, all I had was copies: my copies. If I could get away with the things, our lawyers could tie up the FBI in the courts. Maybe I'd never even be charged.

After all, they had come rushing into our newspaper and we could put an awful lot of editorial heat on the government for that kind of bullshit. That was assuming the paper would support me. I thought about old man March. He might fire me later, but he'd stand up for me in the short term. The thought gave me spirit and I ran on, rounded a curve and, heard a train far up the tunnel. I crossed the tracks.

If I could get on, hang on to a train going the other way, there was just a chance I could get away from the Feebs. They would assume I was trying to make it to the next stop north, in the direction I was running. If I could hang on unseen to an eastbound train for a couple of stops, it would work.

For the first time that night, luck hooked on to me, instead of my pursuers. A second train was coming up. That would hamper the Feds, keep them from finding me on the other side of the tracks for the time I needed. Panting, I pressed my body close into the wall by one of the pierlike supports. It held me just barely within its shadow. The big blinding light swept past me and the train slowed at the station. What the hell to grab on to? At the end of the train, where extra cars might be connected, was a tiny vestibule.

The train came to a stop. Cautiously, because the northbound train was already in the station, I swung out of my hole and clambered up over the coupling and into the shallow opening.

I was crouched in low enough to avoid the trainman, and none of the passengers could see me. The last car was far enough back in the station so I would be equally unseen from the platform.

Still gasping, I pressed into my cubbyhole as the train took on its few passengers and accelerated toward Capitol Hill. At the next stop, I pressed in close again. I could have made it onto the platform and up into the street. But there was the chance that the FBI might cover both stations. I clung in, cursing every second that the train remained in the station. At last, we were off.

In the next station, I could smell *uhuru*. Almost joyous, I swung off the vestibule platform onto the coupling and then scrambled up to the passengers' platform. As I brought my right foot up I felt the muscle in my left ankle wrench with agonizing pain. The odd leap had underbalanced me; the sudden weight had been too much. With a stifled scream, I fell onto the station platform. Goddamnit, I thought, even as the agony shot up my leg. So close. Shock blacked me out for an instant, and then I saw the faces gathering around me. I could hear their voices buzz. Then one: "Aubrey."

It was Black Harvard, Connie March's lover.

"Mark," I said. "Goddamnit! Get me out of here."

He was short, somewhat fat, but he was quick. Getting me under the arm, he helped me up and with those lovely Boston accents assured the onlookers he would get me to a doctor.

"He was hanging on to the subway," one old woman said indignantly to my savior.

"He drinks too much; don't worry about it," said Mark in tones that held more than a little truthful disdain.

"Hurry," I groaned to him. "Hurry."

We were on the escalator. My ankle was killing me. Mark was half carrying me despite a Garfinckel's package in his hand.

"I'll get you to a doctor," he said. "What the hell were you doing?"

"Fuck the doctor," I said. "Just get me to someplace safe. Where do you live? Around here?" He assented. "Just get me in there by your telephone." He looked uncomfortable at the idea.

"It's two blocks from the stop," he said. "I—"

"Mark, please just get me there. . . ."

At the top of the steps he got us a cab. When we arrived at his apartment in the modern building near the old court complex, I saw why he was uncomfortable. Connie March was in his apartment, all dressed up in a see-through blouse and tight white denim jeans, and on the table was a birthday cake and two tall bottles of Rosé d'Anjou. Mark had been coming back from buying her a gift and they had planned a lovely little birthday party.

"Happy birthday, Connie," I said at her shocked thin face, looking at those little custard-cup titties with large dark nipples. "My fucking ankle's broken or something."

"Jesus," she said. "What is it now?"

"He was hitching a ride on the subway," Mark said.

"My ankle is killing me," I said. "Can't I just soak it a little in your tub? Oh, Jesus," I groaned. Nothing had ever hurt so much. "I might go into shock."

Gingerly, I began taking off my shoe. Gently I rubbed and the pain was excruciating. I could hear her running water into the tub. When she came back in, she had a bottle of Remy Martin VSOP.

"Not your birthday brandy," I said. "Just some old bourbon or something."

Some of the initial anguish was fading. The thing still throbbed with pain, though. I drank the fiery cognac and it put things into a pattern. You get hurt; you drink brandy; it feels better.

"So what happened?" she asked. Mark, now that he had rescued me, was looking back regretfully at the table. He was clearly a man of habits who did not like the unexpected imposed on him.

I had another shot of the cognac.

"The FBI caught me and a source with some hot papers," I said. "I got in the subway tunnel and jumped on the back of one of those things and almost was out when I turned my ankle. Mark was there, just like in the movies."

"Am I harboring a criminal?" Mark asked, trying to make it sound light, but I knew there was a self-protective quality in it. As I glanced past Connie March, I saw she heard it too.

"Actually, no," I told him. "You're harboring a fugitive from justice. A criminal is when you're convicted." Still, I was grateful for his quick action in getting me here. "Can I use your phone?" I asked.

Though worried, Mark, with his supersensitivity, had read our vibrations and was realizing that gutlessness would now cost him more than courage. I called Cubbins.

"Where are you, you dumb motherfucker?"

"Don't give me that shit, Cubbins," I screamed back. I expected more sympathy. My ankle began to hurt. "I may have a broken ankle," I added.

"Now do you really think I give a shit if you have a broken back?" he said scathingly. "Do you really?"

I hung up on him, spewing out a steady stream of obscenities. At the end, I said to Mark and Connie, "I'm sorry I screwed up your birthday party."

But my outburst with Cubbins had put us, reporters all, in a condition of consanguinity. It was we against the editors of the world. Mark popped a bottle of the Anjou and Connie brought out the fried chicken she had fixed for him and a big dish of turnip greens. Modified soul food. I wondered if she cooked it as a joke. I thought they were both great now. I ate a piece of the chicken and drank some of the wine and called Cubbins back.

"I ought to write you up in the *Columbia Journalism Review*," I said with sweet calm. "Nobody would believe what you did."

He was controlled, if not contrite.

"Why don't you just start from the beginning," he said.

It was a comfortable way to do it. I told him the whole story, omitting only where I had gotten the original tip on Renardi.

"So Mark Braswell took me to his home and that's where I am. Has the FBI filed anything against me?"

"No, March called the Attorney General at his home and said armed FBI men had invaded his plant without warrants"—my heart bumped with pleasure over that cranky old fart—"and that he was going to redo the editorial page and write something about Kristallnacht, U.S.A. We got a picture at the loading dock of an FBI man with his arm up in the air over one of the deaf guys." Some of our pressmen were deaf. "It looks like he's socking him."

"Was he?"

"No. He was waving 'halt' at the truck."

"Jesus," I cackled despite the pain.

"March is thinking of running it on page one."

"Ah," I said. "That's funny."

Cubbins said, "Mr. March would say the picture is existentially true, if he knew what that meant. What can we say about the documents?"

"Did they get my source?"

"Yes. We got him a lawyer. He's saying nothing and they read him his rights, but it looks like now they aren't going to charge him either."

"Because of—"

"Right, because Mr. March raised hell."

"It's a shitty case anyway," I said.

"Right. What triggered them?"

"Edwards?"

"Could be. That can wait. I'll get you a rewrite man, okay? Give him everything. You trust me to edit it?"

"Yeah," I said. "Why did you say such an awful thing in the beginning?"

"I was wondering why the hell you didn't call in. We're both getting old and crotchety. You want me to say I'm sorry?"

"I guess not," I said.

"What happened to your ankle?"

"I don't know. The FBI won't forgive us for making horses' asses out of them."

"Yeah," said Cubbins, his mind now drifting to production deadlines. "Hold on, I'll get you on rewrite."

After I finished dictating to the rewrite man, Mark and Connie March helped me down the stairs. Mark supported most of me, but Connie's skinny muscular little hands were under my arms and I thought, She's too tough, too good for this guy, even though he's a nice guy.

They got me a cab and helped me in.

"I forgot to ask you what birthday it was," I joked.

"Twenty-sixth," she said.

"Happy birthday," I said. "Next year I'll bring you a present." I could see Mark tightening up. All three of us knew what I was thinking.

"Bring yourself," she said brazenly. As I drove off, I thought for the first time that evening about what Betty Page was going to do to me. To us.

At the office, it was festive. The guard who had stood off the FBI saw me and we embraced, slapping each other on the back. He helped me up to the sixth floor and it was all enthusiasm.

And why not?

The secret police had tried to take a reporter's material, and we'd outfoxed and outslugged them. In my view, it was a fine day for the First Amendment and not a bad day for the Fourth, Fifth, Fourteenth, and Ninth.

I shook hands all round and John helped me over to my desk where somebody brought me my story in takes. The rewrite man and Cubbins had done me up proud. I picked up the carbons, false starts and all.

"Armed FBI agents without warrants broke into the *Eagle* last night and manhandled pressroom personnel in an unsuccess

"Armed FBI agents without warrants broke into the *Eagle* last night and tried unsuccessfully to arrest a reporter and confiscate his notes thereby suppressing the story he was

"Armed FBI agents without warrants broke into the *Eagle* last night and tried unsuccessfully to arrest a reporter and confiscate his notes to prevent him from reporting a news story.

"The agents manhandled two deaf pressmen, and arrested two others who had helped the reporter, Aubrey Warder, flee with his data. Both men were released without charge when Attorney General Leonard Appleton personally intervened to leash the FBI. Appleton promised a 'full investigation of the incident.' "

Then, it recounted how I met with Renardi, got copies of his papers, which were not originals and which were from his personal files as former vice-president of Boles-Panjunk. (Our lawyer, a vinegary woman named

Murtry, felt we had a good case that even the carbons could be called Renardi's.) There was no hint of what the story was about, other than that it involved "alleged stock option matters" at Boles-Panjunk.

It was a nice piece of work, considering how seldom rewrite men get it totally right. And I was thrilled by what a hero it made me out to be. But my leg was killing me all the way up to the knee now, and the adrenalin was going out of my heart, leaving me with dread about what it would do to me and Betty Page.

Hurting now, old and tired, I wanted to go to her, soak my foot in a tub, talk with her, have a cup of cocoa and maybe a peanut butter and jelly sandwich, brush my teeth, and have her ease me in between clean sheets and then ease in beside me.

Yet, I didn't dare call her at home to lessen the blow for her, and thus to us, of first learning of the damned thing in the paper.

On this one, I knew Edwards was going to figure out from the mention of Renardi who my highly reliable source was. If I called and he answered, or she had to try to explain who had called, it would explode them, thereby making things even worse for me.

Several times I started to risk telephoning anyway, yearning to get what coinage I could from alerting her. But I held back. Finally, ankle aching, I caught a taxi home.

5

Renardi

I took two aspirins, and, exhausted, I slept like a rock until about five. Then I woke up, my ankle aching, and my anxieties bubbling sickly along. Old dirty, granular, filthy lifelong guilt! It seeped into all my thoughts, as I lay there in the darkness. For one miserable story, I had fouled up something good beyond my dreams.

Betty Page, bruised as she was, was what I wanted and needed. Slowly she would have come to leave that drunken cornhusker. She would give laughter and love and, maybe, even peace to our getting older. I knew these things. I'd messed it up, betrayed her.

Tough Aubrey Reporter! I turned and tossed and thought of her and how good we were together. Then, about dawn, sick of my anxieties, I began some diversionary imagining about the stringy sexiness of Connie March. In her electric monkey body, I could get patched up again if Betty Page left me, I insisted to myself.

I could glue myself together with Connie March while I demolished that shit of a Speaker who had caused me all this pain. But what kind of rationalization was that?

I whimpered a little, letting my mind drift down to my ankle, throbbing with the more bearable pain. And in the throbbing I drifted off.

When morning came I fretted around, waiting until I could call Betty Page. At ten, I phoned our House guy to see whether the Speaker was in his office. It was a natural enough question in view of my story. Thank God, I learned, he was at his desk. Heart beating too fast, I called Betty Page. She answered herself, knowing it was I.

"I'm sorry," I said, before she could begin. "I'm sorry, and I am paying for it. I—" But she cut in nervously.

"The fat's in the fire, Aubrey. He made all the right assumptions." I tried to break in on her, wanting now desperately to salvage it, but she had figured what to say better than I.

"You made a liar out of me as well as yourself," still nervous, but hardening. "I had to lie to him. I told him nothing about . . . us. Just that you had pushed me and pushed me for news, threatening to do all kinds of stories about him if I didn't feed you stuff on other things—"

"But—" I got in. She was ahead of me.

"On the Renardi thing, I said you'd promised it would be the last one and that there would be nothing about the drinking."

"That's true enough—" I got in, trying to take some of the seriousness out of it. But it wasn't any good.

"So that was my story. He didn't believe it. He thinks we are lovers, were lovers. That I betrayed him. Which I did."

"Did you—" I started to ask her whether she had reproached him for his affair with the Danish woman. She was ahead of me on that, too.

"No," she said. "Soon enough for that." My hand on the telephone was running sweat. If I could just bring her around.

"Why soon enough?"

"Oh, tonight, there'll be a scene when he gets home. He'll be sober, off the booze maybe for a week or two." She was cold now, but wanting to run out the string.

"And—"

"And we'll make up. I'll hint at the girl. He'll give her up, too."

I began to panic.

"I want to keep you. I want to marry you," I said quickly, knowing that it was all wrong, as wrong as that question about the Speaker's drinking at the party, all those months ago.

"Unh-uh," she said, not even dignifying it with a "No."

"Why not?" I pushed. "Why not? I love you."

"Aubrey, there are too many lies around us now. I'm locked in with him. When it was clean with us, you and me, then it seemed sometimes that I would leave him. But now we're dirty, too. I told you about Renardi and you couldn't stand not to do it."

She paused, knowing she was about to hurt me, and even now, thinking maybe she wouldn't. But she was cleaner than I, still. "When you went ahead, misled me —oh, I know how you dodged the outright lie—I've thought a hundred times of what you said. When you did that, it cheapened us." She snorted that little "hunh" without humor. "You made a traitor of me."

"Oh, Christ," I groaned in pain, knowing it was true.

"Aubrey," she said, "you turned out to be no better than him, in a way."

"Yeah," I agreed, stricken and without any words. That also was true. I was no better.

"Okay," she said. "Well, good-by." But still she did not hang up.

"Betty Page," I said, "I'm going to go ahead with the Renardi thing." I wanted to explain that I could not quit this whole fucking business even if she wanted me to. Even if she'd leave Edwards. And even if leaving off on the Renardi story could be an acceptable earnest of my love. I wanted to explain that.

She had loved me for what I was. I wanted her to know something of that old "I sing of Olaf" in me that she respected. And so, telling her that I was going ahead, was really telling her that I was going to redeem myself, by doing what duty (Jesus! Is duty too old a word?) required, that my assholish life as a reporter demanded.

These things I wanted to say, but I did not. Perhaps she knew them.

"All right," she said, quietly. "Good-by."

When I had hung up, I hopped into the bathroom. My nerves had gotten to my bladder. Then I hopped back to the bed and pulled the covers over me. I lay on my face in the bed and tried to cry. I thought if I could have a cry with some of those great racking sobs that had come to me two days after my wife died, when I had come back from desperately screwing some little popsie, that it would purge me. But I couldn't sob.

If only I were a drinking man, I thought. But the idea of a hangover on top of all this pain and anxiety was unbearable. I groaned and groaned aloud, then listened to myself and thought, "My God, you're forty-eight years old and here you are groaning out loud for effect like some seven-year-old." It wasn't funny. But at least it was droll.

I got through the day by being so occupied I couldn't dwell on Betty Page. I started with the doctor who diagnosed a bad wrench and put me on crutches for a couple of days.

Once at the office, I fielded calls from other reporters doing follow-ups on the episode. The wire services did a nationwide roundup of comments from editors, who made it bad for the FBI, for a change.

They were compared to the rabble who had broken up Jemmy Rivington's shop in the Revolutionary War, to the Communists in Czechoslovakia, and the Nazis in Germany. A few editors, notably in Richmond and San Diego, said if the documents *were* stolen, the FBI had acted quite properly. But most papers deplored, spoke with sorrow of, warned, were saddened by, could not help but criticize, were damned worried by, and otherwise denounced the FBI's intrusion, violation of, disdain for, and cavalier attitude toward Freedom of the Press.

By the afternoon, I was getting weary of the adulation but had begun to find it bittersweetly humorous. Goddamn TV. Two stations did interviews with me and both wanted me to make sure I kept the crutches by my chair where the camera could dwell on them. I demurred.

I kept my mouth shut about Edwards, and prayed Renardi would. I couldn't find Renardi and assumed he'd hidden himself after the FBI reluctantly cut him loose. In my TV interviews, I played the outraged First Amendmentist to the utmost. And, damnit, I *was* outraged.

The gray blanket of bureaucracy, meanwhile, began to close over the Attorney General's "investigation." Now, he was saying, "We'll take a look at it, but it sounds like a misunderstanding all around." That would keep him out of more trouble with the FBI, who probably had a file on him like everybody else.

In the middle of it, I called up Brent to find out how the FBI had gotten onto it. But he was off on vacation. I was sure the Speaker had a hand in it, but who could prove it?

The only unalloyed benefit of the experience was that our police headquarters reporter was finally able to get my driving license fixed. The local police hated the FBI. I had to laugh; as long as local cops felt that healthy about the Feebs, we were safe from a national police force.

But in the evening, the frenzy abated, and I thought of Betty Page and me, laughing over wine on my bright balcony.

I went back on the Edwards-Boles-Panjunk story the next day. To write even the softest version of it, I needed to show the tie between Kitticon and Edwards, and Edwards' fine Kansan hand in the oil industry's acceptance of the Boles-Panjunk drill bit. That was where the still missing Renardi had left me, and that's where I picked up.

Kitticon wasn't hard to find. There was nothing in our own morgue. But at our law firm's library, I went through Martindale-Hubbell, the fat, beautifully put-together and costly legal roster of every state. It listed every lawyer in the country, or at least every one who wasn't serving a jail term, bribing Congressmen, sitting on the bench, or something similar.

I found no Kitticon in California, where I'd expected him. Washington, no. New York City, no.

Then I thought, Oh shit, of course. I turned to Kansas, and there he was, a member of the Wichita firm of McFadden—that would be old Congressman Joe McFadden, I'd bet—Wynn, Craid, and Stern. I checked the dates and the funny little Martindale-Hubbell symbols. Kitticon got out of Kansas State ten years ago, LL.B., same place. A local boy. Still, I needed a closer tie, some partnership. Something to make him and Edwards more than friends.

I considered calling the Wichita *Eagle* morgue to see what it had. But that might tip them I was on to something and, being out there, they might even beat me on my own story.

I hobbled over to the national editor, Speedy Mihalik, whose old man was a labor leader but who, himself, was promanagement. He was the man I usually bypassed to go to Cubbins, and he resented me accordingly. Looking at that closed, intelligent face, I thought of how many pricks in this place would love to cut my throat if I ever stopped producing.

"We got anybody in Wichita?" I asked him. The *Eagle* kept "stringers"—piecework reporters—on tap in many cities.

"Flattered you'd ask," he said with mild sarcasm. I ignored it. "Only on the Topeka paper," he went on, looking at his list.

"I want him to run me a check on a guy," I said, giving him the name of Nicholas Kitticon and a short, typed note on his law firm and schools. "If he knows anybody at the Wichita *Eagle*, could he get an unobtrusive check run for me there?"

"I'll have to give him twenty dollars. It counts as an assignment," he said.

"Take it out of the overtime I never got paid for," I said blandly.

"When do you need it?"

"Fifteen minutes. No shit," I said to show him I wasn't just being nasty about it. "It's on the Renardi thing."

"Okay," he said. He was a good newsman but a bad man. Cubbins, I mused, was a good newsman and an indifferent man. In half an hour the Topeka stringer was on the phone to me.

"I got your Kitticon stuff," he said, a little too eagerly. "Can we have whatever the hell it is when you're ready to break it? Can you tell me what it's about?"

I could understand the guy's first loyalty was to his own paper out there, but I was itchy about the story.

"Yeah, Mihalik will wire it to you. It's way down the road. Okay?" He could see I wasn't going to tell him anything and his agreement with us required him to keep his own mouth shut, even to his own paper.

"We got only one clip on him. One of ten Kansas AHEPA Men of the Year. I can't get my friend on the Wichita *Eagle*."

"What's AHEPA?" I said, vaguely recalling something.

"Greek-Americans."

"I thought Kitticon was Siamese or something."

"Guess not," the stringer said.

Nicholas Kitticon. Then it clicked. That little prick who was Edwards' staff chief, Georgie Hedaris. He had to be a Greek, a Kansas Greek. How many could there be out there?

"Look, pal," I said to the stringer. "I'm going to trust you to keep your mouth shut, okay?" He assented, knowing how I was going to have to cut him in on the story. "You can bill Mihalik for what you want on this, okay? Can you find out whether this Kitticon has anything to do with another Greek named George Hedaris? I want to know what Kitticon's wife's name is, too, okay?"

"George Hedaris is Speaker Edwards' administrative assistant," the stringer said in semialarm, the immensity of the story beginning to dawn on him.

"That's right," I told him.

I stopped long enough to call Betty Page again, knowing as I punched the last number that it wasn't going to work. She had a maid answering the phone. When the maid asked who it was, I said, "Roberts with Congressman Bartlow," faking the staffer's name.

Betty Page came cautiously to the phone.

"I just want—" I began. But she hung up.

I was so hurt that I felt the tears burning behind my eyes. For an instant I put my head down on the typewriter. With certain knowledge, I knew I could get her back if I tossed over reporting. That would be the kind of sure gesture it would take. But that was preposterous. Such bargains never held. I shifted gears, wiggled my toes below the swollen ankle, and got back to the story.

For a change, I managed to get a records clerk out in Rockville who liked the Washington *Eagle*. She gave me over the telephone what I had feared I would have to go out there for: the names on the deed to Hedaris' house: he and his wife, Elaine Myros Hedaris.

I called back to the kid in Topeka.

"Crank Myros in along with Hedaris," I said. "That's Hedaris' wife's maiden name. First name is Elaine."

I went back over to the cityside toward Connie March, knowing I could just as well get one of the copy girls on our side to help me. She looked up from her typewriter as I headed that way, then quickly looked down. Well, I thought, feeling a sort of sexual excitement at what the fugitive look said, here's horns on Harvard.

"You want to do me a favor?" I said to her. She'd got her cockiness ready for me.

"Probably."

"No, Goddamnit," I said, "something serious." But she, too, knew I could have easily gotten whatever it was I wanted done over on my side of the room.

"Sure," she said. Pretty teeth, wide lips, and raspberry tips underneath one of those no-bras. Only a wisp of Betty Page clung to my thoughts.

"Call up Edwards' office for me. Ask for Hedaris' secretary. *Secretary.* Ask her if she has a number for Elaine Hedaris' sister in, you think, Wichita. Be very dumb and naive."

"What's her name?"

"You think the last name is Kitticon, or something like that. You know it was Myros before she was married. Say she was your own sister's best friend at school." She shrugged and dialed. I could only hear her side of the conversation.

"No idea at all?" I heard her say. "You must have some idea. . . . Could it be Kitticon . . . ? No, my sister and she were best friends at—"

Connie turned those flat brown eyes up to me. "She hung up. It scared her off."

"Then we're right." I was getting excited. "She hung up over the name Kitticon, right?"

"Right."

"And she was the secretary?"

"Right."

"It takes something for a secretary to lose her cool that much, right?"

"Yep."

"Like Elaine Hedaris being Kitticon's wife's sister and not just Kitticon being some kind of friend."

"I'd guess."

I told Connie what I was up to.

"Ingenious," she said. "Why don't you get me assigned to work with you on that?" Goddamnit, I thought, that's a temptation. But it was also pretty obvious.

"How tight are you with Black Harvard?" I asked.

"That's pretty racist, Aubrey," she said. "Pretty tight."

"You're living with him."

"Not really."

"Can you come drink a bottle of wine with me tonight?"

She laughed outright at me.

"That's not very subtle."

"At forty-eight, with an ankle in dissolution and one heart attack of record, I don't have time to be subtle." I smiled, my voice hearty but my rabbit heart beating in my chest.

She thought a moment, looking at me more speculatively than fondly, like a dentist's aide seeing whether she could work in a patient for a broken filling.

"I'd have to leave about ten," she said.

"So you are living with him." Already I was jealous.

"Sort of," she said. "Eightish?"

"Great," I said, feeling somehow my masculinity dwindle. "White or red?"

"Champagne," she said.

I hobbled back to my desk, wondering if my pants fit in back and whether I might not look merely ridiculous.

The Topeka stringer was back on the phone a few minutes later.

"Mrs. Kitticon's first name is Edith," he said. "Two years ago she was a secretary of the Wichita Wives for Edwards. No maiden name; I'm still fooling around with that."

"Anything else?" Edith and Elaine, I thought. It's got to be. "Where'd you get that?"

"Friend of mine. I still can't get my guy at the Wichita *Eagle*. My friend says Edith got out of Kansas State, he thinks."

"Like Kitticon," I said. "You got a Wichita phone book in front of you?"

"Yep," he said proudly, sensing, I knew, my ploy. "The residence number is 483-1141. You want me to call?"

"Nope, keep trying on the Kitticon background, okay?"

When I dialed Kitticon's home number I heard the woman's voice, hopeful, mannered a little the way a well-educated Greek girl would be out there with those Kansans. I didn't like myself for what I was about to do.

"Hi," I said, anticipatory, youthfully excited sounding. "Is this the same Edith Myros that used to go to Kansas State?"

"Yes," she said, also excited, a little curious, wondering what old beau or friend out of the past had broken her day's housework.

"Edith *Myros*, Elaine's sister?" I said, mocking disbelief. After all these years, my voice said.

"Yes, Edith Myros," she said, more curious, almost cautious now, a trace of that Greek father or grandfather, or even further back, in her voice.

I hung up. Motherfucker! I enthused to myself, forgetting the twinge of guilt my subterfuge had brought. Hedaris' wife and Kitticon's wife are sisters!

The way I could write it, I juggled in my mind, would be "options bought through the brother-in-law of Edwards' top aide." It wasn't the whole story. That was a long way down the road. But it was crucial.

Connie March got to my apartment about fifteen after eight. I was nervous, letting her in. There was something off-center, in my view, about popping a bottle of Moët et Chandon for a girl in a tank shirt and blue jeans, with her hair uncombed and hanging down her back. I looked at her, I feared avuncularly, and thought, what the hell am I doing this for?

She was uneasy, too, more than I would have imagined. The with-it generation, but with some residue Victorianism from Mr. March who had had us print "damn" as "d——" up to a few years ago.

I poured her the champagne and drank Almadén Chablis, cold and solid, myself. It was rude, perhaps, but I honestly didn't like bubbly; I was a little put-out she'd asked for it.

"You're not trying to one-up me, are you, Aubrey?" she asked.

"No," I said. "It's like my wife with Vienna sausages. A can blew up in her face once and it was rotten and she hated them ever after. I got sick on champagne once, for three days."

"Your late wife," she picked it up. "That's a helluva thing to talk about at a seduction scene." She wasn't angry, merely curious.

"Connie," I said, gulping down the wine to cure my nervousness, "I'm only what you see." I smiled agreeably. After all, I had a pretty good story working. I just wished it were Betty Page instead of this little termagant. I could see why Braswell and the shadowy detective had never gotten on quite right with her. She was just a little too much out front, too much her father's daughter.

But as the wine went down, things relaxed. I stopped

comparing it with that wine-drinking day at Angler's Inn, for one thing.

She wanted to know about the story, and I told her that I still needed the drill bit angle. She understood everything, nodding, drinking hard and fast, wanting to get high quickly.

"How could you do this kind of stuff for twenty-five years and not get sick of it?" she asked at one point. I had no answer, but she wasn't really interested in an answer. Her question was for comparison. "I do these damned features and they have an element of sharpness to them," she said. "But they aren't very substantial. What makes them okay is that the material for them is always different. So I don't tire."

"They're good features," I said. They were.

"Thanks, but—"

"Are you going to do features for twenty-five years?" I asked.

"Don't be arch. You know damned well what I'll be doing in twenty-five years. Presiding over the final distribution of your pension fund," she laughed. It was funny.

"Daddy isn't going to give you the paper until you setttle down though," I said, surmising.

"Right. Daddy won't be ready to give it to anyone for ten or fifteen years. And then only if he thinks I'm mature. After that he'll turn it over to me gradually, assuming I want it."

"Want it?" I echoed sourly.

"Well, now, wait a minute. If you had the choice right now of running the *Eagle* or doing what you're doing, being Aubrey Warder with damned few strings on you, what would *you* do?"

Before I could answer, she went on. "The choice for me is between marrying the damn paper and being myself, being free, working someplace else. Put yourself in my shoes and you see it *is* a choice."

Without more ado, she got up from her chair and crossed the room to mine, knelt beside it and kissed me on the lips. I had had enough wine so that I wasn't really taken aback, but it was a little peremptory.

"I didn't have a chance to take a shower before I came over here. Do you mind?" she said.

"No," I said. "I'll come watch you."

She laughed quickly, brittlely.

"That will be nice."

By the numbers, I thought.

Making love to Connie March was mechanical, but fascinating. It was a little like those nouveau art things, with polished ball bearings rolling down inclines, turning on lights, and spinning silvery blades that reflect the lights, all without a sound.

It was a stainless-steel fuck.

She began by kissing me all over my mouth, in the corners, under my lips, my tongue. It was sexy, but almost methodical, a little like a Water-Pic. When I was hotting up, she began to toy with me, skillfully, too skillfully, and took my hand, pressing it to her vagina, selecting a finger to rub on its lips. I thought, whimsically, this phase was like a dentist having you hold that X-ray pad in your mouth, pressing your finger to it while he blips the X-ray machine. Thinking that, my penis fell, buying me a little time.

"What's the matter?" she said.

"Nothing," I said. "I'm just not as predictable as I might be." I wondered if I'd ever be able to tell her what I had been thinking. She might think it was funny.

But she was precociously trying to repair the damage. I thought of some old bit of doggerel about "and tricks unknown to common quiffs." She had read, or otherwise learned, things I had only imagined. Before I knew it she was pulling my foreskin with little pinches, still pushing my hand into her crotch where I was doing the best I could. I felt like a character in a dirty movie, and a vision of a dirty movie came into my mind. It was that, I believe, more than Connie's knowledgeable ministrations that made me swell, and murmur, "Put it in!"

She did, with the efficiency of a busy baseball game concessionaire popping a frankfurter into a roll. And then I supplied the mustard, with some relish.

I was prepared to be cursed by her, candid as she was, but no, she left me inside of her and began squeezing me gently with her vaginal muscle.

"My God, this is unbelievable," I said softly. She kissed me gently on the lips, and soon I was concentrating on the slick caress of her quiff, even as her lips ran soothingly on mine. Incredibly, I began to grow and then become semihard. Ever so slowly, she worked her body on mine, keeping me inside her until I was hard enough for her to move feverishly against it. When she began to come, it was in series, such as had happened from time to time with other women, but never when I was able to maintain any calm about it.

Finally she had come her full and I was hard again. I was willing to waive a second orgasm, but damnit, it seemed such a waste with this slender, active body here and now likely to leave at 10 P.M., a few minutes off.

"From behind," I sighed and she obligingly stuck her tail up like a Corinthian lion, and I slid into her vagina. Weary as I was getting, the friction on the underside, plus her nimble fingers stretching back the foreskin, began to stir me toward orgasm. I turned her over, and heavy on her, came shudderingly into her.

"Nice, hunh?" she said, beneath me. It was a question.

Spent and therefore clearheaded, I almost told her of my images.

"Beautiful," I sighed. "Just beautiful." Yet somehow I wanted to tell her that, spectacular as it had been, there was something missing. Call it the apple tree, the singing and the gold, if you had to. I wanted to say, "Connie, you are not going to get all that much out of life, honest, if life's most explosive experience is so well-tuned." But that was for her to find out from someone else.

She lay beneath me awhile. I rubbed the back of her head tenderly, almost bemused by this kind of coupling. Was it this way for all kids, now? I began to drop off to sleep, still heavy on her, but gently she rolled me off, and out of her.

"I have to wash myself," she said. "I have to go."

Did she want me to tell her to leave Mark Braswell and come live with me? I did not think so. Perhaps, I owed her the invitation.

"Will you come back?" I said.

"Yes," she said. "I liked it. You didn't have to buy Moët et Chandon."

"That's okay," I said, almost adding, "It was worth it." There had been some quality of trade, rather than mutuality, in our making love. Yet, when she left, a little after ten, she kissed me and said, "You're a nice man," and there was something warm, and I felt, even rueful in it. I also sensed she was in love with Mark Braswell.

In the morning, I woke early again and sweated over Betty Page. I felt no real guilt about posting with such untimely haste into Connie March.

They were such different women. Connie: a musical prodigy playing perfectly a single instrument. Betty Page: a familiar town band, warm, diverse, innovative, but maybe not virtuoso.

Thinking of Betty Page, I had that sense again of something that could have been rich all our days slipping away. At ten, I called her house. The maid said she was gone for a few days.

Where? When she had been my mistress, I had known everything she did, almost every trip to the store. Bumbling around the apartment, or in bed, we had talked about the humdrum things as if we had been married. Now she was gone "for a few days," and I had no idea where, and worse, no way of finding out.

Remorse overtook me. I had lost her. Edwards: Had he gone with her? I checked with our House guy again. That would be the last time I could do that without raising his shrewd suspicions. Edwards was at work. Betty Page had, then, just disappeared.

But I plowed on with my story. Now I knew that Hedaris had arranged through his wife's brother-in-law for the stock to be held by Kitticon. That meant it was shady, otherwise Edwards would have held it in his own name, or at worst in some other straw's. In this case, clearly, there was need for absolute secrecy and confidence, the sort only blood relationships could confer.

It was also necessary to tie in the oil companies, Edwards and the Boles-Panjunk drill bit. That would be harder. Webb Renardi would have been helpful, but he was gone, and once burned by that FBI bust, I doubted he would be very brave again.

But I guessed wrong, as I did so often.

The fat little skirt chaser from Boles-Panjunk had some iron inside that pampered meat. I had been working for the best part of the day, trying to figure out from Congressional Record insertions, from reports of speeches, from old clips, which of the Big Oil companies Edwards had touched up on the drill.

Late in the afternoon Webb Renardi phoned. I thought, Well, we'll make it; he has some unburdening to do, and his hate and some hard work will make this damned story yet.

"How the hell did they know to follow me?" he said, once we had made small, brave talk.

"Guessing, I'd bet that Boles called the Speaker and told him you were steaming off, that the Speaker called one of the Big Oil types and got him, in turn, to tip his friendly FBI agent that you were thinking of a little interstate transport of stolen goods, to wit, documents."

"Which I was," Renardi grunted with bitter humor.

"Where can I see you?" I asked.

Things being what they were, the front seat of a car seemed best. I hobbled out to my fine old Morgan, one of the few objects I loved, and drove out Sixteenth Street to where he had holed up in the Woodner. The car—I had bought it on a newspaper ad from a mildly disgraced Labor Department type named Dobrecky, or some such—purred and roared by turns. With spring full in the air, the big trees filling out along Sixteenth Street, I wished only that Betty Page were with me. I harked back to that nostalgic high school feeling: I had the old man's car and no date. Seeing the greens and chartreuses of the leaves, I thought, When shall I see her again, alas, then remembered it came from some long-ago French poem. That made the poignancy twice as bad.

Renardi saw me in the car and quickly came through the swinging doors. We whooshed down into Rock Creek Park and parked in one of the picnic areas. I pointed the car toward Beach Drive so we could see if any Feebs followed us in.

Once we had stopped, I pulled out the Xeroxes of the letters from the oil companies. The Californian smiled. Renardi's guts, or persistence anyway, were making me like him a little.

"I wish I'd never seen those Goddamn things," he said.

"Do you know which of the eight companies Edwards talked to?"

"Unh-uh," he said. "He'd only have to talk with three, maybe, and the rest would go along."

"The biggest three?" That would be Exxon, Texaco, and Mobil, I thought.

"No. It could be somebody else. Maybe Standard of California, Amoco, any of them with lots of exploratory and production work. Look, you know it's a Goddamned good drill. These guys probably didn't even know he was getting anything out of Boles-Panjunk."

"Oh, come on."

"No, no bullshit. Don't ever underestimate the stupidity of an oil company executive. They could have thought he's just trying to do Boles-Panjunk a favor, or even that he was doing *them* a favor. He's done them enough in other ways."

"So one of them might just open up and tell me 'Sure, good old Pom Edwards called me about the bit.' "

"They're not that dumb." He took the letters and went through them. All were just carefully worded inquiries, similar in their businessese. "None of them is going to admit to you they talked to Edwards about *anything*."

"But look," I said excitedly, something hitting me from the old Watergate days, "since these bastards thought they weren't doing anything wrong, wouldn't they write a little memo to themselves, saying, 'Talked to Pom Edwards today on Boles-Panjunk drill head; make inquiry before end of week,' or something. . . . "

"Now you're cooking," Renardi said. "Now you're cooking."

Before I drove him back to the hotel, we had agreed that I would pull every possible string to find out who Pom's tried-by-fire friends were in the oil industry. I would also jerk loose from the FBI which of the companies had sicked the FBI on Renardi. Then, we'd run over the names and see whether he had any friend-of-a-friend that could check through the Edwards' cronies' memos for any record of a phone call or note about the drills.

"Classic," I told him at the portico. "Classic. A classic way to dig it out."

"A classic way to land our asses in jail," Renardi said.

I got my FBI friend at home.

"Drop dead, Aubrey," he said. "Whatever you want."

"Now c'mon, Brent."

"No shit, Aubrey, drop dead."

I was getting angry.

"They had no business—" He cut me off.

"Look, I can't help you. Everybody is so pissed at you over here, there, I mean, that just mentioning your name gets demerits. There is not one man in the Washington Field Office that would not arrest you for running a red light if he could. Except me."

He was calming down, feeling guilty.

"They'll recover."

"Yeah. Look, you made us look like fools." Then he paused. "Were those two guys they manhandled really deaf mutes? I mean *really?*"

"No, just 'deaf.' " I could feel him melting. "They use them because the press noise doesn't bother them. Really."

"Well, be careful about yourself," he said.

Suddenly we were old friends again and I put it to him.

"Which of the oil companies sicked you guys on Renardi?"

"Jesus Christ," he said. "After *this*, you want *that?*"

"Brent, I'm getting old. I hurt in every bone of my

Goddamn body. My Goddamn girl friend has left me. I got a foot that won't heal. I'm old and I do not have time to fuck around. We have known each other for eighteen years. Eighteen years." It was closer to fifteen, but I didn't think he would remember. "If I flub this damned story, I am in deep, deep trouble. Would I hesitate to help you make a case?" The passion of my appeal was catching up with me. I began to feel like a Pagliacci. My voice choked a little. "How Goddamn many times have I gone through our clips for you, used my visitor's privileges to get stuff for you out of the New York *Times* . . . ?" *Vesti la giubba*, I almost said.

"Oh, can the crap," he said.

"It was Shell," I said.

"No," he said. "Wrong first initial."

Ah, I thought, I'll get it. That would also knock out Standard of California and Indiana, too.

"Gulf?"

"Unh-uh."

"Bounty," I said, naming one of the smallest of the eight.

"Could be," he said. "Good-by."

Well, I thought. That meant Edwards was close enough to somebody in Bounty to get them to sic the FBI on Renardi, who didn't even work for Bounty, just on the odd chance that Bounty's papers were included in the general Boles-Panjunk stash.

That also meant that Bounty was one of the companies Edwards had contacted on the drill bit, because even a friend wouldn't take a chance like that if it weren't important. And further, the Bounty guy must have had spelled out to him by the Little Major just why it was important to head off Renardi at the pass.

Blessedly, the FBI had been just a minute or two late, and I still had the Bounty letter among the others.

So Bounty was one. Two, maybe three to go, I thought.

At the American Petroleum Institute, I had one old friend. When he'd been a newspaperman on the *Herald-Trib*, we'd worked a society murder trial together. The murderer was a doctor who had shot his wife in the ass with a drug called Succinylcholine. It had paralyzed her muscles, causing her to suffocate while she was still mostly conscious, eyes nictated stark open. Terrible death, but he'd sworn he never gave her anything stronger than a Black Russian. Both Willy Carmichael and I had come to like the doctor-murderer, who was out on bond during the trial. Now Carmichael was an oil flack.

"Your mind's wandering, Aubrey," I said to myself as I dialed.

"Willy, who does Pom Edwards know in the big eight, I mean well?" I asked.

"Aubrey, everybody in the business knows what you're working on. Jesus, don't put me on this one."

"Nobody'll know you talked to me."

"Everybody'll know."

"Willy, nobody'll know. Jesus, don't you think I get sick of calling up old friends and having them say 'no' to me, like I was some kind of Goddamn leper. Willy, I'm old, tired." It had worked so well a moment ago, I thought I'd try it again. "I have the list of the top corporate officers from each company, right in front of me, right out of Poor's Directory. Just let me run down them. All you got to say is yes or no. Okay?"

He had always been a decent man or he never would have gone down with the *Trib*, but he had always been a weak man or he'd never have gone over to Big Oil.

"Shit," he said. "Go ahead."

As Willy "yessed" and "noed," I could see the Little Major didn't get on all that well with the ARCO bunch, but he knew plenty of people in the rest of them. Willy fingered a round dozen in other companies.

God, I thought, if only I could get Betty Page to winnow down these names. Could I get her to come around just this last time? If I could just get her to tell me the Little Major's very best friends from this list, I would know who he had called about the drill. I would give up her sweet, dear ass forever if she would tell me that.

But then, I thought, no, that isn't true. I would not do that, Betty Page, I thought, I would not swap seeing you again, loving you again for the three or four names I must have for this story. It is a temptation, but I would not, not for a week of front pages.

Relieved that my better self had vanquished the worse, I began to think of her in the apartment again. Once, standing naked in front of my living room mirror, she had combed her blond hair with my comb. "Weave, weave the sunlight in your hair," I had said to her, trying back through all those years to remember the lines from Eliot.

And she had turned, her hands in her hair raising her breasts. "Clasp your flowers to you with a pained surprise," she had replied. And the other line from the poem had come to me about the weather compelling our "imagination many days, many days and many hours." And Goddamnit, I had wanted to cry for love of her.

One of the twelve oil men had retired since our year-old Poor's had come out. That made eleven possibilities. Only one, Emerson Quiven, a corporate president, was from Bounty. That was a good break for me. But the other ten were scattered among the six remaining big companies.

I was sure I was right about the Speaker calling only two or three besides Bounty, only the minimum to get the industry moved toward the bit.

Ordinarily, I would have gone to Boles-Panjunk's competitors for leads. But on this one, with the ass of the Knight of Petroleum at stake, even the other drill bit makers weren't going to risk unhorsing him. The Little Major was as vital to the oil industry as the Man at the Pump.

I called Renardi with the names.

"I can help you on Bounty," he said. "I got a friend there."

Renardi was back to me in an hour; his voice excited and alarmed.

"I *had* a friend at Bounty," he began. "He got the ax today, just because he knew me. Christ, you've got them scared to death just on the rumors—"

"Slow down," I said, knowing this could be our key. "Just start all over with what your friend does there, okay?" Renardi paused a moment and recommenced.

"His job was technical assistant to the president of the place. A hotshot. Played around too much for some of them there, a little too jazzy, you know. . . ."

"Yeah," I said.

"And after I got caught, *we* got caught, by the FBI, Bounty asked him what the hell I was up to and he said he didn't know. But now the word is out it has to do with the Speaker and they don't trust anybody."

"When's he going?" A possibility was coming to me.

"He's fired. Now."

"I mean what's his last day of official work?"

"They said 'be gone by Friday morning.' "

"That means he's fired as of midnight Thursday."

"Yes. What—"

"Will he talk to me if I fly out tonight, we fly out tonight, and talk to him in the morning?" That would be Thursday.

"What—"

"Webb," I said, knowing I could risk it with him now, "he still has a right to go into any files in the office if he isn't off the payroll."

"Jesus," he laughed nervously. "You must think the oil industry can afford two walking suicides. *No*body is going to pull off a shit caper like that."

"You did," I said.

He thought about it a moment.

"Who's paying for the ticket to San Francisco?" he said.

"The *Eagle*," I told him, the old heart beginning to wing up, up, up.

6

The Safe

There, over the big breakfast spread at the Sir Francis, it was easy to see why Renardi and this guy, Drosnahan, got on so well. He was young, twenty-nine, thirty maybe, and he was drinking Guinness with his scrambled eggs and sausage.

"It's full of iron," he told me. "Beats Geritol. Good for the nerves. When all this started, I began to get gut pains so I stepped up the Guinnesses. It helped, but my stools turned dark. Anyway—"

"Christ, Buddy," said Renardi, half-admiring, "not at the fucking breakfast table."

But Drosnahan was enjoying his role as the prime mover in a big story. I knew it was going to be okay if I just let him talk his bravery into full commitment. He went on:

"So I thought I had to have a bleeding ulcer or cancer of the colon and went to the doctor yesterday. He said it was only too much iron in my diet. It was the iron in the Guinness." He poured from the chilly bottle and drank deep.

When the waitress came to give me a final cup of coffee, I told her, "Give me one of those," pointing to the Guinness. Both of the men beamed. This was going to be a piece of cake.

"Have you cleaned your desk out?" I asked him as

123

we sat, wiping the foamy stout from our mouths on the good linen.

"No, I've got until the end of the day. Why?"

"C'mon," I said. "You know."

"You want me to steal the documents."

"I want you to Xerox the documents now legally in your custody as an official of the corporation," I corrected him with a smile. He had already thought it out.

"I will help you with anything I know. But I won't copy anything," he said with firmness. "Besides, the place is full of documents, even Boles-Panjunk stuff. We've been doing business for decades."

"No," I said. "Look, Buddy, I'm going to trust you. Your ass has been fired by Bounty for nothing. You and Renardi are renegades in this Goddamn business, and innocently. You got to start up your own firm even to make enough to live"—the two of them exchanged glances. I could see they were already cooking up some wobbly, perhaps shady, operation of their own—"so I am going to trust you." The stage set, I went on:

"I have reason to believe that there is a memo in there from your president, Quiven, about a talk he had with Edwards on the Boles-Panjunk drill. Bounty and two or three other firms are going to use the drill and we think that it's because of pressure by the Speaker." Obviously this was no news to Drosnahan. Renardi had told him, I was sure. But I wanted to create a feeling in him that I trusted him mightily.

"I want to get that memo. I want it badly."

Renardi shut up. Drosnahan was obviously thinking, What's in it for me? Where do I, Buddy Drosnahan, profit from this?

"I don't know if there is any memo," he said. "I know that Quiven talked to me about the drill bit about three months ago. It was a good drill. If it wasn't, I wouldn't have advised the old man to go for it. But I don't know if anybody called him."

"*If*," I said, "just *if* there was a memo written by your boss for the files, where would it be? I mean, let's begin this way: Is your boss the kind who writes such memos?"

"Yeah," he said. "He's a bookkeeper. That's how he got to be head of Bounty. He jots himself a note in a big ledger every time he cuts a fart."

"So?"

"So, there's probably a memo."

"Where?"

Drosnahan lifted his shoulders in a heavy sigh.

"In the safe."

Oh, shit, I thought. A bloody safe. That killed it.

"Do you have the combination?"

"Man, don't be crazy. I wouldn't go into a safe."

"But—"

"I had the combination. They changed it."

"Ah," I said despondently.

"With my stuff inside," he joined me mournfully.

"Shit," I said, ignoring him. The trip was in vain. How would I explain the two plane tickets to San Francisco? Cubbins would think I was charging off some bimbo on the expense account. I mused dismally on whether I would have to eat Renardi's ticket. *"Merde,"* I said. I wondered if I could talk Betty Page into flying to San Francisco. Or Connie. Dumb bastard, I thought, that's escape into fantasy.

"Aren't they even going to give you back your papers?" Renardi was saying sympathetically. "I mean, changing the dial on a safe with your own Goddamn papers . . ."

I was only half listening, but I heard what Renardi said. Oh! I thought, oh! My pulse was beginning to beat with a superthump.

"Your papers are still in the safe?" I gasped excitedly to Drosnahan, fixing his resentful blue eyes.

"Yeah."

"You have a right to those papers, by law," I said. "Are they personal papers?"

"Maybe a letter or two, yeah, semipersonal, semi-official; the rest is company stuff."

"Hot damn!" I said. "Personal letters."

"I don't believe this," said Renardi, catching on before Drosnahan. Maybe his previous experience with me had given him a bit more insight into the low morals of investigative reporters. Drosnahan looked at Renardi curiously.

"He wants to blow the safe," Renardi said, as I grinned happily.

"Fucking A," I said. "Not blow it; crack it."

Drosnahan, for all his zesty clothes and manner, drew back as if I had deposited a cobra on the table.

"A crime," he said. "A crime."

"No," I said. "Not a crime. Where's the safe?"

"In our office."

"Where in the office?"

"In the conference room, the library. In a closet."

"Did you used to have access to it?"

"Yes, sure. It had pending patent applications. . . ."

"Did anyone say you no longer had access to it?"

"They fired me. Good God, Aubrey."

Renardi joined in.

"They fired him, for Christsakes."

"But did they explicitly say, 'Stay out of the safe.'?"

"They changed the combination. What could be clearer than that?"

"But they didn't say or hand you anything in writing?"

"No."

"And they didn't offer to give you your stuff out of the safe?"

"Well, a lot of it is company correspondence. They could make a case. . . ." He was fascinated, almost hypnotized with the hideous idea I was putting forward.

"But they didn't offer to give back the private letters?"

"They didn't even know that—"

"Did they ask you if—" I catechized him.

"No."

"So, to sum up: The safe to which you retain legal access is in the suite to which you can legally go until today ends. The safe contains your personal property."

"If I asked—"

"You don't have to ask."

"You don't ask; you take," said Renardi parodying me sarcastically.

"No, really," I said, trying to juggle this thing among the three of us. "The law—"

"Christ, Aubrey, you're not a lawyer. If we blow—"

"Crack—"

"Crack the safe, we also destroy private property, company property," said Drosnahan. Renardi looked at him affirmingly. That would be the clincher. But I couldn't give up. I could taste that Goddamn memo. I could read it, feel it, touch it, possess it, almost fuck it. It was the unarguable key to my story. I must have it, I thought. It is as laden with my needing it as a woman when I need her. I could get erect over that memo.

"The *Eagle* will buy another safe in town, have it on the way to Bounty in the morning," I said.

I'll be fired for this, I thought. Mr. March won't stand still for this kind of thing. But I would have that memo. What an absolutely fantastic story, the whole thing. Only the tiniest voice in me said, My God, Aubrey, you're forty-eight years old. Grow up. The rest of me said, I must have that memo!

The two of them were laughing at me.

"Aubrey, you got to be crazy," Renardi said. I tried to get myself under control. It had to be done with a little style or both of these guys would dodge out.

"No," I said. "Where's the hole in my argument? Buddy and I go in tonight. We sign in with the guard; you have guards at night out here, right?"

Buddy nodded, starting to go into mesmerization again. The crazy son-of-a-bitch wants to do this, I sensed. He's as buggo as I am.

"It has to be on the up-and-up. Buddy wants his letters and he is angry that the letters have been locked up and the combination on his own safe changed. In fact, the company has behaved illegally. It has expropriated his legal, private property."

Renardi was still not having any and was trying to warn Buddy off, yet without really wanting it to stop.

"So you want him to de-expropriate it by cracking a safe."

"*Liberating*, Webb," I told him. "Liberating his papers."

"Who can crack a safe?" said Buddy Drosnahan. "This is nuts."

"You were pissed on by Bounty simply for knowing Webb Renardi and you are showing such tender concern for Bounty?"

"He's . . ."

"I . . ." they both began at once. Drosnahan finished. "I'm showing concern for my own sweet ass. A safe-cracking is a safecracking."

"I can have it cracked in thirty minutes unless it's a Brinks," I said. "What kind is it?"

"An old Mosley, I think. It was the old man's father's."

"Mosler," I said. "I've done enough stories on safe-crackers to crack the thing. All I ask is a look at the ledger, or whatever."

"I don't believe this," said Renardi to Drosnahan. "You're actually going to let him do this?" But still the outrage was more *pro forma* than real.

"Why not fuck the fuckers?" said Drosnahan seriously.

"When will everybody, cleaning woman and everybody, be finished at the office?" I asked.

"By nine," said Drosnahan.

"Meet you back here in the bar then, okay? I'll be ready for some more of this cough medicine." I turned to Renardi, my heart beating with both excitement and fear. "Don't you talk him out of it," I tried to joke. But I figured it was okay. Drosnahan could taste revenge.

When I got back upstairs in my room, the first thing I did was to call an old friend in Fort Lauderdale. He had been an arson-and-safe man in the mob and had defected and eaten crap for two years under a new identity given him by the government.

I had done a story about how he had helped lock up four big hoods and had been left to drift by the Justice Department. As a result of my story, he got a book contract offer. He made a little money and Justice gave him a third new identity and now he was running a haberdashery.

He owed me a favor. I got him at the store. In the background, I could hear the chorus singing "Diecimila ah-ah-ni." I wondered what kind of business he did, playing opera in his store instead of rock.

"It's Aubrey Warder," I said. He was effusive, but beneath it was a bed of uneasiness. I told him I needed to know how to get into a safe. It was all perfectly legal, I said.

"If it's a Brinks you got to go in through the side—"

"It's an old Mosler, or something."

"How old?"

"I don't know."

"I believe you had better peel it," he said, and explained in detail. When he had finished, he remembered to be smart. "You're treating me like a source on this, Aubrey, okay? Like on the old story? I could get in trouble—"

"Don't worry—"

"No, I wanna make it exact. You got to be willing to go to jail on this before you let on I told you, okay? I smell trouble on this. Okay, Aubrey?"

His wariness scared me.

"Not that I don't know you would—" he was babbling on.

"Don't worry," I told him. "I take the oath. '*Omertà*' is the word."

That night we three met again, even though Renardi refused to go along for the safe-busting itself. Drosnahan was sweating but game. I had bought a huge vise grip, a short crowbar, a cold chisel, a short-handled sledge hammer, an electric drill, and a half dozen metal-cutting bits. They were in my overnight case. I felt like what I was, a burglar.

In front of the sugar-cube modern Bounty Building, I began to sweat, too. I wiped my hands on my pants leg. I was afraid the guard would want to look into my overnight bag. But Drosnahan, thank God, had a reputation as a hard, afterhours worker, for all his mod ways.

"At it again?" asked the guard deferentially as Drosnahan signed us in.

"No rest for the wicked," replied Drosnahan.

The closet in the library-conference room contained only the safe, but it was close quarters.

As my Mafia friend had advised, I cushioned both the top of the chisel and the sledge hammer with handkerchiefs. The damned safe was incredibly solid. It was two feet wide and three feet high and, for all my pounding at the little line at the top of the door face, at first I couldn't get it open even a crack, much less the big gap I would need to get the crowbar in and a lock on the facing with the vise grip.

It was 10:10 before the steel bulged away even a quarter of an inch. That was only an hour and fifty minutes before midnight when I would clearly be violating the law, assuming it wasn't illegal now.

The steady "thud, thud" of the hammer on the top of the cold chisel made me nervous, and despite the air conditioning I started sweating again. Then my bladder gave me trouble.

"I gotta leak," I said, getting up.

Drosnahan, his face drawn now, too, pointed me to a door off the conference room. I turned, but he said, "Wait a minute; you got to have a key."

When I got back, Drosnahan was also getting shaky. "Can't you hurry it, Aubrey? It's almost ten-thirty."

"Maybe . . ."

I knew he wanted out. But I had a big enough crack now to get the crowbar in. I tried to pry the facing outward, but it was no go. Drosnahan and I both grunted over the bar, and the metal gave enough for us to get a firm bite on it with the vise grip.

"The son-of-a-bitch told me it could be done in forty-five minutes," I said, then realized I had given out a secret. But Drosnahan let it pass.

With him on the crowbar and me tugging on the vise grip, the metal facing gradually began to peel off, squealing noisily each time we gained an inch on it. The droplets of sweat were running down our faces.

My God, I thought, in a few hours maybe some rich bastards are going to be sitting in this library around this oval conference table talking about their safe.

Neat on the shelves behind us were the handsomely bound books on geological law and the proceedings of numerous scientific groups, mostly shills, no doubt, for the oil industry. We grunted with our labors. Bit by bit the black-painted metal peeled off, revealing the fireproofing layer beneath.

To get the facing over the combination dial took an extraordinary amount of prizing and pulling. My chest began to ache. We had worked almost silently, murmuring only, "There she comes," or low curses. But I had to rest a moment. It was 10:47. My ankle was killing me.

"I got a bad heart," I said plaintively, holding my chest.

"You telling me," said the younger man with a grin. You're a tough fucker after all, I thought. He went on: "If you're going to have an attack, slow down. Otherwise, let's go."

The facing broke free of the dial with a shriek. Panting, now, I grabbed the drill and tightened in the first bit.

"Boles-Panjunk?" he asked, picking up the little paper-wrapped drills on the thick rug.

"Funny as hell," I said. My Cosa Nostra consultant had said to drill at three places around the dial to make sure I got the tumblers. Then, the dial would punch out. The whine of the drilled metal was eerily loud. The only other sound was from the air conditioners.

The harder I pressed on the drill, the louder the whine. But the bit was cutting, leaving curlicues of bright metal on the floor beneath the safe where they dug into my knees. I pulled the first bit after it had cut in almost a quarter of an inch and put in a fresh one. It quickly chewed through the door and began grinding into the tumblers. The sound now had a slight resonance from booming around inside the safe. How could the guard not hear it?

I was terribly cramped. Drosnahan, smelling heavily

of sweat through his scent, took a turn at the drill and we punched through the second time. It was 11:30.

"You smell like a sweaty whore, Drosnahan," I told him. "You're a zoo," he muttered.

It was probably true. As I bored the third hole, I thought of the legendary German count who kept a handkerchief in his armpit and withdrew it to remove specks from ladies' eyes. They, taken by his ripe masculine odor, succumbed to his seductions. I thought of Connie March's tight clutching little cunt.

All that I could have: her, Betty Page. And for one cheap piece of fish wrapping, I was busting into a safe, risking prison. I will be dead thirty, twenty, even, years from now, and who will care if I blew a chintzy Speaker of the House out of the water?

The drill pushed through the door and began chewing up the lock mechanism within again. I turned it off and got the chisel set in the middle of the dial. This would be it.

"So here goes," I said and hit it a heavy whack through the handkerchief. The dial did not go a millimeter. I socked it again. Nothing. It was not budging inward, only giving a little outward on the rebound.

"Oh, Jesus," Drosnahan said, almost in tears. I had not realized how uptight we both were about punching through the thing. We looked at the wreck of a safe, a peeled pig of a thing with its little cock of a dial still standing out straight.

Drosnahan took hold of the stubby thing and to his astonishment it turned in his hand with a rattle of broken tumblers inside. He grabbed the hammer and the chisel from me and hit it a rap, forgetting the handkerchief. It sang out with "bing," and went shooting right through the face of the safe.

"Yayyy!" we cheered spontaneously.

As I had been instructed, I tapped the face with the muffled hammer, hearing pieces drop down into the safe. Then with the crowbar in the hole, we swung the door open. It was 11:33.

Inside were neat narrow shelves largely filled with

papers. As I reached out for the first batch, we heard the outside door being touched with a key. At that, my view of the shelves and the stark white of the paper began to blur. I knew what was coming.

"I'm gonna faint," I heard myself say. Vaguely I heard Drosnahan murmur, "Oh, fuck," and I was aware of his getting up, and heading for the door. Then, I was out.

I was already half-to when I felt the icy water splash in my face. I looked up in the frantically twisted face of Drosnahan.

"We gotta get out of here," he hissed. "That was the guard. He was suspicious as hell. I practically had to threaten to fire him to keep him from looking around. He heard those last couple of thumps."

I was woozy, sick at my stomach. My heart, I thought. She's giving out on me. I recalled those statistics about men not dying of heart attacks during intercourse unless it was adulterous.

"Same thing," I said aloud to myself.

"What?" demanded Drosnahan.

"Nothing," I said. "You *got* to get these private letters out to make it all legal." He scrabbled through the papers, looking for his folder. I spotted the Bounty president's ledger and grabbed it out. The Goddamn thing had a small hasp and old-timey miniature padlock on it. Screw that, I thought. Shakily, I came to my knees and popped off the hasp with the crowbar.

"For Christsakes, Aubrey," Drosnahan gasped. "That's his."

"I'm looking for your letters," I explained. "Where's the Goddamn Xerox?"

"Oh, no," he groaned.

"Where?" I demanded. "Where is it . . . ?" I had come this far and I wasn't leaving without the ledger copied. I could see on the cover of the ledger that it only covered the last five months. I hoped that would be enough.

"Where?" I asked and he pointed to a room off the one we were in. Blessedly it was one of those new high-speed beauties that warm up fast and take book pages almost as rapidly as you can turn the page and press down the book.

It was 11:42. We had eighteen minutes to get out if we were going to maintain our feeble legal defense. My heart seemed okay, but I was still blurry. I could not read the bookkeeper-president's tiny, squiggly handwriting in the ledger.

I feared that the fainting had been caused by high blood pressure. With my bad heart, that could kill me, I thought. I've got to take it easier. But not yet, not yet.

On the theory that the entry was nearer the front than the back because it was three months ago that Drosnahan was told about the drill, I worked through the ledger front-to-back.

"Oh, dear God of investigative reporters," I muttered as I Xeroxed the first few pages, "don't let this beautiful machine break down on me now. Keep it in perfect functioning order, dear God." The machine was spitting out a neat stack of duplicates into the tray.

Drosnahan rushed into the room and got me by the arm.

"I've got the letters," he said. "Let's go!"

"Fuck the letters," I said. "I'm halfway through the ledger."

"It's 11:50," he croaked, the words forced through his throat shrilly by the tension.

"Get the tools back in the bag," I said, not missing a page-turning. I polished off the last page.

Time was running fast now. I shoved the raped ledger back into the raped safe. Must remember to send them some money for the Xeroxes and to repair the ledger's lock.

Drosnahan had put everything, even the drill bits and the paper wrappings, back into the bag. He was marvelously efficient.

"Bounty should never have fired you," I said.

Through his tormented face, he smiled. He thought I was talking about the chain of events that led to our safe job.

"You're right," he said.

"No," I said. "You're too good for them."

"Thanks."

I shoved the sheaf of ledger copies into the bag. We loped to the door. It was 11:57. When we got to the ground floor it was midnight on the hop. The guard's face was frozen. He knew something was up. He looked at my bag suspiciously. But he was still worried about Drosnahan's power, not knowing he had been fired effective exactly now.

"Right on the jump at midnight," Drosnahan said to the guard, who ball-pointed the time in himself.

"Midnight exactly," I echoed, looking at the guard to imprint on his mind the time. "The exact time when Cinderella's carriage turned into a pumpkin," I recalled to the stony face as we left.

I knew the guard would be headed upstairs the instant we left. Within minutes, the police would be looking for Drosnahan. I doubted anyone would rapidly find out I was the other safe-cracker. But I wasn't taking any chances.

I had zero time to go back to the Sir Francis and check out. I couldn't risk it. I'd have to call them and have them send the hotel bill to me at the *Eagle* along with the shaving stuff and extra change of underwear and shirt that the burglary tools had displaced in my overnight bag.

"Did you turn off the Xerox machine?" Drosnahan asked as we hustled down the street.

"Probably not," I said. "Listen, you'd better go somewhere tonight that's not where you usually go. The cops will be looking for you, even though I think you're going to be totally clean."

"Yeah," he said.

"And get a good lawyer in the morning, a criminal lawyer."

Drosnahan looked gloomy.

"I wish I'd never pulled this caper," he said. "What the hell did I get out of it?"

"Nothing, maybe," I said. "Depending on what's in the ledger, maybe Quiven's head for firing you."

"Maybe not, too," he said. At the corner now, he

said, "Let's split." I felt regret. I felt I had used him. Perhaps somehow I could make it up to him.

"I'll help you however I can," I said. "You got balls."

He turned from his nervous scanning of the street for a cab and grabbed my hand with a good shake.

"If I don't hang for this, it was a gas," he said gamely.

I let him get the first cab, then walked as briskly as I could with my wrenched foot and the heavy bag for a block or two before I caught one. I had it take me to Union Plaza, then found an all-night drugstore and bought a toothbrush, toothpaste, a razor, a dozen 8 by 11 manila envelopes, some adhesive wrapping tape, and a black felt-tip marking pen. Then, I caught another cab to a second-rate downtown hotel, the Emporia West, which I had seen on the way in from the Bounty Building, and registered under the name "Dudley Kneitschäde."

Even in the cab, I had been dying to pull out the copy of the ledger. Once in the room, I did. Most of the squiggles were legible, although there were many abbreviations and even what looked like codes made up of numbers and letters. It was more a reminder of business activities than any formal memo to himself, or diary.

By 2 A.M., I was so blurry-eyed that I could hardly see. I had reached two and a half months ago when I found the entry "11 A.M., L.M. Call, recs. B-P drill bit, hv K. chek." That was all. But I could have screamed with joy.

"L.M." would be—had to be, for an old pal like the Bounty president—"Little Major," "B-P" would be "Boles-Panjunk," and "K." was Kenneth Drosnahan, my partner in crime, and maybe cofelon-to-be.

There might be more such treasures in the book. I thought I'd seen "L.M." earlier a couple of times and skipped over it, not focusing on its meanings. But that could wait. Despite the excitement, weariness overcame me. I staggered to the bathroom, then returned to the bed. I had my story. It was worth it all.

At seven, I awakened, anxious as hell from some unrecalled dreadful dream. I began to sort things out.

My main feeling was still one of elation at nailing the box shut on the Little Major. But coming up strong was the feeling that I might get fired by the *Eagle*. I would certainly be in trouble with the law. Additionally, I was a long way from getting the documents back to Washington.

I leafed through the copy of Quiven's ledger. Fastidious little Dutchman he was. But the entries were maddening. Initials everywhere, and numbers. Along with such entries as "Magna Constr., $250,000 ck, addition Bluefield Ref.," clearly a check for construction work on Bounty's Bluefield refinery addition, there would be such things as "P.E. 10ht," or "B.B. 5 bb asked but p-up."

Then, I found several more crucial entries. One was two months ago. "K.D. report B-P-bit. Afirm." That would be Buddy Drosnahan okaying the bit from the technical point of view.

And a day later, "3p told L.M. fonely B-P bit okay & will mention D.G., D.A." That would be Quiven calling Edwards and saying he would tell two fat cats in two of the other big eight companies about the drill, I'd bet. So L.M.—Little Major—was not only making his own contacts, but he was encouraging the Big Oil boys to get together on the bit. That was antitrust trouble for him, I'd warrant.

I found two more cryptic ones. "L.M. 5" and "L.M. 15." Could it be some kind of payoff? That was my first thought. We'd see.

Suddenly, I was angry. Here I was, twitchy and anxious, in a hotel room, damned near sure to get arrested and maybe even fired. And why: for turning up a first-class antitrust case involving millions of dollars, a conspiracy by the big oil companies, and bribery on the part of the Speaker of the House. Meanwhile, those bastards scot-free. Crazy justice!

I put the ledger copies down and took a shower. My stomach was almost too upset for food, but I got the bellman to bring me up a big serving of milk toast with a poached egg plopped in the middle of it. I held it down and then had some orange juice and poured out some Sanka. That done, I wasn't feeling too bad, for a man on the lam.

In the Yellow Pages, I located a duplicating place about five blocks from me. Under U.S. Government, I found a post office two blocks the other way.

I addressed one of the envelopes to myself care of General Delivery at the Franklin Station in Washington, one to Connie March at the paper since I didn't know her home address, and wrote on an enclosed second envelope, "Connie: Hold for me, don't open, and keep quiet about this." I addressed a third set to the Reverend Dinan Blathe, care of the National Cathedral, with much the same admonition.

Then, I copied out twice, in long hand, the ledger entries with L.M. in them. I used hotel stationery and addressed them to me care of General Delivery, one to Woodley Station in Washington and the other to General Delivery, Main Post Office, Washington.

I called the duplication shop, found out it was open at 8:30 A.M., and gathered up the various envelopes, the roll of tape, and the ledger Xeroxes. With everything stuffed in my overnight bag, I left the room.

Now was the time of trepidation. I bought two airmail stamps at the desk as I checked out, and walked briskly toward the duplication shop, dropping the small envelopes in two different mailboxes. That way, if I did get caught with the ledger and it was taken away, I would at least have a written record of what Emerson Quiven had written about "L.M."

For an extra three bucks, the woman at the duplication shop put my stuff ahead of the work left over from the night before. I had two copies of the ledger run off. At the shop, I prepared my three neat, sturdy packages for mailing, all double taped at the edges.

Outside, I got a cab to the post office and sent them airmail to Washington. Only then did I feel safe. Maybe I would be caught. But the story was secure. There was no way the Feebs could find all three of those packages, plus the two small envelopes.

That huge load off my mind, I looked up safes in the Yellow Pages and got a cab to the nearest show-

room. The place was small and had that aficionado air
that you find in specialty tobacco stores. Safes, it appeared, were still not being sold in drugstores and super-
markets. The close quarters made me uneasy all over
again.

"What's it for?" asked the tall salesman, a man in
shirt sleeves with an assortment of small arcane tools
in one of those plastic shirt-pocket envelopes.

"An office," I said. He looked patient. I felt panicky.

"Money or records?"

"A little of both."

"A money safe," he said firmly. "How big?"

"Three by two?"

That clue given, he walked me into his back room
where a large collection of safes and vaults were crated,
and a few models stood clear of their crates.

"About that size," I said, pointing to one.

He nodded negatively.

"Won't take a good fire," he said.

At a wooden crated box, he looked at a tab, then
led me back to his office.

"I got one good one in stock," he said, pulling out an
illustrated catalogue, "torch resistant, automatic relock,
and punchproof dial." I winced, then prayed he would
not notice my flinch. "Special drill-resistant plates and
optional mechanical or electric alarm system, cutting
down only a cubic half foot on the interior."

"It sounds great," I said, looking nervously at the
handsomely illustrated catalogue. It showed a picture
of a burglar being baffled as he tried to lay violent hands
on the safe.

"This," he said, pointing to heavy plating on the
front of the safe, "makes it almost impossible to peel
one of these babies. Almost impossible!"

I could feel those droplets beginning under my arms
again. I thought, I've got to get out of this Goddamn
place before somebody calls and says they want to
replace a safe that just got peeled in the Bounty Building.

"Peeled?" I asked uncomfortably. My atonement was
taking a fierce toll on my stomach linings.

But the cognoscente was into his role, and did not notice my malaise.

"Peeled," he said. "The old ones, you could peel like you'd peel an orange. In minutes!" I thought of murmuring a dissent on the time element. "Peel the door right off them."

"Jesus," I said. I looked at my watch. "How much is it?"

He glanced up.

"You'd be taking the business discount?"

"Uh, yes."

"What's the business?" he said, still agreeably.

"Uh, communications," I said, a little more strongly.

"Be 10 per cent off, listing $589, and tax in, about $540, delivery free in the San Francisco area." He tried to look nonchalant, wondering, I suspected, if I'd try to knock him down on the price.

"Guarantee?" I asked, not wanting to sound like an easy mark for his expertise, or too eager.

"One year, all repairs; we come and pick it up. Lifetime on the body, of course. We service the combination changes free as long as it's not too often." He knew he had a sale and began to relax. "It's a fine safe," he said proudly.

"Make it out to me personally, if you would," I told him when he got the invoice out. "I don't want it delivered until I can get the place ready for it."

"Pay then," he said. "I can bill you." Like many craftsmen in this age of dying craftsmanship, he was his own worst enemy when it came to actually collecting the money.

"Take it now," I told him. "You can make sure the check clears." He laughed and looked embarrassed at the idea of bad checks. For him, no doubt, the only worthy crime would be, well, safecracking. "I'll call in the delivery today or tomorrow."

For the invoice, I gave him my real name and the address of the newspaper's San Francisco stringer. It was a mild enough subterfuge. When I gave him the check, he looked as if he wanted to balk at the Washington bank. He stared at my overnight bag. But it was too late now.

"Home office is in Washington," I explained.

I left, wondering how the hell I was going to charge a safe off on my expense account.

Well, I thought, I have protected the story, myself, and the paper as well as I could under the circumstances. Now, I wanted to get back to Washington. I would be easier to defend there than here. I had no doubt I would be in legal trouble.

I wondered if the ACLU would make a First Amendment case out of it. I doubted it. My defense was going to have to be devious and more than a little political. After all, the government had a lot to lose if too much of the Bounty-Speaker story came out.

There would be the three oil companies getting together in an antitrust conspiracy on the drill bit, the doings of the Speaker, the possible widespread payoffs by Bounty and the other oil companies. It could be that even Harry Frieden, the President himself, had not been immune to a few Big Oil payoffs in the past. If I could show my safecracking had been intended only to get a story (and I could make the wobbly concept of Drosnahan looking for his papers stand up), I might get out with a whole skin.

At a rent-a-car place, I picked up a Volkswagen. This story, good as it was, was going to cost the paper a lot of money. I nipped into a grocery store, bought a half pint of milk to drink, got a large grocery bag free, and transferred the tools into it.

Then I drove to the airport slowly on the Bayshore freeway until it was clear of traffic, stopped, and quickly eased the tools over the railing and into the bay waters.

I drove past the vast sprawl of the airport, thinking about all the neat FBI men and local detectives who might be in there waiting for me, and cut into Oakland across the San Mateo Bridge. The flight from Oakland, where I turned in the car, to Sacramento was easy enough. I used an assumed name and paid cash.

I didn't want to wait until I was arrested to give the

safe store people directions on the safe's delivery. It would look as if I was not sufficiently eager to replace it. I called from Sacramento and caught them just before they closed. The man's name on the invoice was "E. K. Stuhler."

"Mr. Stuhler," I said when he came to the phone. "I'm the fellow who bought that safe this morning for delivery later."

"Yes," he said recollecting.

"Could you listen very carefully? I want it to be delivered to the Bounty Building to the president's office. There is a closet up there off the conference room on the eleventh floor." I could hear his breath coming hard now. The safe and vault community in any city was, I suspected, a very close one. By now he had read in the paper, or learned from the police, or even been called in as a consultant to see if he recognized the distinguishing marks of the cracker. The thought made me anxious. I must get to Washington.

"Where are you now, Mr. Warder?" he asked, too honest a man not to be inept in his attempt at calm.

Now it begins in serious, I thought, guts turning.

"Never mind that," I said. "See you." My voice cracked a bit with nervousness as I gently hung up.

7

The Arrest

The FBI did not arrest me until early the next morning, when, after flying in on the Red Eye special to Baltimore, I turned up at my apartment.

Expecting an arrest did not make me any more sanguine about it. As I walked toward the front door of the building, I heard the two cars stop behind me on the street and looked back.

Six or seven neat youngish men in suits were coming toward me. In front, the building's door opened and three more came out. Well, I thought, the skunks are doing it in the grand style this time.

A short fat-faced man was the first to reach me.

"Mr. Warder," he said, showing me his credentials.

"Yes," I said. "Just a minute with that. I want to get your name off it. You don't seem to have read the First Amendment recently. You may be committing a criminal act."

It was sheer bravado. I was scared, even panicky. He held the credentials folder so I could read it, but went on. "You're under arrest," he said.

I got his name, Conrad Prurie, and a rodent-eyed man came up and began tugging at my overnight bag.

"Keep your hands off of that; let's see your warrant," I said.

"This is a street arrest. We don't need one," the fat-faced man, Prurie, said. It was a matter of struggling for the bag and getting nailed for resisting arrest and maybe for striking a federal officer. I let him have the bag.

"What's this for?" I said to fat-face.

"Safecracking, destruction of private property. Flight across state lines to avoid arrest."

"Oh, bullshit," I said. "I want to see my lawyer. You're fucking over the First Amendment. I want the names of every one of these secret-police officers." I asked the man nearest me with my bag what his name was. He gave it, but fat-face intervened.

"We don't have time for that. Let's go."

He pulled my unresisting arms. I could feel my temper running up but fought to control it. I could possibly beat their charges, but if I argued and swung at them, they could get me with a crummy assaulting-a-federal-officer count. I'd seen it happen to many of the FBI's victims, most of them Mafia dons or other thugs. Now it was I.

Think, Aubrey, I said to myself. No resisto. Stay cool. Keep the Constitution out front. Make a record of everything. I started trying to write on my notepad with the ball point.

Fat-face jerked them away from me.

"Now you've done it, you little Hitlerite," I said to him. "Those are the tools of my trade. You've taken my notes, Goddamnit."

I was burned now.

"You have taken my notes without due process, Prurie."

"You'll get 'em back," he said. With his hand on my belt he pushed me across the sidewalk toward their cars. One of my neighbors, a young lawyer at Commerce, saw me as he came out the door.

"Aubrey Warder, is that you?" he looked perplexed as I glanced over my shoulder. Fat-face Prurie gave me a shove.

"Call the paper. Tell 'em the FBI's got me, okay?" I shouted.

He ducked inside the building, hoping the FBI would not see him, but probably willing to make an anonymous call to the paper. Prurie pushed me up against one of the cars. He popped my legs apart and patted me down while another agent held my arms up against the car. The indignity of this bullshit was beginning to get to me. My injured ankle throbbed.

The ferrety man jerked my wrists together and handcuffed them in front of me.

"This is an illegal arrest, not that you guys ever gave a damn about that," I said. They hustled me into the back seat of the car.

"Turn on the sending channel," I said from the back seat. "Since you took my notes in violation of the Constitution, I want to make a statement."

"There's nobody to take it," said Prurie. He was getting exasperated. I wanted to blow his cool. But he knew that he was in a ticklish position. He would push me as far as he dared, maltreat me as much as he could get away with, but no further.

"The hell there isn't," I said. "Headquarters tapes every call you guys make on the radio. I want to record a statement." He ignored me. But I persisted.

"I'm not tying up that radio channel," he said. "How about shutting up until we get back to headquarters?" There was a certain reasonableness in that. But why shouldn't he be reasonable? *He* wasn't being arrested.

"I want my notes back," I said. That was his weakest ground.

The car ran smoothly through the Twelfth Street tunnel and onto Pennsylvania Avenue.

"See what I can do for you when I get back," he replied. I looked around to see whether I recognized anyone from the FBI's attempt to arrest me in the subway episode. None of the three men in the car looked familiar. I doubted the FBI, even as screwed up as they were, would be stupid enough to use the same raiders.

Well, I thought as we pulled up to the old post office building where their squad rooms were, time after time I've seen them make dubious cases against people who had done nothing but cross them. Maybe if I'd exerted myself, I could have exposed them. But I hadn't.

Sometimes they'd made the fakey arrests years after

the imagined offense. One private eye had made public assholes out of them by turning up a witness the FBI had sought for weeks. Years later they'd had him indicted for advertising a little tape recorder that they charged was a "surreptitious electronic interception device." He'd won his case, at a cost of $41,000 in lawyer's fees.

Secret police were indivisible, I realized, now I was their victim. Still, it was hard to believe.

The pack marched me into the building. Five of them crowded into the little elevator with me. At the fifth floor they pushed me out and I stumbled down the hall and into the squad room.

Only there, did it begin to hit me that I was in trouble. I began to see things, just the least little bit from their view: "We got this prick before," they would be thinking, "but this time we have him right. He broke into a safe and fled to escape arrest. Airtight."

There was a hideous rationality to their view. But I kept up the bravado. The first man I saw inside the squad room was Lilly, a beefy, white-haired man with nervous eyes who, I knew, was the assistant special agent in charge of the field office.

"Lilly," I said, "you're violating my rights. I want a form to fill out against police brutality. This thug," I pointed to Prurie, "rammed me up against your police car, although my ankle is under a doctor's care." It was a new idea. He looked at the ankle bulged by its Ace bandage.

Then he looked spitefully at Prurie. I recognized that Lilly did not run a happy shop. Prurie shook his head negatively, meaning he had not roughed me.

"Take off the Goddamn handcuffs," Lilly told Prurie.

"I want my doctor to examine my ankle and I want it written that I have made this request," I told Lilly. "And I want a photographer from the paper to take a picture of the bruised tissue," I added. I was not going willingly into their Goddamn gas chamber.

"Oh, shut up," Lilly said warily. "I don't even want to talk to you." He turned again to Prurie. "Get up a statement on his allegation about his Goddamned ankle, will you. And get the rest of them to witness it."

"I want a doctor."

"Call up PHS and get Doc Grew over here," Lilly said to Prurie. That would be some public health doctor, the kind who would certify to the robustness of a cadaver to please the FBI.

"I want my own—"

But Lilly was an old pro who had handled big-mouths before. I knew the type. He had enough years for retirement and he wasn't so fearful as these younger guys were. He interrupted me.

"Process his ass. Major crimes," he said.

Well, I thought, that didn't do me any good. Major crimes meant that instead of just fingerprinting me, they "fingerprinted" me all the way up to the elbow. They took a batch of extra mugshots, too.

The young agent doing the ink work wiped his hands and looked up at Prurie. Prurie glared at me maliciously. He knew my phony brutality charge against him would go into his folder, even if it was marked "unproved." We both knew it was false and that it would nevertheless successfully put a small cloud over him.

"He's a safecracking suspect," Prurie said to the younger agent. "Fingerprint the bottom of his foot. Not the one in the bandage."

"Aw, c'mon, Prurie," the young agent said.

"We've had barefooted safe jobs. Footprint him," Prurie ordered.

The petty bastard, I thought. But I submitted. The agent slopped the ink onto the sole of my foot. It was cold and tickled. Lilly looked in. At first he was startled, then the old man realized what Prurie was up to and smiled with delighted malice.

"Safecracking," said Lilly.

"Thought it might be a necessary precaution," replied Prurie.

"I want to call my lawyer," I said. "I want my notepaper and pencil back. You are pissing all over the First Amendment."

"There's nothing in the First Amendment about busting safes," said Prurie.

"Shut up," said Lilly to his junior. "How the fuck would you know?" I laughed at Prurie and Lilly cocked his old boar's head at me and laughed along. "Alleged safecracking," Lilly reminded Prurie.

Even as I laughed at Lilly's sally, his enlisting me in the joke, I felt a little shudder. Were they going to "mummy and daddy" me, that old carp? There, one plays good guy, one plays prick, and the good guy elicits facts on the basis of faked kindness. At least that wouldn't work. I had used it too many times myself in working over people on stories.

"I want my lawyer," I repeated.

"Soon as we finish processing," said Lilly and left.

"Since you refuse to call in an *Eagle* photographer, I want you to take a picture of my ankle and the flesh around it," I told Prurie. I looked at the young agent. "I want you to remember that I have requested that you make this photo and that Prurie is refusing. I will call you in the brutality hearing. What's your name?"

"Penn," he mumbled uncomfortably. I knew the Feebs always required their agents to give names on demand. It was one of Hoover's enduring rules. He didn't want them to be accused of anonymity, the hallmark of less restricted secret police.

"Penn, I wish you would note my request so when I subpoena you in the brutality hearing for agent Prurie—"

Prurie was full of hate now. Like any ambitious bully, he was short on a sense of humor.

"Shoot his ankle," Prurie ordered.

From all the walking I'd done on it, some of the bruise tissue had crept up above the ankle.

"There's bruise tissue there," the young agent said.

"I never touched him," Prurie said.

"He jammed me up against the car and struck my legs," I said. "That's a threshold statement by me, Prurie, which I hope you won't forget, since it's admissible in court. I am suffering agonizing pain in my ankle. I implore you to get a doctor." I glowered at the young agent who was beginning to look slightly intimidated. He didn't know the bruise tissue wasn't from Prurie.

"Take a note of that threshold statement," I told him. "Implore is spelled i-m-p-l-o-r-e. Fix it in your mind."

"Can you believe we have to put up with this bullshit?" Prurie said to the other agent. The man shook his head in wonder.

When they had all the fingerprint and the footprint cards in order, Prurie gave them to me.

"You sign here that they're yours."

"Nope," I said. "It would be acknowledging that this arrest was legal." Prurie was weary and bitter enough with me not to argue. He went out and Lilly came in. For an old-timer like that, anything was predictable except a failure to adapt to the standard procedures.

"You won't sign the print cards?" he said, his pale sheepskin face flushing in spots.

"No," I said. "You going to put the thumbscrews on me?"

"You silly fuck," he said, leaving angrily with the cards.

After they had processed me, I got my phone call. I made it to Cubbins. He was expecting me.

"The Feebs called Mr. March. Your ass is in a one million per cent jam," Cubbins said. "I assume this line is being listened to."

"Probably not," I said chilled by his news. "In theory this is a call to a lawyer and if they listen in on a privileged conversation like that, the case gets thrown out."

"Okay, I don't need that feature-story bullshit," Cubbins said sharply. "*I* am going to assume it's being listened to. The lawyer is on the way down."

"Doesn't Mr. March went to hear my side of it?"

"The way the Feebs talked there isn't any your side of it."

"Oh, that's horseshit," I said. "Can you get Mr. March calmed down a little?" I could feel Cubbins wondering on the other end of the line what kind of a story I'd gotten out of the safe. Shifty though he was, he was a good newspaperman.

"I know what you're thinking," I said after a moment.

"Well, don't talk about it on this phone."

"Well, the answer is 'yes,' if there's anybody on the Goddamned paper left who thinks like a newspaperman."

"Don't give me——" he began, his voice rising characteristically. But he must have thought that being where I was wasn't very pleasant for me, because he stopped. "Look, we'll get you out of there soon, okay? But, for Christsake . . ."

When I'd finished my call, the FBI agents began talking to me in earnest. The main interrogator was a Chicano. The Feebs wanted this case with the liberal *Eagle* to have all the earmarks of desegregation about it. I was surprised they hadn't trotted out a black agent.

My interrogator read me my rights. I wouldn't sign the sheet he gave me that attested to the fact that my rights had been read to me. He sighed.

"You must have been expecting something like this would happen to you this morning," he said.

"No," I said. "I didn't really. I had expected to go to bed and rest my injured ankle. I beg you to get me a doctor. I am in agony from the brutality of agent Prurie. . . ."

"You didn't sound like you were in agony when you were talking on the phone," he said. "You sounded like your ass was in a crack for busting open a safe."

Well, I thought, this one is dumb, but he's less of a hypocrite than the rest.

All the while I was being brave, I was thinking of Mr. March. And slowly, I could also feel the fear of the unknown creeping over me. Suppose they *did* make a case on me.

"Did you hurt your foot in San Francisco?" he said solicitously. He took notes as he talked and as I replied and even when we weren't talking. I wondered what he was writing. Maybe it was some technique the FBI taught them to unnerve suspects. Already I was thinking of myself as a suspect.

"Do you know a Kenneth Drosnahan?"

I wondered if they had arrested him. But if I asked, the schmuck would write something like, "subject expressed keen interest at the mention of the name of Kenneth Drosnahan, the alleged confederate in case number whatever."

"Look," I said, to my interrogator, "why the hell should I be agreeable with you people? You've beshat the Constitution by arresting me. Now you're over there in the role of some kind of prosecutor, and I'm sitting here where anything I say you can twist around and swear to."

"I'm just doing my job," he said. That old crap. My temper broke slightly.

"That's what Eichmann said."

The Chicano agent lost his cool, too.

"We aren't that way. We don't kill people."

"It's all a matter of degree," I said.

"There's no third degree here," he said, incredibly misinterpreting me. I realized that he was more nervous than I or he would never have made such a malapropism. "We don't hit people with hoses; we don't torture—" His voice was rising.

"You're not listening," I said. "If you can't hear any better than that, you ought to be retired early. I said with you guys and the Nazis it's just a matter of degree."

"Oh," he said, so discomposed he didn't take it as an insult.

I saw Lilly coming through the squad-room door with our lawyer behind him. Mrs. Murtry looked like a sixty-five-year-old Mother Superior from a slum district who had seen everything and remembered it all.

"Mrs. Murtry," I said.

"Aubrey. I knew I'd find you here one of these days." The light from the fluorescent lamps hit her spectacles. She was straight as a spear and almost as tall as I was. "Where can I see him?" she said to Lilly.

Lilly had not expected a woman and started to take us both out of the squad room. Then he turned to her and said, "How about us getting his name on the fingerprint card now that you're here. It's just a formality."

"Why don't you sign the card, Aubrey?" she said.

"It's an illegal arrest."

Mrs. Murtry turned coldly on Lilly.

"I don't recall much about criminal law," she told him. "And until I do, he's not signing anything at all." She thought a moment. "Not even a receipt for whatever they take from you," she told me.

We went into a little room and I told her fast what had happened. She listened, nodding as I spoke, with no sign of approval or disapproval. I told her about my brutality charge.

"Did they hurt you?" she inquired.

"Not much. It throbbed a little when they put me up against the car." When we got back to Lilly, she was icy.

"I want the full name of this brutal FBI agent," she said to Lilly.

"Now wait a minute," he barked.

"This allegedly brutal agent. He ought to be suspended for the time being. I don't want him near my client. He's a maniac. I want an independent doctor's examination."

"One thing at a time, Mrs. Murtry," he said.

"Okay," she said. "To begin with. The brutality case is under your immediate jurisdiction. What's your name?"

Lilly gave it. She was taller than he, and she kept grinding out questions about his badge number and the persons who witnessed the "brutality" and the time it all occurred. Finally, fed up, he said a bit sharply:

"Lady, this is an interstate flight and California safe-cracking case, not a brutality case. I might add, the safe was both peeled and punched, not a very efficient way to do things." He leered at me. "One or the other would have sufficed. Now, do you mind if we pick up where we left off with the suspect?"

"I want to be present while you speak with him," she said.

"Well, you can't be. We don't have to go that far yet."

"Aubrey," she said, "I'll go get the bond set up.

Don't say anything to them or anybody else until I see you again, okay?"

That said, the formidable woman left.

Lilly looked at me without enmity.

"Tough ass, hunh?"

"Yeah," I said, humiliated that I had overkilled the safe. Clearly I had misunderstood my instructions from Fort Lauderdale.

Now, the indignities began. They took my wallet, went through it, pulling out cards, noting the name of my insurance agent, my bank. I knew what that meant. They would make inquiries everywhere, letting it be known that I was involved in a possible criminal case. They would confiscate my bank records, my telephone bills to check out toll calls, whom they were made to. They would cover my mail to find out who sent me letters. Thank God, I thought, I hadn't ever called Betty Page long distance. Thank God, also, I had long since given up carrying a little book of telephone numbers and kept the safe ones in the office under lock on a Rolodex, the dangerous ones at home with initials and jumbled numbers.

Long ago, I had learned about that. The first things the police did with Jane Fonda and all the others who had been busted for antiwar demonstrations was to Xerox the phone and address books. And it was the Watergate burglars' address books that led the reporters and cops and FBI to the White House.

The Public Health Service doctor came in and looked at my ankle. He grunted a few times, touching the ankle where it was puffing up at the top.

"That's old bruise tissue," he told me.

"Oh, bullshit," I said. "It's fresh. I want your name so I can complain about you to the city medical society."

He was unperturbed and gave it to me. Another one of those old government farts so far beyond retirement age he didn't care anymore.

"Even if it was fresh, there's no evidence it isn't from your being on your ankle too long. Pull up your pants legs so I can see your knees." He looked at my knees and grunted some more, then called Prurie over.

"See there, the slight discoloration. This man has been kneeling for a prolonged period as if in front of a safe." The old doctor laughed up some phlegm, and Prurie joined him. "The kneeling may have cramped him up in the metatarsal region, causing this swelling." He poked at my ankle.

I was outraged.

"I want my own doctor."

The agents, gathered around now, ignored me.

"Can you type that up for me, what you just said, Doc?" said Prurie, relief in his voice.

"Sure, glad to," said the old man.

"Quack, quack," I said to him. The doctor's face flushed for the first time.

"You lying scum," he said to me. "They ought to get you for making a false report to the FBI." He walked out and the agents sat me back down at the interrogation desk.

The Chicano agent asked some more questions, then they handcuffed me again and led me back on the street. I could get a quick hearing at the courthouse, I hoped, and would be free.

At the cell block, the gangling black marshal running the place took away my pencil but let me keep the notebook.

"Don't want you hurting yourself or others," he said. Prurie laughed bitterly. It had not been an entirely happy arrest for him. "Watch his foot," Prurie said to the marshal. "He's a fast man with a brutality charge."

The marshal looked at me hostilely.

"What's he do?"

"Newspaper reporter. The *Eagle*."

I could feel the marshal changing toward me already. "You guys ought to leave reporters alone," he said softly to Prurie. "My father was a printer and he said, once, you don't want to get in a smear contest with a fellow who buys ink by the barrel." Prurie ignored him.

When the marshal handed me over to the turnkey in the courthouse cell block, he said to him, "He's with the *Eagle*. He's got a bad foot." The turnkey, also black, beamed. Thank God, I thought, the *Eagle* stands for something somewhere. I was amazed to find how tense I had been. How grateful I was to these two men. The marshal reached in his pocket and pulled out a felt tip. "Here," he said. "Write a nice story about us down here, Mr. Warder."

For five more hours I sat in the cell as they called the arriving and departing suspects. Because it was the federal courthouse, we got the higher grade crimes.

Of the sixteen men who came in and went out while I waited, there were three narcotics cases, a homicide (gun), two assaults with a dangerous weapon (gun), two grand larcenies, and a fugitive from justice (bank robbery), among others.

Only one, a narcotics suspect, was there long enough for me to get to know him. He had done time and had been made again on a serious heroin-possession charge. He had on flashy but expensive clothes, beginning now to show the wrinkles badly.

"You'll be out and you'll never be back in," he pronounced somberly. "They don't fuck around with them newspapers." I was glad to be reassured by an expert. When I told him I was suspected of safe-cracking, he laughed, unbelievingly, but he was quickly serious again.

"Let me tell you something I been wanting to say to you guys. When you write up a story about some dude being convicted, how come you put in there how much time he can get? You put in there, 'He could get a maximum of 183 years'."

"It's news," I said.

"Shit, man," he went on. "Nobody ever gets 183 years! You put that shit in there about 183 years and it just gives the judge ideas. He figures he *got* to give the dude twenty or thirty instead of just four or five. Don't do that, man."

It was a way of looking at things I had not considered. Now that I faced fifteen or twenty myself, I could see what he meant.

After five hours in the cell block, my case was called

and Mrs. Murtry, still glacial, got me out on personal recognizance—no bond.

I had underestimated the venom of the Feebs. Just to keep me in a cell for those extra hours, they had faked delays with California, with paper work. They wanted to sweat me.

God, I was glad to be leaving that place. But the suspects I'd spent the last five hours of my confinement with seemed a more decent lot than the Feebs I'd spent the previous four with.

"The press is outside," Mrs. Murtry said to me at the table before we got up. "Keep your mouth shut. Cubbins and Mr. March are down here. Just stay with us and shut up." I resented being talked to like some damned kid. But Mr. March's presence upset me.

When I turned from the suspect's table, I saw Cubbins and Mr. March. Behind them were twenty or thirty *Eagle* people crowded into the little federal magistrate's courtroom. I was touched, but Mr. March looked furious. He came up and gripped my arm so tightly in his stringy old fingers that I started to flinch away. His raptorial eyes fixed mine and he hissed.

"I'm defending you with the press, Aubrey. But in my mind you're on probation, understand? Goddamn you; you've disgraced us." I was truly frightened. For the first time, I was convinced I had done wrong. Somewhere in me there bubbled up ever so slightly a desire to tell him to go fuck himself, but it quickly receded. Mr. March had intimidated me, something the FBI had failed to do.

"I'm sorry," I murmured, hating my abjectness.

Then, I thought, Who the hell did Mr. March think he was, bullying me this way? Glancing past him, I saw his daughter, her face lighted up with a sort of exultant pride and sympathy. A sudden image of her cat quickness, her nakedness, jumped maniacally into my head and then popped out.

"Goddamnit," I growled into Mr. March's ferocious visage. "Hear me out before you unload shit like that on me." He was taken aback.

"I'll hear you, all right," he said.

Outside it was dark except for the big TV lights from
the camera crews. I blinked and tried to look composed.
Somebody pushed a mike in my face. The mike hit my
cheek.

I started to wring the mike out of the TV man's hand,
but held my temper. I had to count on these bastards
as allies. Supposedly, we were brothers under the First
Amendment.

Amid the lights, I saw an old friend, Fred Ramos, the
lawyer turned TV reporter. He'd been with the Washington *News* when it folded and then gone to the New
York *Times*, and we had worked stories together more
than once. He was clean despite TV.

Fred and I headed for each other and he got his mike
in my face. March was trying to restrain me, and Mrs.
Murtry kept shoving her leathery old shoulder into my
chest to keep me back.

"What were you arrested for, Mr. Warder?" Fred
Ramos said. Mr. March shoved in front of me, pulling
at the mike. My God, I thought, how the hell is this
going to look on camera? But Mr. March was fine, at
first, as he often was in the clutch.

"I've told him to shut his mouth for once in his life,"
Mr. March said as the light men flooded his face. The
little red eyes on the camera popped on like stop lights
on a long street. "Until this shakes down, he's just going
to be a news reporter like always, not a news figure."

I looked at Ramos and shrugged. But he was facile
at his new trade.

"Did Mr. Warder participate in a safecracking at
Bounty Oil as charged by the California authorities?"
he shot at Mr. March.

"He has participated in a major investigation for the
Eagle," said Mr. March. "The FBI and California
charges will be answered in court and on the editorial
pages of the *Eagle*."

Somebody else had a microphone in front of Mr.
March.

"How about a few words from Mr. Warder?" a
shriller voice said. "You got a muzzle on him or something?"

I felt Mr. March stiffen.

"Next question," he muttered.

"You say you'll answer in an editorial. Whattaya going to say in the editorial?" Mr. March only paused a second.

"That Aubrey Warder has dignified the pages of the *Eagle* for twenty-five years, that I hope he's dignifying the pages for another twenty-five years, and that the charges were whomped up by the authorities to try to stop the exposure of a major political scandal."

Oh, motherfucker, I thought. And he was telling *me* to shut up. A man like that had no business running a big newspaper. Suppose I couldn't deliver on the "Major Political Scandal." I felt rattled.

Mrs. Murtry gasped. I looked at her, beseeching her to get the bit out of Mr. March's teeth.

"What's the story?" somebody demanded. "What story?" said Fred Ramos. "What scandal?" Mr. March composed himself.

"When we're ready to break it, you can pick it up for twenty cents in the daily *Eagle* or sixty if we break it out on Sunday," he smiled.

"Did Warder get it out of the safe?" "How about the safe job?" "Whatcha got, Mr. March?" came the cries. But Mr. March had said his piece. I was awed, but dubious, about his endorsement of me.

"We've got to get back and do a piece of our own on the arrest. I'm sorry, fellows," Mr. March said.

Cubbins and Mrs. Murtry started moving us out through the crowd. Not being a newspaper person, Mrs. Murtry made no bones about dashing the mikes out of our way. She was a most formidable woman.

Mr. March's chauffeur drove an old Buick limousine in deference to the liberal gods who dictated against Lincolns and Cadillacs. Mr. March seated me between himself and Mrs. Murtry. Cubbins sat on the jump seat.

"Aubrey," Mr. March said when we were in the car, "how could you? How in the Christ could you break into a safe? Jesus God! I have been in newspapering fifty years. Fifty . . ." It was an old story. His dad had let him be a copy boy one summer when he was twelve. He started counting his newspapering from then. ". . . and I never heard of a reporter cracking a Goddamn safe."

I explained the rationale of Drosnahan's custody-till-midnight which I had so laboriously worked out. I explained how I had bought a second safe.

"With whose money?" Cubbins snipped in at me.

"Oh shit, Cubbins, I'll pay for it," I shot at him.

"Put it on your expense account somehow," said Mr. March, then thinking about it a moment he said quickly, "No, don't. The last thing I need is to be a Goddamn coconspirator in a safecracking." So, I thought, I pay for the safe.

"I didn't take anything—" I started.

"Oh, don't tell me anything about it. The FBI has briefed me in laborious detail about the whole thing. Including your overkill on the safe. They sent an associate director over. They want your head. They want me to can you so they can hang you."

I looked down at the floor of the car sorrowfully.

"You can't ever do anything like this again, Aubrey," Mr. March said. "Never. Next time it's good-by."

"You're taking it very well," I said. "I appreciate it." Well, I thought, I'm to be spared. I thought of Betty Page. God, to get out of this mess, to get away with her. I was being reduced to a state of infantilism by all this Lord-giving and Lord-taking away by Mr. March and Mrs. Murtry.

What would Betty Page be thinking when she read of my arrest? She'd know what story I was on. Certainly, she'd know that I was after evidence that would fulfill the Little Major's prophecy about Renardi.

As we rode on silently, I began to wonder why the hell this hotshot group of newspapermen wasn't more interested in what I'd gotten out of the Goddamned safe. I glanced at Cubbins. I could read that prick's mind. He, at least, wanted to know, but he was too chicken shit to bring it up. Proceeds of a crime might upset Mr. March. Well, I thought, that was his problem.

"Don't you want to know what was in the safe?" I

asked Mr. March, as conversationally as I could. He looked at me assessingly.

"I know what was in the safe. You got a batch of letters belonging to that Bounty idiot, Drosny or who-ever, that you broke in with. They're looking for him all over California."

Poor Drosnahan, I thought. How disgustingly little I had thought of him. But was that what Mr. March really thought?

"Who said that was all, Mr. March?" I said.

"The bureau." He was perking up.

I looked at Cubbins.

"Didn't you tell him?"

"Tell him what?" said Cubbins from his jump seat.

"You know, what I hinted to you on the telephone."

Cubbins looked uncomfortable. I could rack him up now. I knew damned well he knew I was telling him in that first call that I had the goods.

"I must have missed the hint," Cubbins said disdainfully.

"Tell him what?" said Mr. March, picking up my theme. He was paranoid about people not telling him things. "What was in it?"

"Goddamnit," I said. "I got enough crap out of their—"

"The originals?" hissed Mrs. Murtry. "We don't want to hear about it if it's originals." She didn't want to hear anything about a crime, or rather she didn't want Mr. March to hear anything about a crime, to wit, the theft of documents, lest he be obligated to report it under a law called "misprision of felony."

"Tell me what?" Mr. March persisted.

"Just a minute," she hissed at him. The back seat of the car was becoming a rooster pit with her gasping and calling across me at Mr. March.

"It's Xeroxes," I told them.

"It still may be unwise to hear about it, for you any-way," she said to Mr. March. "He's my client. He can tell me."

"Oh, bullshit, Milicent," he said to her, sailing off the

platter as he had before the TV camera. "My Goddamn reporter steals these documents and *I* want to know what's in them. In fact, I want them. Why didn't you tell me?" he roared at Cubbins. "Aubrey, I want those Goddamn documents!"

He leaned forward as if to give an order to the chauffeur to change directions and head for the documents, but then he realized I held that particular key.

"Where the hell are they?"

"They'll be getting here," I said, afraid to tell him I sent one copy to his daughter. I hoped the ones to Blathe, and to me at Franklin Station, arrived okay. I told him about these latter two.

"Smart thinking, smart thinking," he went on hoarsely. "Now what was in them? Did we get the story?"

"Yeah," I said as coolly as I could. His agitation was upsetting me. When he was like this, he would say and do anything.

"Okay, what is it? What, in a nutshell? About the Speaker, isn't it?"

"Yes, sir," I said now. "It keelhauls him. It shows he took money, lots of it, from a drill bit firm and then got Bounty Oil to use the drill bit in all its operations. It may show that he got the other big oil companies to use the bit, too. It's a helluva story," I said, I hoped reverently.

March's wild eyes hooded over for a moment. He was coming out of it. "Yes," he said. "It's a pisser."

"The safe!" interjected Mrs. Murtry. "You still got them out of the safe. They're the proceeds of a crime."

"Is it defensible? In court, I mean?" asked Mr. March of Mrs. Murtry. She had once been a line attorney at the Justice Department.

"I doubt it," she said.

"Now, hell, Milicent," said Mr. March, exasperated.

"We can try," she said. She looked at me and caught my despairing eyes. My moroseness brightened her. Now that I was penitent, I could be forgiven. She reached around and patted my cheek. "If he's defensible, we'll find a way to defend him."

"When can you write it?" asked Cubbins, knowing now it was safe to act like a newspaperman again.

"What do we have in the way of time?" joined in Mr. March.

"Well," I said, coming out of my funk, "you blew a lot of it talking about a big story to those hyenas back there. Everybody's going to be swarming on the thing. You told the TV people—"

"Damn my stupid mouth," growled Mr. March. "Yuck," he said with self-disgust, moving his hand up for a moment as if he would wrench out his tongue.

"It was in the heat of the moment. Don't feel bad, Mr. March," said Cubbins.

Mr. March glowered at him.

"Don't be such a suck, Cubbins," he said. I grinned. "When can you—?" Mr. March asked me.

"With luck, the documents will be in tomorrow. I can get the reporting done in maybe twenty-four hours—"

"You've got to see the Speaker, in fairness," said Mr. March, remembering his paper was about to draw and quarter an old friend.

"Of course," I said. "I'll have to talk with Quiven and the Boles-Panjunk people and try to nail down another oil firm or two that might have got heat from the Speaker."

"And with a little conning—" said Cubbins. He was very fine when it came ultimately to putting the thing together.

"What about the arrest story?" asked Mr. March. "Treat Aubrey just like you would any other suspect, I mean, in writing the damn thing."

"Of course," said Cubbins.

"But use that quote from me about dignity. You know his twenty-five years—"

"Right," said Cubbins.

"And don't repeat what I said about a major story. Don't give a damn thing away." Even Cubbins had his limits when people began telling him how to do what he knew how to do best.

"I'll say he was breaking in the safe on assignment

from the *Eagle*," Cubbins said, tongue in bitter cheek, but with no hint of the anger I knew had welled up in his chicken soul. It was this point-beyond-which he couldn't be pushed that gave me any respect for him at all.

"The hell you say!" exploded Mr. March.

"He's trying to tell you to let him put the story together, Mr. March," I said, siding with Cubbins. "If, after he puts it together, you don't like it, then you can fire him."

"I'm sorry, Michael," he said to Cubbins, and we all bailed out of the big Buick and headed upstairs.

8

The Speaker

I unloaded everything about my arrest on the rewrite man. By that time, Cubbins had decided to play the thing as if I had been working a legitimate story about the oil industry, but had gotten overzealous. There was no admission of my getting into the safe. Only the California charges and something about me not commenting on the charges themselves on advice of attorneys.

The story picked up wire service copy about me buying a safe to replace the one that was broken into, and paying for it with a personal check, emphasis on the personal.

The wires said Drosnahan was being sought and was reputedly in touch with a California lawyer who would arrange for him to turn himself in. They carried the bit from Mr. March telling what a respected reporter I was and about how under the American system I was not guilty unless proven so, and that therefore I was not being suspended.

They said way down in the story that I had alleged FBI brutality, but that the FBI denied this as a "vicious snipe flight," an improbable metaphor, if I ever heard one.

That saga out of the way, I got down to business. It was still early enough in California to try Quiven. I wanted to con him a little on those damned ledger entries before he was shut up by his lawyers.

Already, he had described the safe job to the wires and local papers as an "outrage and an affront to decent newspapermen everywhere." How would an oilman know about decent newspapermen? I wondered.

As it turned out, the son-of-a-bitch had an unlisted phone number and it was an hour before a friend at the phone company could get it for me.

Then it hit me that there was a better way to go at Quiven. I limped over to Mr. March and asked him if he'd give me a hand with the chore. The old fart was delighted. I told him that, above everything, I had to get Quiven to admit the initials "L.M." in the ledger stood for the "Little Major."

"From then on, I'm safe, because the B-P has got to be Boles-Panjunk and the calls are all dated and square with the dates on the letters from the oil companies to Boles. The 'L.M.' I *have* to have." Mr. March nodded compliantly.

"So you call him and apologize for the safe," I suggested, "and in the course of your talk—"

The crazy, craggy old face lit up with manic glee.

"You bullpizzle!" he said. "Right, right, say no more." He had grasped the whole ploy. "Get him on the phone. Marvelous! Marvelous."

The *Eagle* operator did the secretarial bit, "Mr. Bertram March, publisher of the *Eagle* in Washington, calling Mr. Emerson Quiven," she said in her haughtiest tone to Quiven's maid. Quiven was so impressed that he forgot the gamesmanship for a situation like that, and came on before Mr. March did. I could hear them from the extension.

"Just a minute, Mr. Quiven," said our operator. "I'll put Mr. March on." I heard Quiven murmur "Thank you," and knew he knew he had been had for openers.

"Mr. Quiven, this is Bertie March. I owe you a deep apology," March began. His voice had the resonance of great, humbled power. "A deep, deep apology."

"Well, Mr. March," Quiven began, "I was just—"

"I don't want to get into the merits of the case. We've got a criminal charge to fight, a criminal matter." He came down hard on the criminal, implying that he shared Quiven's feelings about my criminality. "The paper has to be loyal to a man with twenty-five years on it, of course, but as a businessman myself, I am, well, I hope you will not use this against the reporter involved, but Goddamnit, I am just appalled. Appalled!"

"What could have gotten into him?" asked Quiven, sounding now like the president of a giant oil company, in sympathy with a wounded fellow captain of industry.

"Dumb sons-of-bitches," barked Mr. March. "All of them. A great paper. A great paper! My father, my grandfather . . ." You could almost feel the ghosts of earlier Marches rising like Banquo's descendants and passing by, each pointing an accusing finger at Bertie March. "Never in the *Eagle*'s one-hundred-and-two-year history." He rolled out the numbers as if he were intoning the Gettysburg address. "One hundred and two years—"

"Well, it's a crazy time," said Quiven, a little awed now by such abjectness from the personification of American Newspapering. "Why would he do it?" Quiven smelled a rat if only faintly. March smelled him smelling it.

He paused dramatically. I could scarcely believe he was so good at humbuggery.

"I am going to order him to tell you why," Mr. March said in a whisper. "My paper, my family's paper cannot afford to have . . ." overcome by phony passion, Mr. March paused, a catch in his voice. "I am ashamed," he said.

"Now, Mr. March—"

"Bertie," said Mr. March. My God, I thought, he's working it too fast.

"Bertie, I think you should advise him of his right to remain . . ."

"I leave those adjurations to the police, Emerson. I am going to put his fate in your hands—"

"Now, I don't know," began the bookkeeper-president of Bounty.

"Aubrey!" roared Mr. March at no one. "Pick up the extension."

I was quick-thinking enough to press down the button and let up as if I were just coming on.

"Aubrey," said Mr. March, "I am on the phone with Mr. Quiven."

"Jesus," I said, fearing Mr. March would get Napoleonic and overdo it.

"I want you to tell him everything," said Mr. March.

"Everything?"

"Everything."

Quiven butted in.

"I think that's an admission of—"

"I put his fate in your hands," repeated Mr. March. This was too much, even for me. Mr. March had gone crazy. But I saw in the second instant that he had read Quiven well. He knew the genre.

"I would rather not be privy to a criminal confession," said Quiven. "I just—"

"As you wish, Emerson," chimed in Mr. March. "Avoid what you will, but ask at will."

"I just—" began Quiven. "A few questions. I'm not a lawyer. But, a few non-incriminating—I ought to have my lawyer."

"Ask away!" boomed Mr. March. "Aubrey, answer!"

"Yes, sir," I croaked.

"Why my ledger?" said Quiven a bit querulously.

"Answer!" boomed Mr. March again.

"I was looking for a story," I said lamely.

"Did you Xerox his ledger?" Mr. March burst in again. "Did you?"

Ah, I thought.

"Yes, sir."

"How many copies?" asked Mr. March.

"One and then two more."

"My ledger!" said Quiven. "You Xeroxed—"

"Three copies?" asked Mr. March. "Three?"

"Yes, sir," I said.

"I want them in my office the instant you round them up," he roared.

I could almost hear Quiven sigh with relief.

"They will come back to you registered mail with

my personal guarantee that they are intact," said Mr. March. I noticed he didn't say they would come back unread or uncopied.

"Thank you," said Quiven. "But——"

"I am not trying to placate you or to find a way of getting you to drop criminal charges. I am looking to the honor of the *Eagle*," pontificated Mr. March.

"Aubrey," Mr. March's voice softened. "Why? Why?"

Well, I thought, here we go.

"It was on a particular story, sir."

Quiven would be wondering now how many lethal secrets I had found in that ledger. How many encoded thefts from the public, the government, the tax authorities had I discovered in that ledger? How many indictments against Quiven? He would be wondering what "particular story" I meant, knowing it touched the Little Major, maybe, but how? And he would wonder how many others, far worse, I would turn up, for on this particular Edwards story, Quiven would be clean, or at worst, guilty of a little antitrusting in recommending a good oil drill to several other firms. But on the others?

"Tell him! Tell him!" Mr. March said to me, shaking his head negatively.

"Mr. March. I cannot. I have certain——"

"Principles?" said Mr. March. "After this? Tell Emerson!"

"It doesn't even show Bounty did anything wrong," I said.

"What was it, Aubrey?" Quiven now said conciliatingly. He wanted to know badly. And he was relieved that I had found nothing wrong.

"I——"

"Tell!" boomed Mr. March.

"It was only the calls involving Speaker Edwards," I said. "The Little Major."

"What's that all about?" asked Mr. March. "He's a personal friend of mine. I talk to him a couple of times a month myself. What's this about, Emerson? Aubrey?" March went on. There was in the question the confusion of the fallen mighty. Blind Gloucester seeking to know what his eyes could not tell him. "Why shouldn't Emerson talk to Pom Edwards?"

"No reason," I said cravenly. "It was just—"

"Titillating?" asked Mr. March. "Just titillating?"

"I've known him for years," said Quiven. "Why shouldn't I—"

"No reason," I said defensively. "I just wondered, if it was on the up-and-up, why you just didn't use his real initials, instead of 'L.M.'"

"Why the hell shouldn't he?" said March. "The Little Major is what we've always called him, Goddamnit."

By this time there was a circle of other reporters around the two of us. Mr. March was as wan as old parchment. The strain on him was telling.

We were close. But the admission that "L.M." stood for "Little Major" had to come from Quiven's own mouth. We had to be able to write that, "Quiven conceded in a chat with the *Eagle* that the initials 'L.M.' in his ledger stood for Speaker Edwards' nickname, the 'Little Major,'" and "The initials 'L.M.' occur twice in connection with their conversations over the drill bit, etc." That single concession by Quiven on the two initials was the key to my whole story, to everything.

Did they sense it, those others? Their faces were a blur, friendly, solicitous.

I looked pleadingly at old Mr. March. His eyes were squinting with the tension of his own charade. Suddenly, it had all gotten serious. We were at the still point of a story with all the importance of the biggest stories. The Speaker's fate hung on this story. The destiny, in that sense, of a government.

"Why hell, I assume he uses initials the way I do, in my diary," said Mr. March. "Right, Emerson?"

"Of course," said Quiven.

The tension was now almost more than I could stand. We were within one question of it, one last tap of the hammer. I couldn't ask it. I couldn't. It wasn't my position to. Mr. March had to do it. I could see him, his old gaunt hand fooling with his vest buttons. Sound natural, I prayed. Just sound natural.

But he was going a new, more oblique route.

"So, if you write up this call, which I implore you not to, but cannot stop you from doing, in your ledger, the *Eagle* . . ." he changed field again. A flash of magic broken-field running by a long-ago back named Frankie Sinkwich crossed my mind. "I hope you'll make it 'B.M.' for Bertie March, although that sounds—"

Bowel Movement, I thought. I can't stand it.

"Well, B.M. would sound—" said Quiven, giggling a little, relaxing.

"Oh Christ, haven't I been kidded all my life about those damned initials," laughed Mr. March.

"I'll make it 'T.E.' for the *Eagle*," said Quiven, falling in with the little joke.

"You could have made Pom Edwards 'P.E.'," Mr. March said, lightly, no sign of the tautness he must be feeling.

Pull in the fish, I was thinking. Pull in the fish.

"But it would sound too much like Phiz Ed." Mr. March laughed again.

"Right," said Quiven. Did he know now that we needed the knot tied, that we simply *had* to have Quiven acknowledge what "L.M." stood for by more than silence, that his failure to dissent, when Mr. March and I had said it, was not enough. Poor March must be on the brink of a heart attack. Did Quiven now sense something?

"So, Emerson used 'L.M.' for Pom," said Mr. March, belligerently to me. "So what's the matter with that. Is that a crime, a deception? You found nothing wrong otherwise, did you?"

"Not to conceal anything," Quiven picked up, interrupting. "Maybe the Phiz Ed thing did stick in my mind, Bertie," he was explaining. "I guess that's why 'L.M.' seemed better for Pom."

We had done it! I was scrawling feverishly on the piece of paper in front of me ". . . that's why 'L.M.' seemed better for Pom," Quiven's own words tying the Speaker to the Boles-Panjunk deal!

I looked at Mr. March. He still had the t's to cross. His eyes were closed as if he were resting a moment.

The shuffling in that circle of reporters told me that they knew the crisis had passed, that Mr. March and I, mostly Mr. March, had pulled it off, with the grace of a matador.

"So Aubrey," Mr. March was repeating, "what's the problem in Mr. Quiven telephoning the Speaker? What does that show, anyway?"

"Nothing," I began.

"Nothing?" continued Mr. March. "Nothing?"

"It was about the, well, some drill that the Speaker——"

"Oh," said Quiven. "That." Even now Quiven did not know what Mr. March had done to him: Quiven must have been thinking about the other "L.M." entries, if he recalled them. The "L.M. 5" and the "L.M. 15" which I suspected were $5,000 and $15,000 respectively.

It was a toss-up for us now. Mr. March could either try to worm one more fact out of him on the drill, or switch to the $20,000. I listened to see which he would do.

". . . that was a drilling question," Quiven was saying, digging his hole still deeper, as it were. "I can't even——" So now we had a bit more. Gamely, Mr. March was going to try for the last of it. I saw him take a deep breath and put his mouth conspiratorially at the mouthpiece again.

"There were two other——" But Quiven was getting wise.

"I don't want to go into——" So we were finished now and all Mr. March could do was to get out as ably as he had gotten in.

"Say no more," Mr. March assured him. "The copies will be in the mail to you by the end of tomorrow, or anyway as soon as we get them. Say no more." We had what we wanted and Mr. March was trying to get off the phone. But Quiven's accountant's mind still wanted a few more subtotals.

"And——" Quiven wanted to know if another copy would be made.

"I am instructing Aubrey to give me every one of

those copies, with a stricture of immediate dismissal if he discusses them with anyone or attempts to copy a single page. Do you understand, Aubrey?"

"Yes, sir," I said wearily.

"And, uh, Bertie," said Quiven. He was quick enough to notice that Mr. March had not promised to kill any story based on what I had learned from the ledger.

"I cannot guarantee to you in good conscience," said Mr. March, "that we will not be doing a story about our friend the Speaker. I cannot guarantee that," said Mr. March solemnly. The touch of the master interrogator was to end by telling the conned victim the truth at last, gently. I could hear Quiven gasp on the other end. He knew now he was not going to get the whole cake, that there would be no promise of confidentiality.

"But, Bertie——"

"But, I can guarantee that no *other* item in the entire ledger will figure in the *Eagle* in any way," Mr. March swore, steadfastly.

Well, I thought, that's not a bad deal for Quiven, considering all the payoffs and other skullduggery that might emerge if we really tried to decode the entire ledger.

"But, Bertie," said Quiven, "I would think that nothing in the ledger would be used at all."

"Aubrey, I am sad to relate, has confided in others the mention of the drill," said Mr. March. "I cannot in good conscience——"

"Goddamnit," bridled Quiven. "There's nothing in the drill thing. You told me so yourself."

"Bounty is clean on the drill," I said. "It's a good drill."

"You're Goddamned right it is," said Quiven.

"Aubrey," said Mr. March, desperately wanting to wind up, now that we had what we wanted, "I think you may want to——"

I broke in. If Mr. March could be this game, so could I.

"Mr. Quiven. I have been a reporter for twenty-five years, more if you count before I came to the *Eagle*."

I started to say it, finish it, say that I had never done anything for which I was so sorry in all those years. I looked at Mr. March, he was nodding me on, wanting me to spread on the last blivit of bullshit. Screw that, I thought.

"Mr. Quiven, I wish I could say I am sorry that I broke into your safe. But that would be an admission of guilt that my lawyers would not permit me to make."

Mr. March looked over at me with a slightly betrayed expression. But he shouldn't have. My heart was singing. What I really wanted to say was that Quiven had given me a shot at the Pulitzer Prize and that prize or no prize, I would break into four more safes to get what I had gotten out of his. Mr. March raised his arms, as ominous as Siegfried's on his death couch. I did not dare provoke Quiven any further. Mr. March would fire me and the story would never get written by me.

"I am humbled by your decency," I said to Mr. Quiven. "I apologize for causing you trouble," I said. All that safe enough, and at the same time honest, Mr. March bowed out with a flourish.

"I have spoken with you man-to-man," preached Mr. March to Quiven. "The President has often told me, Emerson, that you are the only nobleman in the entire oil industry. I now know it."

Quiven wasn't having anymore. He had thought he was talking to a fellow corporate skunk. Now he knew Mr. March for what he was, something even worse: an alley reporter. He knew we were going to do something about the drilling. He wasn't sure what. But it wasn't going to be helpful to him or to Bounty. Still, Quiven was man enough not to prostrate himself before Bertie March. Besides, Quiven must have known it wouldn't work.

"I can see why you're so respected in your business, Mr. March," he said, putting terminal class into what firmness was left in him.

Quiven would rush to his ledger and recheck all the L.M. entries. He would know we were going to do stories about the entries that read, "L.M. Call, recs.

B-P drill bit, hv K. chek." and the "K.D. report B-P bit. Afirm."~and finally the "3p told L.M. fonely B-P bit okay & will mention D.G., D.A."

He would call Pom Edwards and alert him and also D.G. and D.A., whoever they were. The air-raid horns would be sounding all over the oil industry and throughout the Little Major's command.

Hedaris, Kitticon, their wives and secretaries, Boles of Boles-Panjunk, the public relations men for the big oil companies, their lawyers all, by explicits and osmosis, would be getting ready a reaction to what they surmised we would write. All would be expecting calls from the *Eagle*, and would be framing their comments with a primary and a secondary purpose. Primarily, they would protect themselves. Secondarily, they would protect the Little Major.

Edwards, perhaps with the help of his closest friends in government, would also be scheming up a counterattack on the *Eagle*, on me. The best defense, experience would have taught them, was to go for the balls.

Blathe got the first copy of the ledger I mailed and drove it in to me. I Xeroxed it, stashed a copy in my locker, and took the one Blathe delivered up to Mr. March's spartan lair.

On the wall were a number of plaques the *Eagle* had won, two bronzed matrices from the front pages on the days that World Wars I and II ended, and a picture of his late wife, with Connie as a wayward-looking ten- or eleven-year-old.

Two helmets, on a Roman legionnaire's cap and the other a silvery, closed armet, as I thought they were called, were on pedestals behind his desk. I recalled he had a collection of the things at his country home in Virginia.

To his credit, there were no pictures of him shaking hands with the numerous Presidents whose asses he had alternately kissed and booted. March saw me looking at the helmets and hissed with annoyance. When he was tight on time, he wasted none.

"Where's the rest?" he asked, seeing what I had in my hand.

"On the way, I guess. I'll give them to you when they come."

He fixed his bird-of-prey glance on me.

"If you made a copy of this just now, I don't want to know about it."

The comradeship we had shared the night before had dissipated. I knew the syndrome. Politicians also had it. It was an insulation from others that had to do with egomania. It was what set them off from human beings, what kept the lords safely above their villeins.

It took me no time to find D.G. and D.A. in the Poor's Directory under the major oil companies. But neither of them would come to the phone. Their secretaries took my number. In turn, I left the executives with the hooks of fear in their mouths.

"Tell him," I said to the secretaries, "that we are writing a story about him and wanted him to have a chance to comment on it if he wanted to. So far, we only have one side." Then I double-checked the spelling of their names and precise titles with the secretaries to make it sound as though their mention in the story was a certainty.

Still, if the oilmen were smart, or had good ex-newspapermen for public relations men, those worst and most capable of all oil whores, they would know I didn't have enough yet to name them.

Sure enough, one of the PR men was back to me in an hour.

"Aubrey, they got you with your hand on the safe door, it sounds like," he said pleasantly, trying to put me on the defensive.

"Yeah," I said. "Why are you calling back instead of the guy I put the call in to?"

"He's at a meeting. What can I do for you?"

"Nothing. I need him.

"Can I tell him what it's about?"

"A newspaper story."

"No shit," he said. "What kind?"

"I need him."

"I can try, but no promises."

"Okay, I want you to know we tried to reach him. Don't say we didn't after the facts are out, okay?"

"Don't you want to tell me what you've got? I'll get it to him and get some comment back to you."

"No, I need him."

"Okay, Aubrey, I'll try." Then he paused and got honest. "We don't think you've got enough to name him."

"I know that's what you think."

"Okay," he said. The PR man was good. He earned his $75,000 a year which was more than he'd ever scraped out of the Wall Street *Journal*, where he'd been trained, and well. "Listen, I hope personally you beat the rap, of course."

"I know, Joel. Thanks." And, of course, he meant it.

The other oil PR man was back with much the same performance, though less smooth. Joel had probably called him and told him he thought I didn't have enough to name D.G. and D.A. I could put their initials in the story, but it would be risky to name them.

I got Kitticon on the phone next. He wasn't having any either.

"I don't know what you're talking about," he said.

"I'm talking about your being the owner of record of options in Boles-Panjunk."

"My business is my business."

"You're Hedaris' brother-in-law, right?"

"My family is my business. I have to go. Good-by."

I got Georgie Hedaris on the phone after a good deal of shuffling.

"I can't talk about anything I don't know for sure, right, Aubrey?" the oily little rat told me. I was losing my temper, but slowly.

"Look, do you want us just to write this thing with a string of 'no comments'?"

"That's your job sometimes, Aubrey," said Hedaris. But both of us knew that I had a handle on the Speaker that I did not have on the others: The Speaker was a politician.

The oil companies ultimately could tell me to fry my ass, but a politician could only duck so much. He would have to see me. Besides, Edwards knew that he was the target and that I would therefore have to lay out to him everything I had in order to give him a chance to comment. I could spar with Big Oil, and they with me. But with Edwards, I had to tell him all.

He had to say something besides "No comment." The public knew by now that "No comment" amounted to a confirmation.

"When can I see him?" I said.

"Late next week?"

"No, tonight."

Hedaris sighed, said, "ummnh" a couple of times as if he were looking at the Speaker's appointment pad.

"Up here about eleven tomorrow?"

"Fine," I said.

"Mind if I sit in?"

"No," I said. "Mind if I bring someone or we tape it?"

"Rather neither one."

"I don't want any arguments on what's said," I said.

"We'll tape it," he said.

That night I typed up a summary of all the papers, facts, interviews, speculations, records I had, and all the questions I wanted to ask. It took eleven pages double-spaced just to summarize. But for all the thrill of getting close to my quarry, it was Betty Page Rawlinson Edwards I thought about. I had tried to call her so many times that even the maid was beginning to recognize my voice, despite my attempts to deepen or raise its pitch when I telephoned, and my roster of aliases.

At home, I leafed through the *Star*. Wheatley, a fine young local pianist, was doing Rachmaninov at the Library of Congress. In some other world, I might have picked up a couple of tickets and gone with Betty Page to hear him. Then we could have driven to Georgetown, tired but starving, and gotten a good feed at Jour et Nuit. And so on to my apartment or some apartment of our own or even one of those little Georgetown houses. Then there would be the smooth soft feel of her ass as we lay side by side and I pulled her in to me.

Instead, I was trying to figure out how to mousetrap her husband, and did not even know where she was.

Rather than seeing me in that ornate Speaker's room in the Capitol itself, he saw me in his office at the Cannon Building. I waited in the anteroom in front of the receptionist, looking at the walls full of Kansas and the pictures of Presidents and pens used by them to sign his bills. The office was set up to impress the folks from back home, just as the Capitol office was set up to awe the mighty.

Directly behind the Speaker's head was a window framing the bright dome of the Capitol. There, he was one of the two kings. The Senate majority leader was the other. But, Edwards' power over the marbled ant-hill was much greater than his Senate friend's.

On the desk, as I knew it would be, was the picture of his family: the two kids, one now away from home at school and the other at home, and beside him, smiling proudly, inanimate as a statue, his wife.

"Coffee?" he asked mildly enough. I nodded. "Cream or sugar?" Cream and two sugars, I said.

These were the banal starts for all such big interviews. I looked at the agreeable, longitudinal face, the deep blue eyes alone telling of how capable, cruel, wise, and weak he was, how much he had seen.

I thought of a police chief I had known briefly during the Dominican civil war in 1965. There was a story about how he had interrogated a reluctant rebel, fresh in from the field.

When the rebel had refused to answer the almost kindly questions, the chief had given him a cigarette and lit it for him, and then one for himself. When the man still refused to talk, the police chief had nodded to a henchman who had come from his place by the wall of the dungeon and with a razor-sharp knife had peeled the man's ear from his head and set it down on the desk.

When the screaming subsided, the police chief had

knocked his ashes off in the peel of human flesh, the human ashtray, and said, still calmly, "Now, let us continue." The man had talked.

"I thought I should tell you what I have and give you a chance to comment," I said. Edwards looked over at Hedaris, whose face was blank. He set the recorder on the desk. We all looked uncomfortable about the thing.

Beside it, unused now, was one of those little suction heads, like a rubber arrowhead, that attach to telephones. I wondered whether the Speaker recorded his telephone conversations with it.

"Can I have a tape of it after we finish?" I asked. Hedaris nodded agreement. The coffee came in on a tray carried by a pretty secretary, whom I assessed and whom the other two knew I was assessing in relation to the Speaker. We all relaxed a bit.

"Been a long time, Aubrey," Edwards said pleasantly. Well, a year or two, I thought, since some chance encounter in the House cloakroom. Over the years, I guess I had seen him a dozen times on stories. But he was right to begin it that way.

"Yes, sir," I said. "Sorry to be bothering you on this." I had a manila folder on my knees. It was amazing how fast I forgot the tape machine. I opened up the folder and set my ball point over the legal scratch pad opposite my questions.

There was no use not leveling with him. Quiven would have told him everything he knew from that quarter. So I started in there.

"Mr. Quiven at Bounty says he talked to you about a drill bit," I began. He volunteered nothing, so I pushed it another inch. "That would be the Boles-Panjunk bit." He would already know I had much of Boles angle from the Renardi arrest.

"If Quiven says so," said the Speaker. "I don't have any recollection. Do you know about when it was, Aubrey?" Well, I did, but I didn't want to give it away with any exactitude.

"Be a few months ago, I suspect," I said.

"I just don't recollect," he said.

"You have a small holding in Boles," I went on. That much showed up on the House report, which also indicated that he bought it when it was under ten dollars.

"Hundred shares, I think," he said. "You don't think that Big Oil is going to buy me for a few hundred dollars worth of Boles-Panjunk?"

"No, sir," I grinned with him. "Of course not. That's your entire beneficial holding?"

Not a pause. He was a consummate veteran at his game.

"Yes, sir, whatever the report shows."

"Make any other calls besides the one to Bounty?"

"Now, Aubrey, I said I didn't recall making any calls to Emerson Quiven. You tell me I did. But I just don't remember. What kind of calls?"

"About the Boles-Panjunk drill."

"I don't think so," he said. "I don't think so, that's assuming I made that one. Did Emerson say when it was?"

"I think a few months ago," I fudged again. "But you don't remember calling any other companies about the drill."

"No, I don't," he said. "I don't. I'm not sure I remember they had a drill. Maybe they did." Well, I thought, change of field needed. I leafed through the pages of notes, to make it look as though I had a hell of a lot more than I did. Then, I risked one.

"Georgie," I said to Hedaris, catching him off-guard, "how many shares of Boles-Panjunk do you have?" He paused for a moment, wondering what I had. Then he guessed wrong.

"A hundred, maybe two hundred," he said. Goddamnit, I'd foxed little Georgie.

"Three hundred maybe," he said.

"No maybe," I said amiably.

"Three," he said, a bit sullenly. That meant he'd known the damn stock was going to rise, too.

"You'd gotten it about four-five months ago," I ventured again.

"Right," he said.

"When it was around ten."

"I guess so," he said. He thought I had him cold.

"You informed the Speaker of this?" I asked.

"I don't think so."

"No reason to," said the Little Major. Both of them now thought I had more than I did. And Hedaris had given me a nice paragraph or two. Buying in at ten and the stock up to 85 now. That meant he'd turned $22,500 on it already.

"Nice profit, humn?" I said to Hedaris.

"Not bad," he said, really nervous now for the first time.

"Why'd you buy?"

"A tip. I can't remember."

"You know the people out there?" I asked Hedaris.

"No," he said, "not really." He was wondering whether I knew about his brother-in-law. He figured I did.

"How about your brother-in-law?" I asked. "Did he put you on it?"

"Who?" he said, recognizing I had it now. "You mean . . ."

"Kitticon." I looked at the Little Major. Not a wink.

"Maybe he did. I can't remember," said Georgie.

"Did you know your brother-in-law had an option to buy seven thousand shares?" I said.

"No, hell no," Hedaris said a little angrily. That was an obvious conflict involving the Speaker, and Hedaris got protective.

"Did you, Mr. Speaker?"

"Know what?" he said.

"That Georgie's brother-in-law, Nick Kitticon, had an option to buy seven thousand shares of Boles-Panjunk?"

"My God, no," he said. "I wish I'd had them," he laughed.

"Do you know Kitticon?" I asked.

"I must have met him, Aubrey," said the Speaker.

"But did you have any business dealings with him?"

"I wouldn't think so," said the Speaker.

"You mean, you didn't?"

"Good grief, Aubrey," he was bristling a little, just the appropriate amount for a Speaker being asked an inappropriate question. "I guess business dealings are when you talk to anyone about almost anything. I told you I couldn't recall."

"You'd recall if it had to do with Boles-Panjunk?"

"I would think so." He was getting wary now. I was working very close to a dangerous bull.

"And you don't recall? You definitely didn't have a piece of those seven thousand options?"

"Right."

"Did Georgie have any business dealings on his own or on your behalf with Boles-Panjunk?" Shit, I thought, wrong questions. It's going to get me into a wrangle. I'd lose momentum on this.

"Georgie's right here," he said, knowing I'd misfired.

"I can't remember," said Georgie. "I don't know what you mean, 'on the Speaker's behalf.' "

"I mean did you buy any stock for him or talk to your brother-in-law about it?"

"Aubrey, I can't even remember if Nick gave me the tip." Well, they had me on the can't-remembers. I switched field again.

"Didn't you see in the prospectus that Nick had bought seven thousand options? Both of you got the prospectuses, didn't you?"

"I never read 'em," said Hedaris.

"I wish I had now, Aubrey, with all these questions," said Edwards.

"So you don't know about Kitticon's options, either one of you?" I'd asked it before, but I wanted to tie the knot.

"No," they both said.

Well, it hadn't been my best questioning. But, I'd gotten Hedaris's holdings along with the denials I'd expected. I had thought they'd be too smart to tie themselves in with Kitticon at Boles-Panjunk, and they had been.

From here on in was the dirty work.

"Mr. Speaker, I hate to put these questions to you," I said.

"Don't feel bad about it," he said. The eyes were like blue marbles, now. Both of us knew I was going for his nuts and both of us knew he wasn't going to let me past his first defenses.

"Do you have any beneficial interest of any kind in those seven thousand shares?" I asked him again.

"The records clearly show they belong to someone else," he said coldly. "You're an expert at reading records. That's an insulting question."

Well, I thought, he didn't say no.

"I said beneficial."

"I hold one hundred shares in Poles-Panjunk. That's all," he said, huffy now.

"Did you get any campaign contributions from Emerson Quiven or anyone else at Boles-Panjunk?"

"My finance committee would be handling that."

"Did you know of any?"

"I certainly cannot recollect any."

"Then why would Emerson Quiven have in his ledger two entries about contributions of five thousand and fifteen thousand to you?"

"I'd have no idea of that and you have no proof of it," said the Little Major hostilely. Quiven would have told him there was no solid proof.

"Do you know a Mr. Webb Renardi?"

"Never met the man," said the Speaker. Now I was getting into his bedroom talk with Betty Page. But there was no backing out. There wasn't going to be any second bite of this apple. I drilled him with my eyes, but he looked back stonily.

"Ever hear of him?" I asked softly.

"I read your paper, Aubrey," he said.

"Before that?"

I knew he was dying to say, "No comment," but both of us knew that if he did, I could say, "He refused to comment on whether he had ever heard of a Webb Renardi, a Boles-Panjunk official whose options were transferred to a relative of the Speaker's top aide." He already knew I had him pretty good, and he knew how fatal those "no comments" are to politicians. Eventually, they are dogged into breaking silence. "No comment" was an invitation to endless questions the Speaker did not need.

"I may have heard his name. It is vaguely familiar." He had skirted me well enough.

"Did you call someone to get the FBI sicked on him?" I asked.

I knew the answer was yes, but I knew he knew I didn't have it nailed down and was only asking it to have it in my notes in case I could prove it one day.

"I wouldn't know who I'd have talked to about him," he said. "I can't recall anything like that, but I talk with so many. . . ." I could feel in him the fury at me now. I had fucked his wife and then questioned him about what she had told me between our lays.

For an instant, I thought of saying something honest that would get it all out: her, me, him, his relationship with her, my love for her, why she had told me, how I had betrayed her. It was a mad thought. In Washington, things were not done honestly. Perhaps not anywhere.

I ruffled through my notes. We were getting to a close.

"So, to sum it up, you can't recall ever making any calls for the Boles-Panjunk drill, and if you did, it had nothing to do with any ownership you have in the company. And you only have the hundred shares."

"And . . ." Georgie Hedaris reminded me.

"And you don't know of any contributions from Bounty Oil or Emerson Quiven."

"Right," said the Speaker. *He* was getting out of this without me landing a new punch on him. Hedaris, yes. But the Speaker, no. I did not dare look at the picture on his desk again.

"When would you be writing this, if you write it?" inquired Hedaris.

"I don't know," I said. "I don't know what they'll want to do."

We parted without shaking hands. It was the Speaker's only concession to his hatred for me.

I went back to the office and finished up my reporting, notably a call to Boles. He was a gruff, terse man, but he reluctantly confirmed that Kitticon had not exercised his options, probably since he knew I could get it at the SEC anyway, and because corporate "no comments," too, always looked suspicious.

9

Grand Jury

I took all the material home with me and worked on it late into the night, writing it and rewriting it. The next morning, I was still poking around in the kitchen when Betty Page called me at nine. "Aubrey," she said. As simple as that.

"When can I see you?" I blurted out.

There was her small "Hunh," of laughter assessed. "Have you got time?" she asked, with a chill I knew was false.

"My God, of course," I said, realizing even as I said it that I had this damned story to get down to the paper, to work over one last time before I turned it in. She must have heard the involuntary hesitation in my voice.

"I don't believe it," she said, reading my thoughts accurately.

"Wait!" I said, panicked. "Wait! I know what you're thinking, and you're right. I am thinking . . ." I started to tell her the whole truth about my need to get the story done, then stopped, thinking, "It may hurt me with her," then thought, "No, now I have to tell her. Everything." And I began all over again.

"Betty Page. I am thinking just what you think I am thinking. That I want to, am compelled to, get the damned story down to the paper. But I'm not going to. I will wait over here, all day, if you want. I will stall them. I will do anything if you will come over here." I paused. "Even if we don't screw." Why not say it all, blab it out indecorously as it might come. "If you will just come over here and sit in a chair across the room from me and talk, I will wait."

"Aubrey," she interrupted. But I wanted it all out.

"I am not sure I can give up this nuthouse. But if I can get some Goddamn assurance you will leave that"—I paused again—"that crook, then I will try, if that is what it takes."

"Just a minute," she broke in. "It's him I want to talk with you about. He knows I'm going to—"

"He knows you're coming over here? His own wife?" I was so anxious that I could feel my old nuttinesses coming out through my pores. In my ungoverned mind, the literary image of the king giving up his wife to the savage leader to save the royal skin began to fester.

"Oh, my God," she said. "You're going to get it all so complicated. We'll be fighting before I get over there. I'm leaving right now."

I was flustered beyond belief. I limped around the apartment, cleaning it up, vacuuming hectically, putting the dishes in the washer, while the water ran in the tub.

Once the bath was drawn, I leaped in, burning myself and piteously whining. I particularly washed my loins just in case.

The doorbell rang. I thought one last time about the delay in going down to the paper with my story. Then, I opened the door, and there she was. I had so romanticized her in my mind that, as I pulled her in and hugged her, the fact of her years surprised me. But so what?

"Goddamnit, it's good you're here," I said as she drew away from my grip. She wore a light lime suit, more austere than usual. I thought about how good it would be when I got it off her body and saw her naked again. "I knew you'd come back," I said, trying to hug her again. But she was into the living room.

"Just let me alone a minute, okay?" she said. I looked into her face. It was tired and worried.

"Can I get you coffee? A bloody mary?" I asked.

"Coffee," she said, and I darted off to the kitchen.

She walked with me, falling into our old familiar ways.

"He laid it all out," she said, "the conversation with you up there and Hedaris. He knows what you're going to write."

"I'm not surprised," I said. "He's no fool."

"What is it going to say?" she asked. "Do you know yet?"

"It's going to be mostly stock stuff, a little dull. But it nails him up. On a major conflict of interest." It was the sort of meaty, factual story I loved. "I'll show it to you."

She looked at me somberly, and I brought her the draft, looking over her shoulder as she read it.

"Speaker Pommery Edwards did what may prove to be a multimillion-dollar favor for a California oil equipment firm in which he, his top staffer, and the staffer's brother-in-law have a $629,000 interest," it said.

I knew the paper would make me weaken the lead to distinguish between Kitticon's half-million-dollar holding and Hedaris' and the Speaker's lesser sums. But I always started out trying to get the toughest possible story in, knowing that Cubbins would soften it. It was like a union negotiation where you bargain from an extreme position. The next paragraph said, reasonably, I thought:

"Edwards holds $8,500 and his aide, George Hedaris, holds $25,000 in the firm, Boles-Panjunk. But the husband of Hedaris' wife's sister, Nicholas Kitticon, holds options worth $595,000."

Well, I thought, that's an awkward paragraph. Cubbins could work at it. I thought I'd better check the Wall Street *Journal* to see whether our digging had produced sales by the smart money, driving the stock down. It made me nervous not to be working on the damned story. But I pushed that down into my mind, looking at Betty Page's blondish hair as she bent over the draft.

The third paragraph said:

"The financial dealings in the case are complicated."

That was to alert the reader that the story was going

to be a hard go and that he would have to concentrate. I went on:

"It began some four months ago when a then vice-president of Boles-Panjunk, Webb Renardi, was asked by the company to surrender his options to buy seven thousand shares of Boles-Panjunk stock. The options then cost two dollars and could be exercised if the stock ever hit $11.

"Thus, if Boles-Panjunk languished below $11, the options holder was stuck with a valueless $14,000 investment. But if it went over $11, he stood to make a handsome profit.

"The man to whom the company gave Renardi's options was Nicholas Kitticon, a Kansas lawyer listed in company records as a legal consultant to Boles-Panjunk. Kitticon is married to Edith, the sister of Elaine Hedaris, wife of the Speaker's top aide and confidant, George Hedaris.

"Within a few weeks after the decision was made to sell Kitticon the potentially valuable options, Speaker Edwards made a telephone call to the president of Bounty Oil, one of the 'Big Eight' of the petroleum industry.

"The purpose of the call was to sell Bounty on the idea of adopting a new oil drill bit then being marketed for the first time by Boles-Panjunk. Bounty's president, Emerson Quiven, and the Speaker are old friends and Quiven has conceded the call was made.

"For Bounty to accept the drill would mean millions for Boles-Panjunk and its stockholders. Not only would the orders from Bounty bring income, but the fact that one of the 'Big Eight' was using the new bit would make it a 'hot item' for sales to other firms here and abroad.

"Quiven turned over the bit to his technical experts who reported back to him that it was a good piece of equipment. On the very next day, Quiven called the Speaker and reported to him the good news about the Boles-Panjunk drill bit. There are also indications that

Bounty's president informed other business colleagues of the drill's merit.

"Meanwhile, the fortunes of Boles-Panjunk were prospering. News of the bit had already spread within the industry and the stock was trading at 47 some two months ago. Shortly after the finding by Bounty that the bit was exceptionally well-engineered, news apparently spread even further, for the stock went up to 85.

"Both the Speaker and Hedaris bought their stock while the price was only about $10 a share, it was learned."

I reached over Betty Page's shoulder and put a little "X" in the margin to remind myself to check the present price of the stock. The rest of the story was about when the Little Major bought his hundred shares, and all his explanations, hedges, his denials of any piece of the seven thousand options, and other self-serving statements.

Betty Page read the whole thing through.

"It's as bad as he thought," she said, looking at me. I could not tell what she was thinking, other than that she was serious. She sighed. "It doesn't do any good to reproach you for using Renardi's name." I felt guilty at its mention.

"Pom wants me to talk you out of it," she said abruptly.

I was startled and it must have shown on my face. "Oh, he's not enough of a fool to depend on your sweet character. He wants to know what it takes for you not to use it. Not money, of course, although he would love to do that to you." She smiled up at me ever so slightly. "He's willing to swap you a bigger story. Like we did on the drinking."

I shook my head.

"I shouldn't have gone along with that."

"We'd never have been friends," she said.

"Maybe we would have anyway." But obviously I was curious. "What bigger story?"

"I don't know," she said. "He won't tell me. He doesn't trust me anymore." We had been drinking the coffee, standing in the kitchen. Now she took her cup and went back into the living room. As she sat, I watched the smooth silkiness of her legs cross, the cloth against the skin and the nylon rubbing nylon. It began to give me an erection. "I don't blame him," she said.

"For what?" I said, momentarily distracted.

"My God, Aubrey," she said, exasperated but a little pleased. "I don't blame him for not trusting me."

"Then how can I know if I would trade?" Probably it was impossible now. The story was too far along, too far out of my hands. Good newspapers do not make deals like that, at least not as a matter of policy. They live with them if their reporters make them, but in a way so that the newspaper does not have to acknowledge that deals have been made.

Not that the ethics of editors and publishers are better than those of reporters. Their ethics are, almost to a man, worse. But they cannot *afford* to be caught.

"He wants you to call him."

"Christ, he's not going to talk about it over the phone."

"He wants to set the ground rules on the phone."

I looked at her. We were coconspirators again.

"You got any idea what it is?"

"No," she said.

"Yes," I said, feeling her falter. "You know."

"I don't *know*," she said.

"It's about the President," I said. She looked for an instant as though I had smacked her.

"I don't *know*," she repeated. But I saw she suspected it, and strongly.

"What's his number up there?" I asked, limping over to the chair by the telephone.

Edwards' voice was amiable on the telephone. I began to believe that he would be able to maintain that manner in the face of anything but physical torture.

"Your wife told me you had a proposition," I said, after his greeting about how it had been good to see me again. Recalling the suction cup, I assumed he was recording me.

"Not exactly a proposition," he said. "Aubrey, we aren't tape recording each other, are we?"

"No," I said. "I hardly know how to work the damn things."

He chuckled.

"I had a good story I might be able to give you."

"Oh?"

"I'd have to have some assurances from you. How far has the matter we spoke about gone?"

"Gone?"

"At the paper."

"Mr. March knows about it. The desk. A fair number." I heard only the suggestion of a sigh.

Yet in that sigh Pom Edwards was giving up the ghost. He saw it was too late. Too many knew. In that spectral sigh he was admitting that he was all but finished in politics, or might be. He would fight, would fight as they all do to retain power. But now it would be uphill.

"Ah," he said at last. "That's a problem. Maybe I'd better reconsider the tip." Then he paused again and said very quietly, "There's no way, I gather."

For a moment, I was possessed with sympathy for him. Had he been so bad that he deserved this of a creep like me?

"No," I said. A Roman would have let it go like that. But I could not resist. I demeaned myself at that august moment: "Could you just give me a little hint about what the story was you had in mind?"

"No, Aubrey," he said, with amiable dignity.

When I turned back to Betty Page, she had tears in her eyes.

"Okay," she said. "One bloody mary."

She never got to the sobbing stage, instead wiping the tears out with a Kleenex and blowing her nose. I mixed stiff drinks. I felt so sorry for her, I didn't try to get her to go to bed at that weak moment when it might have been possible.

"What is this going to do to us?" I asked. "We're back together in a way, aren't we?"

"Yes," she said. "In a way." There was no spirit in her.

"How is it with you and him?"

"Bad," she said. "He's back on beer with supper. In a few weeks he'll be back on the scotch."

"I mean . . ." I wanted to know if he were screwing her. She shrugged, not wanting to talk about it. I assumed that meant he was. I wanted her now, badly, but this was not the time.

"He'll still run," I said.

"Oh yes." She smiled sadly. "He'll run and I'll campaign like hell for him. If you hadn't been such a smart ass, he could get voted in with a couple of speeches. I'd be here all summer and we . . ."

She picked up the pale green linen pocketbook that matched her suit. She was controlled now, as she walked toward the door. I did not want her to leave, deadline or no deadline.

"When can I call?"

"He's got a speech in St. Louis on Saturday. I'll call you."

"He knew, I mean, that your coming here would make us lovers again?"

She shrugged, then turned back to me.

"I don't want to talk about it yet." But I knew, thank God, it had mended.

We broke the story the next day. Just as Mr. March had said, it was a pisser. The paper ran it eight columns across the top, with stock pictures of the Speaker and of Hedaris, and one of Kitticon from a Kansas bar annual. Once again, there was all the excitement of the wires picking it up, the TV blabbing about it all day, and the evening news carrying a somber, explaining-it-all-away statement by the Speaker.

"Emerson Quiven is an old friend and I've talked with him about many things from time to time. . . . Anybody who thinks the Speaker of the United States can be bought for one hundred shares of stock has another thought coming," he said, owlishly oozing integrity into the tube.

But there was no explaining away that half-million in Kitticon's name. He was still "no commenting" out there in Wichita. Hedaris had gone into a burrow someplace and couldn't be interviewed.

All in all, it added up to bad news about the Speaker. And the story was not a one-shot job. There'd be the other companies who bought the Boles-Panjunk drill. Might the Speaker *and* Emerson Quiven have called them?

And I still had the campaign contributions to work on.

As with any big story, once the blood was drawn by one of the greater hawks—Mollenhoff, Anderson, Landauer, Nelson, Hersh, Mintz, Stern, me on a rare day—then all the flocks of crows rushed in to drink. Everyone would be out for the Speaker, now we had laid him open.

There would be stories on how he helped Big Oil with the depletion allowance, his behind-the-scenes-doings while he was on Ways and Means.

It would end only when he beat his breast and made a full confession or was driven from office. And I suspected there was too much for him to confess it all.

The whole business was giving me a bad case of nerves. The harder I bit into the Speaker, the more I knew he was going to try to get me, both to end my reporting on him and to avenge himself. I didn't know quite how he would try to nail me, but I suspected it would be through the safecracking.

Mrs. Murtry was working like hell on the case. She was getting equivocal readings from the Justice Department and the FBI who were handling the federal part: the flight, and the two rather dippy interstate-theft charges, one the ledger copies and the other the carbons from Boles-Panjunk.

On Friday, Mrs. Murtry asked me come to her office downtown. In it, she had an antique pinball machine that worked without nickels. It seemed an odd sort of tension-easer for her, but I was in favor of whatever it took to get a person through the day.

She was playing the machine with total absorption

while a colleague looked on, and didn't see me. I stood watching as she gave it a wallop and the ball bounced orgiastically on one of the "Hi-Skor" bumpers.

When she looked up at me, she was slightly embarrassed.

"My only vice," she said.

"Be glad," I told her.

"Try?" she asked kindly. I knew I was in trouble.

"No," I said, "I'm too scared. Bad news, right?"

We sat down, me on the settee and she at her spindly Louis XIV desk.

"Yes. I got word today they want to call you before a grand jury and ask you about your sources."

The thought was fearsome. When a reporter is asked by a grand jury or judge for his sources, he has only two choices. He can tell who they are and stop being a reporter because no one will trust him again. Or, he can shut up and go to jail for contempt.

"They don't even need my sources," I said. So far as the crimes were concerned, either I was guilty or not guilty. Anything I said about Renardi, or Drosnahan, or my ex-safecracking friend, or, God forbid, Betty Page, was superfluous to the issue of my guilt.

"I know. It's clear they want to nail you."

"How do you know they plan—"

"Old friends in Justice," she said, getting up and pacing toward the pinball machine like a giant crane. She thought better of it and walked back. "Some of them down there still believe in the First Amendment. Who do you think has the heat on you?" she asked.

"The Speaker?"

"My thought, too. But how?"

"He wouldn't call himself," I said.

"No," agreed the lawyer.

"He might have old Joe McFadden do it." That would be the appropriations chairman who handled Justice's budget with some personal care, precisely to have a grip on just such power. "He might have McFadden call somebody at Justice or even at the FBI."

"Any way to prove it?" she asked.

"No. It would be done discreetly. McFadden would call the deputy A.G., or maybe Appleton"—the Attorney General—"and just say he felt the source question should be asked to be sure it didn't look like Justice was sucking up to the press."

"Yes," she conceded somberly. She had been at Justice long enough to know how it worked, when it had to.

I thought gloomily and silently of the whole ugly scene. The grand jury questions, the contempt citation and then on to jail: a jungle where blacks terrorized whites and blacks alike. Would I crack the safe again, if I knew this was going to happen?

"When will I know?"

"We'll file all the motions we can to delay it," she said. "If I can get the California thing cooled down, then—" I broke in.

"If you were guessing?"

"A month."

"Jesus, I'd almost rather go and get it over with. A month?"

"Maybe less, if the answer's no," she said. "You could be in jail in a week if the slide is greased enough."

I left feeling depressed, excessively depressed, and she must have recognized it.

"Call me if you get feeling too down," she said, trying to give me a little something to hold onto.

I was nervous enough that night so that I called Betty Page at home. She was still reserved, but at least was interested as I explained the case.

"You sound funny," she said at last.

"Where's your husband?"

"He left an hour ago. They're flying him out in a company plane."

"He never learns," I said. "Can you come tonight?"

"No, my son's at home and Pom will be calling when he gets there."

"Tomorrow morning early?" She paused. Well, I thought, this is it.

"Yes," she said finally, then added with some concern. "What's the matter with you?"

"I'm scared of the grand jury and of jail," I said. "I have the heebie-jeebies."

She paused again.

"Bad?"

"Fairly. I'll tell you tomorrow when you get here."

"Ah," she said. "Poor baby." The hardness was all out of her voice. It was pure sympathy now. "Do you want me to come tonight?"

"No," I said, feeling even more sorry for myself.

Next morning, when Betty Page got there, I was still bumbling around, cleaning up, hoping she would be late enough so I could take a bath. But she was almost always on time.

She came across the room, and hugged me. So fresh from the outside. Her simple dress and her hair smelled of the outside, the spring, and of the soap she had used.

"Oh, Betty Page," I said into her, whiskery as I was and bathless. After so much, how easily we had slipped back together.

She kissed me on the lips, fully and firmly.

When we broke, I murmured, "I haven't even brushed my teeth or shaved and I need a bath. I couldn't sleep. Goddamnit, I'm worried about the grand jury. But you're back. . . ." I wished I could get my thoughts on that and off the grand jury.

She broke and looked at me, her green eyes half worried and half amused. Then she glanced at the vacuum cleaner in the middle of the rug where I'd left it.

"Poor crip," she said. "Here, go take a bath if that's what you want to do. I'll finish." She turned to adjust the vacuum cleaner and I stumped into the bathroom to draw the bath.

In the sounds of a home with a woman in it (the vacuum cleaner, the tub running, the slight bump as the cleaner hit a sofa leg) there was a reprieve from the anxiety.

As the water ran, I brushed my teeth and shaved. The vacuum cleaner went off. She darted in, surveyed me for a moment, then was in the kitchen, putting last night's dishes in the dishwasher. When the bath was

drawn, I started to step in, but I heard her end her
clanking and she appeared at the bathroom door.

"Not so fast," she said. She had already kicked off her
shoes and was pulling her dress over her head. I fell
into the spirit of the thing, helping her get the dress off.
Then I turned her lightly to unhook her bra and knelt,
awkward and naked, to peel down her panties. And, ah,
there it was.

Do all men see women they love in these two ways?
First, as the vague embodiment of all their virtues:
humor, warmth, intelligence, their strengths, vulner-
abilities, looks, habits. Then, in contrast to this inexact,
indefinable catchall, in a second way: as a cunt, with a
precise configuration of hair, of loose or firm lips, of
length, of a measurably large or small clitoris, as a
distinct smell.

She stepped out of the little bikini panties. She eased
her feet apart slightly so that the flesh of her thighs
parted, and I could kiss her close to her vagina, smelling
its hay smell.

"Oh," I sighed. "I'm home."

Lightly, she pressed the back of my head, opening
her legs a little wider.

Damn, I thought, this is as good as anything there is
to life. And crazily, my mind veered years back to those
tapes the FBI had made, saying the voice was that of
the pre-eminent black leader as he was going down on
a girl in a hotel room.

"I am the greatest pussy-eater in the world," had
come scratchily from the tape: it had sounded so like
that enthusiastic voice, whose timber had electrified so
many to courage and decency.

Even I had been revolted to find myself in that little
room on the fifth floor of the Justice Department, listening as the FBI agent giggled over the tapes, revolted
with the FBI agent and with myself, not the black man
who, given the passion he brought to every mission he
undertook, probably *was* the greatest pussy-eater in the
world. And then, of course, it had turned out not to be
him at all.

"I am the greatest pussy-eater in the world," I said.

But Betty Page was so excited that I got no more than a murmured assent. She edged back toward the sink and leaned against it.

Once against the sink, she spread her legs widely. I could caress her buttocks now, run my fingers along the little wrinklings on the inside of her thighs, touch fleetingly her anus, which she liked if only seldom.

Betty Page was wriggling now, all of her, I knew, concentrated in the touch of my tongue. "Aubrey, Aubrey," she said. "Oh, Aubrey." And I was feeling like superman.

In a moment or two, she began saying the little "oh-uhs," that I knew led to her orgasm. Wriggling and pressing my head into her, she came with a thrust of her pelvis.

"I'm sorry, I'm hurting you," she said as the pulses in her began to subside.

I turned my mouth from her, feeling the light abrasion to my lips, and with the side of my head still pressed to her where she slanted down from the sink.

"Jesus, that was great," I said. "You taste marvelous." I was limber, but still feeling extremely lusty. We eased into the hot water.

As soon as I was sufficiently accustomed to the steamy water, I put her hand on my cock, wanting now badly to come. But she started roughly washragging my shoulders and chest.

"No, in bed," she said. She scrubbed me all over, then as she wound up, let me wash her vagina, needlessly soap her breasts, and then rinse them with the warm water.

By now, I was in that imbecile condition where I could respond only with grunts and awkward movements. Out of the tub, she dried me and I inexpertly did the same for her, then limped off to the bed.

There, at last, I could kiss her as I wanted to, and tell her how I loved her. I was afraid to touch her with my penis, knowing I would come, so I kissed and kissed her face, lips, ears, nose until it was no good not doing what we were going to do.

She knew there wasn't going to be any time for her

this go-round, so she rolled me onto her. Still arched upward, my hands on the moons of her buttocks, she let me go as deeply into her as I could. Almost instantly, the great throbbing began. It went on and on, until she felt it end, then she held her body upward against me a few more moments before she eased it down with me on top of her and still inside.

"Together again. I love you, Aubrey Reporter," she said. At peace at last after those long weeks without her, I slipped off to sleep.

In that brief sleep, the fear of the grand jury and jail came back and put their talons in me. I awoke and saw her looking at me, up on one elbow. I smiled and pulled her to me to kiss her. But the dreadfuls were on me. No matter what she did, I could not get another erection. One time, after she had mouthed and caressed me, I was close, but when she urgently tried to get me inside her, I was suddenly soft again.

"It's no go," I said.

"It has you that bad?"

"Yep." I thought about it a moment. "It unmans me."

"Can't the lawyers block the grand jury thing?"

I explained that they were trying to, but that once I was subpoenaed and once I refused to answer a grand juror's question, or the prosecutor, then he could haul me before a judge and get an order that I answer. If I still refused to answer, I was in contempt of court. And the judge was more or less obligated to put me in jail until I did answer.

"That's horrible," she said, genuinely surprised.

"It happens fairly often," I said. "You can thank the crumbums that Nixon put on the Supreme Court for that, and the good guys on the court, who screwed themselves out or drank or ate too much and died. Add in Fortas getting pushed off, Goldberg letting LBJ talk him into going, Clark and Warren quitting too soon, and my ass, as a result, lands in jail."

"You've thought it all out," she said, then couldn't resist. "Aubrey Warder, victim of the historical imperative." I grinned despite the worries.

"So what happens? You can't just stay in jail."

"It's being in jail at all that scares me. I've written so much about it. I got a taste of it that one day. I know what can happen to me down there. Your old man isn't above trying to keep me down there forever."

"He doesn't talk to me anymore about anything," she said.

"I don't blame him for that," I chuckled sourly.

"I have to leave tomorrow to campaign for him," she said. "I can't *not* do it. It's ironic. You make the election tough for him so I have to campaign with him. That means I have to leave you."

"Yeah," I mused. "The final hook would be if the *Eagle* sent me down to cover the campaign and we—"

She rolled over to me, thinking, as I was, about meetings in some Kansas motel room after the campaign day was over. There would be a sort of fever madness to trying something like that which I knew appealed to her, and to me. I put my hand on her buttock, its smooth, splendid curve, and felt again the suggestion of lust.

But the worries came in and squelched it. Betty Page and I were back together again, as she had said. Now, though, there were some new elements. She had not spoken of my treachery in using the information she had given me on Renardi.

But some of her trust in me had gone. Cranked in, too, was the anxiety about the case and what it had done to my sex drives. And finally, things were going so bad for her at home with the Speaker that this added a tension to the affair.

But after she had left, I thought that all in all, we must love each other. There were so many good reasons for it to fall apart that the fact of our still wanting to see each other had to indicate something pretty potent.

Uneasy as it was, I had someone who cared about what happened to me, the way my wife had cared. That afternoon, while she was getting her things ready for the trip, I called and we chattered much as we had in the past. There was a reserve now. But it was still good, and God knows I needed it.

I worked Sunday, coming up with a lovely follow-up

story. A group of Young Turks in the House was going to ask the House Ethics Committee to look into the Speaker's behavior. The committee was made up of weary old whores set up to protect Congressmen's miserable lack of ethics. They would no more think of investigating another Congressman's ethics than they would of investigating their own.

The Young Turks were going to couch their request as being done reluctantly, and affording the Speaker a chance to clear himself of these unproved charges. The purpose was to cut away his power base, of course, and move into the Speaker's chair someone a little more accountable to the younger Congressmen.

It was an important straw in the wind because it indicated that someone in the establishment, well, damn near in the establishment, was willing to take him on.

The fact that twenty or thirty young Congressmen had gotten together long enough to request an investigation by the committee was a major story. The *Eagle* played it very big, and I quietly called our stringer in Topeka.

"What are you guys doing with it?" I asked.

"We're going fairly big with it, but very pro-Speaker, very, very."

"How about in his district?"

"Nothing when you broke the story. The next day they led with his denials of wrongdoing."

"That's par," I said. "Is his opponent going to do anything with it?" The primary opponent, who had been regarded as a joke before my story broke, was the typical reform professor of political science with $3,000 to risk, lots of ambition, and no political skill whatsoever. Now he was beginning to take himself semiseriously.

"So far, he's saying what an outrage it is for the Eastern Press to attack the Great Son of Kansas."

"What a woussie," I said in disgust.

"Not entirely," said our stringer. "After the Young Turks thing, he said he was glad to see the Speaker being given a chance to answer these scurrilous charges."

"That means—"

"That in a few days, if there's another story or two, he'll start saying the Speaker owes it to Kansas to put these terrible rumors to rest."

"Rumors, my ass. That Goddamn scarecrow admitted to most of what I had."

"I know. Look, this is Kansas, it's not the Bronx. What Reese"—the professor—"is saying is that if you provide the stories, he'll provide the war."

Well, I thought, he might beat the Little Major yet. I'd have to come up with another good bomb.

"How's your own case?" the stringer was saying sympathetically.

"Bad," I said, sunk again into my anxieties, hoping that Betty Page would be able to call me at home that night.

By Monday, it was clear that Mrs. Murtry wasn't going to be able to get me off the hook. And in California, Emerson Quiven was insisting on my prosecution, and Bounty Oil was a big power in California.

Mr. March and I had been too smart by half. Quiven knew he'd been had, and he was adamantly demanding my prosecution for the safe bust, for the breaking of his damned ledger lock, and for the flight to avoid prosecution.

I was certain also that the Speaker was behind it. Quiven was sure to keep pressing so long as the Speaker was a powerful man. If I could break the Speaker's power, I might save my ass, for then Quiven would have to desert him. Even Quiven knew we'd made a crook of the Little Major. It was just that he remained a powerful crook.

So I sweated. Quiven, I was guessing, would not in the long run want the case to come to trial. It would mean that he would wind up under oath himself and have to testify about those mysterious entries that looked so much like illegal campaign contributions. But that was a way down the road, and meanwhile he could torment me. And so long as he did not relent on his charges, the federal case in Washington, which was tied to them, could fester along.

Here, the two interstate stolen documents cases were

all too active. Phony as they were, the FBI was moving rapidly. Partly it was malice on the FBI's part. But a friend of old Joe McFadden's had let drop to our House man that McFadden would love to "see that prick Warder in D.C. Jail with a bunch of coons."

If it could be proved that the Speaker or McFadden was behind my prosecution, we could detonate it out of the water. But there was no solid clue to go on. I pulled out every crying handkerchief I had with my old friends at the FBI, Secret Service, even the CIA. But nobody knew anything. My FBI pal, Brent, said he was afraid to talk with me for fear they'd put a lie detector on him and nail him. That's how hydrophobic I had become.

On Wednesday, the bad news came. Mrs. Murtry called.

"Aubrey, the grand jury wants you on Friday. There's no way I can see to block it. Somebody is exerting some very powerful magic," she said.

"The Speaker," I reiterated dismally.

"Probably. Any proof yet?"

"No. How bad does it look?"

"Cold turkey? Bad," she replied. "After I got the notice you were to appear, I checked with a few friends over there. Somebody wants you. They're going to give you immunity on one interstate theft charge. Then they are going to ask you for sources. . . ."

She paused a moment, letting the question of whether I would reveal my sources ask itself, silently.

"No, I can't, of course," I said, a bit tilted by fear.

"They're hinting you can get out of it if you testify against Renardi and Drosnahan. But they really don't want them, they want—"

"Me to kiss their tails. Turn pigeon."

"Yes," she said. "They'd rather have you be a stool pigeon than even to convict you."

"Yeah," I agreed woefully.

"So, there's no way out. You are a witness to a federal crime, as well as a perpetrator. It's not as if you just heard about it secondhand. The best I can do is to get you bond, pending appeals and et cetera. And don't count on that. It's going to be before Frick"—a miserable judge we called "Frick the Prick" because of his uncompromising meanness.

"How'd that happen? Couldn't you have—"

"No. I tried. The thing is rigged. There is just no way. They have not given me one centimeter of bargaining room."

Who could I get to unrig it? God knows I had written enough favorable stories, when they deserved it, about Senators and Congressmen over the years. But most were mavericks of one damned kind or another, those who were still in office, and thus useless to me in such a situation. And the nonmavericks who were sitting wouldn't buck for a man who had tried to do in the Speaker.

I ran through the names of other powerfuls who had profited at one time or another from my exposés. But none came to mind who had the might to make the call that would stop the process.

I thought desperately for a moment of Betty Page. Couldn't she do something for me with the President? He had been to their home. When we first met, she had mentioned her affair in a tone that revealed it was someone highly placed. Could it have been the Goddamn Prez himself, when he was Vice-President. Well, I thought, I'll call her and brace her. Maybe she could call him, or somebody else with some swat. I'd try anything at this stage, I thought. Almost, my conscience added, as I junked the idea.

The grand jury room was like a miniature auditorium. The twenty-three grand jurors were the audience, sitting in ranks of straight, lightly cushioned armchairs.

I sat before them behind a table. Off to the right was the prosecutor, standing in front of an easel with his lawbooks and evidence stacked on a table beside him. It looked like a cozy place. The jurors were serious, not unfriendly. The prosecutor was a shit named Garrigan who was used as the hatchet by Justice. The regular

grand jury man, a decent lawyer named Strudy, had
probably begged off on this stinker of a case.

In a falsely warm voice—the prosecutor's first job
was to get the sympathy of the grand jury so he could
jerk them his way—Garrigan read me the perjury and
false-statement laws.

"So if you don't tell the truth, Mr. Warder," he said
kindly, "then any trouble you might or might not be in
would be compounded. No threat, of course, but I want
you to know your rights. . . ."

"Thank you," I said as convivially as I could. I
wanted that grand jury's sympathy myself. They were
a good mix of old, young, black, white, none of them
stupid, I suspected. Maybe even a librarian or retired
government official among them.

With as much spirit as he could put into the tedious
legalisms, Garrigan read me the charges against me, did
more advising of my rights, and told me they were
dropping the first interstate theft of documents charge,
involving the Boles-Panjunk papers. It was a weak case
anyway.

"So we will not be prosecuting you on that charge,
Mr. Warder," he went on. "Now a few questions." Obviously he had already laid out the bones of the case to
the grand jury, because he didn't bother to put his
questions in context. And obviously the questions would
deal with the dropped charge, where, by law, I would
have to answer or face contempt.

"Mr. Warder, when you met in or near Washington,
D.C., with one Webb Renardi, to the best of our knowledge and belief, you obtained certain information about
stolen goods belonging to the Boles-Panjunk company.
Now will you tell the grand jury whether that is true
and what information was imparted to you. . . ."

Stolen goods, I thought. A handful of carbon paper.

"What do you mean by stolen goods, Mr. Garrigan?"
He had already spelled it out right down to dates and
places in reading me the charges. But I thought maybe
the grand jury would see it all for the put-up job it was.

"Papers belonging to the Boles-Panjunk company,"
he said.

"So what's your question, exactly, again?"

Garrigan nodded to the old man who was sitting at the stenotype machine. He read back the question in an uninflected voice. Well, I thought, here goes. At least it didn't take long. Mrs. Murtry was outside the jury room. And I knew I could go and consult her. But it was all pretty cut and dried: I had no choice.

"I can't answer that," I said. "I can't reveal my source, Mr. Garrigan. The First Amendment says Congress shall make no law abridging the freedom of the press and the Fourth says I shall be secure from unreasonable searches and the Fifth says I shall not have to testify against myself in a criminal proceeding and shall have due process and the Fourteenth says I shall have due process and equal protection of the law. And for all these reasons, I think your question is not constitutional and that, therefore, for these same reasons, I cannot answer it, and won't."

He had been prepared for such a speech, and to keep the jury's sympathy, he had to let me get away with it. But the grand jury hadn't expected a flag-waving. I caught a vibration in my favor from them and went on, quickly, before Garrigan could turn them against me.

"What I'm saying is that the Founding Fathers gave people like me a job to do. It's to keep an eye on the government on behalf of the people. We were told to expose corruption in and outside of government, to tell the people things that the government would rather keep covered up. To set in motion reforms. Of course, this doesn't make the government very happy."

I caught the forewoman's eye. She was a doughty-looking grandmother, maybe seventy, with a sunken chest and those auger-bit eyes that Baudelaire writes about. I didn't want to soapbox it, but Goddamnit, I was right. The government was screwing me.

"Now Mr. Warder—" Garrigan was beginning, but I broke in.

"Mr. Garrigan knows that the only way we can do our job is with confidential sources, and that it's exactly that kind of sources the Founding Fathers had in mind. More often than not, the sources are dedicated, decent people. They've been wronged or they know about wrongs, and they don't trust the government or big industry or the unions to clean themselves up and investigate things. So they come to us, the newspapers. But they won't come if they can't trust us to keep their names secret so that they don't get hurt for telling the truth."

Garrigan butted in again. But I was the one who was headed for the cooler and I wanted it all said.

"Wait, I haven't finished. If you kill off our ability to have confidential sources, then you begin to kill off democracy. The dirty deeds won't get out, causing loss to the Treasury, and injury, even death to many people. It will mean putting us on the road to a police state.

"If the government was trying to nail me up for safecracking, well, that would be one thing. But they aren't! They are trying to shut me up as a newspaperman. When some big shot subpoenas me and demands I tell about my sources or go to jail, then he's cankering the heart of the Constitution, violating the law to cover up something."

I glanced again at the forewoman. She held my fate.

The old lady was unfathomable. But I sensed she was fair.

"The Supreme Court in Branzburg-Caldwell-Pappas doesn't agree with you on the issue of sources, Mr. Warder," Garrigan said. "Now, I'm not here to argue. The grand jury isn't here to argue—"

"You're here to jail me," I said. "For contempt because I must protect my sources. If I talked about one source, then what other source would ever believe me again? Who would trust me? I can't talk. It would take away my livelihood. And I know all about Branzburg-Caldwell-Pappas. Hell, I mean, heck, I've worked stories in competition with Earl Caldwell. It was a lousy decision passed by the Nixon court, a court partly appointed by a common criminal, and then it only went through by a five-to-four vote. I—"

Garrigan looked at the forewoman, caught something of her suspicion on the case and realized he might wind up blowing what looked like an easy win. He interrupted me.

"I won't argue with you, Mr. Warder. Madame Forelady, would you ask the witness to answer my question?" I went weak again. But the old lady had some tempered steel in her. She looked flustered, although the intense eyes were still hotly on me. After drilling them into me, she turned them on Garrigan.

"Mr. Garrigan," she said, "I think we would like to hear a little bit more about what the law says on this matter before we ask that question."

She craned her scrawny neck around at the other jurors. Some nodded, the ones that I might count on. The others were impassive: Garrigan's sheep, the ones who resented the old lady anyway. God, I thought, what a fascinating study of people, if only I weren't the quarry—like a writer condemned to hang at dawn, who could write a great book about it all if he had a little more time.

Garrigan must have thought an instant about going past her to his stooges out there, the ones who would go for the government no matter what, simply because it was the government. But he was too smart for that. Even his own sheep might follow a lead ewe.

"Very well, Mr. Warder, you are excused for the moment."

I caught him with the tail of my eye and gave him that little look that said, You're going to beat me in the end, but by God, here's a nasty splinter under your nail. Outside, I briefed Mrs. Murtry and the *Eagle* people and other press who, by now, had collected around her. There is no stricture against a grand jury witness talking about his own testimony.

"Any chance they'll refuse to ask you?" Mrs. Murtry said.

"No," I said.

Sure enough, in a few minutes the bailiff came and ushered me back in.

"Mr. Warder," said the old lady, "I ask you this question with regret. Regret, because I want to make clear that personally I think this is a shabby way to do business." Garrigan had gone Irish-red. He was thinking about how this bit of honest doubt was going to look in the papers when I described it outside. And maybe how it would look in some appellate brief. "But as Mr. Garrigan has read us the law, we grand jurors do not have a choice but to ask you, sir, to tell us whether you spoke with Mr. Renardi and what if any information was imparted to you on the night in question by Mr. Renardi about any stolen goods?"

Okay, I thought, that's it.

"Madame Forewoman," I said, "I appreciate from the heart what you said about this shoddy business. And its all the shoddier because I'm going to jail for it. But for the reasons I gave before, I can't answer."

She nodded sympathetically, and I picked up ancillary nods from different parts of the grand jury. But Garrigan had what he wanted and said amiably now, "The grand jury is excused for a half hour."

From there, it was the routine I'd read about so often in the papers about ordinary crooks, dissemblers, and the like, but always hoped I could avoid. Garrigan took me before Frick, who granted me formal immunity from prosecution on the single charge, explained that the rest of the charges were still in place, but that my testimony could not be used in the trial of them, and then ordered me to answer the question when I got back before the grand jury.

Like some wretched dog on a chain, I was now led back before the grand jury, where Garrigan explained my grant of immunity to the grand jury. This time, the forewoman didn't even ask the question. She looked sick over the whole thing. A man in the back did the asking for her. Had her own power been shaken by her reluctance? But I was too heartsick by now to ponder that.

When I refused again, still on the same grounds, I was taken back before Frick. With no hint of the relish I suspected he felt, he held me in contempt and ordered me to the city jail "until such time as you will co-operate with the grand jury, or until its term expires"—about two months away. He gave me twenty-four hours to get things in order before I was jailed.

Near numbed as I was by the shuttling back and forth, I could still scarcely believe my ears. A common crook, so long as he was one of the political variety, got out on bond pending appeal even if he had been convicted.

I was being sent to jail for protecting my sources, something that I took as an article of faith from the First Amendment. My hatred for the Little Major was almost unrestrained. I thought of that decaying horseman-of-the-Apocalypse face. Why had I not wielded my club against it instead of against the black hoodlum who had been assaulting him?

Vaguely, I heard Mrs. Murtry making an angry, intemperate argument to the judge. "Mrs. Murtry," crackled the monstrous old crook, "do you really want to join Mr. Warder in jail? I cannot have this kind of uh, uh, extravagance. . . ."

Shaken as I was, I looked back at the courtroom full of newspeople. I could see the holes of mouths in the faces, shocked as I. For it was not just my ass that was going into the slammer. It was theirs, particularly the good ones. I looked hopelessly for Betty Page. She was in Kansas, I knew, campaigning for the son-of-a-bitch who had gotten me into this jam. She would be desolated by what happened. But she wasn't here.

Connie March was, sitting with Mark Braswell. Good Mark. Good Connie. They had come to stand by the decapitee. I thought of her again, teeth and touch and tongue. Then, the fears, the anxieties swept over me so hard that I gripped the underside of the table.

All that Mrs. Murtry's arguments got me was one more night at home. At noon the next day, her final motions would be heard. I knew she already had them written, and I knew they had no chance with Frick and damned little short-term chance with the appellate court.

At home, I tried to call Betty Page to talk out my

fears. But it was no go. I called Connie, even desperately trying to reach her at Mark Braswell's, but she was gone. I started to call Cubbins, but couldn't do it.

I fixed a solid hit of cognac and Galliano, and the fiery mix had its shock value, but soon the thought of jail began to work on me again. That untouchable, vicious man in the robe!

I thought of the story I had written about the rape of a prominent white war protester in this same Washington jail. A half-dozen black studs had gotten him in a cell after lights out, spread-eagled him on a bunk, and buggered him until he was bleeding all over the floor; then they beat him to death with a club. The case had been prosecuted and one of the rapists had saved himself by ratting on the rest. Jesus, I thought. Me! And that pious shit on the bench was sending me down to that, knowing it could happen to me.

I had written of so many nightmares. Now I was one.

The terrible thing was that my fears were so excessive, so surprising. I began cranking out old childhood prayers, promising I would never tell even my journalistic half-lies anymore, or lust overly, if God would lift my anxieties.

I thought of my mother and my wife. If I could talk with them, then the anxiety would go away. Then I realized, it's not that you can't handle jail, it's that you can't handle the thought of jail.

It was nuts that I should feel this way. And I knew that when daylight came, I would never be able to explain my distress to myself, much less to anyone else.

Christ, I had been shot at in wars and riots and had never been this close to panic except for the briefest moments. I started trying to count all the women I had gone to bed with and began to get drowsy. Thank God, I thought, the road to freedom from guilt anxiety. But just the thought of being free of the heebie-jeebies made them come back. I turned and tossed.

I imagined the same young muggers I had beaten that night discovering I was in jail. In gruesome detail, I saw them surrounding me. The hell with this, I thought. I got out of bed and staggered to the telephone. It was almost midnight, but I called up Mrs. Murtry.

"I've got the heebie-jeebies," I said. "I feel like a fool calling you. They got me all of a sudden."

She had come to out of a sleep, and her old mind came awake before her voice did.

"Whas causin it?" she mumbled, then enunciated more carefully. "Do you know why it's getting to you?"

"It's irrational," I said. "It's way beyond what I should rationally be feeling."

"You sound like a psychiatrist," she said.

"I feel like I need one," I answered.

"Well," she said, fully awake now, "if you want to know the truth, what's happening to you is common enough. It's just that nobody knows it except the people who've been through it."

"Somebody ought to put out a guidebook," I said. "It's awful."

"Aubrey, it's infantile fear. I hate to load you up with psychiatry. But I had a case once of a narcotics suspect when I was in Justice. He got arrested, and he killed himself in jail."

"Nice thought," I said, feeling sweaty all over.

"He wasn't even guilty. The thing had just triggered uncontrollable fears in him. I'm serious. Your parents tell you that if you're bad, you'll wind up in jail. You *are* going to jail, so your emotions tell you you're bad.

"You've always thought the FBI were good guys who arrested bad guys," she said. "Now, I'm oversimplifying, but you must be bad because the good guys arrested you. Right?"

"Yeah," I said, some of the pinch going out of my chest. "Yeah." I thought about what little psychology I had ever read and how little I ever thought it would touch me.

What she was saying was that I was suffering from every infantile bit of guilt I had ever locked up, every failure to eat, or to crap by the numbers, the playing off of my mother against my father, probably infant peter-jerking, God knew what else. Aw, I wanted to think, this is arrant bullshit.

I remembered how I had jeered at a woman psychiatrist I had screwed in Chicago. I had been covering a panel on "The Criminal Mind: A Feminist View," and most of the women shrinks had been over sixty, and this one had been a little homely, but in her thirties. I had argued with her about why, if psychiatry worked so well, she was in bed with an unknown male in the Conrad Hilton.

"Because I thought you were a nice man instead of a cruel one," she had said, setting me on my ass. I should have asked her more about that, I thought, a whiff of heavy regret hitting me now.

"I don't believe all that stuff," I told Mrs. Murtry, now. "Some of it, the known, I can handle. But—"

"The unknown, the unimaginable." I could tell she was very tired.

"You could be making $50 an hour as a shrink," I said.

"I'm making $150 an hour as a lawyer on everyone but the *Eagle*," she laughed quietly. "You want to talk some more?"

I did, but she had given me a handgrip and I figured it would get me through the night. I didn't fall asleep until after three.

My palms were still exuding sweat when the judge ended the hearing. Mrs. Murtry, shaken herself, told me she would have a writ of habeas corpus filed within minutes. But I knew that the chances of fast action on that were virtually nil.

Once the paper filings began, there was nothing to do but wait. Still, unaccountably, the panic began to lift and I was merely depressed as they took me down to the cell block.

The same black marshal who had sympathized with me on my last visit was by the elevator when the two white marshals brought me in, handcuffed out of spite.

"You getting to be a regular with me, Mr. Warder," he said, shaking my two hands. He turned to the marshals. "He's mine now. Take them fucking cuffs off him."

This time, he didn't lock me up at all. I sat in his

office, purportedly waiting for the forms to be filled out putting me in the custody of the D.C. Jail superintendent. Actually, it was a stall by my unexpected friend.

"I'm calling over to some of my pals at the jail," he said to me. "Maybe they can give you a hand. It ain't going to be any joke for you over there, man."

His honesty impressed me, but did nothing to buck me up.

"Any advice?" I asked him.

"Don't pick any fights," he said. "Don't trust any low-class niggers. If you got to trust somebody, stick with the bank robbers. The 'king' over there"—that would be the prisoner who ran that jail more than any superintendent—"is a mean son-of-a-bitch named Henry Josephs. He's crazy and somebody may kill him before you even get there, that's how torn up it is over there now." I shivered. My God, what was I going into? My adviser went on, "If he makes real trouble for you, get ahold of a deputy assistant super over there named Sid Barbara." I looked surprised. He grinned. "No, he just *sounds* Italian. Sid's a brother. He likes the *Eagle*, too."

I thanked him and he was gone, off on a round of the cell block. Before he got back, I was led out to the ramp and loaded by the marshal in the jail van with a dozen other prisoners, all black.

Oddly, among them, because they were colleagues in something, if only the indignity of being prisoners, I felt my spirits lift. The group began to break down into components.

"What chin for, man?" a bright-eyed dwarf of a man asked.

"I'm a reporter. I—"

"Shit man, that's enough these days," said another. The van turned a corner and we all rocked to keep our balance on the two bench seats. There was general cackling.

"Listen," said the tiny black man, "I got something I been wanting to say to one of you newspaper dudes." I interrupted him now. I had learned one thing, at least, from my first jail stay.

"Yeah, you're going to tell me newspapers stories should stop adding up the possible sentences because it gives judges ideas."

The little man reached across and slapped me on the knee.

"How 'bout that," he laughed.

"I got locked up before," I explained.

"Be-FORE?" he said unbelievingly. "What for?"

"Safecracking," I said. The van was full of laughter. By the time I got to the jail, I felt enormously better.

We unloaded at the jail, in good spirits, sweaty from the ride through the muggy downtown streets. Then, I began to worry about how I could have protected myself if those good-humored men had intended me harm, instead of merely being curious.

10

Jail

Checking into a jail is not so different from the first day of processing in the Army (or admission to a hospital), or at Boy Scout camp, filling the ticking with straw for a mattress. It was largely a matter of newness and waiting.

In the orientation room, we sat on wooden benches waiting for our names to be called. The benches were not carved, but were covered with deep ink and pencil marks made by those who somehow had avoided having their writing utensils lifted at the courts or precinct stations. It was low-quality graffiti, mostly obscenities, with only one bit of literary brightness. Someone had scratched, "Lemmings, lemmings, on to the sea."

We were already rostered by the clerk. When my name was called, I saw why we weren't already assigned. The processing clerks, bored oldish men, wanted to make sure whites were with whites, blacks with blacks.

When the old man wrote down my cell section, I read upside down the names of those in the same "Section D-11." Instead of Jones, Johnsons, and Smiths, I saw a scattering of Italian and Polish and one Jewish name. It was racial discrimination, of course, but everybody wanted it that way. There wasn't even a plaintiff to get the ACLU interested in ending it.

Also, I found that somebody cared that *I* was different. I wasn't going to be treated like just another poor black, brought in steaming from some vicious street crime. The *Eagle*, just as in the court cell block, *meant* something to people.

It meant nothing to the medical clerk who asked me wearily, "Any communicable disease? gonorrhea? syphilis? tuberculosis?" X'ing my form as I shook my head "no," then repeating the litany to the next man in line. But at the clothing line, an enormous black woman with a pipey, overrefined voice said:

"I read the *Eagle* every day, Mr. Warder. I think it's a shame, a shame what happened." She made a show of plucking a bit of lint from the washed and rewashed blue-gray jail fatigues she was handing me. I could have cried at her kindness.

My cellmate was not there when I was pointed to the two-man cell. I looked at the upper bunk, narrow, pallet-hard. The washbasin was tiny, the toilet seatless and unshielded. But the cell was spotlessly clean.

I cast around for the nearest guard post. But I didn't see it, and a flicker of fear caught me. At the end of the corridor a second section began, and I could see it was predominantly black. Ours was about half and half.

Suppose by some fluke, I imagined afresh, the young men who had mugged the Speaker were here for some other crime? The idea made me quake. My white self was unprotected here in jail. My rights were theoretical, frayed. Did the Speaker's power extend down into jail? Probably, I thought. And was he vindictive enough to use that power? I had perhaps destroyed him as a Congressman, the whole fabric of his life. And I had screwed his wife, a lesser, but still serious crime.

But whom could he work through? Some Mafia friend who had power within the black narcotics syndicate, which could get the word in to Josephs that my being hurt would help Josephs maintain his jailhouse dope supplies?

Or might he do it through a decades-long friend deep in the FBI or the local police? The law-enforcement people would already cherish a man like Josephs as an informer. The jail administration already gave Josephs favors because he controlled the jail for them. The FBI and cops would have, therefore, strong lines of communications with him. And if the Speaker, perhaps through Joe McFadden, could get the Feebs or local cops, at some lower and evil operational level, to let Josephs know I could be hurt, should be hurt . . .

Paranoia! I thought, angry at myself, but feeling the sheet of anxiety being pulled over me again.

I stowed my gear in the little locker at the end of the bunks. I wished I had been given time to find a Shakespeare and a Bible, the two books I had always told myself I would take with me to a desert island. Would Betty Page bring them to me? Connie?

As it turned out, it was Cubbins who got them in later in the day through a friendly guard. Never one to leave a good thing underdone, he had optimistically marked with a paperclip, *All's Well That Ends Well.* Fucking Cubbins! I was touched.

My cellmate was another white man, an elderly check writer so faded and pale he looked forged himself. The next day he was replaced by a sick young man: a borderline hemophiliac. He told me he had been arrested for buying too much cough medicine, depending on a half-gallon of the syrup a day for enough codeine to kill his pain. Actually, it turned out he was busted for peddling stolen pills to pay for the syrup.

The bleeder gave way to a more congenial type, a redneck loser who had never graduated from robbing filling stations in the suburban wastelands of Prince George's County. He had been caught when he tried to stick up a street-wise black in D.C.

For the first few days in jail, I was a sort of celebrity. But like any other news story, I quickly slipped off the front page, and then, out of the paper entirely. Except for prisoners wanting me to write tales of their unfair jailings, of their no-good lawyers, and their general unhappiness, after a week I had come to look on myself as I was usually looked on: a man in jail, doing time.

Yet, for all the tedium, I felt an unanchorable sense of forces assembling to do me harm. It was more the attitude of some of the blacks than anything substantial.

I told myself that it was simply the unjustified fears of a man in a strange place. Still, I wanted some sources among the black prisoners and guards.

The opportunity for contact came easily enough. As a newspaperman, I was the next best thing to a lawyer. A friend of my redneck cellmate's had heard enough jailhouse gossip to be convinced that the search of his car, which had turned up some stolen transistor radios, was illegal.

He wanted a writ of mandamus drafted under the Fourth Amendment. Why not, I thought? It passed the time. And every courthouse reporter has always had visions of Clarence Darrowdom for himself.

The inmate found a copy of the World Almanac, and I used its Constitution sections to draft the God-damnedest writ of mandamus the D.C. Jail had ever seen. We backed it up with two case citations we got from an antique copy of the D.C. code in the jail library. My "client" sent it to court within a filing fee, "pro se" and "in forma pauperis."

That was all it took. The next day, after being shown the carbon of my handsome hand-lettered writ, four or five more clients asked me for various filings: habeas corpus, petitions for rehearing and review of sentence, against an incompetent lawyer (one of my classic Sixth Amendment writs), and even one for mental incompetence in which I was able to recall enough of the old Durham ruling to present quite an argument. Two of the five new cases came from blacks.

One was from the sharp-eyed dwarf, Reynolds, whom I had liked in the van trip over. He was in another part of the jail, but I met him in the exercise yard on another of those steamy mornings.

"You still in here?" he said to me with a laugh. It had been two weeks now.

"*You* still in here?" I replied, shaking his hand. He gave me the various snaps, slaps, and twirls that the blacks invented as handshakes, and I followed him as best I could.

"I already knew you was in here still," he said seriously now. He pulled out a half dozen sheets of paper, each of them covered with fine handwriting.

"This is a big job, man. I don't mind paying you for it." I took a quick look at it. It was already "styled" with the name of the case, U.S. v. Reynolds, and a grand jury and case number. That meant he had already been tried on a major federal crime. The dwarf saw my surprise.

"Man, I'm in *here* on a chicken-shit lottery. *This* one," he said shaking the sheets at me, "is what I'm gonna do *time* on. I mean *time*."

The sheets were a crude appeal from a conviction for conspiracy to commit murder. The lottery charge on which he was now doing a few months in jail was nothing compared to the years he would have to serve for the homicide conspiracy.

"How much?" I asked. His face fell.

"Money?" Already he was assessing me.

"No, Reynolds, you dumb shit," I said. "I don't want your Goddamn money. How much time is this one for?" I pointed to the sheets. His relief was immediate.

"Ten to fourteen years."

"Jesus," I said. "How about your lawyer?"

He shook his head. I knew what he meant. His lawyer had defended him, perhaps ably, on the trial level. But, having attorneyed up all Reynolds' money, the lawyer just slid off the case. I took the documents from him.

"You got all your citations in here?" I inquired, wishing I could dodge the thing. What he wanted was a massive rewrite that would get some attention when it reached court.

"It needs work," he conceded. "If you can do it, I can get it typed, even in here." He paused, looking at me with those keen little brown eyes. "I did a good job on the cases."

"How soon do you need it?"

"Two, three days." The exercise period was ending.

"I'll do it," I said. "I'll do a good job on it." Then, I appraised him. How much could I trust him? "I want another kind of pay for this," I said to him finally. "Something that won't be easy."

"What?"

"I want you to get word to me fast if you hear . . ." His eyes flashed quickly around the yard.

"Okay," he said. "I dig."

"You know something already," I said to him.

"No," he said. "I just know you are in here for something that has got you in trouble up there." His fist at his side, he stuck his thumb upward from it, meaning some high authority, and not God.

"How do you know that?"

"People talk," he said. I decided to risk confiding my fear to him.

"I'm in trouble with Henry Josephs?" I asked. The man's face constricted, but his eyes sparkled darkly.

"*He's* in trouble," Reynolds said. "He's getting too crazy for his own good." Still, there was respect. He had talked enough. "Thanks for the help," he said and we parted.

I went back to my cell marveling at how I underestimated the acuteness of others. The little guy must have smelled trouble on me from the day we were in the van.

My danger came, of course, from the fact that jail inmates weren't equal. Josephs, a man through whom control of inmates could be exercised, would get extraordinary privileges. If he were a switch-hitter sexually, as I had heard, he would get a little from some trollop working part time as a messenger girl or subclerk in the jail. Space would be available. He would also have a large cell to himself where he could entertain his masculine "girl friend," the catamite of his choice.

And he and his terrorist enforcers could roam his jail block much as he wanted.

I, too, got some slight special treatment. I was a newspaperman. When I got out, I would be writing an I-was-there piece. No one wanted to be described in the *Eagle* as a corrupt or sadistic jailer. The favoritism toward me, however, afforded me no pleasures with the female help. But I was a checker at the laundry, an "upper class" job, consonant, Cubbins would have said, with my prejail talents.

Still, doing time was doing time. A prisoner is reduced to the station of an infant. He is unmanned. His freedom is curtailed by guards and by rules over which he has no control. He must get permission, as a child must, to make the most simple departures from regulations.

I wanted a typewriter. I was turned down. ("Mr. Warder, we know *you* would use it when it would not disturb others. But, it would set a precedent. Other prisoners would want typewriters and we would have click-clacking all night long. . . .") I wanted permission to deliver copy to the paper. An agreement had to be worked out so that nothing would be printed while I was in jail. Judge Frick has to be asked for his permission, and Cubbins had to sign a promise, with copies of his promise sent to the mayor.

The bullshit depressed me. Besides I was getting horny. I began playing sick games. For instance, if I masturbated, I had given in to the system. If I could hold out without masturbating, I won. I began to pray for a wet dream to relieve me, and held out.

And the mail. Betty Page wrote me long letters, none of them with any news of the campaign or how her marriage was going, the things that interested me most. She hinted at her love for me. She signed the letters Grishkin Sosostris and gave a postal box number as a return address.

Connie came to see me once, pretending to be my niece. She had a tough time getting me called up from the cell because nieces weren't on the "permissibles list." But a song and dance about driving all night from McKeesport did the job.

I had to talk with her on a monitored telephone through a glass-and-plastic grill partition. I assume the guards recognized she was no niece when I told her how I was so horny I was about to lose my mind.

"Poor Aubrey," she said, smiling. "I wish I could give you a hand."

"A hand isn't what I need," I said glumly.

Finally, after three weeks, it looked as if the full bench of the appellate court was going to let me out on bond. Mrs. Murtry, God bless her, had visited me regularly, even bringing me homemade cookies which, to her outrage, the guards poked through with knitting needles.

"What are the odds?" I asked her when she told me the bond news.

"About four to one in favor," she said. "And I'm no optimist."

"Yeah?" I said, cheered tremendously. "How long will it be?"

"Six days, a week maybe."

"Well," I said, adopting the prison expression used by old-timers, "I can do a week standing on my head."

That afternoon, I got bad news. A black slipped a scrawl of paper to my redneck cellmate with my name on it. It was printed, but the ghost of Reynolds' tiny cursive handwriting was in it.

"Keep cell door locked until your out," it said. "Stay cool."

The note made me sick with fear. Now, within a few days of getting out, I had been targeted. I was panicked. What the hell could I do? I knew that for Reynolds to have taken such a chance he had to have good information. But to get reassigned out of my corridor, out of my present cell, I needed some proof of a threat. I couldn't produce the note; that could identify Reynolds. There were guards who were sucks with the more powerful prisoners, with Josephs.

I flushed Reynolds' note and asked the guard on my block to get me in touch with Sid Barbara. To my increasing fear, it was his day off. I asked to talk with the superintendent. He was on Capitol Hill testifying. Finally, I got to see a milksop white assistant super in his office and I told him I was worried.

"Any reason to be?" he asked.

"Yeah."

"Can you tell me your reason?"

"No. If I could I would. I can't. But obviously I'm serious about it or I wouldn't be telling you about it.

You haven't gotten any complaints from me up to now, right?"

"Well, what do you . . . ?"

"Jesus," I said sharply, forgetting I was a prisoner, however hard that had become. "You're the God-damned expert in protecting people."

"But I have to have a reason."

"I'll tell you something," I said. "Every man in my vicinity knows I'm coming up here to see you and everyone of them knows enough to tell my lawyers I came to you. If anything happens to me, it will be well known that it's your fault. That'll look nice in print for you, won't it?" The man blanched.

"I see what you mean," he said.

"I thought you would," I said sarcastically. "I want out of that cell block and into solitary or up on tier two in one of those one-man cells right under some decent guard's nose, like Bernard or somebody. That's what I want."

"I'll talk with the superintendent about it."

"Talk fast," I said, hating the weakness of this man who was going to stall me into danger. By nightfall, nothing had happened and I was scared shitless. So was my cellmate, the redneck.

"If they come, you want me to help?" he said, with a pretense of bravery.

"If you can," I said. His face fell. He was not such an idiot that he wanted to risk his life. "Well, at least holler as loud as you can," I said.

When I had still heard nothing about a transfer, I tried to get the guard to contact the superintendent for me. He made a desultory call, then reported the office was closed. I wanted to talk to the guard captain, and finally he came to the cell, shortly before Lights Out at nine-thirty.

"I've instructed the guards to keep a special lookout on your corridor," he told me gruffly. "You got nothing to worry about. I hear you're gonna get out of here anyway, soon."

"I hope so," I said.

"I do too," said my redneck cellmate. The four men in adjoining cells, all newcomers, one of them black, all looked worried, too.

"I feel like a contaminant," I said.

"A what?" asked the guard captain.

"Nothing," I said wearily.

The corridor light burned brightly all night and the guard checked by the cell zealously every hour or so, at least until four when I dropped off fitfully.

The next day I was called to the superintendent's office. He was a black, with a Ph.D. in Sociology from the University of Chicago. I assumed he hated his job. He seemed harassed, but I was sure he didn't want a star prisoner hurt.

"Do you want cell block one on tier two?" he asked. That was the location of the one-man cells for death row and the "Special Treatment Unit, Mental"—called STUM.

"Where will I be safe?"

"There, probably. Or where you are."

"Do you think I'm being paranoid about this?"

"No, you got a warning. I'm getting some vibrations on it myself." I chilled with fear.

"From Justice or in here?"

"In here," he sighed. "If Justice or the FBI or whoever wanted to have something done to you, it wouldn't be through me."

"It would be through the convicts."

"Yeah," he said. "Sad commentary, unh?"

That day I moved to cell block one. Tier two was in an isolated part of the overcrowded ancient jail. There, one- and two-man cells were along a single corridor. The men in them had been threatened, or were crazy, or were vicious but sly enough to stay out of solitary.

Mrs. Murtry dropped by and I told her what had happened. She said, "Well, hang on for another day or two."

That evening and the next day, I arranged the notes I had been writing in jail. No one bothered me, but no one gave me any information either. I saw Reynolds, across the yard, but he didn't come near, only nodding slightly at me. I did not know whether he was affirming his warning or signaling me "All Clear." That night, I found out.

Exhausted from my fearful wakefulness of the previous three nights, I fell dead asleep at nine-thirty. By midnight, I must have been slumbering deeply, for I heard no one enter my cell. What awoke me was a soft punch on the shoulder. I gave a gasp of fear and would have cried out, but I felt the prick of a knife at my throat. The instant I was awake, a black gave me a sotto voce growl.

"Sing out and you'd dead, motherfucker," he said. I was terrified. This is it, I thought. Jesus, this is it.

"Who are you?" I muttered, trying not to sound panicked.

"Out of bed," he said. "Not a fucking nother word."

There were two of them. Both big men. The man with the knife walked behind me, the blade now sticking through my shirt at my kidneys. My breath was coming so short I must have sounded like a steam engine. Silently they closed the cell door and edged me down the corridor.

God, I thought, if only someone in one of the cells we passed would report my kidnaping to a guard. But for those who were not asleep, fear would be deterrent enough. And if one of those strangers in the cells did sound an alarm, I knew enough of the savagery and insanity of jail to believe that these two abductors would simply kill me and flee.

I tried to figure the best way to act. These goons didn't care that if they killed me or harmed me the paper would make enough of a fuss so they would be caught and badly damaged: sent off to Atlanta or worse.

Obviously, the "king" would pick men who were so badly in trouble already with the prison authorities that they wouldn't care. Besides, what bribes might he not have promised them? Drugs? If they were heavy users, a series of guaranteed fixes would be payment enough for an abduction, even a murder.

Once out of the first two corridors, with their lines

of barred cells, we were into the ancient hallways of the jail. The lights burned low behind pale metal shields, covered with cross-hatched wire to curb vandalism. I could not see the man behind me. The one at my side was a hulking foul-smelling man in jail jeans with a fatigue hat pulled over his eyes. He gripped my arm at the wrist, twisting it to the point of pain.

Instinctively, I knew neither of them was Henry Josephs, yet I also knew I was being taken at his bidding.

Clutched by fear as I was, some part of my reporter's mind still stood aloof, speculative, recording the event.

The prick of the knife at my kidneys was a reminder that I could not bolt, nor scream out. Yet, even as I shook—the physical evidence of my cowardice—I was a son-of-a-bitch if I wasn't going to find some God-damn way to rage against the dying of the light. I thought if I could get one of the men talking, I could get the knife to relax for a moment, and I could break for it.

"Where are we going?" I said in a whisper. The knife poked harder, breaking into my flesh deep enough so I gasped with the sudden pain. Talk wasn't the way.

Ahead, I could see a guard station. But Josephs would have made sure it was not manned. In the under-staffed jail, this was not uncommon even without contriving. We passed quickly through the momentary brightness of the guard station: the tiny glass-enclosed office with the telephone inside, the small desk with a second telephone outside in front of the big barred door that led into the corridor with its cells.

Before me the corridor was tenebrous, awesome. Most of the lights in the corridor had been twisted loose to deepen the gloom. As we entered the corridor through its unlocked door, I heard no sound from the cells.

This would be the sanctum sanctorum, the place of mysteries of the "king" himself, Henry Josephs. All the men in this corridor would be under his sway, controlled by fear, by drugs, by favors, as strenuously as in any medieval emirate. In all those cells, men would be awake, curious. But they would not breathe. They would glance out through slitted eyes, knowing that something dreadful was about to occur, but fearful of knowing more than that.

Silent as cats, the three of us stalked through the corridor. I felt my hapless bladder ease with fear and release urine onto my leg. Shameful, I thought, shameful. I began to whimper. The knife dug into my side and I shut up.

At the end of the corridor, the last two lights had been loosened. It was all but dark. Crazily through my mind went that awful bass or baritone voice from *The Damnation of Faust*, "Un mystère d'horreur s'accomplit." Oh, Goddamnit, I started to cry, I didn't want to die. I farted nervously.

They stopped me at a cell at the end of the corridor. I could see beyond it only the closed door to the adjacent hallway. That hallway, too, was in near darkness. Could I flee down it? No, I thought, it would be locked. And the knife would rip me up here even more readily than in my own corridor.

But to die like a Goddamn dog. I began to whimper again.

Again the knife jabbed me and I froze.

Inside the cell was a third man. The man gripping my wrist, said to the unseen man inside with rough subservience, "Here he is."

The voice of the third man was cruder and crueller than anything I had ever heard in my life. It graveled out from the bunk where the man sat.

"You gonna die tonight, motherfucker." I was sure it was Henry Josephs. I almost fainted.

"Why?" I murmured. "Why? What did I ever do to you?" I talked faster, still in a whisper when I saw the jabbing was ended. "Christ, I've always written about jail reform. . . ."

"Because I say so," said the voice. A slur in it made me think Josephs was probably well into some drug. God, I thought, not even a reasonable man to argue with.

"Take his pants off," said Josephs.

The man with the knife reached around and snapped

open the jail jeans and pulled them and my underwear down. My God, were they going to castrate me first? Or rape me?

The other man let go of my arm and roughly pulled the pants and underwear over my feet, taking one shoe off in the process. My bad leg ached apprehensively.

"Shit, he pissed himself," said the man in disgust.

The noun, the verb, and my shivering fears loosened my bladder and sphincter again, and I began urinating and farting, and all my will power could not hold them in. The stream of urine must have missed my captors, but they heard it.

"He's pissing again," said the knife carrier with repugnance.

"Motherfucker, you piss anymore and I'm gonna cutcha Goddamn pecker off," said the outraged Josephs. The terror of the threat damned the stream instantly. But the cell smelled of urine as well as the bathlessness of my guard.

Now, I could dimly see the lone figure sitting on the bunk in the two-man cell, not his own for it was empty of any furnishings. I glanced back. The cell door was open. The knife was no longer at my kidneys, but the two big men still held me by the arms.

"Bend him over that bunk," Josephs said.

The two men twisted my arms like corkscrews and I gasped in pain as they pressed my shoulders and face onto the bunk. I collapsed onto my knees, my ears pulsing with fright.

"Get your ass up, white motherfucker, I'm gonna show you something you never seen before," said Josephs. I again had a momentary fear that he was going to castrate me. I was already nauseated at the thought of rape. Rape, castration, and death! Oh God, I prayed silently. Save me! Save me! I began to whimper again, and began to struggle.

They twisted my arms until I thought they would snap out of the sockets. I grunted with pain and stopped scrabbling. I could hear all of them breathing heavily now and Josephs wrestling with his pants.

"Gimme that knife," Josephs growled. "I don't want this fucker rolling around."

"Might snap you off inside," said one of the men with a low laugh. They all cackled. Horrible as it was, I was relieved that he did not want the knife to cut off my balls, which were vulnerable in my ass-up position.

The two men still held my arms, but they had released some of the pressure at the hideous joke. Now, I thought. Now! And break for the door. But almost as if sensing my thoughts, Josephs put the knife point on my side.

"Don't move, motherfucker," he said. I could sense motion and knew he must be masturbating to get an erection. Goddamnit, I thought, the dirty son-of-a-bitch. If he didn't have these two thugs with him, I'd kick or knee him in the balls and be out of here. I could hear him beginning to breathe hard; the others were breathing hard, too. My revulsion began to master my panic.

Goddamn animals, I said to myself. As the "king" built up his excitement, the others seemed to also, as if in sympathy. Josephs' agitation caused the point of the knife to jab at my side, which was already caking with blood from the previous stabs.

Suddenly, the other two men dropped one of their hands each on my arms and began moving their bodies. Jesus, I thought, they're both standing here jerking off while the other son-of-a-bitch gets enough of a hard-on to pork me. The communal perversion was sickening. But the pain in my twisted arms lessened as they writhed and squirmed to their self-ministrations. Josephs, grunting with his low passion now, had all but forgotten the knife in my side.

"Spit in his asshole, you fuckers," he suddenly said breathlessly. "Spit on his ass. The king is getting up for a king fuck!"

The other two blacks began clearing their throats, still pummeling away at their cocks, and hocked globs of spit on my buttocks. Josephs urged them on as if it were part of some obscene ritual.

"Spit on his asshole!" he panted. "Spit on it! The king

gonna do some fucking! The king gonna fuck!" He was trying to chant himself into an erection, I surmised, horrified. The knife dug and fell away. "Spit!" he commanded. "Spit."

The two hoods were falling in with the orgiastic liturgy. They pumped away at themselves and spat, even when all they had was spray. Oh, you dirty mother-fuckers, I thought. Oh, you black miserable cock-suckers! Spit away! Jerk away! This white boy is not going to be your patsy. I was coldly furious now as they spat. The knife pricked and fell back as if in the hand of an epileptic.

The grips on my arm were almost indifferent. The two men's concentrations were in the chant, the spit, and the violent abuse of their cocks. "If it were done," I said to myself, insanely mustering a fierce strength from the fact that I was going to rebel against these animals to the cadences of Shakespeare, I growled, " 'Twere well it were done quickly!"

I wrenched my right hand free from the masturbating savage's grip and with all my strength banged my fore-arm down on the wrist of Josephs, catching it with huge force against the metal side of the bunk. He screamed in pain, but I wasn't listening to his manic voice. I was listening for the clatter of the knife, to tell me where it fell.

As he tumbled on top of me, all his thought now for the knife, too, I slapped on the floor for it and, with feral anger and relief, felt its hard coolness. The thing was made from a single piece of sharpened steel.

My frantic hand first grabbed at the blade side, and it cut across my fingers. Then I spasmodically grabbed it up by the grip. The muscular Josephs must have heard the rasp of the steel as I snatched it from the floor; he began clubbing my head with both his hammy fists. The blows didn't come in solidly because I was half under the bunk. Nothing short of a knockout slug was going to deter me now. I had the fucking knife!

The other two men had fallen on me too, but in the darkness they did not dare to knee or wrench for fear they would injure Josephs.

He got a half grip on my arm. Panting for my life, I tried to break the hold. If I could get the knife turned toward him, I could plunge it into his soft exposed gut by bridging upward.

"Spit on my ass!" I screamed wildly at them. "Spit on my ass, now!" My screams directed one of the thugs to my head. He swung but I moved and his fist caught my left shoulder. The arm went numb for a moment. But the momentum of his blow sent him rolling across me, knocking Josephs off onto the floor.

"Dumb motherfucker!" Josephs screamed. "Dumb motherfucker. He's got the knife!" The man above me drew away so he could swing again. With my right arm free, I stabbed upward, getting my shoulder into it as if I were delivering a right jab on which everything depended. The razor-sharp blade paused a moment on the cloth and skin above me, then sank in like a sharp shovel piercing semipacked snow.

The man above me screamed, and went on screaming even as he flung his body off the impaling stake of steel. I had caught him squarely below the sternum with the blade, where there was no bone to hit, just belly, and I sweetly knew I had killed the motherfucker.

"Spit on my ass!" I screamed. My shout was bloodthirstier than theirs had been moments before. My bestial voice joined the crazed, gasping shrieks of the dying man in a mad duet. I could hear him thumping around the cell, crashing against walls, trying to thrust off the death that was already planted inside him.

I was screaming with triumph now, even as the other two men fought to find my knife arm before it got to them.

"Spit on my ass!" I howled like a battle cry, slashing the air hysterically with the knife. The honed edge cut through a prison shirt, stopped at the bone of one assailant. Then I caught Josephs, the fucker, scraping his skin without much damage.

"Git him in the balls!" Josephs screamed. "In the balls!"

"Balls you!" I screamed, hitting him another glancing blow on the thigh, hearing him gasp as the knife sliced into the fat and muscle. He leaped free with a whinny of pain.

"Guards!" I shrilled. Surely the guards would come now. But there was no help.

Nor was there any sound from the other inmates in the corridor. If the "king" were in a battle for his life, they would not shout to save him, lest he lose and they must answer to a new "king" for their loyalty to the old.

Yet, the ruckus was incredibly loud. The expiring man was gurgling through his screams like a lung-shot animal. My two attackers, both on their feet now, were shouting as they swung haphazardly at me, sometimes hitting each other, sometimes connecting with me.

In the darkness, I flailed with the steel blade, a guillotine gone wild, slashing here, hacking there. When we closed, I felt our bodies greasy with sweat and gore and spit, but I swung feverishly, using the knife handle as a strong-arm thug uses a roll of quarters in his fist to give it weight and impact.

I smashed the nose of Josephs' minion, crunching the cartilage like a well-cooked salmon spine against his face. He screamed and fell off, back against the cell wall. Still sobbing, he slung himself at me again, and this time the knife drove home into his side, not deeply as with the last one, but far enough to send him off of me roaring and incapacitated. Now, I thought, just you and me, Josephs.

He was stronger than I, by far, but I had cut him badly. I thought lunatically, "Beating off makes you weak," so far gone in hysteria that I almost laughed at my sick joke. He flung me on the floor, and fell atop me.

I rolled him over at last, the knife above his throat. He clung now with both hands to my right forearm holding off the blade. With our knees, we worked for a blow to the testicles, but the quarters were too tight.

The sweat was pouring off me and I was giddy from the fighting, but I jerked my knife arm from side to side, hoping his own muscles would give and the blade could plunge down into his throat or upper chest.

Josephs uttered a cry of hate, "White motherfucker!"

"Black motherfucker!" I responded.

Once again, it had come to that.

I could not see through the gloom the face that I knew was intent with determination and hatred. But I knew now it was merely a matter of seconds before his will gave or mine. I pulled downward with all my weight concentrated in my arm and got the knife at his skin where the neck joined the chest. His arms were quivering with strain. His taut muscles wavered.

"Die!" I grunted back in my throat, trying to thrust downward. "Die! Die!"

Now it was he who was grunting with fear. All his strength and mine focused on the needle point of the blade at his throat.

"Die!" I said again. The point bit, but he twisted an inch upward and the blade hit his collarbone. My strength was gone.

Shrieking at the superficial wound, Josephs wrenched to the side and the knife came out of my exhausted hand.

Berserkers, we slapped and pawed for the skittering blade. Both of us gulped in air with rasping breaths. Like two starving dogs snapping for a single scrap of meat, we dared not turn and fight for fear the other would seize the prize.

Suddenly, I was aware he was off the floor. I looked up in alarm as a light blinded me. Although lights were ordinarily controlled at the guard station, the "king" had his own way in his wing.

He had leaped up by the door and found the switch. I could not see for an instant, but quickly focused on where he stood, blinded, too, beside the cell door.

His stunned gaze swept the floor, looking for the glint of the blade, even as he hung to a cell door bar for support. He was the ghastliest apparition I had ever seen. His pants were off, and the blood welled from the slice on his thigh. His body was not huge, but compact and rope-muscled.

His face was opened with a great wound from eyebrow to chin, a Hallow-'een ghoul mask with blub severed harelips running blood. The thick blood had oozed into his beard and dripped from his chin. His eyes, like those of a frightened horse, roved wildly up and down the floor, casting for the knife.

Behind the footlocker near Josephs' feet, I saw the knife! He could not see it, though it was closer to him. If I lunged for it, he would be able to get to it first, or kick the footlocker into my path.

My heart pounded. I saw him follow my eyes to the footlocker. With a sweep of his good leg, he pushed the locker aside and as he did, we both dove for the blade. But he was nearer and came up with it. With a hoarse growl of triumph he faced me, a killer animal. The tables were turned now.

He started for me. Then, with meticulous care, he reached back and closed the cell door. I heard it lock with a click.

"Spit on his ass," he said, softly, inefficiently, his heavy lips curling grotesquely now with hate and derision. "Spit on his ass. You gonna die, white mother-fucker," he pronounced. As cautious as a great spider, he moved away from the door toward where I cringed against the back wall of the cell. I looked frantically for some weapon, but there was none.

Lacking all else, I crouched, watching his eyes, the pupils indistinguishable from the brown around them, the whites red with fatigue and anger.

One slow foot after the other he came at me, the knife held low in his right hand. He would make no mistake this time.

"You gonna die, white motherfucker," he repeated quietly, his strength returning with his proprietorship of the knife. I crouched lower. Should I spring at him, or await the first lunge of his knife? The sweat ran from my body, my palms seemed to spurt it, but I felt clear-headed, ready.

After all this, was I going to die? Not like a sheep, I thought, my eyes following his tarantula steps, watching first the blade, then his eyes.

I took a deep breath as the apparition approached me. I put my right arm up to try to fend off a blow, and dropped my throbbing left arm to my gut. Then my fading body began to give.

I willed myself to get my hands ready for a grab at the lightning arm of my adversary as it plunged toward me, but my muscles were paralyzed as in a dream. In his eyes, I saw an ugly "V" for victory, the reflection of the lights. Oh, God, I murmured, this is it.

Lamely I thrust out my hands and for a split second I seemed to feel my old body encompassing the knife in my neck. For that frozen instant I felt death, gagging death. My brain went wobbly and the man, a single step away from me, blurred.

Then the whole room exploded and I knew I was not dead. I smelled hot gunpowder and almost subliminally saw a collage of scraps.

The front of Josephs' head splattered off toward me. Just on the other side of the cell door, a dwarfish form disappeared through the corridor door that opened on the hallway. Josephs staggered and fell against me.

Pushing his body aside, I saw the wash of gray and red on the wall behind me where his brains had hit. And on the floor, I saw a makeshift zip gun. I started to the cell door, pushed it in vain, and let myself slide to the floor.

11

Replate

When I opened my eyes, I saw sunlight. And I smelled a clean hospital smell, something like the old iodoform smell of dentists' offices before everything began to stink of lilac. I shut my eyes and collected myself. I was alive. I was not in jail. I was in a hospital. The man who had tried to kill me was dead.

I felt for my balls and pecker under the sheet. All there, I thought with relief, and kept my eyes closed gratefully. When I opened them again a few minutes later, I was aware of being queasy in the stomach. My shoulder hurt. My ankle, where it had been wrenched before, hurt badly. I moved my left leg and wiggled my toes. One of my eyes was swollen but I could see out of it.

Gradually, I began to hurt all over, but it was no bad pain. My arms hurt, my hand was heavily bandaged. I tried to think why, then remembered grabbing the knife. I wondered about typing. I moved the tips of my fingers. The gash at the fingers' base made the exercise hurt but the fingertips moved properly at the top.

How long had I been unconscious? It must have been days. My mouth felt sour. I wanted to brush my teeth, but my lips were swollen. I tried to move my body. It ached all over again. At my bandaged right hand was the buzzer for a nurse. I reached across with my left arm, feeling the pain there, too, and rang the buzzer. The nurse was heavy and old, but had a friendly enough face.

"How long have I been here? I want to brush my teeth."

"They brought you in last night," she said.

"No fooling?" I said, unbelievingly. "What hospital?"

"Hospital Center."

"I hurt," I said.

"Be glad," she smiled. "You're full of drugs. You'll hurt worse when they wear off."

"But—"

"No, nothing serious, I mean nothing really serious."

"When—?"

"The police have to talk with you when you feel like it. They're outside. You're still in custody."

"Goddamnit," I said.

"The news says the judge is going to set bond. When they do, the policeman goes."

"I want my lawyer," I said. "Get Mrs. Murtry."

"She's already been here," said the nurse. She smiled again. "She said to call her when you woke up and for you not to say anything to anybody until she sees you." I closed my eyes, suddenly tired again. That's Mrs. Murtry, I thought happily, drowsing off.

Judge Frick set bail as my personal recognizance, letting me out, if you could call flat on your back in a hospital out of bond. Since the grand jury term would expire in a few weeks anyway, that meant I was free of contempt unless the prosecutor wanted to haul me before another grand jury. Things happening the way they did on the first contempt citation, I thought they would drop that idea, at least.

Mrs. Murtry came in before the police. She gave me a hug, pressing her leathery old cheek up against mine as if I were her son. But I wasn't her son. I had not held a woman for so long that I thought momentarily of whether I should fantasize fucking Mrs. Murtry. She was well into the formidable sixties and I felt slightly intimidated about her.

Still feeling that brief hug, I wondered what she would do if I said, "Mrs. Murtry, have you ever thought of fucking me?"

"What happened?" she said.

"Do you really want to know?"

"Yes, I want to know."

"You're going to get knowledge of a crime committed by somebody I'm not going to talk about," I said. "Are you sure you want it?"

Her old prune face with those young, bright eyes surveyed me for a moment.

"You mean about who shot the man?"

"Yes."

"Do you know for sure?"

Well, I thought, did I know for *sure?*

"Not for sure," I conceded.

"Then don't risk harming the innocent," she said.

I smiled.

"Any other advice?"

"Let's hear it up to the point of the shot."

I told her as best I could remember. When I got to where the shot was fired, I paused, then put it elliptically, "So somebody shot him with a zip gun. It must have been with a totally hollowed-out .22 long or something because it blew his brains out."

"Could it have been one of those yeggs on the floor trying to kill you and shooting wild?" she suggested with humorless sarcasm.

"One of them was dead," I said. Then I added lamely, "Well, he seemed dead."

"He is dead," she said, adding significantly, "Now. Were you unconscious at any time?"

I thought, well, Goddamnit, she's just like a Fifth Street lawyer when it comes to hiding the facts from the cops. I thought of the dwarf scurrying from corridor to corridor to get back to his cell. He had not done it for me, at least not entirely, but more likely for the new jail "king." Still, betraying him was unthinkable. I thought, with dark pleasure, that killing Josephs should get him enough cash from the new "king" to finance his appeal. I wondered how I could get him some cash myself without giving away our secret. I looked up at Mrs. Murtry. She was still awaiting my answer.

"No," I said. "But I was in a state of terrible confusion."

"Stay that way when you talk to the police," she said dryly, giving my good hand a squeeze. I did.

After the cops left, the people from the *Eagle* came. Even Mr. March dropped in for a ceremonial visit. Cubbins asked me if I had remembered to bring out his Shakespeare and Bible.

Connie March came in after I had finished supper. I hurt all over now that the drugs were wearing off and grunted as I rolled over on my side to speak with her. I was terribly tired, but touched that she had come.

"How'd you get in?" I said, smiling. "I'm sorry I need a shave."

"Told the nurse I had to cover a story earlier and couldn't come any other time." She pulled from her enormous handbag a tenth of Galliano and a tenth of Remy Martin and said, "Where can you hide them? You look like a busted up old man."

That hurt my feelings. I pointed at the cupboard at the botton of the washstand. "Put them way back. I don't feel like an old man," I said. She had on a nubby cotton Levi shirt and I could see vaguely the outline of those small tits.

"I think I'm in love with Mark," she said.

"Oh," I said. "What does that have to do with it? If you feel that way, why'd you come over here when nobody would be here?"

Her lips pursed, drawing the skin even tighter on the mobile face. I thought of her body that night I had had it, and bent my knees modestly so she would not see my erection. Why had she mentioned Mark? Simply for the record?

"Goddamnit, I'm so horny I'm about to die," I said.

"Poor man," she said. "I can't get in bed with you. Besides, I fell off the roof yesterday." I smiled at the archaism.

"Who the hell cares about that?" I said.

"God," she said, her face flushed despite her sang-froid. "What a clown."

"Bullshit," I said, "I'm a hero." How good I felt to be out of jail and with a friendly, even loving woman. "What's new over there?"

We gossiped for twenty minutes, liking each other, laughing. I told her more or less what had happened, skipping past my killing the man. Yet that lingered in the back of both of our minds. I could feel her thinking, "He killed a man."

Evening visiting hours came and more *Eagle* people arrived. Connie peppily told them to make me go into my liquor closet and give everyone a snort. We passed the brandy around, and I slugged the sweet Italian liqueur.

When they all had left, the old nurse came in and, smelling the alcohol, gave me a peeved look. I could feel her thinking, "Drunken Newspaperman." I didn't try to argue with her. And in any case, the telephone rang. It was Betty Page. I was embarrassed with riches.

"Where are you?" I whispered.

"Downstairs," she said. "With dark glasses on."

I imagined her down there in that cold, dirty lobby. What a chance she was taking! Her face was well enough known in town to be recognized even with the shades on.

"Why aren't you in Kansas?"

"I heard about it on the news. I canceled my speeches and got on an airplane." That meant the Goddamned Speaker, the cause of my horrors, would know of it. The terror of my forced march through the nighttime jail gripped me, but I was lifted out of it by the excitement of Betty Page's visit.

"Come up," I said. I looked at the nurse. "Make sure you let them know you're my sister-in-law or they won't let you through."

In contrast to Connie March's cat freshness, Betty Page looked weary, more tired than I had ever seen her. Campaigns are always tougher on women, I thought. The nurse was gone.

"You look beautiful," I said. And to me, it was true. She walked briskly across, ripping off the glasses and dropping them on the foot of the bed. She grabbed me in her arms.

"I was so Goddamned worried," she said. "I heard the broadcast wrong and it sounded like you were killed. I called the radio station to find out." She began to cry. Her tight grasp and my efforts to get my arms around her made me ache all over.

Momentarily, I thought of Connie, but this time with guilt. I loved Betty Page. As long as I lived, I was going to love her.

She sat in the chair beside my bed and we talked feverishly, of the campaign, of my terrors in the jail, of how the legal case was going, of her husband's slipping back into alcoholism.

"Aubrey, now anyway, you'll get out of the damn thing? I *will* leave him, if you want me to. I'll make him get his own place, right after the election. All right? If you'll get out of it."

"Well," I said hypocritically, "I want to get out of reporting. But I want to get some things done. Like burying the saucehead that sicked those bastards on me! Do you know—"

"No proof," she said, anticipating as she often did my questions. "I don't have any proof." She held tightly to my hand. "Will you—" She was hesitant to repeat it, knowing she had hit some resistance in me. "You once said . . . at least writing editorials."

And how really sane it would be to leave reporting to free-lance a little maybe or do some PR work for some small college, teach a course or two in journalism, or even get Mr. March to put me out to pasture on the editorial page: all the alternates I had run over during the thousands of times I had thought of doing something else.

"I keep going back and forth," I said to her honestly now, reaching up to caress her blond hair. "When you asked me a moment ago, I thought, no, I don't want to. Then an instant later, I saw us up in Pennsylvania, say a place called Spruce Run I went to once, an old hotel in a depopulated town in the mountains. Or a long summer in Europe, your youngest son will soon be in college. I mean, there would always be some way for us to make money. . . ."

She took my bandaged hand away from her hair and kissed it.

"So it's a maybe," she said. "So let's think of it."

"The options—" I began.

"Are different now," she picked it up. "They're different because now I'm ready to get him to leave. And maybe will anyway," she finished. We were unwinding. I thought if she could only snuggle me off, how well I would sleep, ache and all.

"You're horrible-looking," she said. "You smell of strong drink." She laughed, the face breaking up into little wrinkles the way it did. "You need a shave. I must be crazy to think of having anything to do with you."

She got up from the chair and gave me a long kiss, and I felt the passion begin again, the old demon lust which was exclusive when it could afford to be and indiscriminate when it couldn't. The nurse knocked on the door.

Betty Page gave me a hot look as we broke.

The nurse knocked again, stuck her head in and said it was time for the visitor to go.

"Can you have breakfast with me?" I asked Betty Page, breathless from the quick passion her kiss had stirred after my long weeks of continence.

"Sure," she said.

"When do you have to go back?" I asked as the nurse waited.

"After breakfast," she said with a sigh. And I knew that when she left it would be a cold, empty time.

When the lights went out, I had a nightcap of Galliano, and then brushed my teeth to get the sweet taste from my mouth. If Betty Page wanted me to quit the reporting side of the business, if that was what it took to keep her beside me as my wife had been beside me, then I would quit. But could I trust my constancy?

I shut my eyes. My mind shuttled from Betty Page to Connie to jail to my present hurts and back again.

Two women, I mused, loved me after a fashion. And

I was alive when two of the men in that jail cell were dead. My mind came to rest on the dead men. I knew I would not sleep until I tried to deal with their deaths.

Who had set Josephs on me? I recapitulated my thoughts of that first day in jail. Edwards! But I could not prove it, would never be able to. Presidents and other tyrants or semityrants suggest and the suggestion becomes an insistent order as it traverses the chain of command.

The Speaker would rage at this churlish priest to Hedaris or McFadden, and the word would pass through distorting septic layers of police or the Mafia or renegade FBI agents. The rewards for Josephs would be as I had speculated: the promise of drugs, for his own use or for controlling his jail satrapy, or money paid into an outside bank account or a hint of early freedom.

Or could Josephs, for an obscure reason unknown to me, have done it on his own? God knows. I had built enemies enough in my reporting: politicians, law-enforcement men, the Mafia, local gamblers . . .

What I was certain of was that Edwards had conspired to see me jailed instead of cut loose on bond pending my appeal. That I knew from his old friendship with Frick, and from the head of the Justice's criminal division replacing the regular grand jury prosecutor with that skunk Garrigan.

So even if the Speaker hadn't ordered me killed (and I did not believe that even he would have let himself think he was doing that), still he had pushed me into the road where the trucks ran.

In the huge quiet systole and diastole of the hospital, I thought of my terror during that walk down the corridor, of the pressure of the knife point at my kidneys.

Yet, suddenly up from the guts something soared. *I* was alive! *They* were dead. I tested whether this great fierce joy would cancel the fact of my stabbing the man to death.

I graphically reconstructed my killing him. Did it sober me? No. It thrilled me. My assailant was a cruel animal, a sawfish, a shark, a mad, ravening tiger. He intended my rape and death. Shit no, I wasn't sorry!

If anything, I felt a vague discomfort over not having been the one to kill Josephs. If I hadn't killed one of them, if I had been cheated of killing either, after the indignity they had tried to inflict on me, then I would have been left badly deprived. Their deaths had been redemptive.

Maybe if my life had been less subject to violence, I would feel a bit differently about it. But, the past had calloused me. I thought of the gobbets of human bodies after a plane crash south of Culpeper years ago: a head with one open eye asquint, a few intact feet, the cutlets of unidentifiable organ, all lying upon a tarp spread out on the field near the wreckage.

From outside, the parking-lot lights gave a sort of violet impressionism to the hospital room. The bars at the bottom of the bed cast a faint shadow over the sheets. So much for death.

Well, I thought, what about Betty Page?

Was it so crazy that she would leave a Speaker and marry a reporter? Jackie Kennedy and Ethel Kennedy had both gone out with newspapermen after their husbands were killed. And there was that British lord's wife who married a Washington reporter.

Now suppose I were a big-shot editor?

Suddenly, like a huge bird beak, lust bit me. If I married Connie March, I would be an editor. I snickered to myself so loudly I was afraid a passing nurse could hear me. An editor! Cursed race.

Why had Connie told me she was in love with Mark Braswell? Why had she burst out with that? To see what I would do? Obviously that was part of it. Maybe she was really in love with me. Ah, bullshit, I thought, vanity, vanity. Then why had she come to visit me when nobody else would be there?

She was twenty-six, twenty-two years younger than I. When I am fifty-eight, she'll be thirty-six. I figured I would be a viable lay until I was about sixty-five, if I didn't die first of a heart attack.

Well, I sighed, if I am going to settle down with Betty Page, then I shouldn't think of Connie. But on the other hand, I considered traitorously, Betty Page would be out in Kansas until November, doing her final thing for the Speaker.

I thought about getting back to the paper.

First, I saw with annoyance, there was going to be the First Person account of the attack in the jail, dully bowdlerized of all spitting on asses, wetting of pants, tri-whacking-off rituals, breaking of nervous wind, and so on.

I would also have to do a series on jail reform from an insider's point of view. There was going to be, therefore, a hell of a lot of "duty work" before I could get down to destroying that Goddamn tent pole who had almost destroyed me.

I could feel my heart pumping. Watch out, I thought. If I hate him too much, I will get too eager and blow it. Cubbins and Mr. March would take me off the story. Suddenly, I was terribly weary. The recognition of how much I hated the Speaker had crushed me with fatigue.

Ah, I was tired. But I was alive.

I slept stonily, but was awakened early by the hospital noises and my physical aches. I came groggily to and gave an orderly a dollar to cadge up a cup of coffee for me.

The private room, which Mr. March must be partially paying for since the insurance only covered a semiprivate, had a full bathroom. I showered, washing off the jail, the touch of those obscene killer hands.

The hospital provided a little shaving and toothbrush kit and I drank the still-warm coffee as I slowly shaved. I splashed some of the alcohol rub by my bedside on to my face as aftershave, feeling clean and fit despite the softened scabs on my hands and side. By the time Betty Page got there, the nurse had my open wounds powdered with some antiseptic and bandaged again.

"Yippee," I crowed with delight when she came in carrying a bag of fresh-baked croissants, butter, a jar of Dundee orange marmalade and a styrofoam quart container of steaming coffee. She was dressed in a trim summer skirt, pressed and ready for the plane trip.

As she spread out the goodies on the table, I reached from the bed up under her dress and felt the soft nylon-encased flesh of her inner thigh.

"Damnit," she said tartly. "I'll spill the coffee." Then she turned, laughing and added, "Missed me, didn't you?"

"Yes," I said. "I did. I do."

Betty Page and I ate all of the croissants, me four and she two. I felt snug and full.

"I've been thinking about what I said last night," she began after we had eaten. I took her hands, the left one carrying the Speaker's big diamond on it. I gave the ring a small tug, but it didn't twist off easily. She laughed at the shallow symbolism.

"I am going to separate, right after the election."

"Yes," I said. "I know. So let's start thinking again about getting married." She tightened a bit.

"Let's *think* about it," she said.

"Let's think *hard* about it," I said. "When will you leave him?"

"I'm working very hard for him," she dodged. "I think I prefer that he win," she mused. "I'd feel a little less guilty about asking him to go. Then, there's our son."

Well, I thought with some humor, we are getting to the sticking point when we both start worrying about the son, me last night and she this morning. Realistically, I saw no insurmountable problem. The wrench would upset both her kids. But I thought Pom would give her custody. The oldest would soon be twenty-one. And the youngest, within a year or so, would be home only summers. Maybe I could get to like the idea of having a sort of son, if the kid ever forgave me.

But first, she had to make the decision to leave Pom.

"Pom knows you're here?" I asked.

It seemed weird to me that he would have tried to get me killed, or at least played some role in it, and yet, once I survived, acquiesce in his wife rushing to see me. I also resented her staying with him until November.

"He must know I'm going to leave him," she explained. "He can't stop me. He won't. Besides, being a politician lets him slip past difficult things."

"Particularly if there's something more important at stake," I said cruelly. She looked up sadly.

"That's a lousy thing to say." She dropped my hand. "That's why I want to try to get him elected. If he wins, I've discharged all my debt to him." She paid out some of her own hostility. "You know, it was my telling you about Renardi and your being so untrustworthy that got him in this trouble."

I had betrayed her confidence. I also lusted for her. I looked at her eyes, seeing the liking for me at the bottom of it all.

"I wish we could fuck," I said.

"That would be nice," she said. "But crazy."

She reached under the cover and found me suddenly erect. My God, I thought with wild but unspeakable humor, in a hospital room. But the humor quickly burned away in desire. She looked back at the door to the room and must have seen quickly it had no lock.

"I wish I could get in bed with you," she said. "For both our sakes."

"It doesn't matter," I said, out of breath. "I mean it does, but . . ."

She pulled a handful of Kleenex from the box.

12

The Primary

Aubrey Reporter stepped haltingly back into the city room. Invictus! I thought, allowing myself the momentary luxury of slopping around in pride. Old gray Aubrey Reporter, I gloried, Abbot General of the Little Friars of the First Amendment.

Old gray Sir Aubrey, upon his dirty, manure-stained White Horse, his armor creaking and somewhat smelly, his lance infirm, his maiden's handkerchief actually a pair of Molly Murphy's drawers, and his flask of clear Camelot spring water really cheap brandy.

Old Peter Zenger Aubrey. Unvanquished, unbowed, and even unbuggered, by God. Old Aubrey, we-precious-fewing it up. A couple of dozen reporters gathered around and shook hands and insulted me in the most lovable ways.

"How did you like that funky black stuff?" said one black, not Mark, who simply gave me a good honest shake and a slap on the back. I figured Mark sensed something cooking.

"Well, our own Lovelace," said a wiry, spinsterish deskwoman who reviewed poetry. I smiled. "I honestly thought it was by Marvell," I said.

"End of my vacation," said Cubbins. "Where are my books?"

I was ready for him. The jail had sent my belongings to the hospital. I handed him back his Bible.

Then I gave him the Shakespeare, all wrapped up. I had sent it by cab to a bookbinder up near the Capitol who had done a rush job on it for me. It was bound in red leather, with "Works of Shakespeare" embossed on the center of the cover. Down in the left-hand corner, in gold script, was "Cubbins loves Goneril." Cubbins scanned it with an embarrassed smile of pleasure. For once, I'd one-upped him.

It took me a week to clean up the First Person Jail and the prison takeout. Down there, meanwhile, the police had first arrested Josephs' surviving factotum for attempting to murder me and for manslaughter of Josephs. There was no thought of charging me with the stabbing.

When the cops analyzed the trajectory of the bullet that entered Josephs' cranium, they realized it had been fired from the hallway, and that the survivor could not have done it.

There the trail ended. I resolved that I would send $200 in twenties, held by their edges when I got them from the bank to skirt fingerprints, to Reynolds. I could mail them anonymously care of whoever he listed on his bond application as next of kin.

By now, the Kansas primary was getting close. As I expected, Cubbins was torn between keeping me off the Speaker-Quiven story because he knew I was prejudiced, and letting me go back on it because that same prejudice and my knowledge of the story's inner workings made me the best reporter for the assignment.

As with all weak men, the best approach to Cubbins was to get him to let somebody else make the decision. In this case, I pointed out that Mr. March had made certain agreements with Quiven on the phone, and that, therefore, Mr. March should be personally consulted. After all, the Quiven ledger had mentioned what looked like $20,000 in contributions to the Little Major, and a story before the primary vote could make a difference.

Blessedly, from my point of view, the old man was feeling venomous when Cubbins and I went into his office. I looked past him at the two helmets from his collection, let my eyes roam to the matrices again, and allowed Cubbins to lay out the problem of whether to further breach the secrecy of the ledgers.

"I don't recall making any agreements about not using the ledger with that son-of-a-bitch," Mr. March said. "Aubrey, you were on the phone; didn't you take any notes?"

I had. They showed unequivocally that he had "guaranteed" to Quiven that he would not use anything from the ledgers I had copied except the drill bit story. I told Mr. March so.

"I don't recall the word 'guaranteed' being used," he grumped. "Quiven's venality is costing me a fortune in West Coast lawyers, trying to get this damned thing dismissed. And all he has to do is call off the dogs, say he doesn't want to prosecute, and we're done with that blither-blathering."

"Maybe my notes are wrong," I suggested somewhat sarcastically. "Maybe you didn't say 'guarantee.'" He got up from the desk and looked at the notes. They said clearly "gn'tee" in my makeshift speedwriting. He grunted and went back to his desk.

"You think he tape-recorded us?" said Mr. March.

"No," I said. "We got him at home. Besides, it's against the law in California."

Mr. March thought a moment.

"I don't remember 'guarantee,'" he muttered. "Not the kind of word I'd use." He looked at me with those ancient predatory eyes. "What else is in the ledger?" I could see Cubbins tensing. "Can you remember?"

Mr. March must have known I had Xeroxed a copy before we sent them back. But he wanted to be sure.

"Yes."

"With *exactitude?*" he asked. "I don't want any bull-crap about us misquoting him. Is there good stuff in those ledgers, yes or no?"

"Yes," I said. I knew we were safe now. Cubbins looked at Mr. March and Mr. March glowered at him.

"If Emerson Quiven did wrong, it's not the *Eagle's* role to shield him," he pontificated. "Or that bean-pole crook of a Speaker either. I gathered they had a falling out, perhaps over something totally unrelated to the case. I don't recall any guarantees, Aubrey, and I'm worried about the quality of your note-taking."

I started to bite back. I didn't like him justifying his duplicity by accusing me of sloppy note-taking. I sighed as I recalled he was paying my substantial legal bills.

"Then, shall Aubrey work on the story, Mr. March?" said Cubbins.

"Why not?" replied Mr. March wickedly.

After we got in the elevator back to the sixth floor, Cubbins observed sourly, "Mr. March will eventually be sorry he let you back on this one; I can *guarantee* you that." I wasn't sure Cubbins, who was capable of subtlety, was using the word "guarantee" on purpose. It might simply be due to his parrot disease around the mighty, a sort of verbal psittacosis.

"Fuck you, Cubbins," I responded.

In the ledger, I went back to where I had left off. I reviewed the numerous initials and numbers. The place to focus was obviously the two putatively illegal contributions from Quiven to Edwards. The other entries could wait.

Was there any way I could prove, other than from Quiven's or Edwards' mouth, that the money was paid? I finally located Drosnahan.

The criminal safecracking charges had depressed Drosnahan; he had no sugar daddy like Mr. March to pick up his lawyers' fees. He could not add anything to the story. Mainly he tried to get me to get the *Eagle* to help him pay his bill. I promised to ask Mr. March, knowing it would not work. Mr. March would call it a conflict of interest.

Renardi might have been some small help, but I could not even locate him. Finally, through the court docket, I found the name of his lawyer. The man told me he'd let Renardi talk with the devil himself before he'd let him talk with me. In a way both he and Drosnahan were right. I hadn't exactly brought my partners in crime good luck,

I thought of calling Betty Page to ask her if she had any idea how I could get more information on the $20,000. In the back of my mind was the idea that

Hedaris or Edwards had kept a list of illegal contributors as the Watergate bunch had.

But calling Betty Page to sneak-peek on Edwards' private files would have been sick. Again, the plodding began.

I went up to the Securities and Exchange Commission and went through the endless filings of Bounty Oil. What I sought were the names of dissidents who might have made "stockholders proposals" at the annual meetings. These whacky or idealistic types sometimes had inside sources in the company itself.

At the same time, I took notes from the SEC file on the officers going back five years, hoping that the ones who had dropped off might have a hard-on about Bounty or would know somebody still working for Bounty who would spill the beans.

I also listed the directors and their companies. Just possibly I might run across someone I knew or someone I thought someone I knew might know. Only one man jumped out, and that one unrelated. An ex-football star and one-timer Congressman from Oregon turned up as a director. Dutifully, I recorded it. On the SEC docustat, I ran off a copy of the last annual report, just for reference, and went back to the office.

I called one name after another, confiding more or less fully with the dissidents, playing it cozier with the ex-directors and officers.

With them, I used some ploy like, "I understand you have knowledge of certain contributions made by Bounty to politicians during your tenure, Mr. Whoever. I thought you ought to have a chance to comment on it."

They'd say, "I don't know what you're talking about," or some such, and I'd come back knowingly, "Well, I'm talking about the $20,000 the company provided to Speaker Edwards."

If I could even have squeezed a "no comment" out of one of them, I would have known I was on the right track. But not a one of them bit that day. Everyone denied it out of hand with varying degrees of outrage.

By the time I was into it a day and a half, the expected call from Emerson Quiven's lawyer came to Mr. March. Mr. March called me on the phone.

"Quiven's lawyer, a mug named Beemers or something, called. Says I had promised Quiven not to do any more stories on him. Says he hears we're working on another story."

"Yeah," I said. "On the $20,000, you know, the listings. . . ."

"Yeah," he said.

"Dead end so far," I said. "They're going to sue?"

"I doubt it," said Mr. March sourly.

The primary was a week away. The original few days of journalistic bloodletting which my last story had unleashed had been long stanched; it had cut into the Little Major's confidence, but he remained a shoo-in. Reese, his professor opponent, was gamely but repetitively beating the integrity drums. Another story was needed if Edwards was to be threatened.

For me, it was labor of hate, you might say. I began working at home and not putting in overtime for it, even though I disliked Sweet Alicing. As I worked on the contribution story, I kept a couple of others in the air.

One was a reprise on the young mavericks who had asked for some action from the House Ethics Committee. After they had signed the first request, it had been "taken under consideration" by the ethics unit, and no more had been heard of it. I dead-ended on it because I couldn't budge anyone on the ethics group or fire up the mavericks again.

A third story was who sicked Josephs on me and, along with that, how I could prove without doubt that Edwards had stuck me with Judge Frick and Garrigan so I would go to jail.

Again, I touched base with my old Justice sources, but no one was talking. The word was only that Garrigan got his orders on the case from the head of the criminal division. It petered out there.

I worked the stories at the same time, keeping them going like the circus performer with his sticks and plates. Like most reporters, I had developed my rhythms, so that the two clanging phones on my desk, the barrage of call slips, the pads filling up with scribbled notes and more numbers, the "X'ing" out of leads and "starring" of others as good bets, all had no more effect on my nerves than mowing the lawn.

By three days before the primary, I had a few good clues, but no solid stories. One ex-Bounty man, who had been pushed off the board by Quiven, had offered to meet me in St. Louis and tell me about some dubious contributions Quiven had made five or six years ago (the Speaker not among them). I got him to agree to give us an affidavit, with my promise we would not surface it unless we were sued. He said he would have it in the mail to us.

Ideally, a story on the Speaker should break right now so it could get down and canker around in his Kansas district for two days, rotting away a few hundred votes. I needed something desperately. That night, I got Brent, my FBI friend, at home.

"I'll never bother you again," I swore.

"I can't, Aubrey. You're too hot."

"I've got to show you something."

"I don't want to see it."

"It's evidence of a crime."

"I don't want to see it."

But the combination of old battles together, his decency, his recognition that I really needed him, his curiosity . . . finally, I got him to meet me.

"Where?" Brent said as if asking the site of his execution.

"Natural History, by the Seminoles?" It was an obscure enough exhibit in the Smithsonian, and near the FBI.

"No, too close."

"The Freer?"

"The art gallery?"

"Yeah."

"Where is it?" he said with some embarrassment.

"On the Mall, by Agriculture. I'll meet you at three-thirty in the Whistler Peacock Room."

"Jesus," he muttered, then leavened a little. "Sounds like a fag bar."

What I planned to do to Speaker Edwards was one of the dirtiest tricks in investigative reporting and one I had shied away from except for two similarly desperate times in my life. Cheap-shot reporters did it fairly often. It was to take data which was insufficient for a story, turn it over to an investigative agency, the FBI in this case, and then do a story saying, "The FBI is investigating reports that, etc." In other words: I was going to generate a story where none existed.

I Xeroxed a copy of the Quiven ledger, folded it, and stuffed it in my coat pocket.

Brent, in his honest two-piece suit and conservative tie, the old Hoover uniform, was at the Freer, the worry showing even through his dark glasses. Amid the gold and teal blues of the Peacock Room, poor Brent looked like a butter-and-egg man at a big-city house of joy.

"Not going to see any other Feebs in here," I reassured him.

"No, or *Eagle* reporters either," he rejoined.

We stood uncomfortably in the bizarre little room and I pulled out the ledger. Hastily, I explained that it was full of initial codes and numbers that looked like cash, along with all the day-to-day doings of the president of Bounty Oil.

"I'm not taking it," he said flatly.

"I don't want you to," I said a little tartly. "Look," I pulled out the two pages with the apparent contributions to the Little Major on them. "These two relate to 'L.M.', the Speaker. That's his nickname, the "Little Major.' See, $20,000."

"How'd you know who Quiven means by L.M.?"

"Quiven told me and Mr. March who 'L.M.' is."

Brent looked at me dubiously. "We mousetrapped him," I conceded, "but he *did* say it. I would give you an affidavit."

"Would Mr. March?" That was getting dangerous. Mr. March lacked scruples, but he was unpredictable about standing up bravely for his lack of them. Quiven was costing him legal fees now, though.

"I think so," I said. "I'd be willing to bet he would." I tapped Brent's shoulder. "Look, I know I can't give this shit to you and get *you* to investigate it, can I?"

"No, you're right there." He got up and started to light a cigarette. I halted him with a hand. He would discolor Whistler. "I got to have a smoke," he said, "let's get out of here." We walked rapidly out from under the countless eyes of Pavo, into the sun and around the corner of the building where he lit up and breathed in an atmosphere or two of smoke.

"I know what you're doing, Aubrey, and I'm ashamed of you," he finally said.

"It's the third time I've done it in my life."

"Can't you make the story some other way?"

"Nope," I said.

"Well, I won't take it."

"What would you do?"

He paused and said, "I'd give it to Lilly."

I laughed. It was ingenious. Lilly would have to take the stuff. His agents had arrested me, and any show of a lack of interest in *my* report of a crime would be the grossest kind of prejudice. Then I could write my fakey story.

"Okay," I said. "Now seriously. Is there enough here to investigate? I mean if somebody came in off the street and said, 'Look, I have this book showing apparently illegal contributions, and I've checked the contributions in the public files, and this $20,000 doesn't show up, and here is one, maybe two affidavits that the alleged contributor, Quiven, identifies the entry as relating to the alleged contribution receiver, Edwards, and here is some evidence of their drill transaction, and friendship, and so on' . . ."

"Yeah," nodded Brent. "We'd have to take a look."

"Okay," I said excitedly. "Couldn't you tip Lilly that I have some good dope and ask him to come to me instead of me going to him? I'd give it to him." That would avoid my being the moving party, shift the onus a little.

"Not on your ding dong," he said. "No sir. *You* give it to us, to Lilly, I mean. Goddamnit, Aubrey, you may be able to force the FBI to fuck this duck for you, but we aren't going to seduce it voluntarily."

With any sense of gratitude, I should have let him go. He had told me exactly what I had to know: that Lilly was the man and there was sufficient evidence to begin an investigation.

Still, I pushed him a bit.

"How much is the Speaker responsible for getting me?" I asked him.

"All I know is this," Brent sighed, looking over his shoulder, "the talk is that somebody very heavy is pushing the case against you. We got word to work with our California offices closely on the two stolen documents cases, which as you know are bullshit cases. It came down through Lilly who looked disgusted about it and said, 'Don't blame the bureau on this one.' That means it came from Justice."

"Who?"

"I don't know."

"How about—"

"The jail thing? Josephs was an informer for us. One of the thugs handles him." The "thugs" were FBI agents who were pariahs even in their own agency, the *de facto* dirty-tricks crew. "That doesn't mean it was us that sicked him on you," he said hastily.

"Which agent?" I ignored his caveat.

"Don't ask," said Brent. "Nobody knows who those bastards really work for. All I know is what you already know: nobody can fire them."

Even there in the sun, I felt chilled. Someone had put Josephs up to trying to kill me. Somebody in Washington, a government person perhaps, walking the streets just as I did, perhaps even eating in the same restaurants or going to the same parties. And the FBI itself had an agent who *might* have conspired in it.

"Goddamnit," I said, in anguish now. "It was so awful." I looked up at that homely worried face, hooded by its banana-republic-cop shades. "How could a guy do that to another person?" I asked him.

"I don't know," said Brent. He shrugged. "Maybe if I had any balls, or the rest of us did, we'd make an issue of these guys." I could feel the defeat in him. He looked me in the eyes and I thought he was going to cry a little for shame.

"Look, you're not all like that, damn few are," I said. "Here you are risking your ass for an old pal." I hit him on the upper arm, trying to be convivial, but I was still affrighted by what he had told me of Josephs.

"When we get out of this business, you out of yours and me out of mine, Aubrey, we'll have some stories to tell." His voice broke slightly.

"We'll laugh and sing and tell tales of gilded butterflies," I said, quoting or misquoting the Shakespeare I had so freshly read.

"Forget what I told you," he said, meaning it in many ways. As I watched him plod toward headquarters, I thought, "A good cop is the noblest work of God, because it is so hard to be a good cop."

I went to see Lilly late that day after calling ahead to tell him I had some information to give him. He was no fool and saw quickly what I was doing.

He took the copies of the ledger as if I were making a gift to him of rotting shad guts on a hot day. He and a junior agent took my statement, including my hint from the ex-Bounty official (unnamed) that Quiven had made earlier contributions. I waited while the younger man had it all typed up.

"You'll never make a rewrite man, son," I said to the young agent, as I read the statement he had typed up.

"Does it or does it not reflect what you stated about the alleged facts of your call to Quiven and the rest of the crap you gave us?" asked Lilly. "If we wanted poets in here, we'd hire them."

I looked out on the squad room and wondered which of his men was the "thug" Brent had referred to.

"It's okay," I said. "What are you going to do with it?"

He rose from his chair and sat on the desk looking

down on me, a stocky man's obtuse trick. I pushed back from the desk to feel less intimidated.

"That's my business," he said. "Now get your ass out of here. I know exactly why you're giving me this. You are now going to write a story about how we're investigating the Speaker of the United States. I am going to ask our public relations department to do everything they can to make you look like the asshole you are. They will say that *you* turned over the material to us, that we didn't ask for it, and that we look into every lead, however spurious it may appear."

I was rightly chastened as an asshole, but the leads were not spurious, Goddamnit.

"Screw you, Lilly," I told him angrily. "You don't hire poets. Okay, but I don't hire killers. A blind man could follow the leads in that ledger. Next time I'll bring you some dope about how your boys procure the death of jail prisoners."

The pale lambskin face streaked red along the drink lines. I had got him hard in the ballocks. But he held it in and wheeled away from me, leaving me alone.

He was the sort of goaty old man it was easy to hate. But I was glad I had gotten it off my chest, put him on notice.

I went back to the office and began to write the story. The phone rang late that day. Once again, I found out that when it came to judging people I could misjudge with the worst of them. It was Lilly.

"I want to say one thing, you miserable cocksucker," he bawled. "What you said about killers, I know what you meant. It wasn't me that set that guy on you. It might not have been anybody from here. But it could have been. I want you to know that. And I feel God-damned awful about it, maybe worse than you." Before I could decide whether to apologize to him, he had hung up.

What the story said was this:
"The Federal Bureau of Investigation is probing $20,000 in mysterious transactions between House

Speaker Pommery Edwards and Bounty Oil President Emerson Quiven.

"The alleged payments are recorded in a cryptic ledger kept by Quiven about both his business dealings and his numerous arrangements with politicians.

"This is the same ledger that lead the *Eagle* to its exposure of how the Speaker, his top staffer, and the staffer's brother-in-law benefited from a $629,000 stock deal involving Bounty Oil. The money represents holdings in a firm which had made a crucial sale of oil drilling equipment to Bounty with an assist from the Speaker.

"Quiven and Speaker Edwards are old friends, and the coded entry concerning the $20,000 transaction is written in Quiven's executive-version shorthand. At one point the ledger simply says "L.M. 5" and at another "L.M. 15."

"Quiven has confirmed that L.M. stands for "Little Major," the nickname of Speaker Edwards derived from his days as a World War II hero in the Air Force. The numerals 5 and 15, stand for $5,000 and $15,000 based on similar shorthanded entries throughout the journal.

"Quiven refused to speak with the *Eagle* about these newly discovered entries and the Speaker has said he was unaware of any gifts to his campaign from Quiven. There is no public record of any such contributions, as is required by law for all campaign contributions."

Then came the real manure-spreading:

"The *Eagle*, after going through the ledger obtained through an employee of Bounty Oil, turned it over to the FBI for investigation. In view of independent evidence that a Bounty official had made dubious contributions in the past, the FBI has undertaken the probe."

That official, of course, was Quiven, from the St. Louisan's affidavit. The affidavit named the recipients but I had not had time to check them out, so I left out their names and Quiven's. Details on that could await a follow story.

It was a piss-ant story, iffy and contrived, barely

legitimate, and I knew it. Cubbins wasn't happy with it, either. He played it with a suitably modest two-column head on A-3. Everyone on the paper knew it was a cheap shot, but they all understood what we were doing. We wanted to knock off the Speaker in the general election and to do so he had to be bled a little more in the primary.

This story would get the opposition bubbling in the last two days before the primary. The local press, which had at last begun to ask a few questions, would more or less be obligated to demand of him whether he ever had a $20,000 "transaction" with Quiven. I was sure it was a campaign contribution, but others would have to prove it.

AP and UPI picked up the thing for their regional wire in Kansas and got comment from the Speaker and from Quiven later in the day. The Speaker said it was just more of the *Eagle*'s criminal campaign of slander against him. He could recall no such transaction with Quiven as described by the *Eagle*. But he didn't say he couldn't recall any $20,000 transaction at all, and his opponent was quick to point that out. The professor was reckless with the false smell of victory.

Quiven said the story was based on stolen goods and he wasn't commenting while the case of his pilfered ledger was in the courts. But he didn't deny a $20,000 deal. I knew we had hit a nerve.

Mr. March called Cubbins and told him, "I'm glad the FBI is onto this damned thing. Keep me in touch." That meant he was going along with my nasty tactic, for the moment, anyway.

I tried to call Betty Page the day the story broke, but the chirpy little voice of the volunteer manning the phone said, "Mrs. Edwards is in Petrie with the Speaker. Could I take a message?"

I left the name Sosostris and a Kansas City number, her own sad little joke, hoping that if the Speaker saw the note, he wouldn't spook over the name. And if he called the number, he would get a wrong number and just assume someone had goofed somewhere. It was one thing for him to know his wife was sleeping with me, but it was another for him to think I was checking with her for his reaction to my stories.

It was eleven that night when she got me.

"I'm in a hotel lobby phone," she said. "I can't talk long."

"Did you see it?"

"Yes."

"Well?" I pushed her.

"It wasn't your cleanest bomb," she said tensely.

"Will it hurt him?" I asked.

"Aubrey, I told you I'm torn on this. Don't ask me things like that. Can you come out here?"

"I hope so, after the primary. He's going to win, isn't he?" We were batting back our words like a ping-pong ball. I could feel her fearing he would catch her on the phone.

"Yes, I think. But maybe close."

"Anything new? Something I could use as an excuse for coming down there? God, could you shake him long enough for . . . ?"

"Probably." She paused. I could feel her holding back a secret from me.

"What is it?"

"I'd tell you, except I don't trust you." But I would not play her false again.

"Never, Betty Page, I swear it. I don't want you ever to leave me like you did."

"That's sweet," she said, meaning it. Then she went on. "He's talked the President into coming down to campaign for him if he wins the primary."

"Good story," I said. "I won't touch it, I swear. When is somebody going to announce it?"

"After the primary. Good-by, here he comes."

Well, I thought, after the primary maybe I could talk Cubbins into double-barreling it. I could go out to Kansas and do the political stuff that one of the political reporters would usually do, and take the opportunity to poke around in the records. Cubbins would get two for the price of one, particularly since I was running dry on a Washington angle.

The night of the Kansas primary, Connie March and Mark Braswell had invited some of us to a grand guzzle at Connie's apartment. A number of primaries and other elections were also on, and the TV would give us a hint about how the country was feeling politically.

At the party, Mark had that mother-hen quality toward Connie I had seen before. He really loved her and I felt like a shit for lusting after her. On the other hand, I had a four-week prison edge on me. I had assuaged it temporarily with a call girl I had once rescued from a phony narcotics charge. She was both gratis and genuinely glad to give me her best wares.

But I thought, as I lolled in her like an old shark in a wave, that even though I was horny, there was something sordid about this casual sport-fucking.

Connie wore her usual jeans, and instead of a light shirt, a Levi work shirt with that embroidery all over the shoulders and down the buttons. I kissed her on the cheek, my hand touching her at the waist.

You little whore, I wanted to say. You have this nice Harvardy guy who will be an editor if he marries Mr. March's daughter, assuming old March could stand the trauma. And I have this most relaxing and beautiful and sexy vintage woman whom I love. Whom I really love! And both of us know we are going to do it again.

My old faulted heart bumped up and I wanted to laugh, thinking of the limbering down in my crotch, and of being in this apartment with my colleagues to watch whether Speaker Pom Edwards got a close run for his money in Kansas, birthplace of the Kansas Korn Kween.

The others had been thinking of Edwards, too, because one of them had had a guy in the art department sketch a scroll-like award on which it said, "Pulitzer Prize for Safecracking." Connie gave it to me with a little speech when she served me up the first glass of Galliano and soda on ice.

Even I was beginning to think Pulitzer. If, eventually, the Speaker was beaten or maybe indicted, then I would be a contender. And the *Eagle*, as it had been known to do, couldn't claim the damned Pulitzer for itself rather than submitting me for the individual award, because it was *my* story.

The editors and academic types who gave out the award were always notoriously sentimental toward reporters who had been locked up as a result of their stories. On the other hand, the Pulitzer bunch would not be too enthusiastic about my safecracking. They might even feel a little uncomfortable about my stabbing the guy to death in jail.

The booze and pot began to flow and blow and I thought these were the good times, all of us knowing that reporters really were different from anyone else, and that daily newspaper reporting was better than the wire services or the news weeklies or broadcasters.

"Jameson"—the city editor—"came up with the funny today," Connie said as she fine-tuned the TV to CBS, flicked quickly to NBC just to be sure we didn't get a better picture there, then came back. "He made me cut down a sixteen-inch feature to a three-inch mutt box"—a small "box" of type used for cute features with white space around it, but no byline.

"What's so funny about butchering a feature for a mutt box?" I asked her. She turned back with her open lips pulled over her white teeth, smiling in anticipation over her story about the mutt box.

"He said," and she imitated his high, whining voice, " 'And be Goddamned sure to make that mutt box bark.' " She shook her head this way and that, knowing she had not quite brought it off, but pleased with her effort.

More shop talk percolated through the room: speculation on a homosexual cabinet appointee's chance of confirmation, the inability of the cops to catch the nut who had threatened to bomb our presses if we did not denounce the Jews, a feature story someone was doing on life in a blimp. Newspaper-party chatter.

Connie had toasted huge quantities of Ritz crackers with bits of cheese and garlic salami on them. The whole room smelled of cheese and garlic and grass and tobacco. The tube was telling of one dashed hope after

another in the city elections, with occasional breaks for
the voting around the country. Kansas, with four House
seats (McFadden's was not even challenged), a Senate
seat, and the state house up for grabs, got a fair amount
of attention.

I sat back from the TV, making small talk. The first
tallies on the Speaker came in at eight from his county
seat. There was an even split there since it was also a
university town.

"Looks good, hunh, Aubrey?" said one of the reporters.

"Naw," said the copy-desk man I often shared supper
with. "The rurals will gobble up that poor professor,
just like always."

But he was wrong. Reese, the prof, held steady with
the first farm votes. I switched from the sweet liquor
to brandy and water and nervously munched the crackers. At ten, NBC did a brief remote from Kansas. They
were covering it with a very young guy out of Chicago
whom I didn't know, but he had gotten the Little Major
in front of the stick mike and might as well have been
beating him to death with it.

"Did the issue of integrity hurt you, Mr. Speaker?"
said the correspondent baldly. I laughed out loud. It
was a measure of how much we had hit Pom Edwards
that anybody would dare to ask a question like that.

But the Speaker, looking tired and greenish on the
color tube, was still resilient.

"I don't think anybody ever questioned my integrity,
Peter," smiled the Speaker. "I think the eastern press
was jealous that I'd turned a little profit on a hundred
shares of stock. I was surprised my opponent made
such a fuss about it," he tcched. "Now, I don't think
a small, good investment ever hurt a candidate," then
the big smile, "or anyone else."

Next, it was the professor's turn. He was as gauche
on TV as I imagined he had been on the stump. The
NBC man minced him.

"Do you feel the charges that you ran a scandal-
mongering campaign were fair?" asked the correspondent. We all giggled appreciatively. It was so rare to see

a TV type really stick it to a politician. The kid would
not last long.

"No," he said. "I never did get answers to the questions I raised. I think it's a tribute to the campaign that
we're doing so well in the voting."

Reese would have loved to spend some more time
on the network, but the reporter cut him off, and the
TV was galloping on to the Kansas senatorial race
which was also neck and neck, as predicted. Then it
was the state house race, and I saw something interesting.

The governor, who had backed Edwards strenuously
during the primary campaign, wasn't winning as big
himself as he was supposed to, though he was winning.
When the TV man asked him what he thought of the
Edwards-Reese race, the old pol said it had been a
tough race between two fine candidates. I looked over
at the copy-desk man to try my assessment against his.

He nodded.

"Two fine candidates," he recited, picking up, as I
had, the obtrusive quote. "Good-by, Pom."

What the desk man was saying was that the governor
would never have said "two fine candidates" if he did
not think the Speaker was a goner—if not in November,
then two years from now. He would have said, "Our
distinguished Speaker and his opponent." The governor
scented disaster for the Speaker.

Connie had sensed the excitement and came over to
sit by the easy chair where I had come up from my
slump. Mark Braswell lingered behind her, a worried
ghost.

"What's up?" she said.

"The governor of Kansas doesn't think Edwards will
be in office two years from now," I said.

What did this mean to Betty Page, I wondered, even
as I looked into Connie's small, brown birdlike eyes.
What, I mused, would Connie March think if she knew
the Speaker's wife and I were lovers? A shrug? A semi-
indifferent I'll-be-damned?

"Are you sure?" she asked, excited now herself.

"Pretty much," I said, looking for a nod from the copy-desk man.

"Then—"

"Then I better break my ass between now and November to nail him." I thought of the jail. I wished I had a new good lead to follow up. I glanced at the longish fingers on Connie March's capable hands. I wished I were in bed with Betty Page Rawlinson Edwards.

I looked up in Connie's eyes again and saw a speculative glance. Well, I thought, I can't go to Kansas yet. But I can't get to Connie tonight either, not when it was her party and there would be much to clean up and Mark would be helping her, wondering whether in that quick look she had compacted with me for something.

By midnight, I was tired and a little smashed and the TV was telling us how Speaker Edwards had apparently weathered the upset challenge of his career.

I thought, I will try to call Betty Page in the morning and try to get Cubbins to let me go down there because that will keep me away from Connie March. And, if he won't then I will try to get Connie to come see me again.

And, I thought, I would have to find a way of sitting down with the man who would oppose the Speaker in November, because he would now know that he had a chance to win, so he, as I, would be looking for the big butcher's knife to chop off the Speaker's tenure.

13

The Campaign

Betty Page called me early at home. I was hungover, hating alcohol and telling myself that I ought to stick to wine and maybe even forego that for virgin mary's and other juices.

"Is he finished?" I asked her.

"I don't know," she replied. "I feel awful about it."

I felt a weakness in her and wanted to be with her. It was no good, her whoring it up down there, discharging guilt by campaigning for Edwards.

"The governor—" she was beginning.

"I know," I said. "I heard him."

"Frieden"—the President—"still may pull him out of it. Any more stories . . ." she was totally absorbed in her husband's campaign. "If Harry Frieden lets him down—"

"Any chance of that?" I asked, sensing something.

"I think he'll come across," she said.

"You really want him to win, don't you?" I demanded.

"Yes, I do now."

"Where is he?"

"In bed. He's back on. Bad. After Reese conceded around midnight out here, he just— Even I felt sorry for him." I could tell by the way she was talking that she had given him a little while he was drunk, which I knew she disliked herself for doing. She was upset

270

enough so I did not chide her, but I felt jealous and a little angry. Rationally, I knew I had no right to protest a husband and wife going to bed together, but, damnit, I hadn't even made the pass overt at Connie.

"Get some sleep," I told her.

"Aubrey—" She was going to explain and it would get sticky.

"It's sick, you doing this," I said. "I mean killing yourself on the campaign for him. Now it'll be three more months, and even worse for us seeing each other."

"I know," she said. "Can you come out?"

"I hope so," I said, depressed by our talk.

But Cubbins put me off.

"Can't you work that Young Turks angle?" Cubbins asked me. "This would show that the only thing that saved him from a defeat in the primary was his pals back here calling off. . . ."

"I'd rather—" I began.

"You'd rather go out to Kansas where you think you can pick up an easy story than go back to an old furrow," said Cubbins with nasty accuracy. "I want the Young Turks piece." Cubbins was feeling his oats. "And if you can't do it, then—"

My temper flared at this busher Mussolini.

"You cowardly shit," I said, cranking up a few really good blasts. I knew I had gone red. But Cubbins roared.

"Out! Out! Out! The Young Turks or fuck you! Deal with Mihalik anyway. Why can't you just—"

I stomped out. Old hates had suddenly been gasolined, and my heart was pumping wildly. I went back to my desk and sat down, astounded by the explosion. When I calmed slightly, I realized that the wonder was Cubbins and I had had so few of these lately. I went to the urinal and, while I leaked, grew calm. I really should try the Young Turks story, dull as it was. But I wanted something bigger, say the story Edwards had offered as a bribe to block our first major exposé. What had it been?

Most investigative reporting was a tedious kind of gumshoeing, building a story with small, square blocks. After you did it a long time, what little pleasure it contained was in technique rather than product: a little like a good bricklayer working on an ugly, unworthy building.

I went up and saw the Young Turks' leader, a bay-windowed civil rights lawyer from Wisconsin. He was friendly enough, but he seemed turned off on the idea, particularly now that Edwards had squeaked through the primary. I dropped in on several others who had signed the petition. Ditto. I smelled a rat, and got our House man to go to still another, who I knew might lie to me, but would level with him.

"The Turks got calls from other members," he told me. "Different ones, but all sort of senior nice guys."

"Saying what?"

"Well, this is pretty interesting. The young guys were all told just about the same thing, that the senior member could understand their dissatisfaction with the Speaker, but that just before a primary wasn't the time for a fight."

"God, if that isn't, when is?"

"Aubrey, I'm just passing on what I was told. The guy I talked to felt the senior member would back some reforms in the leadership in the next Congress if the Young Turks backed off now."

"Can you talk to the senior Congressman?"

"I've got my own stories to do," said the House man. I understood. I had stepped on plenty of his sources in the course of my muckraking, and I had little claim on his time or his sources now. I had stopped being a crybaby over it long ago. He was a good man. We just didn't play the same sport.

But what he told me was important. Someone had put some subtle heat on the Turks to ease off. I bet it was McFadden calling the senior members, carefully picking the right one in each case to put a few fatherly words in each young reformer's ear. That was the way it had worked.

I had a few old friends in the House myself, and a few staffers even in the dens of my House enemies. But the House members I knew were eccentrics like me, outside the system. They were often the last to know what was going on. McFadden or Edwards wouldn't trust them to fix a ticket for a leukemia victim.

So I jotted down the names of the Young Turks I had not reached and resolved to take one or two out for meals, separately, where I could get that old Sans Souci glamor working and squeeze some juice. I set up a supper with one that evening, and a lunch and supper with two others the next two days. Cubbins would piss when Speedy Mihalik brought him my expense account for the week, but fuck 'em. News was news.

Maybe feeling a twinge of conscience, our House man saw his source in the lunchroom that day and got permission from him for us to call the senior member who had put on the heat. The senior member turned out to be a ranking minority subcommittee member and one I had *not* attacked. The House man wrung from him a confession that McFadden had indeed put him up to backing off.

"Great!" I said excitedly.

"Not so great. You can't quote him by name."

"You couldn't wheedle McFadden a little, Leon?" I ventured.

"Shit, Aubrey," he said.

But our House man had given me a wedge for use with my Sans Souci companions. The restaurant always intimidated me. In the first place, I felt I had to say "Aubrey Warder with the Washington *Eagle*," to get a reservation. Then, I got the cooing French maître d' saying, "Ah yes, Monsieur Warder, what time you want?" Without the *Eagle*, it would be one forty-five at best.

When I got there, the maître d' had already looked over his list. I think he did it by memory, but I wondered if he didn't have some code to distinguish those on the way out from those on top or on the way in.

"Ah, yes," he said again, as if I were a long-time patron. I looked around at the first platform, where a half dozen fairly "good" tables were. The steps led down to the general eating area with its banquettes along the wall and the booths, the two sites for the real hotshots, depending on how much they wanted to be seen that day. Then there was the second platform in the rear where such peons as could get reservations sat. That was where they had put me and my wife when I had called years ago two days in advance for her birthday supper.

The food was good in Sans Souci, but its sense of being the best restaurant in town, its bland costly paintings, its few, rich touches of drapes and wood panels, its ever so slightly snotty waiters made me want to investigate its ownership, just for the bloody hell of it. The maître d' gave me a booth—grace, I was sure, of the *Eagle*. As in the jail, the *Eagle* had, selectively, cachet.

My companion was a two-termer from New York, a lawyer named Abramowitz who'd beaten out another reformer in a tough primary and then won the general. Since he wasn't from the Speaker's party, he could in theory talk to me openly. But the "old boys" network didn't allow it to work that way. For a young Democrat to talk about a Republican leader, or vice versa, was just as disloyal as besmirching one's own party leader.

Still, Washington had its magic, and I was at worst a minor thaumaturgist. I had made sure the maître d' knew my dinner companion was a Congressman and hoped he would not check out Abramowitz's seniority.

From my booth, I saw him come in, a little nervously, as new Hill people are when they get this physically close to the White House. But the maître d' had gone into his egret dance, swaying, smiling, squirming slightly, bowing. The waiter, picking up the cadences that signified a "presence" was among us, began a diluted imitation of the egret dance and swayed and wooed the Congressman to my booth.

I ordered a Galliano with a little soda on the rocks and the waiter treated it expertly as if he were accustomed to that from Aubrey Warder and maybe even had a little Galliano bottle someplace with my name on it.

This sufficiently unnerved Congressman Abramowitz for him to order a very dry martini. The waiter got that momentary look on his face that a good French waiter sometimes does when anything that strong is ordered before a superlative French meal. But the expression flicked off even as the Congressman realized he should have ordered some kind of aperitif, or something freaky as I had, or simply cold beer.

We devoured venison paté, tournedos, and garlicked spinach and allowed the *Eagle* to buy us a bottle of good bordeaux. By then, my interview was going pretty well.

"Your rabbi on this thing was Worcester"—the first and last of the upstate New York liberals, I guessed. "One of the senior members tells us they got their request to intervene with you junior guys from McFadden. Same for you?"

"Who told you?" said Abramowitz, knowing he was getting close to fire.

"I'm sworn not to tell." He agreed to keep my confidence on it. "But it was a Connecticut Republican, okay?" Since there was only one Connecticut Republican, I was in a sense giving up our House man's source. But it was in a good cause, and Leon would not mind so long as I didn't put the name in the paper. Abramowitz nodded conspiratorially. I had struck a good chord.

"But on me you're wrong. It was not Worcester," he confided. "Worcester's friend from—"

"Staten Island," I said, guessing right the second time.

"Right."

"Did you push him on who put him up to it?"

"I think it was the same guy."

"McFadden."

"Right."

"What makes you think so?"

"My friend from Staten Island," Abramowitz went on, "said McFadden would help me cash my chips on Appropriations if I went along." Abramowitz quaffed the last of the bordeaux. "I'm only telling you this because I feel like a sell-out."

Well, I thought, you are. But McFadden's involve-
ment was still third hand, even if reliable third hand.

"You don't mind my talking to your friend from
Staten Island, do you? I mean so long as I keep it away
from you? I'll say I picked it up from somebody on
Appropriations."

"Wish you wouldn't," he said. Then he sighed again.
"Oh go ahead, Aubrey. I don't give a shit. Just protect
the hell out of me, okay?"

When we left, I was full of too much good wine and
heavy food, wishing I'd eaten a salad. But I had a bite
of the news story along with all the expense account
surplussage.

I worked the two other members the same way. The
maître d' knew something nutty was going on when I
came in the third time, but he was too discreet even to
suggest I'd been doing a lot of Sans Souciing in the last
three days. Even my Congressman knew something was
up.

"Mr. March is going to be broke the way you're
wining and dining us junior members down here," the
third man chuckled.

"Who told you?" I laughed, hoping to seem nonchalant. My guts were crying out over the sumptuous
food. I was sick of drinking good wine. I wanted a bottle
of soda water and some lettuce, if that.

"Staffers tell staffers," he said.

"You should've been a newspaperman," I said agreeably.

"You should've been a restaurant reviewer," he
parried.

But the joke had made it easy for him to talk. If
everyone was talking, as I had tried to convince
Abramowitz and was now suggesting to my new connection, then there was some protection. Besides, the
narrowness of the Speaker's victory had made him
vulnerable to more than just nasty press questions. The
House foot soldiers were restive.

"So you know what I need," I said amiably even
before the entree.

"Yep," he said and went on to lay it out for me. "Just make sure you keep this damned thing away from my door." So now I had the names of four senior Congressmen who had been approached by McFadden, and who in turn had got the Young Turks to call off their pre-primary assault on the Speaker.

In the next days I went to the senior members' offices, catching two of them there. I got two more elusive ones by going to the cloakrooms and sending in my name.

"I wouldn't be crazy enough to let you put my name to assenting to that," was the way the first one, the Connecticut patrician, answered my first questions.

"But it's true, isn't it?"

He just smiled.

"Look," I said. "The Chairman"—McFadden—"talked to enough of you so that he won't know who leaked. I already have it from one of you"—I told a half-truth—"as an absolute fact. But the desk says we have to have it from two sources."

The New Englander was listening carefully, now.

"I can do one of two things, Mr. Addison," I said softly, but firmly. "I can print that you went to your young friend at McFadden's bidding—can print your name right in the story, 'Perry Addison, R-Conn.'—or I can leave it out like I'm doing with my other source."

He thought a minute about this gentle blackmail.

"Leave my name out, too," he said.

"You're confirming it."

He gave me one of those looks that ask whether you can be trusted. And I knew what to tell him on that.

"I've already been to jail for a source," I said ungently in a low voice. "I've been in this town too long to start screwing over my sources. My kind of work depends on a tight trap."

"You're a good man," he said, disliking me, still a little nervous. "You can leave my name out," he repeated. "It was McFadden."

Two of the others came across the same way, but the Staten Islander was too tough to crack, even when I let him know I was going to put his name in the paper.

"I'll deny McFadden talked with me or that I talked with anyone," he told me, picking at the leather in one of those deep chairs off the cloakroom where we sat.

"You'll look like an asshole," I said. "Yours will be the only name in the story." He smiled cockily.

"If I'm the only name, McFadden will know I didn't talk and all the rest did." Well, I thought, he was right, really. "You ought to be ashamed of using this kind of blackmail," he continued.

"Oh, don't give me the pious horseshit," I said. "I already have the damned thing nailed down."

"Then why do you need me?"

"You can't nail one like this down too hard," I told him.

"I can't help you," he said. "Next time maybe."

I sort of respected him for hanging tough. "I'll leave your name out anyway. That way he'll think you talked just like everyone else."

He was a tough Irishman and I liked him.

"What a bunch of pricks," he marveled and shook my hand without warmth and went back to the floor to vote.

I tried to get an appointment with old McFadden, but no soap; The *Eagle* had bruised him too many times. Besides he had gotten word by now about what we were up to.

When I got his press man on the phone, I used the time-tested ploy of, "I'm going to print it anyway, but I thought the Chairman might want to clarify or comment on it."

The press aide came back to me after talking with McFadden. "The Chairman feels that you have to print what you have to print and he doesn't want to go any further than that."

So we popped it loose:

"Speaker Pommery Edwards' primary victory was guaranteed only at the eleventh hour when his Kansas colleague, Rep. Joseph McFadden, managed to cool off an embarrassing revolt against Edwards in the House. . . ."

I attributed it to "senior Congressmen" which would make them all sweat and also would keep my junior

informants out of trouble. It would even give the Young
Turks a chance to regroup and try again, a move that
seemed possible now.

As I worked on the story, the newsroom electricity
that always runs high-wattage from September to November in an election year had me nervously burning
for Connie March. Across the city room, I could see
her neat head with the hair tied in a long pony tail.
When I looked up from the typewriter I could see her
laughing on the phone or drinking coffee or studiously
typing or joking with someone at her desk.

Sometimes I caught her glancing toward me and I
met her eyes and laughed. She knew I was thinking of
how I wanted her and how I wasn't making a play for
her. I supposed that she thought it was out of regard for
Mark Braswell and, in part, it was. I supposed, too,
that she figured I had somebody else.

Because she had come to my hospital room and,
when I was at her apartment on primary night had
tacitly consented to see me again I believed that she
would come to me if I asked her.

Also I did not think that she felt screwing somebody
else was necessarily disloyal to Mark. For my part,
however falsely prudishness might seem to sit on my
brow, it struck me as unfair for her to screw me while
she professed love for Mark. Even more importantly, I
really loved Betty Page. I wanted to be faithful to her,
at least with everyone but an occasional bimbo *de
convenance*.

Still, watching Connie, seeing the nimble, small doe
way she moved, seeing, when I was near her, the articu-
lation of her long fingers, thinking about the shudder
in her breath, when she spun out a sentence too long
and had to inhale, I was afraid.

In Betty Page, I had what I wanted. I had in her
another wife, as my wife had been. I had safety, a companion for the long haul. If I fooled around with Connie,
it was just possible that the mix of tension, and softness,
and, in a way, adulation she brought to me might cause
me a tough emotional time.

In a word, I did not want to fall in love with a

Goddamn twenty-six-year-old, and I knew I was still enough of a windbroken romantic to do just some stupid thing like that before I settled down with Betty Page.

I felt both relief and a sense of loss when Cubbins finally cut me loose to go to Kansas. I tried to call Betty Page to let her know I was coming, but missed her, rushed home to pack, and then caught a cab to the airport.

Coming down toward Wichita with the sun high over us and the plane's shadow running raggedly across the fields, I felt an immense freedom. Washington was behind me. All the shackling of the paper, of the criminal case, of Cubbins and March and Connie were struck from me.

Flying into Washington meant the broad Potomac and the postcard layout of marble domes wheeling under the plane as it skimmed toward National Airport. Here it was broad patchworks of fields and the sluggish Arkansas River and way up north, the hint of haze and hills; it was openness.

Edwards and McFadden had adjacent districts, with McFadden in the city and Edwards in a Wichita suburb and on out into the country counties. Both of them had their campaign headquarters at the Holiday Inn Plaza. But for the nonce I wasn't interested in showing my face there.

I stayed in a second Holiday Inn, ten blocks away. Sitting on the enormous double bed I called up Edwards' headquarters and asked for Betty Page. She was fifty miles south in some little town at a Wives of the Founders luncheon, or something.

"Tell her Gabby Sosostris called," I said. "I was in town and thought I could help."

"Where can she reach you, Mr. Sosostris?"

I gave her the hotel number. Oh God, let her hurry, I said to myself as the chipper little voice said she'd pass the message on.

But I couldn't wait. I called the local police in the town where she was, knowing they'd have to provide the escort to and from the luncheon meeting, and thus would know where the Speaker's wife was. I misrepresented myself as a reporter from Topeka and the police told me she was meeting at a church in a neighboring town.

But when I got the church, she'd just gone on to an afternoon tea. Wasting *Eagle* time and feeling guilty about it, I chased down her hostess at the next scheduled stop and left the name Gabby Rossetti. The lady said she'd give Betty Page the message and asked me if I were named after the poet.

"Yes," I said, impressed and rebuked for being such a smart ass. I had assumed just because no one read poetry before sleep or on the toilet in Washington that the same applied in Kansas.

I turned back to the story. My first job was to find out what had been written out here on the Speaker, both so I did not rehash old news and to avoid duplicating someone else's work. I knew when the original story broke on Kitticon in Wichita, the local papers had given him a fit for a few days. Then they had dropped the Kitticon angle.

If, since then, anyone had undertaken an in-depth investigation, the *Eagle*'s Topeka stringer would have called Speedy Mihalik, who would have told me. If, on the other hand, there had been a fruitless investigation, then I also wanted to know about that. It could save me much unnecessary work. I called the Topeka stringer.

"Where are you?" the Topeka newspaperman asked. "This is a good connection for Washington."

"That's because I'm in Wichita. Just forget I'm down here, okay?" I told him what I needed and he agreed nervously and was back to me before I could even read the two Wichita papers as a means of acclimatizing myself.

"The Wichita papers did a couple of interviews with Kitticon, that's all," he told me. "Kitticon's in McFadden's law firm, you know."

"I know," I said.

"So, that gets pretty close to home," he needlessly explained.

"Well, that's good for me," I told him.

"You got anything solid?" he asked, still uneasy.

"No, I'm just going to snoop around," I said. The young fellow seemed to have good instincts. He was properly worried about an outsider coming into his territory.

I started to invite him down to give me both help and a cover. But that would complicate things with Betty Page, assuming she could find a way to see me. Now that I was down here, it didn't look as if it would be all that easy.

Pushing her out of my mind, I turned back to the story. Obviously, my first job was to tie Kitticon more closely to the Speaker, if I could. Already I had shown that Kitticon got the options for seven thousand shares of Boles-Panjunk in a deal involving Edwards. I also knew in my heart that Edwards would be getting a sizable piece of that $500,000. But I could find no way to prove that.

In this complex world of payoffs, there was a good chance the Speaker would be getting his money in some way totally unrelated to Boles-Panjunk. Perhaps Kitticon would keep the option money and pay off Edwards elsewhere. What I wanted to find was a second deal in which both Kitticon and the Speaker participated, say a land or stock deal or building purchase, where lots of money was changing hands. It was in such transactions that a seemingly proper increase in the value of land or securities could be, in fact, a cover for Kitticon to transfer money to Edwards.

Wichita's broad streets and sidewalks threw back the sunlight, and I bought a pair of cheap sun glasses. The Sedgwick County courthouse was only a good walk away. In my light-colored summer suit and shades, I felt like a Mafia hit man or private eye or FBI agent.

All of us, I thought as I walked along, are cops of a sort, caught up in investigation or enforcement. All of us feel that surge of excitement when we're in a new town on a fresh investigation or assignment. All of us are unclean, though I liked to think that the Mafia torpedo was the dirtiest and the newspaperman the cleanest.

The ugly blue courthouse had the sort of beautifully kept files you'd expect in a Midwestern state. The wonder to me always was how such well-kept courthouses could wind up breeding so many crooked lawyers that became crookeder politicians.

In the grantee-grantor files, a good index of land-holdings, I found Kitticon was very big. That could mean that he served as a straw for other transactions just as I suspected he had for Edwards with Boles-Panjunk. I took down the page and *liber* numbers for the deeds so I could check them out at the recorder of deeds office and thus find out their money value.

Kitticon also showed up in the equity court civil files. One case touched his law firm, while two others involved him as an individual. They might be useful, but what I really was after were cases where he was sued as a corporate officer.

That would give me the names of corporations that he served as a director or officer. It was in corporation files that I expected to find the names of his associates and, perhaps, of his other companies.

Under Pommery Edwards' name I found nothing. But this was not his county. I would travel downstate to his county seat later. In Wichita, my research could stay anonymous awhile. In the little town of Petrie, I suspected, I would be found out much sooner.

The Wichita courthouse closed before I had gotten all my notes together. I telephoned the hotel from the courthouse, and found Mrs. Sosostris had called. She would call back when she reached Wichita at seven. That meant I would see her tonight, if I could somehow finagle her into the hotel without her being recognized. Ah, joy, I thought. Then I thought soberly it might only mean that she had an evening appointment for the campaign.

The mix of anticipation and anxiety upset me. Nevertheless, on the way back to the hotel, I bought two bottles of good claret and found a delicatessen where

I got some lox, bread, pastrami, Tilsit, thinly sliced Polish ham, and sweet butter. I bought two candles.

Near the hotel was a florist where I got three roses. Excited as a boy now, I set up my feast for Betty Page. By half-past six I had one of the bottles of claret breathing and the roses in separate plastic tumblers in different parts of the room. I had the candles, ready for lighting, stuck inside two ashtrays at either end of the Holiday-modern dresser-table-desk.

By seven, I was showered and shaved, and several times had envisioned Betty Page's delight when she saw how I had turned a Wichita Holiday Inn into a betrothal bower.

At last, the phone rang.

"Aubrey," she said quickly. When I talked with her now, it seemed her voice was always pressed. I knew from the single word that she couldn't come.

"Why can't you?" I asked, hurt the more because my preparations, the fun of them, had made me expect her instead of merely hope for her.

"I can't," she said. "I can't. I promised him I'd go to a meeting with him, McFadden, and the big backers. The President's coming tomorrow."

I didn't give a shit who was coming.

"What do they need you there for?"

"Oh, Aubrey," she said, "they want his wife there. They know it looks bad for him and they know things aren't going well with us, and they want—"

"To see the Speaker as family man."

"They want to be sure I'll keep speaking for him," she said. "It's going over pretty good for him, better than his own speeches. I'm pushing Equal Rights—"

"You sound like you're enjoying it."

She paused.

"If it weren't—" she paused. "In a way, I am," she finished.

I could feel an argument coming, and collapsed.

"I bought two bottles of St. Emilion and Tilsit and cold meat and bakery bread and sweet butter," I said. "I've got the wine breathing and I have two candles ready to light." I didn't have quite the self-pity to tell her about the roses.

"Oh," she breathed into the telephone. "I'm sorry."

"I have three red roses in water tumblers," I said, feeling self-pityingly enough all of a sudden.

"I'll come. I'll beg off," she said. I started to let her do it. But that really wasn't the way. We both had to play out our game.

"No," I said. "When can I see you?"

I could feel her thinking.

"Do you care if he knows?" she said. Well, I thought, she does love me. She's saying that she'll just tell him after the meeting that she's going to sleep with me.

"Is it that far gone between you two?"

"No, not quite," she said. "But I would do——"

"No, I don't want him to know I'm here," I said.

She paused again.

"What I meant by enjoying it," she said, now that it was settled she would not come, "is that some of it has nothing to do with Pom. I can feel the women I talk to, good crowds sometimes, caring about what I have to say on Equal Rights, about other things touching women. I mean, I'm no militant, my God you know that, but these women are interested in me as me. They seem to give a damn about what I say about economy or foreign affairs, even though they believe, accept the fact, that Pom is just another politician they trusted who deceived them. Do you see?"

Ah, indeed I did. I had seen it often enough in others.

"Betty Page for Congress?" I asked with dour amusement.

She laughed, a little nervously.

"Well," she conceded, "that's the *feeling* even if the idea is absurd."

And suddenly it was all right again.

"You'd be making enough to support us both," I said.

"No, I wouldn't run. I'm not crazy. But you know the feeling. And knowing that by speaking for him I am no more than a whore for him isn't really inconsistent with the free feeling."

"Backing his stands . . . or non-stands?"

"No, Aubrey, not even that. I just say, I believe he will go this way on an issue. If he doesn't, I say I will give my own views anyway, even if they disagree with Pom's. They like it."

Well, I thought, that would be Betty Page: The brightest girl in the class, and the one who was hardest playing at volleyball, and who translated her God-damned pantoums or whatever and got them published. And so now she was back home in Kansas telling the women how to cast off the bondage of their minds if not their bodies. All for Pom Edwards, ultimately.

"When can I see you?" I asked, feeling very supernumerary. "I feel like the groom whose bride goes off to buy a pack of cigarettes on the wedding night and doesn't show up again."

"Look," she said, "why don't I just tell him?"

"No."

"Then tomorrow night. Here."

"Where's here?" I asked.

"The Holiday Plaza. Call from downstairs, okay?"

"How much time will we have?" I said.

"An hour, two," she said. "We can—"

"Is it going to be like this the whole time I'm here?" I realized she hadn't even asked me how long I was staying. She paused again.

"I don't know," she said seriously. "It will be over in November."

"Don't sound so sad about it," I said a little nastily.

"Ah," she said. "Not that nonsense." She was right.

"Why not longer than an hour or two?"

"The President is coming in tomorrow night. Everything is scheduled tightly until about midnight when I can drop out of it. Then he and Pom will be talking up in the President's suite, probably until two."

"You aren't in the same room with Pom, are you?" I asked, not really accusing but simply curious about whether I might not pilfer a few extra hours.

"No, but it's the same suite and—"

"He might come in," I finished for her.

"Yes," she said. "Even at midnight it's a risk." And so it sounded to me.

"Goddamnit," I said.

"I know," she said. "Look, we won't get caught. We can take that much time. If he comes I'll keep the door locked and tell him I just don't want to see him. I can do that. It's bad enough for that to be natural. There's a door into the hall you can leave by."

"Jesus," I said. "This is terrible." But it was all we had.

When we finished talking, I poured out a wallop of wine and called the *Eagle*. The White House already had tipped reporters that Harry Frieden was heading for Wichita so I wasn't betraying any confidence from Betty Page.

The thought perversely crossed my mind that betraying her might make me feel better, pay her back for enjoying the Goddamn campaign trail. No, I'd never do that again. But I thought of Connie, even wildly considered calling her to come on a night plane and share my feast at breakfast.

Speedy Mihalik came on the phone.

"Want me to save you some money?" I asked him. "I can pick up Frieden when he comes down here. You won't have to send anybody down with him."

"Yeah," he said, never one to accept an offer gracefully. "I was going to ask you to do it as soon as I got time to call you. Can you handle it?" There was just that touch of snideness that said, "Can a gumshoe like you write a White House story?" But I was too depressed to take the bait.

"I'll call you a 'situationer' about three," I said. "I'll pick up the arrival at the airport and I'll call you in a freshener about ten, okay? Can the wires do for you from there on?"

"Okay," he said.

"And, Speedy," I said, rallying, "if you don't like my copy, don't hesitate to fill with wire copy. This is a

big new area of endeavor for me and I might screw it
up by putting in something besides the hand-out material."

"Fuck you, as usual," said Mahalik efficiently. "Do
we know where you are if we need you?"

"Holiday Inn," I said, and gave him the number. I
lit one of the candles and ate what I could of the good
food, washing it down with the claret. I missed Betty
Page, but it was still nice to be away from Washington.
I could get a lot of work done in the morning on
my investigative story, then switch over to the political
thing. It would surface me with the Speaker sooner
than I wanted, but not that much sooner. I slept like a
tired child.

Betty Page called me at seven-thirty.

"I wish I were waking you up from next to you," she
said. "I wish I were with you." I told her to save it until
midnight and we joked. We weren't together, but at
least we were in the same town.

"Can you tell me anything I can write about the
President, something that enough others would know so
it won't look like you gave it to me?" I asked.

"Is your name going on the story?" she asked.

"Yes." She paused, then sighed a what-the-hell.

"Pom is going to accompany him out to the Coast.
You know, interrupting his campaign to confer with
the President on affairs of state. The Russian trade talks
and the HEW reorganization bill mostly. Okay?"

"Has it been spread around enough so that it doesn't
get back to you?" I didn't ever want another Renardi
episode between us, even with her witting.

"Probably," she said.

"Anything else?"

There was, but she wouldn't let me use it. She said
that the President had wanted to make this his only
quasi-political stop in the Speaker's district, but Edwards
had really put the heat on him in a telephone call to
the White House two nights ago.

Now the President had promised also to come out
again just before the campaign ended. Edwards had to
agree to go back to Washington and bang some heads

together on the new consumer legislation package that the President wanted and Edwards didn't. It sounded like a brutal horse-trading session.

"How long did they talk?" I asked.

"Forty-five minutes. But you can't use it."

"I wish I could."

"I know," she said. "But don't."

It would have been the best story of my visit. It meant that despite all the damage we had done to the Speaker, the President was willing to dirty his own skirts by campaigning for him. Edwards, obviously, was still a long way from a Kansas has-been.

The West Coast trip wasn't much, but it would still be more of a story angle than the White House reporters would have. In the morning, I got the rest of the routine name-gathering done at the courthouse and the recorder of deeds' office.

I skipped lunch and made a few calls to the Kansas reporters and the state party headquarters, the police, the local Secret Service and FBI offices, the hotel (Frieden was staying a floor above the Speaker), the student paper, and a black leader to see if there were any protests planned. That gave me enough on the schedule, the security, and the city atmosphere to put together a fairly good yarn, with the help of the two exclusive and harmless tidbits from Betty Page.

I called it into the dictation bank at the *Eagle*.

From there on it was just the mindless, to me, reporting of the White House regular: I was loaded into a bus to go to the airport. At the door of the plane, I saw the Great Man, his blond head looking left and right, the football physique still there, larded a bit now.

War hero, football star, he had married into an old rich New England family, become the governor of California, spawned four children, three of them successful, one a hippie tragedy of the sixties, and been elected Vice-President, then President.

He had weathered a minor scandal or two about his non-marital screwing. Between November, when he was elected, and January, when he was sworn in, he had rested a number of weeks in West Palm Beach. There, he had made so many indiscriminate passes at women reporters and, at presumably less vocal other women, that we called him the President-erect.

I had once mused over him as being the man Betty Page had talked about as her lover. But since she never brought it up, and *I* was hardly in a position to reproach her for infidelity to the Speaker, I never asked. Besides, from our first talk of it, I was certain only that her lover had been highly placed.

While I was jealous of him, whoever he might be, the idea that it might have been the President was both titillating and intriguing. For one thing, I wondered whether he was all he was cracked up to be in bed.

14

The President

As Frieden came down the plane's steps, the gangly figure of the Speaker moved out of the crowd to meet him. The two men, one big and husky, the other big and skinny, talked for a moment, then their two heads, both above the governor, mayor, and McFadden, moved toward the microphones.

The notables made the usual witless remarks—"Great son of Kansas" was as eloquent as Frieden waxed about the Speaker—and were whisked off to the hotel. I called in from the airport with a quote or two from the speeches, and then headed to town, wishing that Betty Page had been at the airport.

If the President's quick visit had not been so clearly to benefit the Speaker, the party could have raised a fortune with it. But that was Harry Frieden's way. Nevertheless, a quick meeting of pols from Kansas, Missouri, Iowa, Nebraska, and Oklahoma plus a smattering from other nearby states had been turned out in the hotel auditorium.

The next day, Frieden would make a short appearance at the football stadium in Petrie, the Speaker's county seat, endorse him up one side and down the other, and then speed on to California, where he had a major address in Los Angeles.

Wearily, we reporters waited through the pols' meet, got the briefing and called in what news there was from it. "The President discussed prospects for Republican victory in November. The consensus was . . ."

The "lid" was put on by the White House press man, meaning that everything from now on would be in private. Between now and 2 A.M., the crowds would be narrowed down, the really big contributors from the five-state area would each get a few minutes with the Great Man, share a funny story, maybe put in a pitch for a special business enterprise.

The Speaker would endeavor to stay sober, I suspected, and he and Harry Frieden would talk about where the legislative program was going in the few months, before November, how much time the Speaker would have to spend in Washington on it, what bills would be winnowed out, which pushed through.

I finished calling in to the paper. It was eleven. I was so tired that I almost wished I were simply going to bed. And it was still more than an hour till midnight. I trudged through the lobby.

The place was full of Secret Service men with their buttonhole rosettes and local police with their identification pins. There were enough walkie-talkies to jam a 50,000-watter, and the local cops, perhaps because out here the frontier was a bit fresher, bulged at hip and chest with the .38 Cobras that the Secret Service seemed to hide more discreetly.

I went back to my Holiday Inn, bathed, shaved again, three times in less than thirty hours, and, zombielike, grabbed a taxi and headed back to the hotel. "Betty Page," I said aloud to myself, "this is no damned good."

I called her on the house phone. She was alone in the suite and I hurried up, wondering if the Speaker's floor would also be aflood with Secret Service men who feared, perhaps, that someone would plant a bomb in the room beneath the President's and blow him out of bed and into history.

Betty Page was in a dressing gown, a long one that cloaked her short body down to the heavy rug. With a quick kiss, she led me through the suite's big room, which stank of stale tobacco smoke and into her bedroom, locking the door behind us.

In her bedroom, it smelled only of her, her perfume, and the slight steaminess from the bathroom where she must have just showered. It was only from the bathroom door that light came into the room.

Well, I thought, throwing off my coat, one hour or two a week, what does it matter? I haven't touched her for so long and I have stayed away from Connie March at least in part because of Betty Page. And here we are.

"Too long," she said, echoing my thoughts. She hugged me and then reached with tender efficiency down to reassure herself of whatever women reassure themselves of when they do that. She started to pull down my tie at the same time that I tried to hug her and her hands were crushed awkwardly into my chest. We laughed softly together, pecking kisses while she undid the tie now, unbuttoning my shirt as I worked one shoe off with the other.

Once out of my clothes, I unzipped the long zipper of her dressing gown, and lifted it carefully away from her shoulders and eased it from her back. And there in the low light from the bathroom was Betty Page, breasts full and the amphoral curve of her hips centered by the vee of hair.

"Oh, God," I said to her, "I don't ever want any more than this, just being able to take off your clothes and find you naked and clean."

I pulled her to me, standing up because we had time to stand up a few minutes before we went to her bed. She swayed against me rather than rubbed, and broke from her kisses just for the moments it took to draw in deeper breaths.

The telephone rang in the living room of the suite and I pulled away for a moment, but she shook her head "no," to let it ring, so I did.

God, I thought, the ripeness of her. It flitted through my mind that a French professor in college years ago had said the slang for ass was "*poire*"—pear—and feeling her buttocks, slightly tautened against me, I thought of a pear, and whispered "poire." She withdrew long enough to look at me quizzically and I said, "Poire, in French. . . ."

"Oh," she nodded and kissed me again, this time reaching around to draw my tail to her own body. I knew, heavy for her as I was, that I was not going to last if this kept up, so I edged her over to the bed and with a big sweep threw back the sheets and we rolled into it.

"Can you last," she murmured, not touching me now. "I'm not there yet, almost but not—"

"No," I said, "I can't." We had been lovers long enough to change pace, and kissing her, I began to fondle her mount and she rubbed it hard against the heel of my hand. I knew that soon she would be there, and then after that maybe all night long . . . maybe two, three, five times, I fantasized; it had been so long away from her. Another minute or two, and nothing, not anything at all would have mattered.

I heard the slam of the door that led into the suite and drew away. I lay still.

It had to be Pom. She eased from me, listening with all her might. It couldn't be more than twelve-thirty. By all rights, he should still be up there horse-trading with the President.

My heart was beating so loudly I was sure it would be detectable. We heard him walking, I thought unsteadily, in the suite, then the door to his bedroom swung open with a bump. That would peg him as drunk. I listened, heard him pissing copiously into the toilet, heard it flush and then nothing for a few seconds. Was he steadying himself?

I started to get out of the bed to put on some clothes, but her hands on my wrist held me. Both of us still lay dead still, listening. In a moment, he began to move again, this time down the short hallway toward her door. I took her hand off my wrist and gingerly climbed from the bed and felt for my pants.

If he threw that long frame against the door, drunk or not, he would wrench its tongue from the latch plate, and I would be discovered naked unto my enemy.

I found the pants and was silently trying to pull them over my legs when I heard him very gently try the door. My racing mind assumed he was looking to get into bed with her and figured the best way was as a thief in the night.

I wanted to say this to Betty Page, but of course dared say nothing. I wanted to tell her that he was the sort who picked locks rather than drilled safes and punched out the dials.

From the bed, she faked a sleepy groan, thumped her feet on the floor, and walked past me to the door, putting her hand in my hair for a moment.

"What do you want?" she said grumpily, drowsily.

"I want to come in," he said, his voice slurred.

"No," she said, firmly. "No."

"I want to tell you what he said."

"Tomorrow, Pom, please."

"What's the matter?" he said, sparring.

"Come on," she said. "Go to bed."

"I want to pass on to you what the President said," he repeated, more demanding now. "Just to talk to you," he said, drunkard-sly.

"Tomorrow," she said.

"Now," he countered. She paused.

"Pom, I'm tired. I am going back to bed. Please go to bed."

"I want to come in," he said more demandingly.

"No," she said, her voice sharper now, too. "Look, go to bed. I'll talk with you in the morning." I stood now with my pants on, listening to this ritualistic dialogue. The light from the bathroom ran liquidly along Betty Page's back and buttocks. I eased softly to the door and put my hand on her hip. "I'm going to bed, good night," she said.

"I'll push open the door," he said cautiously threatening, but with a timid note still in his voice.

"No, Pom," she said. "You won't push open the door. It's locked. If you break down the door, I'll call the police, and that will be that for the election."

I marveled. How many years had it taken for these two people, who must once have been in love, to get this way? How many affronts had it taken Betty Page, whose toughness and sweetness I loved, to get to the point where she talked in this calm way of calling the police on her husband while her lover stood here with his hand on her naked hip?

Would she ever speak in this matter-of-fact, totally affectionless voice to me? I moved my hand up to her breast supporting it gently, feeling an erection returning even now with her husband on the other side of the door.

"That's pretty shitty," Edwards was saying, "pretty shitty."

But there was no life in him. It was a scene that had, except for my presence, been enacted numerous times before, I was sure.

"Well, Goddamn you, good night," he said, trying to summon up an element of huffiness, as he turned from the door. What lust he felt had obviously dissipated. We listened as he went back to his bedroom and slammed the door. Within seconds, we were lying nakedly in bed again, silently kissing.

I dared not speak to her or thrash around in the bed. Still, even if I had wanted to I could not leave until we were satisfied he was asleep, lest he hear the door to the outside hall shut.

What had amazed me, and in the process, chilled my passion somewhat, was how little the dangerous scene with her husband had affected her love-making. She fell back into my arms as naturally as if she had been interrupted by no more than a gentle belch. Her hands flicked over me just as if Pom had not been warning her a moment before that he would break down the door.

Obviously the Speaker had gotten so drunk that the President, even though he was known to take a few himself at the end of the day, had figured talking to him was a waste of time.

How stupid, suicidal even, Edwards was to have missed that chance to forge a stronger union with the one politician who might pull out his chestnuts. Instead, classically alcoholic, the Little Major had gotten himself stewed at the worst possible time.

These thoughts, drumming in my head, upset the

balance of my sexual desire. Betty Page sensed it, stopped her caresses and rolled over on her back, holding my hand as if we were in conversation. Silently and briefly we lay there, then my lust stirred and I turned to her.

I knew now that it was going to be fast, that it was no good trying to stretch out the love-making this time. And that this would be unsatisfactory for her. But, ungenerously, I thought, she brought it on herself by not meeting me at the Holiday Inn, by agreeing at all to campaign for Edwards. Goddamnit, we could be lying now together, talking, kissing in my own apartment, with a whole night's sleep ahead instead of a hairbreadth escape from her hotel room my only prospect. I went limp again.

"I'm sorry," she ventured a whisper in my ear. For an answer I squeezed her hand. Again, I could feel passion building. But I was now horrified by the possibility that after so long I would fail her, and I went limp again.

Caught in a nightmare of impotency, there was no awakening, no shout that would bring me into reality. The impotency was reality.

"I'm sorry," she said again.

"I have to go," I risked now. "I can't screw and we can't talk." She pulled me to her sharply now, hugging me so that I could not leave her arms, wrapping her legs behind my legs, not from passion, but simply to let me see that she would not let me go.

And then, blessedly, I relaxed. So, I thought, what a nice lady. And just as she says, one day after November we will be back where we can make love all night. And, I began to firm up again, thinking of the humor of it, knowing I wouldn't be any particular good for her, but that she would be glad simply that it had happened at all, under the circumstances. She was slipping me into her hastily, both of us on our sides, when there was just the slightest knock on the outside door.

"Holy God," she murmured and sprung from the bed. "It's the police." The thought terrified me, my relations with the cops and FBI being what they were. More likely, I thought, some private eye from the Speaker's opponent.

Whoever it was, I knew this could finish me with the paper. The publicity I had stirred up with my subway chase by the FBI, the safecracking, and my jailing had already got me perilously close to being a news event instead of a news reporter. That way led to a few talk show appearances and then reportorial death.

As quietly as I could, I rushed to the bathroom, as she threw on her dressing gown. I realized I could not hide there, then scrabbled up all my clothes and carried them into the walk-in closet. I could hear Betty Page whispering at the closed door. She would stall the police as long as she could.

Good-by, Aubrey! I thought. Good-by, Speaker's election chances! What a helluva thing, my feverish mind said to itself on one level, to see him get beaten for all the wrong reasons: because his wife was a whore, which she was not. I turned on the closet light.

All the clothes she had been using on the campaign were racked up neatly. In the back of the closet was a suitcase. I managed in a few totally silent seconds to stuff my clothes behind her dresses and then to get the suitcase out to where it would hide my legs. I loosened the light until it went off, then scrunched down half behind the suitcase, with the top part of me behind her dresses.

No more, my poor heart said to me, no more. I could feel it beating too fast, throbbing in all the pulses of my body. Suppose I faint, I thought. Over a fucking bedroom farce. I could hear her now in the silence whispering at the door.

"Damnit, you're crazier than he is," she said and I knew suddenly that it was not the police, but indeed that, God save us, it was the President of the United States. And in the next split-second instant, I knew that he had once been her lover. I gripped the clothes bar to control my vertigo. It had been one thing to suspect it, but another to know it.

His voice was no more than a purr. Where the hell were the Secret Service? I wondered. Well, of course, he'd tell one of them, and that would be that. The one agent would be able to keep the elevators from letting anyone off at this floor for the few minutes it took Harry to talk his way into the room.

She opened the door and I heard his "Thanks" whispered.

"Now you're staying here for just that one damned minute, Harry," she said. "That's all. And right here. He'll wake up."

"You smell wonderful," he said. "He won't wake up. I do know that much, you know. I had to see you alone."

"You got in by extortion," she said nervously.

"I didn't," he said pacifyingly. "I didn't."

"Oh, Harry," she said, "you implied it. That you wouldn't help him. Cheap, cheap, cheap!"

"Rawly," he said. Goddamnit, I could stand the idea of his having been her lover, but the use of a pet name to which I was not privy infuriated me. Or was it simply, as had happened once when my wife weepingly threatened me with an affair, that it was easier to conceive of infidelity than to have proof of it. "Rawly, let's not have—"

"A quarrel," she broke in.

"A lover's quarrel, I was about to say."

"We aren't lovers." I was furious, tempted to come out, with whatever I could find wrapped around me and say, "Get the fuck out of here!"

"Anymore," he said. He must have reached for her.

"Harry, get your hands off of me." Would she have been so angry, I wondered, if he had not unwittingly testified to that old affair while foolish Polonius listened in the clothes closet? If I weren't here at all, would she have resisted him?

"You've always been prettiest when slightly put out," he whispered to her.

"Always!" I caught it, my reporter mind snapping on the key word.

"Always," she picked it up. "Don't make it sound like it was some long romance. It was a lousy romance. We both knew it."

"You never gave it a chance," he said. "Never."

"Harry, will you go back to your room," she said. But it was not with the same coldness that she had told her husband to go to bed. The trouble with amoralists like Frieden is that they were nice, bumbly men. Charming. That's part of what charisma was.

"Goddamnit," said Frieden. "Rawly, I risk my political career for a few hours with you. I've always half-loved you, I—"

"Half is right," she whispered, with her soft snort of laughter. "At least that much is honest." I could see she was enchanted by the combination of his glow and the sheer outrageousness of it. There was something of the wanton in Betty Page that even I did not like to admit. "You're half in love with whoever is nearest you at the time."

"Not true," he said. "I'm fully in love with Emily." That was his wife. "And maybe I have been two or three other times. I would have been with you," he said softly, "if it had worked."

There was no way the seducing prick was going to get Betty Page to go to bed with him, not with me in the closet. But I was afraid that he might be finding some way of establishing a later relationship. I imagined again coming out of the closet, confronting him. Maybe just do it in the buff.

"Hi, Mr. President," I might say. "I'm Aubrey Warder of the *Eagle*."

Betty Page's insistent words broke my fantasy.

"Well, Harry, it *didn't* work," she said. "And it *won't* work now."

The President apparently wasn't used to getting a "no" so persistently. In an existential way, I felt sorry for him. After all, his line was failing in part because of something about which he had no idea, namely a witness in the closet: me. I wished he would go. I was getting cramped.

I began to wonder how much he had had to drink.

Any normal philanderer would recognize he wasn't going to score. The cramped position made me want to urinate.

"Let's try it again, pick up where we were," Frieden said. Ah, I thought, he has been drinking. Nobody sober would persevere this way. But then, perseverance was how he got his job. "I know it isn't working out with Pom. You *need* somebody."

Up to now he'd had a sort of boyish charm about him, but this was getting corny, serious, and a little nasty. Suddenly, I heard him pushing at her and their feet moving on the floor as if he had caught hold of her and she was trying to keep her balance. Well, I said, if he strongarms her, I'll cold cock the schmuck, football star or no football star, Secret Service or no.

But she was quick enough on her own.

"Okay, Harry," she snapped. "That's it." Her voice was even icier than it had been with her husband. "Out!" I could hear his feet scuffing now. She was pushing him out of the room. "Out! Out!"

"Now, just a Goddamned minute," he said, the President speaking. One more mini-decibel and Pom would wake up and then we'd all be in for it, all of us. "Now just a Goddamned minute. You do want this election, don't you . . . ?"

Betty Page was nothing if not politically quick. The pushing stopped. She was breathing hard, but I heard her say with neither warmth nor coolness:

"Harry, nobody blames you for being a big lovable man. But before you say stupid things like that, think. You'll be . . ."

And by now the alcohol had chilled in him, too.

He was breathing hard. But he was back under control.

". . . just like the rest of them," he said. "I'll be just like the rest of them," he repeated. "I'm sorry, Rawly.

"Well," he closed, scrambling to recover, "you can see how much I want your sweet ass to say something as stupid as that."

"We tried that once and it didn't make sense," she said.

Having failed to get what he wanted, Frieden did not want to stay around and argue the philosophy of love.

"Toodle-oo," he whispered, slipping out the door.

Once she had closed it, she slipped across the room as I unfolded from behind the suitcase.

"Aubrey," she whispered, "I—"

"First I have to go to the bathroom," I said.

"He—"

I went to the bathroom and then came back to the closet and got my clothes.

"You're not going," she began, genuinely worried. I looked up at her and smiled. Her dear face was full of worry. She did love me.

"No," I told her. "I just want to get my pants spread out so I can get into them if anybody else flies into this Goddamn airport."

"It was only four times with Frieden, not 'always,'" she said. "And—" She was going to tell me it was no good with him, but I really didn't want to hear it.

"Don't worry," I said. I looked at my watch on the table.

"And you aren't going?" she asked, still concerned.

"Are you kidding?" I whispered to her. "And give up fucking somebody who just said 'no' to the President of the United States?"

The first time, it went very fast. Then we lay in bed whispering to each other about all the things we had not been able to talk about for so long. Yes, I told her, I would think of leaving reporting. No, I had never been so happy in bed with anyone. Yes, she told me, she recently had intercourse with Pom several times when he was sober. No, she had not enjoyed it. And for him it had been just a way of relieving tension.

Yes, she explained, the affair with Harry had been while he was Vice-President. They had gone to the house of one of his friends in Bethesda. It had been lousy—for one thing because she had been uptight about it, doing it in part as experimental revenge on Pom for some affair or another he was carrying on at the time. And then, Frieden had been ungentle, proprietary almost. No, she had laughed, no bigger. Shorter and fatter.

Yes, it was definitely over with Pom. Maybe, she thought, we should get married and maybe not. Maybe we should just be lovers and we should see how it was. Or live half apart. We could see after November.

And by then, since we were kissing between the whispered stretches of talk, I began to come back. I felt marvelously lusty and proud to be with her velvet self.

At about five-thirty, punchy with exhaustion and bedazzled with love and gratification, I crept out of her door into the hall. Downstairs, the desk clerk looked at me suspiciously.

There were some half-dozen Secret Service types around the lobby dozing, a few walking around with their omnipresent earplugs. They, too, stared at me. No doubt they suspected I had just come from some couch of love, but as long as it was not the President of the United States, they did not care.

15

The Speaker's Country

Thank God, I thought, I need not be on hand for his talk in Petrie. Poor Betty Page would have to be there, all unslept as she was. But by the time I got up, the President would be on the way to Los Angeles for his major address.

That would be the lead story on him for the *Eagle* tomorrow morning, just as Kansas was the lead this morning. By tomorrow morning the Petrie appearance for Edwards would be a three- or four-paragraph drop-in in the Los Angeles story, and the paper agreeably was going to pick it up from the wires so I could be about my business.

Still, it was rare that I slept late on Mr. March's time.

I got up and out and finished up my note-taking at the Sedgwick County courthouse. All told, there was a fair amount of property around town held by Kitticon. The only curious thing was that he held much of it as trustee. Trustee for whom, I wondered.

I rented a car and drove south to Petrie to see whether the court records there would yield anything on the Little Major. I expected to find new material. A powerful politician seldom facing anything but reverential competition often got a free ride with his home town newspapers, whose editor and publisher were part of the county establishment.

As a result, the "establishment" of the counties usually remained just as corrupt as the establishment of the country. Often worse, because a few big papers run by establishment types in cities like New York and Washington and Boston, and lately Philadelphia, now sometimes bit the hands they broke bread with.

My God, Kansas is flat and hot, I thought, as I drove down the straight wide strip of interstate concrete that Pom had, no doubt, finagled with the help of old McFadden years before any other state got theirs.

The wheat stubble began just off the highway and stretched forever. I opened up the window and the cool conditioned air rushed out and was replaced with the baking smell of the empty grain fields, shaved like a prisoner's head.

Because I had drunk nothing the day before, my body, though wanting sleep, felt sound and clean and cleansed by a motel shower and by its remembrance of the annealing it got from Betty Page. The warm air poured over my face with a dry smell of cooking dirt and stalks.

The sky was bluer than in Washington, yet here too, it had the sort of feckless quality I had seen there so often; a feeling that it was made up of layers of insubstantial gauzes until it was so deep that it was eternal and infinite.

The highway's white and the sky's blue and the open harvested spaces, so still and hot, set me singing. These intense colors of America. Dull green and ocher fields stripped of the waving grain: It was beautiful land, full of all magic.

And now, almost twenty-five years, I had been in the heart of it. Soon the *Eagle* would be throwing my twenty-fifth anniversary party. Would Connie come?

I pushed my thoughts back to the land and to me. To be sure, my kind of reporting fed on whatever hostilities I had brought into adulthood. The hostilities were useful, keeping me bubbling with the sense of outrage that was the only sine qua non of investigative reporting.

And yet I had done some small something for the land. I had rid it of some crooks, and was now, slowly and surely, finding the taproots of another one. The

men I had knocked out of office had not necessarily
been worse than the ones who followed them, but they
had been more powerful. The successors had thus been
less dangerous crooks.

If I could knock Edwards out of his seat, the man
who would succeed him, an ex-Attorney General of the
State named Dennis Marthas, would be less able to
afflict the weak and pamper the strong. Seniority would
see to that. And, he was probably slightly more decent,
not as smart, and thus, again, less dangerous.

Though I had been singing "America," I now began
shouting "God Bless America," at the top of my voice,
as the Kansas air gushed through the fast-moving car.
I was forty-eight and in love with the body and mind
and spirit of Betty Page Rawlinson Edwards, the former
Kansas Korn Kween, and I lusted occasionally for, and
genuinely liked, Ms. Connie March, electric daughter
of my publisher. And I was healthy in body and mind,
and my motives, while hostile, were not unuseful. And
the sight of all that warmly colored Kansas land lifted
my soul and made me love America to which I had
contributed at least one tiny bit as a garbage man or
tree pruner or ragpicker or soil conservationist.

"Gawwwd Bless Ah-mer-ee-kahh," I Kate Smithed it,
thinking I would not live forever, but that life was very
sweet and had been very sweet to me. Now if Mrs.
Murtry could save me from the pigs, I would feel
apotheosized, at least as a very minor god.

It was in Petrie that I found the surprise I had hoped
for, even though the explanation was still missing.
Again, here in Blaine County, there were properties
owned by Kitticon as trustee. In Wichita, it made sense.
He might have a lively real estate practice where the
beneficial owners wanted to hide behind a straw. But
not here unless he was a Blaine County boy and I did
not think he was. No, I recalled, pushing my memory
hard, he had gone to school in Wichita.

I took down all the entries and checked out the
properties. They were small town holdings mostly, a
few acres here, another one or two there. But the tax

stamps showed they were good sites, improved by stores or gas stations probably. There was a slow turning over of the properties, almost always at a solid profit. Whoever was behind the dealings knew his land.

It had been the same in Wichita, where the percentages of profit were the same, and the profits themselves higher because of the greater value of the land.

For whom was Kitticon trustee? It could be anybody, any rich banker or speculator. It could be little Georgie Hedaris. It could be a second straw for the Speaker or series of corporate veils so impenetrable that I would never rend them to the point where I could see the Speaker himself.

At lunch in the town's new pride and joy, a Ramada Inn, I ate a club sandwich and drank a heavy milk shake in the "Renaissance Room." It was filled with copies of British, Dutch, and Florentine landscapes. I started to sneer at the pretensions, but I remembered the Kansas hostess for Betty Page who had caught me up on Rossetti.

I tried again to think how I could find out who Kitticon represented as trustee. After bolting the lunch, I went to the motel's phone and called our stringer in Topeka.

"How the hell do you find out who a lawyer is trustee for?"

"Where are you?" he said, worried.

"Look, I'll personally telegraph you the story if I ever get it done. You can break it at the same time as the *Eagle*. Okay? You're making me nervous with that eternal whine in your voice."

"I'm sorry," he said. "It makes *me* nervous for you to be out here. I keep thinking you're going to turn up something I should have."

"I hope I will. Just consider that you were never given the time to look," I said. "It will make you feel better. It may be your paper is happier that you don't slash up all the local dignitaries anyway." I made up my mind to try to get the *Eagle* to hire this guy. He was the kind of neurotic worrier we needed.

"There's no way," he said. "The only obligation is

that he must declare the trusteeship on his taxes if there's any income from it for him. And when he assumes the trusteeship, it's made public record only if it's for an estate or something else that has to be done in open court."

I told him what my problem was.

"You think he's the trustee for the Speaker."

"Or something like that," I said.

"Can you get his federal tax stuff?"

"I doubt it. Can you get his state tax stuff?"

"No, it's tightly held."

"Any other public filings? States securities com—" The first syllable was only out of my mouth when I thought of where I could try. "Securities and Exchange Commission!" I said loudly. "Listen," I said, "thanks a lot. See you."

I went back to the courthouse. I took down all the Kitticon holdings, then I checked the deeds for the Speaker's own home in Petrie. It looked all on the up-and-up, with a standard mortgage. By that time, the clerk of court was sniffing around. He was a pallid old man the color of the yellowing writs he catalogued and filed.

"You from Wichita?" he asked agreeably.

"No, sir," I answered.

"Kansas City?"

"No," I replied.

"Can we help you?" he went on.

"No, the ladies here have been fabulous. Their files, your files, are in beautiful shape." I felt like a gynecologist must feel when he pronounces a set of ovaries particularly healthy.

"What kind of research do you do?" the persistent old prick went on. I knew now I was talking to a political patronage appointee of long and dedicated standing. The women, who, in a nicer way, had also been inquisitive, were listening to see whether I would break on their boss's gentle rack.

"Real estate, mostly," I said. That had been apparent from the time I had spent on land indexes and deeds. I wondered whether he was aware of the two harmless suits filed in connection with the Speaker that I had had to request by number from his clerks. One was a debt suit filed by him, another against him, a tort suit involving an injury on his property. If the women had checked the titles of the suits, which they would have, they would have seen what they needed to know.

The old bird was getting cross. I had made it tough for him.

"See you requested two suits touching on Speaker Edwards."

"That so?" I inquired, getting my papers together. I did not want to spend any more time in Petrie now.

"You with the government?" he asked.

"Not in the usual sense of the word," I hedged.

"Not CIA, are ya?" He laughed. I smiled.

"Thanks for the help," I said to the ladies. They were looking at me dourly now, who had been so friendly before. The rooster crowed; the hens cackled.

Well, I thought, good-by, Petrie. I wanted to get back to Wichita fairly fast. Small towns being what they were, the clerk might have the local cops bust me on a cheap traffic offense just so they could find out who I was and report it to the Speaker.

The clerks watched me leave. I could feel their eyes like small bullets hitting my back. Sure enough, a municipal cop car picked me up, moving up fast as I left town. But I stayed five miles under the limit, making a show of taking down his plate number as he trailed me back onto the interstate.

The policeman did not stop me. I assumed he had merely taken the tag number. By the time I turned the car in at Wichita, the leasor would be giving me a funny look. The Petrie cops would have called to find out my name and everything else on my leasee forms. A few minutes later, the Speaker's local "ole boy" in Petrie would know my vitals and would be calling Hedaris in Washington or the Speaker's campaign chief in Wichita if he couldn't get the maximum Brownie point effect by reaching Hedaris.

"Fuck 'em," I said aloud as I drove again through that great, flat land. Fuck 'em. America, I love you, but you have got some Fascist overtones. Still, pulling in at the rent-a-car office, seeing the leasor's face dart from the glassed doorway, I thought, I would do the same thing. In effect, I was doing the same thing. It was the same cops-and-robbers game: It only depended on point of view as to who was the cop and who was the robber.

I checked out of the Holiday Inn, whose address appeared on the rental form for the car, walked a block with my bag, and caught a cab to another equally anonymous, new, and clean motel. Why risk a bag job or a tap if I could avoid it so easily? I registered under a fake name this time.

I called the *Eagle*'s business editor who stayed close to the Securities and Exchange. He was already home and feeling guilty about it. Thank God, because he was a grump.

"It's a big favor," I warned him. "A big, big favor."

"What is it?" he said warily. His main job was to make up the business page with its maddening collection of stock tables, one-column cuts of businessmen, straight news, columns from outside, tiny and large ads (many of them dangerous because they might contain illegal security claims), and three-line fillers. He was sickeningly probusiness.

I told him I wanted him to pull a string at the Securities and Exchange to find out whether Kitticon had ever made a filing and thus had been obligated to list *all* his business interests. The SEC was lovely on that sort of thing, but highly secretive except for what was ruled necessary for a prospectus. I liked the SEC and was sorry I had never developed any sources there I could truly call on.

"That stuff is in the prospectus," he said.

"Sometimes," I said. "But you have got to get somebody to run the guy's name through a computer to find out what prospectus it's in." He said he didn't know that.

"They don't like to do that for a reporter," I said. "It smacks of Brave New World. But it's a very fine computer." Brent, at the FBI, had got something out of it for me, once, in more halcyon me-FBI days.

"I'll try," he said. That meant he wouldn't do it. I played a cruel, wild card.

"Look, I have to have it. If you can't do it, I'll call Cubbins and see if anybody else will." That meant Cubbins would call him and ask him why he wouldn't do it, and that would reinforce with Cubbins, a powerful man on the paper, the fact of his probusiness attitude. He caught on.

"Okay," he said. Now I could be honest.

"I also need what's not in the prospectus," I said. "I want to know mostly about any operations he's a trustee for."

"That's impossible," he said. "They can't legally give out that information."

"I need it," I said. "There's no place else to get it. I need it by noon tomorrow when I call you, okay?"

"Is it that important?" I could feel him thinking about how he would have to put the arm on some golfing buddy, some social friend, and how that friend would recognize that good ole business editor was just like all the rest of those snoopy, suspicious reporters.

"Yes," I said. "If I could do it myself I would. Instead I have to call on you which is uncomfortable for both of us. I'm sorry. But it's that important."

"Okay, Aubrey," he said, resigned.

I left my fake name, "Mr. Pantoum," and the new motel name at Betty Page's room number in the Holiday Plaza, musing that I would soon be running out of instantly recognizable fake names. She called about nine.

"I'm in Petrie," she said. "I gather you were down here. I called the hotel and got your note."

"Oh?" I said, fascinated and a bit pleased.

"Pom asked me what you were doing here. And I said I didn't know. Do you want to tell me what you were doing here?"

"You don't have any crazy vow to tell him, do you?"

"No, of course not," she said a bit sharply. "If I had I would tell you, wouldn't I?"

"Yes," I said. "I'm trying to tie him to some land deals with Kitticon. Know anything about them?"

She paused. I half-wished I hadn't asked her. But it could save me much time.

"Yes," she said quietly. "But I don't know how they've got it working. He gets a lot of money from it." She stopped. "I feel like an informer or a spy," she said.

I was excited by what she told me, but upset at what she felt. She was right. It was improper, unethical really, for her to be going night and day to get that totem pole prick elected, and then for me to ask her to help get him defeated.

"I think you should stop working for him," I told her. "That's the sickest part of it. You could just tell him he's a shit and that you love me and I love you and that if it means blowing him out of the water, then you are going to blow him out of the water. Tell him he has it coming."

"I can't do that," she said, and, of course, she could not.

"I shouldn't ask you questions about him," I conceded with a sigh. "It's a mess."

And it was. There had been an element of alienation in our talk, and well there might be. Both of us were doing something dishonest, something that each recognized was unfair to the other. Afterward, I loved her a little less and knew she felt that way about me. There had been those kinds of times between my wife and me, I thought. And it was then that we had talked of leaving each other.

That night I computed what Kitticon had paid for the properties he held in trust, the profits he had made on those he had sold, and made a crude estimate of what the ones still held in trust were worth. It added up to about $2 million to $3 million in property for which $800,000 had been paid. In addition: as trustee, he had already taken $960,000 in profits over the last decade. That was almost a million in hard-cash profits and way over a million on paper.

If that kind of money had been going into the Speaker, as Betty Page believed, it would explain his big house in Wesley Heights and his general affluence.

With money coming in at other times from Big Oil and such deals as he and Kitticon had going at Boles-Panjunk, Edwards was a rich man.

But how to prove it? The land was where the money was, and it was precisely that which he did not have to report to the House. Even if the "trust" that Kitticon presided over as trustee was really a partnership, say, between the Speaker and Georgie Hedaris, still the House need not be told. He could get around it.

Only the IRS would know and the Kansas tax people. I had to assume he would not chisel on his taxes in a land matter. On Boles-Panjunk, maybe, but not on land which left behind so many records.

After breakfast, I looked at some of the Wichita properties. All were improved with apartment houses and stores and office buildings. Their owners must have leased the land long-term from Kitticon as trustee, and I suspected they would know who really owned the land beneath their investments.

At eleven-thirty I called our business editor and he had the information for me. Kitticon was the trustee for the Wichita Landmark Trust. That's all they had and it was in a public file on a filing he had made as an officer and major shareholder in a parcel-delivery corporation that had been set up and failed. It was nice to know that something of Kitticon's didn't turn into gold. The business editor had been acute enough to look into the other officers, directors, incorporators, and whatnot in the parcel outfit. None touched the Speaker that I could see.

All I'd have to find out now was who was the Wichita Landmark Trust. I plodded around the courthouse, feeling like a familiar. No record on it anywhere, not among the suits for and against, nor as an incorporated entity in the Corporation files. I called the Secretary of State's office in Topeka. No record.

Goddamnit, I thought, it's bad enough for a court to let a deed be registered just in the name of a trustee without naming the trust. Still, doggedly, I bumbled along. Land left records. It always did. And if there were a record, I'd find it. I got our stringer to check his and the Wichita papers' morgues. Still no soap. But it gave me an idea.

"You know the name of a seedy Topeka land broker?" I asked him.

"You've decided to stay?" he said a little testily.

"Look," I said, knowing how glad he would be when I went home, "get me the name and bill Mihalik $25 for 'special assistance.' I want somebody who would make an inquiry for me and not ask too many questions about why he's doing it."

He was back in an hour with the name and I called the guy blind, saying I was a real estate man from Pennsylvania and was interested in a property in Wichita where a client firm could open up a Midwestern branch office.

I gave him the address of the newish office building on one of Kitticon-Wichita Landmark Trust's properties. No, I said, I distinctly did not want any Wichita people in on the deal. My client wanted a reasonable price and if local people knew the name of the client it would go sky high. I would want him to handle the deal. His name had been given me by friends as a discreet businessman, I said, and both a finder's fee and commission would be his when we closed the deal. We didn't talk cash, but I was imperious enough to make him feel there would be good money there.

What I wanted as a first step was the name of all persons with a share in the building and the land. And I wanted it fast, I told him. Yes, he could consider himself retained. I gave him my phony name Pantoum and the hotel number and, as a reference, my brother's name and the respectable old manufacturing firm in Philadelphia he worked for.

"That is the man in the client firm I am working with," I said, "*if* you need references. I would insist that you and I deal directly, however. The name is *only* for reference."

That was the sort of talk I knew he would understand. He would think I was protecting my own cut of the action and probably would not call Philadelphia. But I called my brother quickly and told him what I was up to. He was huffy about it as I expected.

"Please, Arv," I whined, "you just have to say that you know me and that my credentials and bank situation are substantial. Now that's true enough. I never borrow money."

"Yes, but indirectly it sounds as if the company is endorsing you, and by a phony name. Your sucker gets the switchboard, hears the firm named, and assumes I'm speaking for the firm."

"Fuck," I said, losing my temper. "Then tell him you don't know your own Goddamn brother." He was two years younger than I and we loved each other, but we always fought.

"Now don't start that," he said calmly.

"No, I mean it. Just screw it!"

"Oh, shut up, Aubrey," he said. "I'll tell the man I've known you for years and your credit is sound but that I am not speaking at this time for the firm."

I was soothed and ashamed that I had shouted at him. "I'm sorry, Arv. I know I shouldn't do this, but I need it badly. Honest."

"When will you be up to see us?" he said, and then it was all right again, or as all right as it ever is between brothers who went different ways.

When the man called back, he was guarded. But I smelled it was from a sense that there was money to be made rather than from any loss in my credibility.

"My associate insisted I call your reference," he said. "Your contact at the company said he could not speak officially for the firm." The real estate man was trying to get me on the defensive fast.

"Did you expect him to just tell you he was about to sign a multimillion dollar deal for a new branch office, just like that, just out of the blue?" I hottened up. "I thought you were supposed to be discreet."

"I had to call," he said stiffly. "He gave you a good reference."

"You're fucking 'A' he did," I said, leaving the implication that dear old Arv was going to get some kick-back action, too. I could almost hear the lip-smacking on the other end.

"I have the information. Shall I bring it to Wichita?" He had nostrils full of money smell and he wanted to get closer to old Mother Lode Aubrey.

"No," I said. "The damn thing's delicate and I need it now. Besides, I will be frank. I am not happy with you knowing the name of the company involved."

"I understand," he said. "We are talking about a standard 5 per cent commission on the gross, are we not?"

"We are talking about 3 per cent," I said, "assuming the deal goes through. I estimate the land for about $200,000 and the building about $800,000, so I am talking about $30,000 for you just for a few hours negotiations and then the closing. That is, if they'll sell at our price."

"Let's say that's okay tentatively," he said. "If it takes more, I can let you know."

"Who are the owners? Go slow," I said.

He gave me the name of the office building owners just as I had it and then the land, "N. Kitticon, trustee for Wichita Landmark Trust. They own a lot of cats-and-dogs stuff around the state. The office building's land is one of their better properties."

"Who *is* Wichita Landmark Trust?" I asked. "What is a trust doing with a batch of landholdings? I mean one estate maybe, but—"

"No, no," he pacified me. "It's fairly common out here. The land trust is actually just a dodge, a legal dodge to shield the owner."

"Shield 'em? Who are they, the Mafia or something?"

"No, man," he said. "The Wichita Landmark profits go into a couple of family trusts, ordinary families, I mean. They are the beneficiaries of the Wichita Land-mark Trust."

"What families?" I asked, trying to sound suspicious. This was where I was going to get my "yes" or "no." "I told you I needed the whole ownership picture."

"I got it for you, Mr. Pantoum," he said. "The two

family trusts are the Edwards and the Parian Family Trusts."

I involuntarily inhaled, shielding the noise of it from the phone with my hand.

"Who are they, any idea? I'm worried about this trust business."

"No worry, no worry," he said. "I don't know who they are. Just local people. I got this stuff from a little girl in the city real estate office who just reads it off verbatim from the confidential files. She doesn't know anything. Just that they're local people."

"Well, who are the trustees for the two *family* trusts?" I asked. "Did that show up?"

"Two banks. Both of these trusts are subordinated to the Wichita Landmark Trust."

"What banks?"

"Wichita Prudent Savings and First Kansas Farmers. The last was for the Parian bunch, the first, for the Edwards."

"And you don't know who the families are?"

"No," he said. "There are Edwardses all over the state and a few Parians. The biggest Parian was a lieutenant governor about ten years ago and brokers corn now. A millionaire or better."

The Topeka chiseler was remarkable. He should have been a reporter. On one swoop he had gotten everything I needed.

"Now lay low," I said. "I want to check this out very carefully. I don't like the idea of the trusts and the banks and all that." I wanted now to ease out of it in such a way that he would not screw up my brother.

"You've spent good time for me," I said. "I want to have a small fee on the way to you tonight. Can I include $25 or $50 for the City Hall girl?"

"No," he said, knowing that this meant at least $250 for him for his one phone call to her and the one call to me. But I could feel the greed in him for the bigger deal that he must now sense I was worried about.

"I'll take care of her," he said smugly. "When will I hear from you?"

"Within two days is my best guess," I said.

Now I was sure, but I still had to prove it beyond a doubt.

Edwards, it was clear, had a fat trust set up that could be dissolved at any time by Kitticon, the trustee, who could then give Edwards whatever Edwards wanted. The interest from the trust would be what Edwards used ad interim. And that interest would be substantial, not just from the land, but from whatever else went into the trust.

I was excited over my discovery, but now I had to get the bank to admit that it had an Edwards Family Trust and that it was the Pomery Edwards and not old John Doe Edwards. I went down to the bar to get a stiff drink and to think.

Ignoring the fact that it would call attention to me, I asked for a Galliano and brandy on the rocks and when they didn't have Galliano I ordered brandy and Strega.

It tasted sweet and exhilarating and I wanted Betty Page or Connie there to brag a little about my ingenuity. I had to remember, too, to get an anonymous money order for $250 off to the real estate man.

Well, I thought, looking around the near empty bar, here is what I can do: I can call the bank's trust department and say I want the trust officer handling the family trust of Pommery Edwards. Bold, outright. But I had to have an identity that would get me immediate action from a suspicious banker.

I could get Mr. March to get some banker friend of his to call. But why get Mr. March into it with his potential for eccentricity? I could pose as a federal investigator. But impersonating a federal agent was a crime and I didn't need any more of those.

I picked up my drink and went to the pay phone in the bar and called the bank. I asked for the trust department and when the secretary came on, I said I was calling from San Francisco. She commented on the clear connection and I drew back from the telephone a bit.

"This is Mr. Aubrey," I told her stiffly. "I handle certain matters for Bounty Oil." That was honest enough, in its way. "I'd like the trust officer who handles the Pommery Edwards Family Trust." The girl went off the line and in a minute a firm, suspicious voice came on.

"This is Mr. Laurie, can I help you?"

"Aubrey here," I said briskly. "I work on some of the Bounty Oil matters. In Mr. Quiven's office." True again. Fuck 'em, it was all true with a vengeance. But I was nervous.

"Yes, sir," said Laurie, nothing daunted.

"The Speaker probably has called you," I said, risking all.

"No, sir," said Laurie, softening. I could feel him thinking, "Did the Speaker call and was I out to lunch or home early or did the message not get to me?"

"You are the Laurie who handles the Edwards Family Trust, aren't you?" I asked.

"Yes, sir." The middle-level Wichita banker began to yield fractions to the San Francisco tycoon's factotum. I lowered my voice.

"Mr. Quiven of Bounty Oil has asked me to reach you." Well, that was a lie, which I did not like.

"Mr. Quiven?" he said nervously.

"This is the trust officer for Speaker Pommery Edwards' Family Trust, is it not?" I asked, feigning sudden caution on my own part.

"Why, yes, sir," he said. "But hadn't you better get the Speaker to—?" I hung up and gulped down the rest of the sweet strong liquor.

"Roll dem presses," I said to myself. "Aubrey Reporter has struck again."

There was still cleaning up to do.

Kitticon didn't return my call, but to my surprise the Speaker did. It was late afternoon. I lay on the soft, wide bed.

"Just got your call," he said. "How are you, Aubrey?" Not a trace of rancor in his voice, although he knew I was trying to demolish him and was making some headway. But then there wasn't any venom in my voice either, and he had tried to have me killed, or at least had left me open to being killed.

"Fine, Mr. Speaker."

"Working on me, I guess?" he said in those firm tones, so different from the petulant whine coming through his suite door three nights ago.

"Well, I was down covering the President's appearance and did scout around a bit," I hedged.

"What can I do for you?" he said, tiring of the bullshit. I wondered if he had been drinking, maybe even had a jolt or two to brace him for our talk.

"Shall I put it to you straight?" I asked.

"Sure," he said. I could hear him waiting, knowing that this one, whatever it was, could divebomb him out of the House, that now almost any big one could finish him.

"Do you want to talk about your land deals with Nicholas Kitticon?" I asked.

"You've got to be more specific than that, Aubrey."

"Nicholas Kitticon is the trustee for a property owner named Wichita Landmark Trust which in turn controls two more trusts, one of them the——?"

"I'd rather have you——" he cut me off.

If he could block my question, now that he knew what it was, it would make it harder for me to write that he had refused comment on any specifics.

Now, I cut him off. I wanted it on the record that I'd asked him the key question.

"The Edwards Family Trust, right?" I finished.

He was angered.

"I told you, Aubrey, to go through Hedaris. I want you to have a full chance to——"

"Who is Parian?" I interrupted again. I had nothing to lose.

"Goddamnit," he said, his voice louder. "You can call——"

"Is money from land deals——?" I recommenced.

But now he was almost beside himself. Something that must be in every politician came roaring out of him.

"No!" he shouted. "No!" There was honest anguish in it. A man against the wall, saying, "No! This far, no farther."

In a flash of memory, I recalled a funny, tough California Congressman who had confided to me he was quitting because he was sick of it. "And in the last few months I'm in the House, I'm going to start sending a wire to every one of those drying-up old Orange County kooks who keep bitching at me. And the wire is going to say, 'Fuck you. Detailed letter to follow.' "

"No!" the Speaker bellowed in the phone. "No!"

I was awed enough to shut up, if only to hear what he was going to say next. I surmised now he had some drink in him. In the wordlessness between us, I could hear him breathing hard, getting under control. When he did, he said in a low, tense voice simply this:

"How did you like jail, Aubrey?"

I was too stunned to answer him for a moment, which was all he wanted for an answer. Then he hung up.

I tried to chase down Betty Page, hoping I could be with her one more time before I left, yet also ready to get the hell out of Wichita, particularly with the Speaker's strange threat, if that was what it was, hanging over me.

But she was at another campaign tea. I suddenly resented the teas, the coffees, the bilge of her speaking for a cheap and discredited politician. I did not want to hurt her, or hurt myself with her, and so composed a half-dozen short cautious notes to leave at her hotel. Finally, I simply wrote, "Mr. Pantoum has gone home," and called it in to her hotel message box.

For days in Washington, I had dreamed of coming to Kansas and reporting all day and being with her all night. It hadn't happened that way, not from either of our faults.

I loved her, but circumstances had spread our love thin. I would be glad when November came.

I made my call on Edwards' opponent, Marthas, at his campaign headquarters just within the district on the outskirts of Wichita. He saw me in his cluttered office on the third floor of a shopping-center office building. The ex-State Attorney General looked like a young Victor Mature.

But up above the Ultra-Brite teeth, there were some

brains and cunning. He laid out the platitudes and the generalities, but if he knew anything about the Speaker's land and other deals, he wasn't telling me. He knew that if it ever got out that he had helped the eastern press put the gunpowder to Edwards, it would backfire and burn him up.

Maybe if he got desperate in the last days of the campaign, he would help a reporter. But it would be a Kansas reporter. I shook hands with him, a bit startled by how he was sweating, and caught the plane home.

Back in Washington, the Speaker's aide, Hedaris, gave me a predictable answer:

"We have been so harassed by the *Eagle* and Aubrey Warder's inaccurate, distorted, and outright false reporting, that we will decline in the future to answer their questions. In the past even our efforts to respond to their queries have been distorted."

Well, that was their prerogative.

By deadline, my story was in:

"Speaker Pommery Edwards has used secret financial trusts to amass a fortune from land deals in Kansas with the help of the brother-in-law of his most trusted aide.

"None of the hundreds of thousands of dollars in real and paper profits has been reported by Edwards to the House Ethics Committee as appears to be required by House rules.

"The complicated deal uses the cover of trust funds to make money.

"One is the Edwards Family Trust, an unregistered private fund whose trustee is the Wichita Prudent Savings Bank. An old family friend, former Kansas Lt. Gov. Marlow Parian, is proprietor of a second trust.

"These two trusts are controlled by still a third trust called the Wichita Landmark Trust. It, too, is unregistered, and its trustee is lawyer Nicholas Kitticon of Wichita. Kitticon's wife and the wife of George Hedaris, Edwards' administrative assistant, are sisters.

"Kitticon is the key mystery man in the deal.

"In Wichita and other Kansas towns, numerous pieces

of property are deeded to 'Nicholas Kitticon as trustee,' for the Wichita Landmark Trust.

"The value of this property is estimated at between $2 million and $3 million based on current prices for property in the area. It was bought for less than $1 million.

"Tax stamps and land records indicate that the Wichita Landmark Trust also already has made real profits of almost $1 million during the past ten years of buying and selling.

"These profits go into the two family trusts. There is no indication of how much Edwards has actually taken out of the funds or how much interest he has received over the years. But this interest is clearly substantial.

"Kitticon and Edwards refused any comment on the trusts and Parian would confirm only that he maintained a small trust fund for his family. Parian conceded he and the Speaker were old friends. Parian is now a wealthy grain broker."

Then I went on to describe in detail the earlier deal between Kitticon and Boles-Panjunk and the Speaker's role in it. There was no legitimate way that I could imply the Speaker was getting a big chunk of the land as a payoff from the Boles-Panjunk deal and perhaps other activities. But I thought maybe the conjunction of paragraphs would raise the question.

At the end I told about the FBI investigation which the FBI was doing everything it could to commit infanticide on. I also had a couple of paragraphs explaining why the Speaker should have reported the money to the House Ethics Committee. After all, he had been partly responsible for setting up the committee to monitor Congressmen's outside income.

All in all, it was a helluva lot better story than the one I had written on the FBI investigation. Still, it set up the inevitable reaction. Cubbins came out to my desk next morning wearing his it's-my-painful-duty face.

"Mr. March feels we look like we're conducting a vendetta against Edwards," said Cubbins. "We aren't, but he feels we look like it."

"I was wondering when this would happen," I said. "Don't tell me the rest. We aren't going to do any more stories on the f'ing Speaker unless it's the one that blows him out of the water. Mr. March has gone flat, right?"

Cubbins, who had come to me proud of being the direct emissary from Mr. March, was now softening toward his better self, the newspaperman he was at his best.

"It makes me uncomfortable, too," he said. "The new story was a good story."

"Yes," I said, "and I had to bribe a real estate man with $250 in *Eagle* money to get it."

"I don't want to know," he sighed.

"So what now?"

"Have you got anything good enough to polish him off?"

"No," I said. I was furious. "Why the hell does this always happen?" I had seldom liked Cubbins more. He looked around as if he feared Mr. March might be listening.

"Because the *Eagle* conceives of itself as having a mission," Cubbins said. "Because we put on the hair shirt to be fair. Look, it doesn't mean we won't do another story, just that it has to be a very big story."

"Don't explain," I said gloomily. "This was a fine story. I ought to quit. Working for that erratic madman wears on a person. I get tired of beginning to grind down the crooks, and then somebody says back off, we're not being fair. You know there might be a Pulitzer in this."

Cubbins laughed harshly. He felt he had commiserated enough. Now it was time to get on with putting out a paper.

"You can still putter with it," he said. "There's something else I wanted you to be the first to know."

Well, I thought, what turkey is this going to be?

"The Speaker's wife is running quite a campaign for him down there. I don't know if you picked it up?"

"Humm," I said neutrally, my heart suddenly beating faster. What the hell was up?

"She's doing a sort of modified women's lib thing, even disagreeing with him on some issues, but saying that he is the sort of man who comes around, listens to people. Good national feature. She's a good-looking broad." Amen, I thought.

"So Connie March is going down to do a feature piece or two on her campaign."

Jesus, I thought, what next in my nutty life? I parried with suitable sourness.

"To show how fair we are to Edwards by kissing his wife's ass," I said. "Why Connie? She's cityside."

"Why not Connie," said Cubbins. "She writes well enough. And there's a poetic justice in it. It was Speedy's idea, not mine. Besides," he said, "Mrs. Edwards sounds like what Connie might have been if she'd been born twenty years earlier."

Well, I thought, it may be logical to Cubbins and poetic justice to Speedy Milhalik, but it was irony for me, and chilly irony at that. Also Cubbins was wrong about Connie being a young Betty Page. "*Merde*," I said and turned away.

Here was the kind of bullshit that reporters put up with and that never made the papers. I remembered thinking once, in my cityside days, that the actual reporting of a story took only 40 per cent of my time; the rest went toward contriving ways to get the story in the paper.

I had been at the *Eagle* long enough to know that Mr. March had acted on some impulse or as a result of a call from a friend. Moreover, the fanciful old fuck probably did not mean entirely what he had told Cubbins to tell me.

As I always did, I pondered quitting, but sighed. Even the image of an open, howling resignation scene had paled after so many revivals in my mind. I looked up from my low-grade self-pity as Connie came to my desk.

"You've heard?" she said more hesitantly than was her way. She wanted me to tell her what I knew about Betty Page from my days down there. I was touched, thrilled a little by the danger and deception of it, and somewhat uncomfortable.

Like so many feature writers, Connie was unsure of her reporting, the actual gathering of the facts as opposed to the writing of them.

An old night city editor, gone years ago now, had said of my copy when I was on the police beat:

"There are reporters and there are rewrite men." What he meant was that I would never be much of a writer. But what he also meant was that rewrite men were different, were not reporters. There are bright chinks of insecurity in men whose only job is to rewrite the copy of other men. They are always called on to make it read a little better and there are more drunks among rewrite men than among reporters.

Feature writers fall in between and that morning the chinks showed in Connie. She was wearing a dress instead of slacks. It made her look particularly vulnerable what with those thin, nicely muscled, almost adolescent legs showing and the seemingly flat chest beneath the demure print.

She sat by my desk in the single chair each of us had, like cops in squad rooms. She'd brought over a cup of coffee for me. It was morning, the tempo of the gigantic city room was largo. With so much hectic activity behind me in Kansas, the President, the crazy Speaker all but revealing he had gotten me jailed, my frustration with Betty Page, there was something homeportish about sitting in the city room and talking with Connie March.

She was wonderfully intuitive about news, and even people, and I worried that I might give away my affair with Betty Page. She was young enough to ask the blunt question. Betty Page was old enough to know there are some questions just better unasked, better left hanging in the limbos, the empty spaces, of every relationship.

I told Connie first about Kansas, about the Speaker's drinking and his efforts to overcome it. I talked a little about Dennis Marthas, the former attorney general, a gutfighter who in the end would try to push Edwards to the wall on corruption.

She nodded gratefully, and I felt valuable and useful in her eyes.

Lately, I told her, the papers had shown a little more guts, and had nipped at the Speaker just as if he were any other cheap chiseler, and had found his blood tasted just like that of the local conniving probate judge.

Connie made no notes about what I said. But I could see her computerizing it in her head and I was flattered. She pursed her lips to blow slightly across the coffee. I thought of how I would like to get her in bed before she left for Kansas. She was so sleek and so adept. And how many more years of either screwing or reporting did I have left? Did I dare ask her to come see me that night? I passed the impulse.

As to Edwards' wife, I went on, I had met her a couple of times at parties. I reminded myself I must be sure to call Betty Page and think up some reason why I should tell her to be cautious with Connie. Betty Page would not be indiscreet under any circumstances. For one thing it would be suicidal. But Connie was so fast.

From what I recalled, I told Connie, she was tough— she would have had to be, married all these years to Edwards—and bright and had a slightly intellectual reputation.

"Does she play around?" Connie asked, looking up from her coffee. I felt a grab in my stomach. Watch out! I thought.

"Don't know," I said. "Never heard anything one way or the other. He does."

"Bet she does, too," Connie went on.

I changed the talk to her campaign style which, so far as I knew, I said, consisted of these earnest talks at coffee and small groups about more freedom, always within the family structure, of course, for women.

At the end of it, Connie asked me bluntly, "Are they sending me down there because my father is going through one of his we've-got-to-be-fair episodes?"

"Well, that's why we're doing a *feature* on Mrs. Edwards. I think they're sending you because you write good features." I paused, looking at the earnest brown eyes. I figured, hell, I may be working for her one day and I certainly intend to go to bed with her one time before I marry Betty Page, if I marry her, forsaking all others. Therefore, I thought, this is no time to lie to Connie. So I added, "It may be that you're going because you're your father's daughter and they're playing some little Byzantine game."

"Okay," she said, badly hurt that I had confirmed to her that perhaps she was being used. "Okay on that. But if my father weren't Bertie March, would my being assigned to this be within the range of potential assignments that I would have been given? No bullshit, now."

I thought a minute.

"Possibly," I said. I breathed deeply, and went on, "Will you come to my apartment when you get back?"

Connie gave a start at the suddenness of it. She looked at me and I felt she was weighing how old I was and something more. For some reason, since I had been in jail, we had been staying away from each other. It was partly, I saw, because now it would not be just a jingle. Dreiser talked about love being a kind of chemistry, and I tended to believe him. Clearly, now, some kind of chemical thing was happening between Connie and me. When she told me in the hospital that she loved Mark Braswell, something had begun catalyzing.

What she had said then, I now recognized, was not just "I love Mark Braswell," but, "If I stop being faithful to him so I can do what I want and go to bed with you, then it will be because I am going to stop loving him. And if I stop loving him, then I may fall in love with you." The thought sent a thrill of youthfulness through me.

"I'm trying to keep it all for Mark," she said. I looked at her now, really wanting her, wanting to touch her bony hips and softer thighs and forearms and to kiss her on the mouth and then wherever I could. How very damned young I felt, almost giddy.

"Maybe you ought to," I said with a little nervous croak in my voice. But she had recognized what I was thinking and the wires in her were beginning to short out. I could almost smell it.

"Maybe I should," she said. "I'm worried sick about doing this story right," she switched subjects purposefully.

"When are you going?" I said.

"This afternoon."

I knew that both Connie and I were wondering if we had time to get it on somewhere, maybe at lunch. But there was too much for her to do. She had to pull the clips. She had to pack. Besides, she was still worried about her first out-of-town big assignment.

The pregnant moment passed chastely.

"I'll be back in a few days," she said, her voice a bit dry now, too. "This isn't very smart," she ended.

I watched her, as she knew I would be watching her, walk across the city room. I thought of that lithe, young ass, the cleavage above the bikini pants, and the unexpected heavy, almost coarse brown nipples. I will have that, I thought.

Then, I thought, I must call Betty Page.

For a change, I was able to reach her. She was at campaign headquarters and had to talk softly. I told her about Connie coming to do a big feature on her and planning to follow her on an "average day."

"It could help if it's good and it's reprinted down here, you know," she mused.

"It'll be good," I said. "Anybody doing a fair job on you, it's bound to be good. And Connie is fair."

"What's she like?"

God, I thought, both sides of this hypocritical coin within an hour.

"Tough, bright, good writer, very fair."

"You sound like—"

"My God, Betty Page, she's only twenty-five or twenty-six or something. . . . She's also the publisher's daughter."

"That's a new catch," she said. "Why—"

"Well, maybe she would have gotten the assignment anyway, but old man March feels we've been too tough on the Speaker—"

"So his daughter is going to do a puff job on me—"

"No," I said, defensively. "If there were a place to get a knife into you, Connie would put it there. It'll be fair; therefore, it'll be good. Goddamnit," I said, feeling again her zest for the campaign, "you really do hope he wins, don't you? I mean, you told me you did, and I see now you really want him to win. You want a good *Eagle* story about you because it will help *him*."

"Yes," she replied. "Yes, I do. If only because I've put so much time into it. And it will be my way of paying him . . ."

She was starting that again.

"Yes," I said, "but don't you see that if he wins, I lose? I've done all these damned stories and if he wins, then my stories have lost. And now I can't even do any smaller stories, ones to chip away at him—just a big one, if I can get a big one."

"Aubrey," she said quietly, "please don't start talking about a campaign to purposely destroy him, as opposed to doing straight stories that might in the process destroy him. You'll be as bad in a way as he is."

I thought about that a moment. I knew she said it with love, if also with some wariness. But Goddamnit, why shouldn't I feel vengeful toward him? What was so bad about a newspaper vendetta if the object of it was a skunk?

"The fucker got me thrown in jail," I said irritatedly. "I'll blow him up on the sand any way I can."

She laughed, rising above it as I was unable to do.

"And in a sense now, you blow me up on the sand, too."

Instantly, I cooled down. Valiant, clean Betty Page.

"I'll drag you back off the sand and into deep water again," I said, not recognizing the pun until we had said good-by.

Three days later, Connie March called me from Wichita.

"I'm coming home tonight," she said.

"How was it?" In my imagination's quick study I saw not Betty Page, but Connie.

"Great, she's a great lady." Well, that I knew. "I'll

tell you about it when I get there." I felt the rush of anxiety and lust.

"When will you come by?"

"In the morning?"

"Why not tonight? Mark?"

"Yes," she said. "Is nine-thirty okay? Can you—?"

"Yes," I said. "God, yes."

I left that evening at six o'clock, to get the house cleaned up. I told Speedy Mihalik I wouldn't be in until noon next day. I had so much time Sweet Aliced that nobody really asked me about hours. The company was afraid I might ask compensation time and be off for six straight months. And the union feared it would have to censure me for failing to put in for over-time compensation days. That would be embarrassing to them.

After all, I had led the strike of '03 or whatever year it was when we got a "Guild Shop" clause in the contract.

On the way home, I bought flowers, mostly wild-flowers, to decorate the apartment. I had dressed up the Holiday Inn for Betty Page and she had not come. Now, I was doing the same thing for Connie March. Before, when she had come, it had been Moët et Chandon and it had all been experimental for us. Now, it was something different.

That night, the apartment clean, I tried to think about myself. Why was I so youthfully happy at the idea of having Connie March come to me when I was com-mitted to Betty Page? *Was* I committed to Betty Page? Goddamnit, she'd gone back to bed with that miserable, booze-filled tube of skin, her husband. Was I committed to anyone? Or simply to screwing, while there was time, and reporting?

The shadows marched across my room, as they had that night when I was in the hospital, as they had when I was a boy, lying frightened in my room sometimes, and sleepless. Had I always been this way? No.

In all those years with my wife, there had been strong, good solid love—when it had been good. We had liked each other, enjoyed it when we had traveled, she getting away from the speech clinic she ran and her work on her Ph.D., and me from the paper.

Then why had I not been faithful to her? Ah, what did it matter? I thought, with a dreadful, longing pang. She is dead.

And since then what? Reporting and screwing. Oh, I had dressed it up. I put the Mozart and Bach on the phono when I came home and let it play until I went to bed.

And when I could, I read before I dropped off to sleep, sometimes even the Bible and Shakespeare and from the Oxford books of English and of American poetry, which my wife had given me.

And the other things, dipping into the past for a snatch of Voltaire or into the present for a good female gig, like Barbara Raskin, or whatever new thing Updike or Barth might write or, rarely, non-fiction.

And some evenings, with a woman, or alone, I had gone to the Kennedy Center. But even there often I used my binoculars to ogle Salome's nipples or the upper thighs of the prima ballerina or the bounce to the tits of some aspirant in the corps de ballet.

Why had it come to this? The young fellow from Hamilton who had gone to Paris and tried halfheartedly to be Robert Lowell or Karl Shapiro or Tate or among that host of other medium-good poets. But I had chosen a second-best field. I had tried to tell Betty Page why it had happened and she had understood. Yet now, having found her, something was happening or about to happen with another woman.

I reached down and felt my limp organ. Soon, soon, I thought, seeing the slit of Connie March with its sparse hair and the chicken leg plumpness that creased in from the thighs.

But it wasn't just cunt. She was a person who respected me, even though she clearly saw me as I was. She venerated—I backed off from the word for a number of reasons, and substituted "idolized"—me. She saw in me the old woolly mammoth, outrun by a smoother new breed of rogue elephants. The old hairy beast of the Ice Age, trumpeting and bellowing there among the herds of young reporters, the Woodsteins and Marros and Cloherty-Owenses I had encountered on stories.

Aubrey Warder. Aubrey Reporter. It even sounded like an old winded mammoth's gravelly sad call. Bleat! Bleat! Bleat! And where in the name of God would this youngness I felt with Connie March ever get me? I thought, as I had before, at fifty-eight, she will only be thirty-six. At sixty-eight, forty-six. The last time I had thought it, the difference had seemed obscene. Now the gap seemed less great; we seemed more of an age.

My God, I imagined wildly, if I married her, old March, crazy man that he was, would feel he had to make me part of management. The prideful old monster could not have his son-in-law being bossed around by Cubbins and assigned by Speedy Mihalik to Secretary of Commerce luncheon speeches. Speedy Mihalik? Being Speedy's boss was enough to marry Connie for, I laughed. I could fire his ass.

A dream of Betty Page interposed:

"I am thy father's spirit, doomed for a certain term . . ." she seemed to say, only she was rushing in the door of my apartment in a midsummer linen dress, smelling of something fresh-flowery that cost much and that she would have just happened to have touched also to the inside of her thighs as a small joke.

"Hamlet's father?" she said, laughing with that slight grunty tone. "Are you crazy?"

But Betty Page was in Kansas. Again, my resentment stirred. Sleeping with Edwards! And she could have come back to Washington more often to see me. Even though I had gone all the way to Kansas, in part, to be sure to butcher her husband, she had only managed time to see me once. And she really *wanted* the man reelected who had jailed me and almost got me raped and killed, . . . really wanted him to win against stories I had written to bring about his defeat. I knew my resentment was unfair, but it was heavy enough to fight her from my mind. That way, I could think of Connie March coming here.

My sleepy mind drifted to fantasy again. Suppose I married her, I would stop working for Cubbins and

Mihalik. I would be an editor with a team of young investigative reporters whom I could train. I could be editor-in-chief later on, much later, when I finally conked out as a reporter, if I ever did, and my beautiful wife, Connie, would then be showing a little gray (she forty-six, me sixty-eight). And we would drink Bernkasteler Doctor Auslese and make occasional love and have very good seats at the Kennedy Center. I would get the Pulitzer for my . . . well, for something, and would be straight and heavy with honor among my colleagues as I walked through the city room of our thriving paper.

And shortly before I retired to fish and to dream over my grandchildren, to be respected by worshipful young reporters, all Galahads good and true, I would prove that I had not become stuffy like Cubbins. I would write a well put-together non-fiction work about all the good stories I had covered, and also about all the ones I had failed on, and about all the fine women I had fucked or tried to fuck. And in this deceit I fell asleep.

16

Connie

When Connie came in the apartment door, she seemed grown up. At first it did not hit me that she had arranged herself so by design. Her long hair was done up in a French twist and she wore a dress. It was light cotton, sort of Peck and Peckish, with a cap sleeve and a thin dagger throat line that plunged down to just above her breasts.

"Hi," she said bouncily. "I finished a first draft of my story last night on the plane, and I wonder—"

I was dressed in slacks and a sport shirt, feeling very uneasy in my role as wily old seducer. I had coffee and orange juice and apricot juice and even a melon ready as back-up troops.

"Sure," I said. "Absolutely." Reading her story was a way to break this awkwardness between us.

"I . . ." she began. And then I saw all the bounce was artificial. Her face turned plain, the animation that made it so pretty given over to fear. "I don't think it's very good, Aubrey," she said.

"Well," I said, "let's take a look."

She had a light calfskin briefcase, and she walked toward me with it in her hand, half held out. When she got to me she started to unzip it. She looked up at me now with that same worried look, only intensified.

"It's not good," she said.

335

"Then, we'll make it good," I said. "C'mon, show a little guts."

She dropped the briefcase on the floor and put her arms around my waist and I looked into the unprepossessing young face with its unhappiness at having failed. Then, gently, I kissed the fresh mouth, which seemed touchingly soft. Gone was the ardor of the efficient female animal she had been last time.

"Don't be so afraid," I told her. "Half the stories I've worked on I've screwed up one way or another. You've got enough notes?"

"Yes," she said. "With me."

"Then we can patch it up."

The tears ran into her lower lids.

"I hate to fail," she said.

"So do I," I said. "I do all the time."

"Would you like to go to bed first?" she said, a bit less wretchedly. I was surprised until I thought about it an instant.

Yes, I thought, I certainly do. I kissed her again and, out of gratefulness that I was going to save her, I guessed, she kissed me warmly and steadily, slipping her tongue tentatively between my lips.

Here, at least, she was on her home field. By comparison with her previous near rape of me, she was surprisingly docile. Her dress unzipped easily at the side and I reached inside and touched her bare skin there at the waist. While before, she had reached for me like a monkey for a banana, she did no more than pull my hardening loins into her stomach.

"Come," I said, and took her hand and led her into the bedroom. I sat on the bed as she pulled the dress carefully over her head and then turned so I could unsnap her bra.

"This is new equipment," I said of the bra, then was upset for being what might seem indelicate. Her little bottom was just as I had imagined it above the cotton pants. I slipped them from her body and she stepped out, then took off her sandals, and started unbuttoning my shirt. Her breasts with their dark quarter-circum-

ferenced centers dangled over me, and I took them
gently in my hands.

"Beautiful," I said. "You're beautiful."

"No," she said.

I finished undressing and crawled into bed with her
and she kissed me and pulled me atop her and reached
to where my cock should have been. But I was barely
alive.

"Don't panic," I thought. Don't! But in such cases
the imperative is invariably the passive voice. I was
suddenly a noodle. Connie saw what was happening
and tried womanfully to caress me into a suitable condition. I kissed her and she gently kissed back, then tried
more passionate kisses and more vigorous massages.

But it was no go.

"Now," I said, trying to be funny, but sounding
hollow, "you see what failure is."

"Is it me?" she asked.

"No, baby." But now she was on top of me, gently
rubbing to and fro. "It's me."

"There's nothing wrong? Last . . ."

I was afraid she was asking me if I were getting old.
I wanted desperately to assure her that I had performed
three times in four swift hours only a few days ago with
the very subject of her Kansas interviews . . . but instead, "I've always had this element of unpredictability,"
I said with embarrassment. "I'm surprised no one told
you," I said wryly, thinking of some of my other egre-
gious flops with her older colleagues in the Washington
press corps.

She chuckled a bit at that.

"Is there anything I can do?"

"Well," I said, "to be exact, the best thing is for me
to stop thinking about how awful I feel about failing."

"It's my fault for talking about failing when I came
in," she said with, I felt, considerable generosity, and
perhaps truth.

"Any little thing puts me off," I said. "I feel like the
Wizard of Oz when they pulled the screen back."

"Ah, not to worry," she said. "It will come back."

Just at that moment I had been relaxing into the state where I felt I could get erect. Her assurances undid me again.

"You liked her?" I said of Betty Page. She fell in easily.

"Yes. Can I get us some coffee?"

We lay in the double bed, our coffees on the night tables, sipping and talking, still naked. I looked over at her and she smiled back.

"Well," she said, "I don't feel so nervous any more."

"Me neither," I sighed. "I wonder why I am this way."

I had doped it out hundreds of times. It had something to do with my mother's hints about the hazard of sex which were so vague I could never grab at them and strangle them. I knew that it went back that far. But I couldn't thoroughly define it and thus I could not eradicate it.

"Don't you know?" she asked.

"Something about my mother," I spoke from my musing. "I just don't know what."

"Pop is my hang-up," she said.

"Surprise, surprise," I said and we laughed.

"So how was she?" I said, coming again back to Betty Page. It was odd that I felt no guilt about lying here in bed with a young rival. Part of my lack of shame was the burnt offering I had made to Betty Page of my initial impotency with Connie.

"You'd like her if you knew her," she said innocently. "Once published some poems, French translations." Funny, I thought, that Connie would alight first on that. "One kid at home, another off to college. Won't even talk about Edwards' drinking. Not a single disloyal word on him. But you feel she is moving away from him. I saw them together at some afternoon barbecue.

"He does the big political thing, you know, pride-in-the-wife shining out of his eyes when she's around for the handshaking. But once I caught a look in his eye as he just glanced at her among some women. Looked at her like she was a rubber duck. The only thing he was thinking was that she might be lining up a couple of votes for him."

Well, I thought, that's the way they all are, politicians. To them, women are things that vote and fuck in that order. Politicians are worse than I am, I consoled myself. At least I love women.

"She's saying all the low-key feminist stuff, still pretty advanced for out there: second careers, share the housework, joint tenancy for all stocks."

"What does Edwards think of it?" I asked, wondering how Connie had perceived it.

"What can he say? He gave me twenty minutes. Knew we were doing a favorable piece on her. Why couldn't I make it fall together, I wonder?"

"Don't worry," I said. "It may be fine and even if it isn't, we've got all day to patch it."

She crossed her legs sedately at the ankles and took a draught of the coffee, her mind on how it had been in Kansas, lost in the recounting of the story. I looked down at my graying chest, and on to my poor crippled member. Reporting is an odd community, I thought: me in bed with my publisher's daughter.

"What he *says*," Connie went on, "is that he thinks it's great for her to be part of the women's movement during the last quarter century of the second millennium, or some such drossy bull. He's all for her boosting equal rights and thinks there's a lot to them . . . in moderation, and et cetera."

"And," I added, "he will defend to the death her right to say it." Both of us rebelled at the purity of the cynicism of politicians talking about their wives. Her rebellion came out a bit more raucously.

She stood up on the bed, her head almost touching the ceiling.

"He takes Betty Page's rights to be self-evident," she said, erect as a stiff orator in a junior high play. "That all men and women are created unequal. Yassuh!" she said. Now her high spirits were taking hold.

She saluted the wall, her arm lifting her breast even as Betty Page's had been lifted when she combed the sunlight through her hair. I felt a momentary qualm at the recollection.

"Hup, two, three, four," she said, now gripped with the mimicry of militancy. "We shall not be moved," she said, and began to march in place on my bed. I quickly put my coffee on the night table to avoid its being jousled onto the clean sheets.

"For God's sake, Connie," I said.

"Give me some men," she started singing in her pipey voice, then switched to still another parody:

"Give me some men who are Hamilton men," she sang,

"And I'll get you ten girls from Skidmore."

I struggled to my feet on the boucing bed. My God, here she was singing a bawdy Hamilton College drinking song. I joined in the marching, my old flesh flopping beside her fine, young breasts.

"Cornell is colder and Harvard is bolder," we chanted, marching along.

"Hamilton men always score."

She laughed and kicked her feet out, doing a trampoline sit on the bed. I toppled beside her already in a sweat. Her body was slick with it.

"I never knew you went to Hamilton," she said.

"Did you go to Skidmore?"

"Yep," she said. "Sure did."

She kissed me now seriously.

"Want to try one?"

"One what?"

"One Skidmore girl."

From the heavy kiss, which would almost certainly have sent me into the purdah of impotency again, she pulled her lips away slightly, brushing them now gently. The dampness of her back and her buttocks was arousing. Ah, I thought, now maybe.

The stoutness was beginning in my groin and she must have noticed for she reached down ever so lightly and touched the eye of my penis. Then, she ran her fingers under the glans, pulling back the foreskin gently, fondling my balls and then moving her finger with the faintest of traceries back along its path.

I slipped my own fingers now behind her and into her vagina which was also moistening and held the lips gently between my fingertips, running them back and forth as if I were carefully creasing paper. "Yowwee," she murmured and she bucked against my touch, already hotter than I. Don't fade, I said to myself, and wavered slightly.

She must have felt it, for she stopped touching me and took my fingers in hers, moving my hand around to the front of her. She arched her knee, opening her vagina and took my two forefingers between the lips, pressing them lightly against her clitoris, a hard little pea. I knew that she meant to come now whether I was along or not. Actually, it was something of a relief to me. So I tweaked and pulled at the hard little organ, lubricating it with the oozings of her vagina. It felt great and she closed her eyes, concentrating entirely on my touches.

As I masturbated her, she reached, found my thigh and moved her hand up to where my touching her had gotten me hard. With a twist of her body, still without letting my hand stop, she moved her head to where she could mouth me and I thought, well, this is the next best thing to heaven. I had wanted to screw her a long time now, and I looked down at the serpentine curve of her body, the breasts firm and rounded even though she was half on her back and the tautness of her muscles straining for an orgasm.

"Get it in there," she urged in a hurried way. "Get it in there, it's important."

I wheeled over her and eased my slightly overripe erection into her, dropping my fingers away as the underside of my penis first creased upward, missing her vagina. Then I pushed the head of it down across her clitoris, slipped into her vagina, and pushed my groin hard against where I had spread open the labia.

That should do it, I thought with inappropriate satisfaction at my handiwork. Neatly joisted! But there was no further time for any thoughts at all. The effect of this cockmanship was to set her to bucking again against my groin, grinding and writhing with great intakes of breath for such a slender body: OH-ah; OH-ah; OH-ah. "Hurray," I thought. I came with dispatch and great enjoyment, but more with pride that I had finally connected with near perfection after such a calamitous beginning.

She kept me inside her, as she had before, and affectionately squeezed me after her spasms were over. And then my pride in doing something fairly special for her turned to gratefulness to her for bringing me back from shame.

"Thank you, Connie," I said. "Thank you; thank you."

And she, pleased at so much gratitude, replied:

"Thank *you*, Aubrey."

Poor Mark, I thought, as I dozed off, aware that my aging flesh was too heavy on her, but knowing that at this time she would like me there, heavy as I must be.

When we had both come out of it, I asked her to go get her story. Both of us still naked, I poured us huge glasses of orange juice and we went back to bed, which now looked like a spin-dry washing machine barrel. She primped it up and we got in, me with a light lead pencil.

"Have you read the paper?" I asked.

"No time," she said. "I'll read it now. It makes me nervous to have you working on my copy while I'm sitting here reading."

"Put on some Mozart," I said.

"I'm not crazy about him," she answered. "What else?"

I looked at her, her hair down now and her face flushed, her full lips fuller than ever and her eyes brilliant as marbles. She had been plain. Now that changeling face was indisputably beautiful. I was entranced.

"Put some of the quartets on," I said. "You'll *get* to like them. You're too beautiful not to."

I could see I had hit a place where she had not been touched much.

Her cop-lover must not have told her very many nice things about herself, and I wondered if Mark weren't a little uptight, perhaps embarrassed at expressing his feelings about her.

Well, I thought, that wasn't my problem. "One day I will put a pearl necklace on you," I said, "and you must put your hair up just as it was when you came in and we will play a string quartet in the next room and fuck and fuck."

She looked as though she were going to say something smartassed, but instead she blushed and got out of the bed and headed for the phonograph. When she came back, she gripped my shoulder in her wiry little hand.

"You are a nice man, Aubrey Reporter," she said, looking into my eyes to see what I thought of her.

And it was easy for me to repeat honestly, "You are a beautiful lady, Connie." I paused. "Somehow I hope this keeps going, whether or not it's wise."

But it was too early to define it. "Read the paper while I work on this stuff."

She was right. Her story was no good.

Most of her feature stories had the hard, perceptive glitter that her talk and even her love-making had. She tried to maintain the same kind of sheen in this one. But, in parts, it got sentimental, and then to compensate it turned maladroitly cynical. Besides that, her transitions were bad.

When I finished reading it through the first time, I reached over and put my hand on her bare thigh where she was reading the paper. She jumped nervously.

"They sent you out of town and you got rattled," I told her.

"How bad?" she asked. Then I thought, as shitty a writer as I am, who am I to judge anybody?

"Patchable," I lied. I told her what I thought was wrong as clinically as I dared. "Take another bite out of it," I said, finally being honest. "Try this. List all the elements in the story on a piece of paper. You know, 'Mrs. E. at coffee.' 'Speaker on abortion,' 'Mrs. E. at outdoor rally,' 'Mrs. E.'s hair, dress, looks' "—I had a moment's twinge on that one—"and so on, in any order it comes to mind. Then number each element by where it's going to be in your story. So, you know exactly what the order of your paragraphs will be."

It was an old wire service trick for dictating an orderly story rapidly. I still used it on complicated features, when I did them. Connie bobbed her head.

"How about the writing?" she said, gutsily facing up to the story's problems at last. But my role as critic still upset me. I knew my hesitancy was rankling her and began to feel unworthy. "God, Aubrey," she remonstrated, "you're such a Goddamned weakling in some ways."

I cleared my throat, fearing I'd sound professorial. "Get your order of paragraphs up, like I said, and then just write through in a breezy way. How it *feels* to be in a small Kansas town. Start it off saying something like 'Betty whatever-her-middle-names-are Edwards is blank years old, lovely to look at when she's animated, and likes Washington, Kansas, her husband, campaigning and the French poets, though not necessarily in that order.' Then say, 'Whatever the order of her likes, the order of her priorities is clear: to get her husband Pommery Edwards re-elected so he can continue to be second in line for the Presidency of the U.S.' Then, 'At a coffee klatsch in whatever town a few days ago, while her hostess kept the homemade sweet rolls passing, here's the way Mrs. Edwards stumped for Mr. Edwards.' "

She looked at me a little acerbically.

"Maybe you ought to write the fucking thing."

"It's just a suggestion."

"It's a good one," she said glumly. "You ought to be an editor."

I had spent a few months as a relief man on the desk fifteen years ago. "I can't handle people," I said defensively.

She leered. My inadvertent pun had broken the tension that had come up between us.

"You've been handling the hell out of me this morning," she said.

She rolled to the side of the bed and sat up.

"I want to work on it now while what you said's

fresh," she said, looking questioningly at me. "Do you mind?" I felt vague tugs of sex, but told her "no," and she went to the bathroom to shower. I finished the paper and, in a few minutes, she came from the bathroom pinkly, a towel around her waist.

Warmed by this domesticity, I got up, hugged her, and found for her a terry cloth robe, realizing as she slipped it on that Betty Page had worn it and that it might even still smell of her light perfume.

I watched Connie gather up her copy and walk briskly to the living-room table where she sat down with her briefcase in front of her and began scattering papers like an absorbed schoolgirl doing homework.

I felt that propriety dictated that I get dressed and not try to inveigle her into more sex, when she should be working on her story. By the time I had showered and was in my office suit, she had gotten her list down and was finishing up the organization by the numbers, as I suggested.

I walked to where she sat, and parted the top of the bathrobe so that I could reach down and cup her breasts in my hand. I read the small neat list of subjects with the numbers, some scratched out a time or two, in front of them. She held my hands against her breasts.

"Is that right?" she said of the list.

The organization looked good now, moving from the lead through the anecdotal coffee klatsch, then into the issues of the campaign and how bad publicity had made a sure thing into a horse race. After that, she was going to get some more good color, the wind and the flatness of Kansas as Betty Page spoke to an audience at the courthouse steps in Petrie.

The interview with Betty Page would come next. Then some background on her, the poems and the family, and then the interviews with the Speaker, the Speaker's opponent, and, a nice touch she had omitted from the original piece, a few lame words from the opponent's wife. She polished off with one of those "political observers believe" bits.

"Good skeleton," I said. "Just hang the flesh and clothes on it and you've got a lovely feature." But the shock of seeing Betty Page all but committed to paper made me feel uneasy again.

"You are very affirming, Aubrey," she said chipperly, taking one hand from her breast and kissing the fingers. "Can I show you the next-to-last draft?"

"Yep," I said, still thinking Betty Page. Connie re-arranged her papers to pack them in the briefcase, then looked back and up at me, assessing whether I wanted to go to bed again. How frank she was about such things.

"No," I said. "Get your copy done and give me a look at it in the office." Now was the time to get things straightened out, I thought, all but telling her of Betty Page.

"What does this do to you and Mark?" I asked.

"What do you want it to do?"

"It was very nice having you here," I said. "Not just the screwing which made me feel very young, but having you rattling around, drinking my coffee and reading my paper and marching on my bed." She smiled at the memory.

"So you want me to come back?" she said.

"Yes."

"But you aren't sure you want me to move in."

"Do you want to?" I dodged again. I felt as evasive as a government press officer.

"I don't know," she said. "I am very fond of Mark. He's a good heavy person." But "very fond" was one of those eternal code phrases. For an instant I felt panicky. If I invited her, she might leave Mark.

"Why don't we leave it that if I ask you to come see me, you come if you want, and if you want to come see me, then you tell me."

"That's an old-style gentleman for you," she said a bit sarcastically.

And before I knew it, she had dressed and, with a look as spic-and-span as when she had arrived, she was leaving.

"I'll be along later," I said needlessly as we kissed. When she was gone, the place seemed empty. I opened the door to the balcony and watched as she came out and got sprightly into a cab. She did not look up so that I could wave to her.

Autumn was unusually soft that year. The sidewalk cafés were still filled all through October. The leaves changed late and the suggestion of coolness that is first felt in the brackish air off the broad Potomac had not touched the city.

Why try to lie about its sweetness? Betty Page came home on a flying-visit and lay in my compromised arms as I told her honestly how I loved her, and wanted to spend the rest of my life with her. Then not thirty-six hours later she was replaced by Connie March. I was embarrassed with riches.

Although I had not come up with anything big on the Speaker, the local press in Kansas was giving him a fit. And on Saturday night, crazy old Mr. March was throwing my twenty-fifth anniversary party at his Tudor mansion in Fairfax County. All the guests were going to sleep over.

To the younger reporters, I supposed it seemed corny. But, Goddamnit, I was excited. I had gone over the select list with Mr. March's secretary: Cubbins, the prick, if only for the longevity of our mutual distrust; Mrs. Murtry, God bless her for her balls; my old colleague-rivals at the White House, State, and the Hill; the desk man I often ate with who was genuinely touched, perhaps the only one to be; the chief librarian; a half-dozen others who'd manned one barricade or another with me over the years. Their wives, those who had wives.

The tradition for these parties was that only *Eagle* or ex-*Eagle* people came, otherwise I would have had a few good cops, my preacher friend Blathe, a long-time source who was a private eye, a couple of maverick congressmen and Brent from the FBI and Knowles from Secret Service. The last two would have been fired merely for getting an invitation.

I wanted to have Connie, but so far we had kept our slippery affair to ourselves.

I underestimated her deviousness. Mr. March's secretary, who had survived for an amazing five years with the madman, said conspiratorially to me two days before the party: "I hate to mention this, but Connie is going to be out at Eaglesmere"—believe it or not, that's what the place was called—"this weekend and—"

"Could she come?" I finished for her with a pout.

"Would it be a bother? Her father . . ."

"If he wants her," I conceded grandly, thinking whackily that perhaps I could roger her under the very nose of her old man. "No problem, no problem."

"Mark Braswell . . .?"

"I'd want Mark, anyway," I said, disappointed, but in a way relieved that it had been forced on me. He had pulled me out of that damned subway. I respected him for his progress toward becoming a tough-assed reporter. But another voice in me said, "and you want an anniversary-party black."

The day of the party, Cubbins' wife was sick. I picked him up and we drove across Memorial Bridge and on up the south side of the river, that most beautiful of Washington's scenic drives. I had the top down. The midafternoon sun reflected off Cubbins' balding pate, and the wind had my graying locks flying.

"Grow old along with me, Cubbins," I said to him as we wheeled northward. His potato-face smiled and he gave me a companionable clout on the shoulder.

As we ascended, the towers of Georgetown were ahead to our right. The Morgan roared and throbbed, its ancient motor straining upward. Below was Theodore Roosevelt Island, its trees, all golding and browning in the sunlight.

We'd lost the battle there against the highway lobby who had cicatriced the island with a bridge complex years earlier. Cubbins had been a reporter in those days.

Then there were the Three Sister islets where the highway lobby had tried to build another bridge. Cubbins, then city editor, and I, as a reporter, had beaten back the bastards by showing skam was going to a Northern Virginia politician. We won that one. The *Eagle* had given the conservationists enough breathing space to cinch the victory.

"It's our city in a way, isn't it?" reminisced Cubbins, knowing I was thinking the same thoughts. "We helped get it better and we helped fuck it up."

"Yeah, man," I said. "I helped get it better and you caved in on the big issues and got it sicker."

"Goddamnit, Aubrey," he said sharply, nettled. "Even when a person tries to be nice to you, you have some nasty, asshole thing to poison it with."

"That's why you got to be an editor and I stayed a reporter." But I knew he was right.

"Along with all the other reasons," he said mildly. "Is Mark going to marry Connie?" he asked me out of the blue. Did he suspect? I thought not. But he had the true rat's sixth sense.

"*You* ought to know that," I said. "Why?"

"Mark'd be managing editor in a few years," he said soberly.

"Ah, Mr. March wouldn't push you aside," I consoled him, secretly thrilling at the idea that if I married Connie, I might keep on Cubbins, but eventually would push out the old man and be editor-in-chief. It was a crackpot fantasy. But I wallowed in it briefly, wondering whether, if I really wooed Connie, I could marry her. In practice, it likely was not what politicians called a viable option.

"Yeah, March'd move me aside," Cubbins went on. "He's very big on family. I've always thought there was a racist streak in him for all the liberalism. But if Connie married Mark and the old man could bring himself to accept it, it wouldn't be long before he'd have Mark in as editor."

"He'd keep you as number two," I said.

"Maybe." Then he mused, "What do you suppose she's like in the sack? I mean there was that cop and now—"

"Finger-licking good, I imagine." I told him that Mr. March's secretary had said she'd be at Eaglesmere this weekend. "Mark, too," I added. "Maybe you can put some horns on Mark," I said. But it was a sorry joke.

We hooked south on to Virginia's endless winding roads. As the afternoon faded, the old oaks and maples

cast long shadows, striping the asphalt. The sun was
alternately bright in our eyes, and subdued as we crossed
the bars of shade.

"Will we ever get out of this, Cubbins?" I said. I felt
comfortable with him now. "Should we free-lance?
Write a book? Something?"

"No," said Cubbins. "You won't quit unless your
heart cuts you out of it. I've still got a kid in college,
so I can't quit."

"I wanted to be a poet," I told him.

"Yeah," he said. "I remember. You must have told
me that once. You don't write well enough, so forget it."

I barked a short laugh at him.

The posted forests of the March estate had begun
on our right. Some old March must have bought the
land for a song a hundred years ago. The Tudor heap
on it had been abuilding for a century. We turned in
between two stone pillars. Other guests must have
come shortly before us because the sun-slanted dust
from the graveled road was still hanging above the
long driveway.

It ran between rows of poplars, a little gapped from
time to time from storm or disease and replaced with
younger trees. To either side, the fields were used for
grazing by some neighboring farmer whom, in exchange,
Mr. March would dock for the taxes, I suspected.

The end of the road funneled out onto a circular
drive that branched here and there for guest lodges, a
tennis court, a swimming pool, garages, and outbuild-
ings.

"Eaglesmere" was three stories high, with a fine
wood-shingled roof, numerous gables, a large screened
porch. Each new March had added to its eccentricities.

The present publisher had converted the small ballroom into a museum for the family collection of helmets. At Cubbins' twenty-fifth anniversary party two
years ago—March lavished these things mainly on editorial employees, and then only a few of us—the
museum was just being built. Mr. March opened it up
from time to time to the public which gave him a
gigantic state and federal tax write-off. I'd once play-

fully offered to do Cubbins an exposé on it, or to write one for *The Progressive* magazine.

Damn, I tickled myself as I pulled up to where the other cars were parked. I wonder if I'd have to change my name to March if I married Connie and became heir to all this. Aubrey March sounded better than Mark March, I grinned to myself.

Cubbins and I got our cramped bodies out of the Morgan just as Connie appeared at the house's doorway, as if she had sprung corporeally from my thoughts. Her father was behind her, tweedy as the Lord of the Marches had a right to be, in tightly woven slacks and a big Shetland sweater.

Connie, to my astonishment, was in a tailored Donegal tweed pants suit. She looked like something out of Vōgue, standing there in front of that sagging old house. Her silken blouse was a pale brown, the color of her eyes at their lightest. The sharp creases of her pants and the severe cut of the jacket made her look older from the distance.

As I walked nearer, I saw she had her hair in the same French twist she'd worn when she came to me after Wichita. Her full lips were coated lightly with pale lip paint that softened her face into beauty.

"Lady of the Manor, hunh Aubrey?" said old March, noting my entranced stare. "Takes after her mother, not me."

"She's your spitting image, Mr. March," said Cubbins.

"My God," I demurred, shaking Mr. March's bony muscular hand, then I took hers and it was soft, but with the same kind of sinewy squeeze. "Thanks for the anniversary party," I said to both of them.

"You don't mind me crashing?" she said.

"Brings a little beauty to the beasts," I said to her, meaning the part about beauty. I was dazzled at how lovely she looked out here.

"Come in, come in," snorted the old man. "People are already here." He looked up the road to see if any other cars were coming, his old eyes piercing as an ancient bird's. "Your cottage is over there," he pointed. "Come in first."

As I passed in, I heard a thump and saw it was a shingle falling off the roof onto the front walk.

"Happens all the time," he said. "Even though I have it patched every year." Sure enough there were wooden shingles fallen in front of the house like leaves. "Place would be a firetrap, inside and out, except for the sprinkler system," he said. "Had to put it in for the insurance." I thought momentarily of the summer's arson threats.

Inside, the guests came forward to shake my hand. When Mark came up I saw that he knew. In his eyes, there was more hurt than anything else, no hate. I guessed he'd been pissed on enough times in his life to have built up a defense that would take anything.

Still I felt guilty, unmanly, and I did not dare look at Connie to see what she was thinking.

"I'm glad you could come," I said to Mark. I didn't know what to add, and he didn't say anything to make it easier for me. Looking at that Negroid face and the careful intelligent eyes, I felt like a shit. To me, Connie was an exciting toy. To Mark, she must be someone he had risked intense love on and might now lose.

I got a glass in my hand quickly, brandy and soda. If it were going to be a long night's drinking, I didn't want anything sugary. Mr. March was hitting a bourbon on the rocks. It flashed on me how shy he was. He was hoping, like the rest of us, that the booze would break down the barriers.

"Connie says your pieces may beat Edwards," he muttered, grabbing me by the upper arm. He sounded apologetic, so I got in my licks.

"I wish you hadn't cut them off," I said.

"Aubrey, Goddamnit," he rose to the remark. "You were dishing out chicken shit. I don't mind if you can come up with another Boles-Panjunk bombshell, like you and I did on Quiven. But this sort of penny-ante illegal contribution and real estate deals and so on, it just seemed . . ."

Well, he had some good arguments. I hadn't produced another bombshell.

The enormous hearth in the living room opened on

a smoothed-out fieldstone floor. Rugs and sofas and low wooden tables were scattered around the hearth. Beechwood burned in the fireplace. The two of us walked to the fire.

"The *Eagle*'s a *reporters*' paper," Mr. March said. "Whatever you think."

There was truth in that. Otherwise Mr. March wouldn't keep a weak editor like Cubbins. A stronger editor would make for a more homogeneous paper, one that reflected less of its nutty publisher, and would give less freedom to its diverse reporters. "You've done good work for the *Eagle*," he went on, "but you'd be too ornery for most papers. Look what I put up with from you." He laughed. "I mean just the legal fees alone."

That reminded me to ask about Mrs. Murtry.

"She'll be here. She'll be here," Mr. March said.

He looked around the room at the women, most of them unhandsome, but a few good-looking, none more so than his daughter.

"Gawd," he sighed. "I wish I were younger. I wish I had made it on my own without all this just given to me." The comment surprised me.

"Don't get sentimental on me, Mr. March," I said. "You've kept the paper going. That's something. If you'd just been a rich man's son, the paper wouldn't be as good as it is."

"That's right, Aubrey, that's right," he said, brightening.

But I couldn't stand to let him get away with too much.

"I don't want you to think I agree with you about my stories being a string of chicken-shitters."

He started to say something imperious. But then he sighed ponderously. "Heavy sleeps the head, Aubrey."

Mrs. Murtry arrived, gave me a tall embrace, kissed Mr. March familiarly, and gave a quick hug to Connie.

We drank some more, Mr. March belting them down, then he went upstairs and changed into a suit, the sign that dinner was going to begin. With all the money he had in paper mills and forests and land all over the east and his TV station and his newspaper, it would have been surprising if he hadn't done the dinner well. Still, once inside the rich dimly candle-lit dining room which looked out on fields and woods, I was awestruck.

"I told you it's a reporters' paper," he said gleefully. "I've picked the food soft enough so old fossils like you and Murtry can gum it." He cackled.

We went from watercress soup to fresh artichokes both with an Anheuser-Bernkasteler, a wine I didn't know. It was light and sweet, like Mr. March's beautiful daughter. I could hardly keep my eyes off her, for all my guilt over Mark.

Then, he had veal with a veronica sauce and magnums—magnums—of a good Chablis. It was ostentatious but sensational. Everyone was guzzling wine and wolfing down the food as if they were having the last expense account meal before retirement.

The more I drank the better time I had. I was at Mr. March's right, with Mrs. Murtry on his left.

Every time Mr. March stopped talking about the vagaries of lawyers, antique-armor dealers, and insurance men, Mrs. Murtry and I got in a few good words.

"If we can get the state charges dropped out there, the federal things will go away," she said.

"Why don't you concentrate on Quiven instead of the Speaker," interrupted March. "If you terrify Quiven then he'll get the state case dropped. Now on that kind of story you would have my backing, Aubrey." The old hypocrite, I thought.

"Yes, Aubrey," chimed in Connie from catty-corner across the table, "why can't you find another mutineer on the Bounty?" Mr. March looked at her with wonder.

"That's actually funny," he said evenly.

"You can imagine your daughter as a queen of the manor," snapped Mrs. Murtry to Mr. March, "but you can't imagine your daughter or any woman with a sense of humor."

"You're right, Milicent," he said. "The only funny woman I ever knew was Dorothy Thompson and she was too old for me."

"Cut him loose to work on Quiven," Mr. March loudly and suddenly ordered Cubbins.

Cubbins looked at me from down the table. He did not know what was going on and didn't know how to react. I pulled up the side of my lip indicating Mr. March was talking nonsense. There was nothing I could do on Quiven that hadn't been done. It was a waste to put me on it now. Cubbins got the message.

"Could be a wise move, Mr. March," he answered equivocally. That meant it would be dropped. I sighed. A crazy March idea dead aborning, thank God.

With the cheese, there was an old Chambertin.

"Look," I said to Mr. March, "this is too much."

When the coffee came, Mr. March clinked a glass. I recalled his kindly, drunken speech at Cubbins' affair. I wished he wouldn't say anything. He had said it all with the dinner. I wanted to cry a little. Goddamnit, I was touched. Chambertin.

The babble died. Mr. March stood up. I got one more glance in at Connie as Mark turned to his own left, and then I regarded the old Eagle. His eyes were looking off into the dark fields. They contemplated a dream of newspapering.

17

The Marches

"The *Eagle*," he began softly, "is a reporters' paper. In all its years, its strengths and weaknesses have stemmed from that fact. We were first to report the end of the Spanish-American War. A lousy week too soon" —he was still looking beyond us to the twilight fields— "because we believed the madman reporter we had on the scene. Our goof is now a newspaper legend."

March paused to let the horror sink in. It did, and now he forced a smile. "Eighteen years ago, when we got our last Pulitzer, why did we get it? We got it when Samuel F. Richey, may his soul rest, went out and physically dug up, in violation of the law and despite his editor's disapproval, the body of Senator Avery Lenneman and removed from his coffin the Lenneman papers."

It was another legend. Richey, a reportorial hack until then, and almost seventy, had been tipped by the widow that papers showing Lenneman's deals with the big utilities had been hidden in his coffin, to be dug up under a secret codicil fifty years after his death. Mr. March recapitulated, at colorful length, the whole saga.

"The *Eagle*," he said quietly, "is a reporters' newspaper." I was beginning to fall in with the spirit of the long-winded speech. Damnit, it *was* a reporters' newspaper.

"And in all of reporting, there is no finer calling than

356

investigative reporting. For those who do it are most often exposed to insult and lawsuit and arrest. They are the assault troops of newspapering, the first onto the beaches, the earliest casualties.

"They are the first victims of a vengeful administration or company or union. When the screws are put on, they are the first whose tax forms are pulled, who are hauled before grand juries, who are jailed and sometimes injured. Theirs are the first reputations to be smeared."

I was entranced and flattered. The cawing voice aspirated on. Then he stopped, reached down for his water to wet his throat, but instead darted his fingers to the cognac and took a mighty swig.

"Investigative reporters are the dirtiest by the end of every day, from mucking among the corrupt in power, from the dust of old files, from the grainy seepages of police precincts and police courts.

"A fine reporter, Warren Rogers, once said of his friends, 'Good reporters, in the long run, have no constituencies. They are the purveyors of truth and nobody likes the truth deep down unless it is about someone else.'

"But"—and he looked for a moment outward to where the stars were beginning to speck the sky up above his forests and fields—"but, that is the risk that must be taken to keep this intricate democracy breathing. That should be the *Eagle*'s credo."

He gestured to the glass windows where, faintly, the candlelight and our ghostly faces were reflected. For all the passion of his speech, the liquor was beginning to get a hold on him.

"Out there," he went on, "past the mirror of your faces, are the voices of my fathers." His lips pursed tightly with the poetry of his vision. A March Hare, I thought, and was ashamed of myself for the unspoken cruelty.

"All their compromises, all their buckling to the powerful, to the advertisers which they did, which I have done, to my remorse, were to keep our paper strong," he said, as if explaining to us.

"Oh," his voice quavered, "like them, I have let Presidents talk me into killing stories 'in the national interest,' as they put it. Never trust 'em!

"But I have fought, too. The *Eagle* fought that evil man from Yorba Linda, even though it meant that we were blocked from acquiring two TV and four radio stations that would have given us financial security!"

He rambled briefly about other Presidents the Marches had tangled with over the decades, then interrupted himself and stared again at the reflected faces in the window.

"But so help me"—and he waved to the fields as if he would pacify those ghosts of his ancestry, trumpet them like a reverse Gabriel back into their graves—"I have never, never, never lost sight of what the *Eagle* is."

Old March was now the picture of humble age venerable with honor. He let the silence speak for him. Then with a great sigh, he drew himself up.

"The *Eagle*"—and now there was a catch in his voice, and he reached up and wiped a genuine tear from his eyes—"the *Eagle*," he stammered. And suddenly, in my own eyes I felt a tear leap. The fucker, for all his theatrics, was right. He was right. My heart jumped with a kind of hot joy. There wasn't anything else in the world like being a reporter.

Oh, I knew the fighting with the desk, the scheming for stories, the dreadful squabbles within the union, the union against management, the editorial staff against the printers, against advertising. But March was right. He, we, had been right to be in this business. Because there wasn't any other.

"The *Eagle*," he cried. And to my amazement, Mrs. Murtry patted his old hand with her old hand, and I heard Connie scrape back her chair and could see she was about to start down the table to him. He leaned forward, and went on in a tense whisper.

"The *Eagle* is a reporters' newspaper."

Well, of course, we were drunk. Of course, reporters and editors and all of us in the business have deep down in us that totally sentimental, romantic chord. And old March had reached down in us with his old clever fingers and had plucked the be-Jesus out of it.

"And, so, this is Aubrey's anniversary," he said. "And I have a gift for him." The gold watch, I thought, feeling a bit ashamed of myself for the cynicism after his rush of emotion. "Come with me."

There was a lot of shuffling of chairs. I should have known old Mr. March would never let a good thing come to an end if he could find a way of squeezing it out some more. Before we could begin to chatter, he said:

"Bring your drinks." He looked back at the three waiters who had been standing at the end of the table. "Bring more drinks to the museum." Mr. March led us out of the candlelit room and through the arch. We crossed the living room.

Mr. March switched on a light and I looked in at his museum. Two long display tables of helmets ran the length of the room along the walls; two more, equally long, stood in the middle.

On the walls hung old swords, broadaxes, halberds, maces, clubs, and the like. It was all newly, handsomely done, right down to the sprinkler system along the ceiling.

On the near table a Greek job with a brush plume and bronze cheek guard was beside a Roman gladiator's affair, à la Spartacus, with the face cage, the rudderlike crest, and the scalloped steel brim.

There were domes neatly labeled "Spangenhelms" and "Conicals" and "Norman Casques." All were polished handsomely, many of them marked, to March's credit, "Copy from original" in such and such a museum.

With Mr. March ahead, silent, like some cranky old chief priest, we filed through the museum. The party had strung out, some reading the markers. Mr. March was losing his audience before I could find out what my gift was to be.

To add to the confusion, the waiters were now passing out more cognac and liqueurs and some of the more

dedicated guests were getting back to the bourbon and
scotch where they began. When they got to Mr. March,
he dashed down a cognac straight and then took another
for sipping.

"Here, here," he said, in his hoarsened bossy voice.
"Get a drink and gather round." He had stopped in
front of two identical helmets, one labeled "Jousting
Heaume, 15th century." The other had on it a small
brass plate. I saw now what the old bird was going to
give me.

Before he did, his eyes darted around until he spotted
Connie, and he said to her, "Connie, get me the Italian
Burgonet." She brought him a gold-plated helmet with
a long beak, a neck protector, and an embossed crown
on the front of two bowls intertwined with garlands. It
was some sort of king helm.

Connie, far from being embarrassed by her father,
seemed relaxed to see his eccentricities in full flower.
My God, I thought, this is the way he really is.
The trappings of ordinariness were the pose, not the
kookiness.

The old man took the helm and put it on his head.
Even with the load of alcohol in him, he must have
been aware of its incongruity with his clothes.

"Aubrey Warder. Aubrey Warder," he said, looking
at me, "is an investigative reporter, and far, far from
that ideal I painted. He stays at the best hotels when
he is on my expense account.

"He is immoral and has chased every woman we
ever had on the paper, at least in his younger days."
I didn't think Mr. March knew about me and his
daughter, but maybe he did. In any case, he was a fine
one to be making a big thing of woman chasing.

"Lately, he has cost me much money in legal fees.
He has cracked a safe, an illegal act far worse than
Samuel Richey digging up Lenneman, far worse."

Goddamnit, this was a helluva way for him to brow-
beat me on my anniversary. I yearned for him to get
to the point.

"But through it all, Aubrey has been a reporter," he
said, and I felt better. "He has brought to the paper

all the prizes a reporter can bring except the big one. He has never shirked a story, nor given less than his best to it."

The decency that so often lies hidden in people was beginning to come out of Mr. March like sweat, whether from the drinking or from his excursion into the mystique of newspapering. I felt him warming to me, liking me.

"Aubrey"—Mr. March dramatically put his hand on my shoulder—"is a reporters' investigative reporter."

There was a little round of clapping, and I was overwhelmed, despite myself. I wished I were a first-rate reporter instead of a good second-rate one.

Beaming now, the old man dropped his hand from my shoulder and picked up the helm with the little plate on its brow.

"Here it is, Aubrey. A damned good copy. It cost me $400." Mr. March had no sense of niceties. "I chose it because—" Connie was still standing near. "Connie," he said, "get me that sword up there." He pointed to an old broad sword with a big grip.

"Aubrey," the old man said, calling my eyes back to the helmet, "this heaume here was not the most versatile of helmets. It was subject to only a limited development. While other helmets went on to become the helmets of modern soldiery, the heaume became a sort of saber-toothed tiger among helmets. Highly efficient up to 1500, then archaic." The wicked old eyes tipsily twinkling.

I interrupted him at last.

"What you are saying with this kick in the ass, Mr. March, is that I am a dinosaur." Mr. March, an odd mix of soused humor and seriousness, nodded.

"That's right. That's right. In a way you are." He paused, seeing he had hurt my feelings. "I am, too," he said. Everyone was fidgeting, fearing Mr. March or I would lose our temper. I looked up at that weird man in his burgonet with the heraldic emblem of Italian kings on it.

"Still," Mr. March started up again, hiding behind his pedantry, "it is the helmet of the Round Table, and of the early rough-and-tumble knights who were never above a little pillaging in a good cause.

"And you, God knows, have pillaged a good many villages in your days." He put down the helmet and gave me a pat on the shoulder, then looked for his sword. "Kneel, Aubrey."

Well, I thought, why not, it's no crazier than some of the other things I've done in my life. He lowered the heavy helmet over my head, and its bib came down over my upper chest.

With diminished clarity, I could hear him talking. The slit for the eyes showed me only the side of the table. I felt creaky in the knees.

"I knight thee Sir Aubrey of Underwood," he said. I wondered where he'd learned about my old typewriter. Connie? Not likely. Maybe Cubbins. "Knight Lecher! Defender of the First Amendment! Bane of the Speaker Sinister!" I reached out and grabbed the underside of the table to take some of the pressure off my knees.

Connie interrupted him, in a peremptory voice that surprised me.

"He's getting tired of being inside the damned thing," she said. I knew her sharp tone would irritate him, but as I listened for his reply, he unexpectedly hit the side of the heaume a great whack with the sword. The clang was like an explosion, and I let go of the table and toppled awkwardly to the floor.

My ears were ringing so loudly, I could not hear a thing. But I tore the damned heaume from my head and looked up to where Connie had pushed her father up against the table, and was taking the sword from him.

"Goddamnit!" she snapped. "You did that out of spite!"

He pushed her off, and sword still in hand, reached down with his other arm and helped me onto my feet. I picked up the helm from the floor and looked to see if it had been dented. Mr. March, seeing I was not hurt, called Cubbins.

"Cubbins, get over here. You never got knighted on your twenty-fifth." But Connie had calmed him down and now he merely looked at me with a lopsided smile.

"Are you all right?" she said to me. My ears still rang, but I nodded.

Around the room, the guests were standing a little tentatively with drinks in hands. Mr. March, his hostility discharged by his terrific blow to my helmet, turned mildly to Connie and handed her the sword.

"Ah, Connie," he said quietly. The old brows furrowed beneath the golden burgonet. Mr. March looked searchingly into her eyes. Had he ever understood her, or really ever thought about her as a grown person, I wondered? They stood there, a *tableau vivant*, facing each other.

Something curious, we were all aware, was about to happen.

Then he took the sword from where she had leaned it against the case. She still stood by the table, thin and erect.

"Lady Constance of Eaglesmere," he recommenced, his chest rising and falling with a heavy sigh.

Again, the tears started from the mad eyes, and he choked up. "All that's left of us Marches, Goddamnit. I wish you'd never marry and have some fine little bastard who would keep the name going, and the paper—" He stopped and continued his charge to her. "Heiress of the *Eagle*. May you do no worse with it when I'm gone than I did."

He backed off and hit her a shocker on the shoulder with his sword. She staggered back a step, and I could see she was tearing up, too, but not from pain.

In effect, he was announcing that when he left, far hence, she would run the sheet: that it would not be a consortium of editors, as with the old *Times-Herald*, or of the employees, as with some papers, but Connie March.

She was blinking, but all she said to him was:

"Put down the sword, Daddy. You'll hurt somebody."

Back in the big living room I read the brass label riveted to the helmet's blued brow: my name, The Washington *Eagle*, my dates at the *Eagle*, the words *Tenere lupum auribus*. I didn't know what the words meant, only that they would reflect Mr. March's odd humor.

An hour later Mr. March was thoroughly gassed, and headed upstairs, after he had made a disjointed but cordial exit. I was flattered he'd chosen my party to get smashed at. I knew he didn't often drink that much.

It was a good party. I was hugely proud of my heaume and allowed various friends to wear it. Connie put on records. We danced to tunes out of our youth, holding more closely the wives of our colleagues than we should have.

Mark and I behaved politely toward each other. It was hard for him to hate me since he knew I was coming to respect him as a reporter. I liked him and felt guilt toward him for my affair with Connie. Yet, after all, I, too, had come to love her, if not as he did.

By 1 A.M. we were all exhausted. The lights were low. The fire was guttering. The less hardy, or the lonely, had already gone to bed, Cubbins among them. I danced one last time with Connie, to an old song about Indian summer, one I had loved even before I had known my wife.

Her jacket was open, and I thought that even through my coat I could feel those hard little bubs. What with the drink and the minor lionizing I had received at the party, I felt I might be able to bring off the unlikely.

"You sleep in the big house, right?" I whispered, afraid Mark or one of the other endgamers would hear me.

"Mark already asked," she said. "I told him no. If he found out, it would hurt him."

"It's not his twenty-fifth anniversary," I muttered. "By the time he has his, you won't have to even worry about me anymore."

She laughed.

"God," she said. She thought a moment. "Can you stay up until two-thirty?"

"Of course," I said. I could see she didn't like the idea very much. But she had decided to do it anyway, and now it was just a matter of the means.

"On the button. Okay? At the front door."

"Yummy," I said, pulling her close into my wanton, mindlessly rising member, and humming the old Indian summer song. It had a rhyme about something coming *after* spring or summertime *laughter*, a rhyme that had made the whole song stick with me.

I took my helmet with me when I left them—Mark and Connie and a few others—by the last of the fire. I wondered if she would give Mark a little bit before I got to her. The thought gave me a twinge of jealousy and of something else uglier.

I walked across the front yard, feeling the brisk wind that had come up. My tiredness said to go to the cabin and get a good night's sleep, that I'd be hung over enough in the morning anyway. But a quick nap (I knew I could "set" myself for an hour more or less) was all that stood between me and Connie in some soft bed.

The wind had the old mansion creaking and groaning. The friction of the poplar limbs against each other in the faint moonlight was eerie.

I had been assigned a room on the ground floor of a guest lodge. Except that Cubbins shared the room, it would have been easier for Connie to come to me.

I put the helm carefully on a chair, took off my shoes, and lay down in the bed. Wake up in an hour, I said, to myself. More likely it would be a half hour. I looked at the dial on my watch to reinforce the limit on my sleep.

"So she'll get the newspaper," I mused. And she had seemed more grown up, more sure of herself tonight, than I had ever seen her. I imagined her slender, smooth body moving across my old tired one and fell sound asleep.

My head was blowsy when I woke up, forty-five minutes later. The bad taste of the alcohol in my stomach had not taken long to work up into my head and mouth. I wanted a shower, but settled for a tooth-brushing in the dark.

As I left, I thought of my helm and took it with me. I wondered how it would be mounting Connie from behind with the damn thing on, particularly if she had a mirror in her room where I could see it. It seemed a marvelous, kinky idea. Maybe we could get a helmet out of the museum for her.

The front door of the main house was open a crack. I put on the helmet and opened it a bit more. She was inside, waiting, but started at the sight of the helmet.

"Sir Aubrey of Underwood," I said, "soon to be rampant on your field of gules and argent."

"Are you drunk?" she asked rather coldly. I was surprised again by the tone.

"No," I said defensively. "I thought this was a chivalrous mission, and besides, I love my helmet." The whole downstairs was dark. I took off the helmet and whispered to her the idea of her getting a helmet so that we could do it in armor, Corinthian style.

"No," she snapped. "I just had a helluvan argument with Mark."

"I'm sorry," I said, feeling I had made a fool of myself.

"Besides," she said, reconsidering the frivolous even while she brooded over the break with Mark, "we might clank and wake up my father."

"What happened with Mark?" She was holding my hand as we edged to the big staircase. She gave my hand an admonitory squeeze and "shhhed" me.

Once inside her room, while we stealthily removed our clothes, she whispered about Mark. "He said if I were going to play games with him, he didn't want to be my lover anymore."

"I'm sorry," I repeated.

"He also gave me some bilge about now that I was going to be running the paper, I'd be, you know—"

"He did not want to tup the putative heiress?"

"Goddamnit, Aubrey, be serious. He didn't want to tup the putative heiress if she were also being tupped by the aging ram."

"Touché," I said, beginning to breathe hard. I had taken off all my clothes. The helm was nearby. I meant to carry out my scheme willy-nilly, heiress or no heiress.

"You don't care who's tupping me as long as you are?" she said. Uh-oh, I thought, this way lies trouble.

"No," I said. "I sort of wish you would tup only

me. But I recognize your rights to tup whomever you please."

She was young enough to be satisfied, if not flattered, by this pat answer.

She rolled in close to me. The bed was as soft as I had imagined it to be. The room was very dark. The little light that came from outside showed some narrow triangular patches on the wall. I assumed they were pennants left over from her tomboy days.

We began kissing, and I smelled the liquor on her breath. If I were married to her, would it soon be down to that? Or to why she didn't brush her teeth before she screwed, and menstruations, and minor skirmishes? In other words, a marriage. For some reason, even in bed with Connie, it seemed easier to think of Betty Page in terms of these little marital acceptances.

"I think I'm beginning to love you," she said.

I reached down and found her vagina.

"It's because of the flap with Mark," I said, breathing stertorously. "I don't think it's a good thing to talk about love with me."

She pulled my body atop hers, and I felt her sink sweetly into the deep bed. In this strange house, with her father only a room or two away, I wondered whether the exoticism would overcome me. Would I be able to last?

"Ummm. Why not talk about love?" she said, beginning to lose herself in her own images of passion. I pressed harder into her. No time to talk now, anyway, but I thought for an instant of my plan for the heaume and pulled gently out of her, right on the verge of coming.

"What's the matter?" she asked, reaching down to touch me.

"No!" I said. "Don't! I'm on the brink. Look, Connie, I wonder if I could put on the damned helmet, you know like I suggested, and take you from behind." She gave a little exhalation of laughter.

"In the—?" she questioned.

"No," I answered with some disgust. "Right where I was. It's just—"

She laughed very quietly again, rolled over and came to her knees. I reached down and got the heaume and fiddled with it until I got it on my head.

"It's worse than a rubber," she said, patting me in the darkness to find where I was and to get me into position. "Here."

The heaume was uncomfortable, resting as it did coldly on my bare shoulders. It was antierotic, but I was so close to orgasm that I didn't limpen. I thought of an elaborate pun, "Oh, go not knightly into this good gentile." But it was so obscure I decided not to say it. Betty Page, maybe. Connie, no.

I could feel my pulses throbbing within my ears, themselves within the iron globe. This is going to be a helluva quick come, I thought. I imagined the sudden thrust and the soft pressure of her cunt on the underside of me. I touched her smooth buttocks, getting my knee in between her calves. It would be like a rocket launch and my head inside the control capsule.

At this instant I could hear or think nothing, only feel the splendid premonition of orgasm, but Connie suddenly squirmed around and stage-whispered. "Aubrey! Somebody's outside!"

I wrestled off the helmet with loud clankings, thinking she meant outside the door, but when the thing came free, she bit into my arm with her fingers and tugged me out of the bed's downy fastnesses.

"Outside the window!"

Then I heard it, too, shoes abrading on the wood shingles down below our second-story window.

I peered out the window. There, moving in the gloom, were three or four figures. The light sheen of dimmed moonlight and starlight hit an object of glass among them. The threats against the paper and March had been real!

Fire bombs! I saw the flare of two lighters, one directly beneath my window and the other down the side of the house about twenty-five feet.

"Fire!" I roared, knowing as I did that there would be hell to pay before this night was done. "Fire!" Simultaneously, I heard a gunshot, felt the window crash around me as glass struck my chest and saw garish yellow flames from two ignited fuses.

There was a confusion of shots, and then the whole room was alight as a Molotov cocktail flashed through the window. I had no time to shove Connie out of the way, but caught the quart bottle in my hands, ripped out its torch still flaming, and chucked the container of gasoline back through the jagged glass.

The whole room was afire. As I had heaved the unbroken bottle out the window, much of the gasoline had spilled on the curtains and floor. Miraculously, I had gotten the flaming wick clear of the bottle. But knowing my hand was wet with gas, I had dropped the wick, and it had ignited the thin skein of gas that had spilled.

"Fire!" I bawled, leaping up onto the bed, away from the sudden flames. Connie was rushing toward the door. She looked like a lithe devil, her glistening body orange-lit by the gasoline flames.

"Fire!" her shrill scream reverberated. As I crossed the bed, I stumbled on the helm, gave it a kick, painfully, with my bare foot and heard it rattle toward the door.

Just above me, the sprinkler system spurted on, and the cold water hit my sweaty body, scaring the hell out of me.

The fumes had us both gasping and coughing. There was no time to put on clothes. We rushed into the hall. Suddenly, I thought of the second fire bomb.

"Your father," I choked at her, catching at her thin arm.

"Daddy," she gasped, running up the hall to his room, her white ass ghostly in the light from her burning room. I stubbed my toe on the damned helmet again. She pulled open the old man's door into the hallway, and a gush of smoke and fire poured out.

In that room, there had been no one to catch the bottle of gasoline. The thought of those napalmed kids in Vietnam flashed through my mind.

She started in, naked as she was, but was scorched back. I grabbed her arm and flung her down the hall as if she were a bundle of rags.

"Get out!" I yelled. My heart was pumping dangerously. But I couldn't just let the old fart burn to death.

I ran back into her eerily lit room. The fire was confined to flickering pools. The bedspread was dripping wet from the sprinkler. I ripped it off the bed, scratched crazily for my shoes, and jammed my feet into them. Connie was standing at the doorway, her face frozen with fear.

I flung the bedspread out into the hall and grabbed up the heaume. "Help me!" I shouted at her, unfreezing her enough so that she helped me latch the damned thing over my head.

Once out of her trance, she moved rapidly. I felt her hands wrapping the bedspread around me. Down below on the first floor there were cries of "Fire!", babbling voices and shouts, and then the thud of footsteps on the wooden stairs. For an instant, I thought: Why not let the other guys do it?

But now Connie had me swaddled in wet, cold cloth. I gripped the material tightly to me, and lumbered down the hall.

As I reached Mr. March's door, I was pushed aside. Mark Braswell rushed to the door, swung it open and thrust himself into the flames, clad only in his plaid pajamas.

It was impossible to force one's body to take that kind of heat and pain. He was thrown back, as if by a giant's hand, singed and smoking like someone fresh from hell, grunting in agony from the burns.

"Get the fuck out of the way!" I growled at him, bumping by in my heavy wet bedspread, like a wrapped squaw or poorly shrouded corpse, crowned by my blued helm. My words reverberated around in the kettle.

"You can't do it, Aubrey!" he screamed at me.

Connie grabbed the back of my shroud and gave it a pull to hold me back. I turned and pushed her onto her ass again. Then I wrapped the bedclothes around me and threw open the door.

I felt the heat on my hands, and tucked them into the

wet cloth. By now the hall was full of people and someone was shooting powder from an extinguisher all over
me and the Goddamn fire.

I barged through the fire like the killer mummy in
that old movie. The bottle in Mr. March's room had
gone clean through the window and struck the wall
nearest the hallway. Once I had breached the wall of
flame, the floor of the room at its middle was compara-
tively free of fire. The sprinkler had washed the gasoline toward the walls.

What I feared most was a burst of fire flaring up as
I went to the bed and roaring up the chimney of my
skirts to my unprotected balls.

"God save them," I prayed hollowly from inside the
helm. I was coughing and my eyes were full of smoke,
but so far the Dutch Oven on my head had not gotten
hot enough to bake it. Without sticking out a hand, I
bumped my way to the bed.

The sprinklers had wet down its top, but the steam
was coming up from the foot of it where a pool of
gasoline had not washed away. Smaller fires were burning under the bed itself.

"Mr. March," I called, reaching out for the bed. I
paused and heard him coughing and gasping for air at
the top of the bed. I did not know whether fear, or
caution or some sudden heart attack, had immobilized
him up there.

I reached out of my protective sheath with one hand
and found an old hairy leg. "Wrap in the covers!" I
shouted. But then I inhaled and started to cough. He
seemed paralyzed in the fetal position. I tried to wrap
him in the wet bedclothes.

But I was getting dizzy from the heat and fumes.
Letting the bedspread unravel from me a bit, I scrabbled
him up in the covers on his bed. His hands feebly
helped, so I knew he was at least semiconscious; he
was also probably still drunk.

"Fire!" he croaked with his old chanticleer voice.

Fucking A! I thought, not wasting any breath.

With him half wrapped, I shoved him off the mattress

toward the door, but the flames from beneath the bed nipped his legs and he screamed in pain. He jumped back on the mattress.

Crouching low, I dragged at the mattress with Mr. March aboard. Maybe, I could get it to the door and push him through those flames.

The heaume banged one of the bedposts and I grabbed at the back of the mattress, dumping the whole thing on the floor. Mr. March fell into a small pool of fire and let out a fierce scream. Again he leaped back on the mattress. At least, I had it on the floor.

Turning my eyeslit toward the door, I still saw only fire. There was less flame between us and the door than there had been, but more than enough to keep us away.

I gagged with smoke. It's all up, I thought. I looked at the window of the room. Surely in moments someone would have a ladder up there. It was a rectangle of flamelessness. But between the window and us were small fierce fires.

My hot shoes began to hurt and I jumped on the mattress with Mr. March. I was retching and coughing, my lungs trying vainly to expel the smoke.

I knew the smoke could kill me as rapidly as the fire. We could die on the steaming mattress that isolated us from the greater pain of the fire itself.

"Alley oop!" I coughed to Mr. March, dragging him off the mattress with my hands in his armpits, trying not to loosen his wet bedclothes and yet to keep the spread around me.

Coughing violently, I let him drop screaming into the fire for a moment, then grabbed him up again. With what was left of my strength, I kicked the mattress toward the door to make a bridge across the low flames. Then I rolled him onto it and started crawling, dragging him along. But there was too much flame ahead. Through the slits in the heating metal, I saw no exit.

My eyes were shutting up from the heat and the burning outside. "Help!" I tried to gasp in my last panic.

Then, I felt a blast of powder on my bedspread and aching ankles.

I wheeled my body and saw someone wrapped as I, but with a big extinguisher. It gushed powder all over me, the mattress, and Mr. March, setting me to gagging again. Then, another mummy was beside us carrying a spare bedspread.

Fumbling there in the fiery, fumy room with its barricades of flame, we got the old man wrapped and half walked and half carried him back to the doorway.

On the other side of the flames, I fell, letting him go. With a clang, my heaume hit the stair railing.

I lay on the hallway floor until numerous hands lifted me up and got me down the stairs. My eyes were so burned I could not open them.

"Get the cloth off him. He's burned," someone authoritative said.

"Who is it?" said another voice, perhaps a servant.

"It's Aubrey," said someone else. "Get his helmet off."

Gently, I was unhelmeted. Feebly I clutched at the bedspreads with my burned hands hoping to hide my nakedness. But wiser hands unwrapped me.

"My God!" a woman said. "He's naked."

18

Election

Connie told a credible half-truth about how I came to be in her room. She said we had been talking downstairs, which was true. She said we were concerned about her father, which was true, but not for the reasons she implied. She said she went upstairs to check on him, which was half-true, or maybe a quarter-true. She said we had heard a noise outside, totally true. She said our clothing had caught fire, and we had torn it off.

The cops were dubious about the clothes and seemed most curious about why I had the helmet upstairs. I told them the heaume was my highest award, and I had not wanted to leave it where Cubbins might subject it to some crude practical joke.

The police and fire inspector, who after all were supposed to catch arsonists, not fornicators, were discreet about unnecessary questioning. It may also have been that Eaglesmere was very big on the local tax rolls, or simply that old March was regarded with awe out in the county, as he was nationally.

On the other hand, the sight by experienced, callous, and sexually curious newspeople of me naked and Connie wrapped up in a sheet made at least the general outlines of our activities pretty clear to them.

When I called in the next day from home, where my feet and parts of my hands were recovering from the burns, Cubbins was chilly.

"It'll be a couple of days more before I can get back," I told him.

"Who's taking care of you?" he asked.

Connie had been by, and we had finished rather gingerly what we had begun, only with me on the bottom and no helmet on my head. She was not there now.

"No one," I replied. Cubbins paused, thinking, I knew, that my bedding down Connie made the relationship between him and me a little less that of would-be master and recalcitrant servant. But he must have decided to brave it out.

"You are literally trying to fuck me out of my job," he said peevishly.

"I wouldn't want your job," I retorted with little spirit.

Connie was more embarrassed than I had expected her to be by our colleagues' assumption that we had been in bed. "Maybe they'll think it was just a one-time pop," she had said hopefully. I had laughed, thinking how funny it was that a young woman would rather be thought promiscuous than to be having an affair. Although, of course, that oversimplified it; my age and her father had something to do with her feelings.

The *Eagle* offered a $10,000 reward for information leading to the arrest of any one of the arsonists. Papers around the country deplored the fire-bombing, and Mr. March, who was burned worse than I, called me from the hospital.

By that time I was back in the office, doing routine stuff by telephone. I was heartened to hear the raspy old voice.

"Aubrey, I want to thank you," he said. "Helluva way for a good party to end." He told me he was still going to be in the hospital for a few more days. When he'd jabbered a bit, he blurted out what was really on his mind.

"I surmised what you were doing up there," he said. "She's too young for you. She won't develop into a decent newspaperwoman if she keeps bouncing around this way."

I made a few non-committal, "Wells" and "Uhs."

"I'm not telling you to stay away from her," he said, and for the first time there was a note of pleading in his voice. "But—" He was suddenly at a loss for words. I thought of saying something like, "She's a big girl now," but didn't.

Still, I didn't trust him enough to outright confess it.

"She's as much as told me," he recommenced. "I don't give a shit whether you tell me or not." He paused, on the brink of anger. "Don't be a prick, Aubrey," he said instead. "There are so many others."

But I liked Connie. And he must have sensed that to try to push me away from her would just make me want her the more.

"I'm sorry I mentioned it," Mr. March now said. "I'm a silly old fart."

"I wouldn't worry about it," I said. "It'll work out."

In Kansas, the Speaker was in serious trouble. My friend in Topeka, after an *ex voto* of ass kissing on his managing editor, had gotten permission to follow up on my land-deal story.

It seemed the Wichita Landmark Trust, in which Edwards had a half interest, was also doing business in several neighboring states. Through Kitticon, it had chalked up another $1.6 million there. In addition, the Topeka reporter had turned up an obscure civil suit deposition establishing that a sudden cash flow into Edwards' family trust had originated from an out-of-state property company.

The papers were pressing Edwards for a full accounting, something I knew damned well he couldn't afford to do. There were too many pearly skeletons in his closet.

So far, his dodge was the old chestnut of "every man in Kansas or any other state is entitled to financial privacy, and a Congressman is entitled to no less." But his opponent, who was reasonably broke, had made a big thing of his own full accounting.

Back last winter, before the stories began, the Little Major had been looked on with awe by the voters. Now the whirlwinds that had whipped around him had eroded that awe. The citizenry forgot the jobs he had brought to his district through government construction. Edwards was becoming a cheap pol in the voters' eyes, and thus expendable.

Yet even wise Betty Page, as with politicians and their wives everywhere, was blotting out the bad, adhering to hope. Mostly now, she based it on the potential impact of the President's visit.

The governor, as we had predicted on primary night, had given Edwards only the most perfunctory support. As a result, Edwards had virtually deserted Washington to campaign in Kansas.

Betty Page, as part of her intense, but narrowly defined loyalty, was breaking her back for him. How many coffees, I wondered? How many visits to the small towns on that flat land? How many churches could there be in his district for her to drop in on during the social hour?

Edwards had pulled all his power strings, she told me. The Secretary of Agriculture had come out to honor "the man who helped shape the future of the American farm." The Secretary of Defense had praised "the man whose anvil of patriotism had forged our country's strength."

But the Little Major's opponent kept plugging away at the issues of public accounting, vast out-of-state land-holdings, the code words integrity-in-government, and friends-of-the-oil-magnates (though withal a "great Kansan"), and beneficiary-of-a-secret-family-trust.

During one of Edwards' brief visits to Washington for some meeting with the Secretary of State, Betty Page managed to come to my apartment. It was indicative of how far things had gone with Connie that before Betty Page got there—early in the afternoon—I had searched the apartment thoroughly for any earrings, pieces of clothing, or anything else Connie might have left behind during her increasingly long stays.

When we were finally in bed, I popped off like cheap, homemade champagne. And for all that we had two hours together, I had not been able to come back. I knew it was guilt.

"You must be feeling guilty about something," said Betty Page with acuity. "I don't want to know about it," she had said lightly.

When she was back in Kansas, we called each other often. On the telephone with her, I could imagine touching or being with no one else, even though she was usually wrapped up in the campaign. But once off, I was avid for Connie's near and fervent arms.

I did not like the role of liar. And although I had not verbally lied, still the fact of my dishonesty with both Betty Page and Connie rankled in me What my lips could not volunteer, my honest tool had revealed in pantomime, at least to Betty Page.

With Connie, for good or ill, because I was intoxicated with her youth, her abandon and openness, her toughness and her comparative innocence of life, if not of sex, I was insatiable. And she was ardent. If Plainspoken Prick thought I was being a liar with Connie, he did not make his thoughts known.

I learned about the great disaster for the Speaker before he or Betty Page did. That was unusual; his antennae's sensitivity was one of his assets He had friends to tip him off to events, and to confirm or deny his own intuitions. Yet they had begun to fail him.

Bothild, the *Eagle*'s White House man, an old rival since our days on cityside, caught up with me one day as I crossed Lafayette Park.

"Aubrey," I heard his voice. There was a nip in the wind that had chilled loose some of the leaves from the old horse chestnut and flicked spray from the fountains onto the sidewalks With the sky overcast, the birdshit on Andrew Jackson's shoulders and horse looked to my fading eyes like a preview of snow. "Gotta minute?" We sat on one of the benches.

"I get a vibration about your man Edwards." He paused, watching a pigeon drawing nearer and nearer.

"They give you a disease ending in 'osis,' " he said. "About the Speaker."

"Whatcha got? Can you write it?" I asked, excited about what it was, but first wanting to establish its degree of probability.

"No," he said. "It's sort of gooey so far."

"Ah?" I encouraged him.

"Had you heard the Prez was thinking of going down to do a speech or two for Edwards at the end of the campaign?"

I knew it only from Betty Page. And I was sworn not to speak of it.

"Oh, a rumor or two," I fudged. "Is he?" God knows I did not want another Renardi case with Betty Page.

"No," said Bothild. "I don't think he's going to. But since I wasn't ever aware he was going to do it in the first place, I'm getting this thing sort of like a denial of a statement that I never knew was made. You know what I mean?"

My pulses throbbed with excitement.

"So, he's not going, right?"

"That's what I get."

"How much work would it cost? To get it?"

"Too much, probably," said Bothild, "unless I can tie it up as a broken promise sort of thing. Right now it's so—"

"Vague . . ." I said. I had the cutthroat's urge for the purse if I saw it first. I knew more than the White House man how much the Little Major's campaign depended on the President going. The President had promised to come, and his failure to do so would be an absolute rejection. The voters would read it as the President turning his back on the Speaker because he was a crook.

A story on how the President had first agreed and then reneged would finish off the Speaker. It would also show what kind of prick the President was. I thought of his horny pressure tactics in Betty Page's hotel bedroom. The President and the Speaker deserved each other.

"Like you say, if you could show a promise had been broken because the President decided the Speaker looks like a thief, it would be a helluva story," I told him. "It would be nice to have somebody else break one on the Speaker, just so I wouldn't look biased."

"Let's not lie about it, Aubrey," said the White House man, suavely. "Let's plan." I looked at the shrewd little man and gripped his arm.

"If I can come up with the promise," I said, "I mean something hard, like when and where it was made, that you can use for a lever, then can you break loose the fact that he isn't going to go now?"

"You mean you want to split the byline?" Bothild said.

"Well, yes."

"Who'd be first?" It seemed petty of both of us, grown men with more than fifty years of newspapering between us, to be quibbling over who came first on a byline for a story we didn't even have. But we both knew that's the way it was.

"We could flip," I said. Then I thought of Betty Page. It might just be better if my rival went first. It would be better yet if I wasn't even on it. But, shit, I thought, if this story kills him off, and it very well might, then it could go in the scrapbook for the Pulitzer submission. I doubled up my fist and gave the ferrety White House man a friendly poke on the upper chest. "You go first," I said.

We parted, he walking toward the new executive office building. As soon as he was out of sight, I started walking fast, like one of those marathon walkers on his heels. My feet still hurt from the burns. I was out of breath when I got to my desk.

Betty Page was hard to locate, but I said it was urgent, a matter of a near relative at death's door. As usual, there was an element of literal truth in it. I left the name Tiresias Eliot.

She called a half hour later.

"Can you talk?" I whispered.

"Yes, I'm in a pay booth. But I've got a time jam. What's up?"

"Betty Page," I said, "get a grip on the side of that pay-phone booth. The jig's up for Pom."

"What do you mean?" She'd gone cold, offended by my excitement.

"The President isn't coming."

I could hear her gasp.

"How do you know?"

"I don't *know* 100 per cent." Now I would strike a bargain, and a loveless one. "You have got to protect me," I said. "Can you only tell Pom what you've heard, since I assume you feel you'd have to, but not saying *where* you got it? Can you not even hint?"

"He'd know it was you," she said.

"Could you conceal where I got it from?"

"Yes," she said. "From the Secret Service?" She had gotten a feel for my sources: all cops, like me.

"No, from our White House man."

"How solid?"

"He sounds pretty solid."

"Christ," she said, assessing the damage it would do. "It will finish him. Probably, anyway."

"I'm sorry," I said. "At least I'm sorry about the part that you invested in it."

"That doesn't matter. What will the story say?"

"I guess that he's reneging." I did not tell her that the only evidence of the original promise was what she had told me and what I had sworn not to reveal. And I would not reveal it unless I could get her to release me from my vow. That's what I set about to do.

"You know that my telling you this and you telling Pom means that Pom can call the Prez and maybe get him to change his mind. That means I'm scuttling our White House guy's story."

She stopped, thinking of what the ethics of it all were, probably from my point of view. I felt like a terrible heel. Here I was trying to trick her into releasing me from a confidence, and she was thinking of how to preserve my soul from a breach of ethics with my colleague.

"Maybe I'd better not tell Pom," she said. Her decency made me feel even a worse skunk.

"No," I said with mock gloom. "Let the skinny son-of-a-bitch know. Let him try to reverse the President. All I ask, Betty Page, is that if he *fails*, you cut me loose from my vow and let me report about the original promise from the Prez."

"Doesn't the White House man know about that?"

"Oh, I'm sure he has a bit of it, but not in detail, you know, about how the bargain was struck by him in Kansas over the phone to Washington that night."

"That could only have come from me," she said. "I—"

"I know that. Tell Pom that in exchange for my tipping you, and him, to the thing, I want that one little smidgen of detail. He understands such things."

"He hates you," she said.

"Shit, I hate him. It wasn't *me* that damn near got *him* bungholed and butchered in a Goddamn jail cell. I hate him, but what's that got to do with it?"

She seemed defeated by the news already.

"I'll ask him," she said. "If the President does come, if Pom can change him, then I can tell you and you won't be running the story, right? It would just be courting a full denial from the White House. You'd look silly. . ."

"Right." It was possible that the Speaker could convince the President to come. God knows what kind of secret pressures he had on Frieden.

"How much time do I have?" she asked.

"I don't know. Our White House guy is not noted for being slow on a good story."

"Jesus," she sighed. "I'll be glad when it's all done. Can we get off somewhere when it's done?"

I thought of Connie March, of how it would feel to lose her.

"Yes," I said. "We're going to need to get our heads screwed on again. This whole business is fucking up my loyalties." I knew she thought I meant my loyalties to the White House man, the paper, and to her. That was the least part of it. But, devious as it was, I had finally told her a full truth, and as much of it as I ever wanted to.

Betty Page called back late that night.

"The son-of-a-bitch won't come," she said.

"Jesus," I said consolingly.

"Pom talked to him for almost an hour. He gave Pom the usual lies about scheduling problems. We tried everything."

"Why didn't he threaten to botch up the legislative programs?" I was sympathetic now that I knew we were going to get our story. Also, two phone calls in one day was all it took to retie me to Betty Page.

"He did. He tried everything."

"Everything?" Pom must have some blackmail stuff on the President. I saw an angle for myself in all this, if I could find out what it was. She stopped.

"Oh, God, Aubrey. Not now. I don't know what he used on him. Whatever Pom has on him, he probably has worse on Pom. That kind of thing is a stand-off."

"Why don't you come here? Leave him now." Would that not save me, too?

"There's only the last two weeks," she said mournfully. "It would help if your White House man didn't write anything, you know."

Only two more weeks with Connie, I thought with a pang.

"I don't think I can stop him," I said. I felt guilty about pushing her to release me from my promise on Edwards, taking the last ounce of blood from the situation. Then I felt angry over my guilt.

"Goddamnit, Betty Page," I said, "what right have you to protect that prick? What kind of crazy masochism is it for you to try to get me to kill off a story about a couple of lousy, cheap crooks . . . ?"

"I'm not trying . . ." she started up in a wavery voice. Well, I thought for an instant, I don't think I am a bully. But I wanted it said.

"The hell you aren't," I said. "To save that lousy

shit you want me to kill a story. He's no good for the
country and he has merded on you a foot deep and
you're out there sniveling around to get him elected.
You ought to beg me to write the truth about him. And
about that cheap prick-on-legs of a Goddamned President, too. I mean, I'm scheming around, kissing your
ass, striking bargains to get you to let me use one lousy
little fact, and it's making me into some kind of cheap,
lying whore. You're too good for him. Even as bad as
I am, I'm too good to be conniving around this way."
I knew I was being self-righteous, and that poisoned my
satisfaction at getting it said.

She began to cry, and I waited for it to stop. I
couldn't remember ever hearing her sob so. What I had
said was the truth. But I was plenty bad myself, plenty
devious, and I was heartily ashamed. What I should
have done was to just blunt it out to her in the beginning; to tell her: the White House man has a piece of
the story, and I want a release from my vow not to
tell about the President's promise to come out.

But I had played a seedy game with her, whom I
loved.

"It's all the truth," I repeated stoically when she
paused.

"I know it," she said. "I'm just so damned tired. I
just want a bath and a good drink and to be with you.
I'm sick of it."

"So am I," I said, softened. I was heartsick enough
over my duplicity, which had probably not even been
necessary. Now I was also sick of the story.

"Oh, the hell with that," she said, beginning to come
back. "Go ahead and write the Goddamned thing. I
should never have agreed to be a middleman between
you and him. That's sick. He says he doesn't give a
damn now either. Go ahead and use it. It'll get out
anyway. Pom figures"—she paused, and a little sunni-
ness was there, that thing in her, that rising to brightness that made me love her—"he figures that a skunk
like you will stink up the President as much as you

stink him up. Go ahead and use it," she said. "Can you remember what happened?"

"Yeah," I said. "I love you." And God knows I did, and not just because I was about to nail up a truly good story. "As I remember it, they talked for a half hour or forty-five minutes—"

"Forty-five minutes," she interjected.

"—about him coming out there a few days before the end of the campaign, and the Prez promised with no 'ifs,' 'ands,' or 'buts,' right?"

"Right."

"And Pom agreed to help him with the consumer package, or HEW appropriations or some damned thing."

"Consumer package. And Pom did, and it got through."

"Right," I said.

"Okay?" she asked.

"Anything else?"

"Not on the story," she said. "I love you."

"I love you, Betty Page," I said, my old heart full of joy.

It was 11 P.M., too late to put together the whole thing. I was afraid we would lose it by the next day, but it was better to take the chance than to come out half-baked. The next morning, I got the White House man at home, fresh out of the shower.

"It's all true," I said. "Your stuff is solid, and I got the details."

"I'm getting the same kind of vibrations. I made a couple of—"

"Fuck your vibrations," I told him. "I have it nailed down."

This irritated him, and his voice got cold.

"Then why don't you just sit down to your little typewriter, Sir Aubrey of Underwood, and write the Goddamned thing?" I could tell he was about to hang up on my jubilation.

"No, no, no, no," I said, laughing. "Don't get a hard-on, assuming you still can. It's your baby. Honest, if I hadn't had the stuff you got, I'd have never nailed it down."

"Secret Service?" he said dismally. Everyone surmised my sources.

"As hard or harder," I said equivocally. "It's your story." I could afford magnanimity. "Just let me give you what I have and you put it together." That was the greatest compliment I could pay him, to give him my notes and trust him to fold them into his story.

"Let me get a notepad. I'm dripping in the hall." He was mollified anyway.

"I can call back," I suggested.

"No, no." He would be on the phone, I knew, as soon as he had his clothes on, to tie up the loose ends and to crank in who the President was going to schedule instead of Edwards, what the White House thought of the Speaker's record in Congress that year, what the White House thought of the financial scandal —all the non-essential background at which he was so fast and good. I knew he would let me see how he used my stuff before he showed it to the desk. And I knew my name would go on the story, though in second place.

When I had finished telling him of the President's early promise and that Frieden had given the final "no" to the Speaker last night, I called up Connie March.

"Got a good one coming," I said. After we had chattered about it, I realized how natural it had become to call Connie about whatever was on my mind. Whatever my longings for Betty Page, Connie March had become both friend and lover.

I went into the office and returned to the story I had been picking at for the last two days: a rip-off by a big utility company of some little municipal power facility in West Virginia. Finally, about noon, Speedy Mihalik came to me and asked, "How hard is the shit you gave Bothild on the Prez?"

"Hard," I said.

"Did you call the Speaker?"

"Just say he wouldn't comment," I said. That would

leave the impression with Speedy that the Speaker or someone next to him had given the information. But even in this town of intrigue, Speedy would not believe that *I* could get anything out of Edwards or his entourage.

"Do you mind telling me where you got it?"

"Yes," I said. "You'll just have to take it on faith, Speedy."

"You're sure of it?"

"Fuck it," I told him, bristling. "I told you it was hard. I don't ask you about how often you beat your meat. Don't ask me about my Goddamned sources, okay?"

He left angrily. I was hot, too. One advantage to marrying Connie March, I mused again, would be that I could fire Speedy Mihalik.

The White House man did his usual adequate job on the story. I would have done it nastier.

"President Frieden," he wrote, "has reneged on a tentative agreement to make a last-minute campaign appearance for Speaker Pommery Edwards, in the wake of charges against Edwards of financial irregularities."

The White House, of course, said if the Speaker thought the President was going to be there, it was due to a misunderstanding. I had hoped the White House man would have made more plain that the President was turning down Edwards because of the political consequences of campaigning for a crook. I would have said the President reneged "*because* of charges against Edwards of financial irregularities." But when you have a double by-line, somebody has to call the shots, and this time it wasn't I.

I called Betty Page and read her the whole thing when the proofs came up, an hour before the first press run came out.

"Is it going to beat him?" I asked her.

"I don't know. We've got a backfire going on Marthas"—their opponent. "He was still handling a couple of estates after he was sworn in."

"That's not much," I said.

"It's all we have," she replied. "With things this close, it may be enough. Probably not."

"I hope not," I said, bridling at her "we."

"I know," she said wearily.

Because I had done so much on the Speaker stories, Cubbins wanted me in the office on election night. He had made a career of setting up his special squads, teams, centers, and Christ knew what, to get complete and varied coverage in the paper. As a result, the *Eagle* ran on a skeleton staff during most of election day. The "Election Team" began to straggle in at three, many of us in casual clothes instead of the respectables we wore ordinarily, clinging, as we did, to the notion that we were professionals and not artisans or tradesmen.

In the old days—the early fifties—"Election Central" was three TV sets and the three wire services tickers. Three tickers, not because the now defunct INS ever beat AP or UP, but it had its great pieces by Considine and the like, if there ever was "the like" of Bob Considine.

There had been also the unpainted plywood tables with their newly wired telephones for calls from our reporters in the counties covering the local elections. I'd done journeyman rewrite on the Prince George's Fairfax, and other county elections, and it had been zesty stuff for me.

Now Cubbins had computer printout equipment and zippy little jobs that gave quick digital readings. There were also the wire machines, TVs, facsimile machines, and so on. Instead of the results being set in hot lead, as they once were, they were now blipped out by the computer and photo-set just as they came out. The printers sneeringly called the serifless printout script "Computer Bodoni."

By 5 P.M. we had damned near as many electronic technicians screwing around with the lenses, scanners and computer reels as we did editorial staff.

I was in an area identified by a big sign on a one-by-one stick as "Congress." The other election night "desks" were similarly marked "Governors," and in the cityside section were "DC-Md-Va."

Connie had been brought in to do features. She was fixing her hair these days in that same grown-up way. As she bustled around, I saw the slender throat above the opened collar, and her head, a sort of bouncing ball with a life of itself, like the emphasis balls on those old sing-along movies.

The copy kids were in second heaven. This was NEWSPAPERING: election night on a metropolitan daily. I still felt the excitement of it, wishing I could be more blasé about something that had happened to me so many times before.

But there *was* a thrill when the copy people came running up with the first piece of wire copy (so far the wires were running ahead of our vaunted computer), from a tiny polling place showing Marthas ahead of Edwards 21–19. Because the Edwards race was an important one, we had the past performances of most of the precincts in his district cranked into the computer.

I had the copy kid get me a reading on the same polling place two years ago. But it came back "n.r." which meant either "not recorded" or "not relevant." Either the polling place was too small, or it covered a different territory last time or it was newly set up.

Fidgeting for something to do, I thought of calling Betty Page, but I knew that whatever she felt about Pom, she would be with him now. They, not she and I, had been the unhappy companions of that Long March, bound together now like Ugolino and Ruggieri in political ice.

Along with the Edwards race, I would have to write up side pieces or excerpts of overall pieces on half a dozen other states out that way, too. Soon, enough of the copy and printouts had rained on and cluttered my desk for me to begin. I clipped them together by state and district, and rattled off a fast "trends" story for the first edition. It was too early to tell anything at all about Edwards' district. It had been sufficiently changed since the last election so that the big national TV computers couldn't predict with accuracy.

Because of the time difference, only a few scattered sites had reported. The vote was now 190–167 for Edwards.

From throughout the room, the copy was beginning to gush toward the desk for the first edition. The enormous city room, which earlier had buzzed with low talk, the yap of the TVs, the muted. sound-proofed rat-a-tat of the teletypes, now began to take on different sounds.

The volume picked up around the three areas where the copy was actually being knocked out. There was the tic-tic-tic of the typewriters, or for those younger reporters who used electrics, the thuck-thuck-thuck. The rhythms of our typing were as individual as our patterns of speaking. Without seeing, I could distinguish the White House man's fastidious trickle of sound from the authoritative key-socking of our top cityside rewrite man.

The small talk subsided. The early deadline men writing the lead stories shouted "Copy!" now and then. The copy and news desks were so long now that a clanking conveyor belt ran news copy from one editor on down the line to the next. It was Cubbins' technical masterpiece and, at huge cost, actually did speed things up a bit. The flashy little plastic clips for attaching the copy had begun to disappear and the belt was now at least humanized with various kinds of clip-on clothespins.

When the machine was first set up, the medical reporter had sent a grisly story on the vice president's enteritis operation down the belt attached with a small surgical clamp.

The conveyor tended to rumble at either end and to squeak in between, giving the city room cacophony an atonal quality. As deadline got nearer, there were more shouts of "Copy!", more running of copy kids' feet, a subdued bass rumble of grumbling from the copy desks and headline writers, and a diminution of typing.

At deadline, the "Copy" howls crescendoed, the various editors running each "area" swore frantically, the technicians loudly explained the failure of their electronic machines, the reporters spread discontent and spite as far as they dared at the editors, who were now feverishly macheteing copy to make it fit.

Then, suddenly, it was all over. The edition was "down," and you could feel the place relax. There was laughter, a relieved chatter. Chairs scraped as staffers went to the coffee machine. There were shouts across the room to friends eager to cut out for a fast drink, a shriek or an oath of excitement from near the TV and wire machines when an unexpected result came in. If it reminded me of anything, it was the launch of a rocket in the old days when the TV picked up the sounds of the control rooms in Houston.

We'd launched the *Eagle*'s first edition. We'd gotten something on the street. The basic framework of today's paper was now being fixed in shimmering metal below in the composing room.

In a short time, the building would come to life, pulse even up where we were on the sixth floor, and those gigantic presses, the great driving balls and cock of the paper, would begin to rumble out the edition.

I wondered if newspaperwomen thought of that first press run as metalanguage for giving birth. God knows, *I* felt it as a sexual thing. I looked around for Connie to ask her, then realized I'd do better to ask a woman reporter who'd had a baby.

But no time, no time. One of the subeditors had called me and was pointing at the TV. "C'mon," he shouted. I walked gingerly over on my gasolined soles and just caught the tail end of the broadcast from Wichita.

The TV reporter, in a motel ballroom somewhere, was saying, "And so for the first time in his twenty-six years in Congress, the Speaker of the United States is in trouble." He signed off.

"What did he say?" I asked.

"It's neck-and-neck in Petrie where Edwards ought

to be winning," said someone. "It's going to go against him."

My heart leaped. Jesus, I've beat him. I thought nightmarishly of that cell and the big black coming at me with the knife. I wanted to hate Edwards, so I could be happier. But I wasn't a very good hater. I began to feel slightly sorry for him, for Betty Page.

Another network was beginning its Kansas cut-in. I recognized the face of the fellow we'd seen slicing up the Speaker at the primary. He'd mellowed.

The small-town vote was coming in more heavily for the Speaker than expected, and it looked as if it would handily offset the surprise in Petrie where the Speaker had only equaled his opponent.

Well, I thought, that small-town margin would be Betty Page's doing. I wanted to beat the Speaker; I wanted that slightly sick feeling of power, the knowing that my stories had made a mighty man fall. But I feared both the liking in me for the power, and the sense of having toppled a figure of authority.

Complicating it was knowing that Betty Page would be distressed. Now I had a feeling of blah too soon after the first exhilaration. I felt emotionaly jerked around.

I went back and looked through the wire copy and printouts, then clipped them together again, fresh stuff on top. There was a good deal of bustling now from the "DC-Md-Va" area. The next edition was the "State," which went as far north as Baltimore, southward to Richmond, west into West Virginia, and east all the way across the eastern shore to the ocean beaches.

It was loaded up with wire copy from just outside the Washington area. Even with the circulation problems, it made money because it was a "split run," meaning it had a special page or two of advertising for those outlying areas along with the regular ads.

I banged out new leads and did a safe, short piece on the Speaker's race being a toss-up as of "last night," since the paper was dated for the next morning. But soon the trend was going against him. I smelled his defeat. I walked over to where Connie was beating away at the machine.

She looked up, saw me, and then went back to whatever it was she was typing.

"What's the concentration?" I said. I saw something in her face I did not understand and it worried me.

"I just called Betty Page Edwards," she said, and then, I knew what it was. "I'm doing a sidebar on her and I got through to her."

"Yeah?" I said, sick at my stomach.

"Why didn't you tell me?" she said. "I wouldn't have cared if you'd been straight with me." Now I felt even sicker.

"How'd you find out?" I asked lamely. Her eyes narrowed now.

"So it's true, you prick." My God, I panicked, I've been taken in by the oldest ruse in newspapering.

"You mousetrapped me," I said. She had teared up.

"It was a dirty trick," she said, meaning my not telling her about Betty Page.

"I was afraid it would turn you off to me," I said. Now, I could see we were getting down to the basics. It had been, always up to now, warm, but superficial, loving but uncritical.

"It would have, too," I said gently. I could see her going from me, something I had known would happen. And now I was wrung by the sadness of it, and a feeling that I did not want to hurt her.

"Oh, bullshit. I'd have let you have what you wanted anyway," she said. "Which was a good, young lay." The tears dried up in her anger. "It would have been no problem."

"It's no problem now." I could see we were being watched by some of her cityside colleagues. I desperately wanted to get her out to a restaurant, over a bottle of wine, anything.

"No problem for you," she said bitingly.

"How'd you find out?" I said, feeling a little colder now that she was giving me such a hard time. I won-

dered if she had told Betty Page about her affair with
me.

"She said, 'I guess Aubrey Warder will be happy
about the early results,' and there wasn't any hate in it
like there should have been. There was something else.
Then I thought about the way you talked about her
that day when I brought you my story on her. I remember feeling then that you knew her better than you
let on." She had sandbagged me with a look and one
question. "You're a crappy liar," she said. "And I'm
a damned fool."

"Are you—?" I started.

"Am I what?"

"Are you going to see me again?" Now I did not
want to lose her. She looked up, the anger controlled
in her constricted eyes.

"I don't know. I'm going to finish this story. And
when I get time, I'm going to decide whether an old
bag of shit like you is worth fighting for."

I felt completely demoralized. But she wasn't totally
finished with me. She fixed me with a hard look, her
father's daughter look.

"Aren't you going to ask whether I told her about
us?"

I realized I was so broken by my dishonesty and her
assault that, after the first instance, I had not thought
of that. Before I could phrase the question, she had
answered it.

"No," she said. "If you had any balls, you'd tell her
yourself. *She's* too good for you, too."

"You're right about that," I said. "You both are."

But she was wrong about telling Betty Page. It might
be disloyal, weak, even treacherous to have an affair
with two decent women at the same time. But to tell
either about the other was worse: It was cruel. That
much, at least, age had taught me.

"Oh, Aubrey," she said, but now the anger was at
least diluted to irritation and disgust, "don't be such a
milksop."

I left her desk and went back to my own, so disconsolate I didn't care whether Edwards won or lost. Now I was found out.

The returns were stacking up against Pom Edwards, but for part of me it was anticlimatic. I kept looking over at Connie March but she had no glance for me. By 11 P.M., with the deadline for our first really big press run, the "three star," only forty minutes away, Cubbins and Mihalik came over.

"The TVs aren't calling it yet," said Cubbins. "Do you want to?"

"No," I said gloomily. "He might pull it out. Wait'll next edition. Let's just say, 'appeared to be in serious danger of defeat,' okay?" The two of them looked at each other.

"You don't seem very happy for a giant-killer," Speedy said.

"I've got mixed feelings," I said, glad to be honest at least on this point. "How many inches you want?"

"Make it twenty-four or twenty-five," said Cubbins, "for out front"—the front page. "For the next one"— the four star—"let it run longer, okay?"

An hour later, it was all over for the Little Major. I felt a dizzy shock of elation and justification. I had beaten him who had deserved to be beaten for so many reasons! When the stammer of excitement had left my brain and arteries, I shook my head to clear it, and went into a trance of work.

In my story, I tried to weave the spot news of his defeat with the background of the campaign, the stories we had done that destroyed him, the weathervane of the primary.

All concentration now, I threw in the national significance of his defeat, a fair amount on Betty Page's part in the campaign, and how it might have saved him, if the farm vote had not wavered. I did it totally without passion. My climax had passed with that lightning strike of joy. The rest was an elevated kind of routine, and I knew a letdown would come after the story was done.

When I had finished it, the copy boy running my

stuff to the desk in "short takes," I was wrung out with sweat and weariness. I had beaten the Speaker, but there was little satisfaction in me now, more nagging personal despondency over my unspoken lies to the two women, and the fouled-up feelings I had about the hurt there would be in Betty Page over the vote.

I looked across for Connie. I wanted now to try to mend things a little with her. But she was gone. Her features would be done, the kind that could be juggled to fit victory or defeat.

At 1:30 A.M., Edwards made it official.

I looked at that drawn, emaciated face now on all three tubes. Every Congressman, I thought, no matter how often victorious, must carry graven on his voice box the words of a concession speech.

The Little Major went out with class. He even seemed sober, and, heartbreakingly, there beside him was the tired face of his wife. The two sons, one in from his college, the other in from the boarding school in Washington, were beside her. Pom and Betty Page looked as if the campaign had rewedded them with its pain.

"For twenty-six years, Betty Page and I have had the good fortune to represent our district in the Congress, Kansas in the community of States, and our country on international occasions," he said.

"We were ready to go on doing it," he said the platitudes with a sad smile, "but the board of directors of our district, the voters, decided to try a new executive team.

"My opponent fought hard, the way Kansans do, and I would be dishonest with you to say I thought he fought a campaign purely on the issues. But, Betty Page and I had our crack at the constituency. Our views got good publicity in the press and broadcast media"— and here his voice caught a bit—"and the voters simply decided they didn't want Pom Edwards around for two more years.

"So be it. You have elected an energetic public servant. I wish him well. He has given the state good law enforcement as attorney general. He is young . . .

and he is alive to the main chance." Well, I thought, thank God for that single, muted note of bitterness.

"To those who have worked so hard for us . . ." the camera panned out on the young and old wheat-belt faces, some crying, some staring stolidly into the red eye of the camera.

I wanted the camera to come back to Betty Page. I wanted her to be with me, not Pom tonight. And yet, I wanted Connie March, too, and the realization of my duplicity made me sick of myself. I quietly got up and went home.

19

The Tapes

Next morning I tried to call Betty Page at the headquarters hotel, but the Edwards' room did not answer. I left my real name. I wanted no more games, at least not ones I could avoid.

I also called Connie March, but her phone did not answer. I figured she'd gone back to Mark Braswell, and I sure as hell wasn't calling there.

When I got off the phone, my own phone rang and, with hope that it was one of them, I swooped up the handpiece. But it was only some dippy baby from a New York media magazine called *Turn Rule*, journalistic slang for another page coming up.

"Do you think the defeat of Speaker Edwards puts you in the running for the Pulitzer?" she asked.

"I don't know," I said.

"How do you feel about it?" she persisted.

"I feel shitty, but about other things," I muttered. "Besides, I don't want to answer an asshole question like that. If I say I'm glad Edwards got beat, I sound like a vindictive monster. If I say I'm saddened, I sound like a hypocrite. If I say 'the voters have spoken,' I sound like a shnook. By the way, what do you look like?" I asked her.

"What kind of chauvinist question is that?" she sneered.

I hated that kind of New York woman.

398

"Forget it," I said. "I don't like being interviewed."

After I dodged a few more of her questions, she gave up, and I wondered how she would shiv me in her sheet. Newspapering is a first cousin to cannibalism, I thought, gloomily pouring some orange juice.

I still couldn't get Betty Page and began to wonder whether she might have surmised from Connie's voice what Connie surmised from hers. All three of us, not just me, were lousy liars.

The next day, wanting to restore communications so I could resolve my life a little, I went to Connie's desk. She looked up at me with inscrutable eyes.

"Can you come see me after work?" I asked.

"I'm back with Mark," she replied, as if she'd rehearsed it, but she hadn't rehearsed much beyond it. "But that's no good either," she went on. I hurt for her. Had I really thought we were that wired into each other?

"Just come, even if we don't do anything. I'm having my troubles, too," I said.

"No fun, is it?" she said, smiling with chill sympathy.

"No," I said. "Would neutral ground be better?"

"No," she replied.

"Okay," I said, the anxiety clawing me.

I tried again to locate Betty Page, but all I got from Edwards' clean-up campaign headquarters was that they'd gone away for a few days. *They'd* gone away, I thought. Well, it's all over up there, too.

But in my heart I knew it wasn't so, that she might be traumatized by the defeat or by whatever she thought I was doing with Connie or whoever, but that we would see each other again. I got our House man to call Edwards' office. Mr. Speaker was coming back in a few days, his office reported, to try to make a good legislative record as a lame duck.

That's what they all say, I thought. But at least he— they—would soon be back in town. I had already written the "follow story" on Edwards' defeat. The *Eagle* was genuinely building a scrapbook for the Pulitzer now and wanted my name on Edwards' stories.

They would be collecting clips from papers crediting

us with his defeat, from political scientists willing to give us letters commending us and from TV editorials and commentaries. Getting up a Pulitzer entry was like an ad agency putting together an ad presentation for a prospective client.

At home next morning, longing for Connie, longing for Betty Page, I looked out into the gray morning. To the south, the leaves in Potomac Park's fat old trees were dull brown, dull orange, deadened by the overcast. The brown Potomac reflected the skies. Choplets, all dirty white, had set in with the north wind.

I was feeling sorry for myself and for my age. One of my molars needed a root canal, that first sign of failing body. Another was going to have to be pulled because it had an abscess below it. The tooth hurt, vaguely.

What is the salt, when it has . . . I began to think, then saw the birds wheeling in the dismal sky and thought of some line about seagulls and gray waters from Hart Crane, and then rummaged in my desk for a translation of Betty Page's that she'd managed to get published twenty years ago in a magazine and which she'd Xeroxed for me. It was Baudelaire, and she'd given it to me half in jest, but I remembered it now as appropriate.

I see in autumn's pall the fall of all my dreams,
   [it said]
Who knows if laggard flowers sprouting in my brain
Can find in this soil drained like beaches by the
   rain
The magic sustenance to make a strong new
   start . . .

Well, I'd show it to Connie to make her feel sorry for me, I thought, then realized the last thing I ought to do was show her one of Betty Page's poems.

I put the damned poem back in the drawer and went out on the balcony again, feeling that this soil was not going to sustain any strong new starts.

If I hadn't felt so sorry for myself, I would have been impressed with Connie's pride. I knew she had seen in me something better than I deserved, and that my action at the fire had bolstered it. I knew that she even felt—oddly, considering the abandon and guiltlessness of her screwing—that I was somehow fatherly. Maybe that's why her discovery of my affair with Betty Page had bitten her so hard.

At the office that day, about eleven, I got up and walked to where she sat, running through notes on some chicken-shit feature or another. She glanced up, her eyes looking as if she wanted to be friends, then filming over hostilely.

"Come on," I said. "Enough of this bullshit. Let's go get a cup of coffee and get this settled." It was firm enough so that March or no March, she got up and went with me.

Despite the rumors that had begun the night of the fire, we had been discreet around the office. But now we found a table in the sterile cafeteria, which was filling with the classified women and subscription people who'd come to work on the early shift.

"I never said anything explicit about love, and whatever I felt of love for you, you sensed it all anyway, right?" I said to her as she blew across the surface of her coffee.

"Maybe I sensed more than there was," she said.

"Oh there was enough. Is enough," I corrected myself.

"Enough for what?" she said tartly. I ignored the tone.

"Enough to be troublesome," I said. When she did not reply, I went on. "I was in love with Betty Page before I even met you. When you and I jumped in bed that day, it was because I was horny, and you were curious. And it happened to work despite the age thing. And then the fire tied it a little closer."

"Right," she said. "So why didn't you tell me?"

"Because I didn't want you to leave me," I said. She fixed me now with the back-lighted brown eyes.

"Is that true?"

"Yes, I was having double dreams. I dreamed of a farmhouse and a weekly somewhere up north with Betty Page, and I dreamed of being editor of the *Eagle* with you."

"I dreamed of being married to you, too," she said.

"Well," I said, helplessly, "it was a possible dream for both of us."

"*Is* a possible dream. What's wrong with it? When I'm thirty-seven—" she insisted.

"Don't," I said. "I've already done the arithmetic a hundred times. It counts down to ten or fifteen good years, if you didn't fuck me to death with my bad heart."

She laughed. The face, which had seemed so plain with its lipsticklessness, brightened, and the glamour of that night at supper poured into it. But it dimmed to caution.

"It's good, isn't it?" she said.

"Yes." I drank the cooling coffee, bitter and strong, and thought, one day fairly soon I'll probably have to switch to Sanka. "What do you want to do? Is it marching with Braswell?" The bad pun went past her.

"No," she said. "I don't know what I want to do." She sighed, her thin chest rising up to where I could perceive the breasts beneath her blouse, and then falling, her shoulders hunched over.

"Why don't you move permanently into your own pad?" I asked. "Be your own damned person. You don't really have to keep latching on to some damned man just to keep yourself secure."

"Yes," she said, agreeing that was what she did, without agreeing that she would live by herself in her own place.

"I've thought out that whole Oedipus shmeer," she said. "Maybe I will try it again, living by myself." She shuffled in the chair, making up her mind. "Okay," she said. "So let's say I move out on Mark to get my shit together. Then what about us?"

I thought of those lean, warm shanks and grinned at her. If Betty Page had not seemingly simply deserted me for these three days since the election, I might not have weakened. But I said: "Let's see each other and see what happens."

"At least it would be with knowledge aforethought," she said, adding, "now." She shrugged. "My God, I must be nuts to fool around this way. I'd be better off married to the Goddamned paper, like Daddy."

And, I thought, you will be. Connie, I suspected now, had considered marrying me only when it was safe from happening. Mark was possible: close to her age, a defiance of her father, yet withal, capable, and toughening. I was less possible. I had probably been a vineyard worker too long to inherit Château March.

I touched her shoulder as we got up, friends of a sort again, a truce if no real peace. "You will, if he has his way," I said, aloud this time.

Two evenings later we were in bed again: precise, filigreed love-making, platinum and bright light, just as before. Only the mystery of where our affair was going was out of it. We were seeing, really, if Betty Page would go away, although neither of us said the name.

I tried to reach Betty Page through the Speaker's office, disguising my voice as best I could, but no one would say where either of them was. My feelings jumped between fear that Pom was using some unknown leverage to keep her with him and jealousy that she might voluntarily be trying to make another start with him, now he had failed. I prayed that he had not gone on the wagon, thus giving her an excuse to stay.

At bottom, my resentment of Betty Page's failure to call me made it easier to forget her when I was with Connie, whose bed and board were now her own. Mark no longer called her, and she told me she was sleeping with no one but me.

When she spent the night with me, our love-making had the reckless quality it had before. But, the feeling that it might come to something more than that was gone. In the morning, we still talked compatibly of the stories we were working on, as we cleaned up the place together. And we laughed quickly.

One night, after we had screwed wildly and well, she had nuzzled into me and said, "Nice, hunh? Do you . . . ?" She had stopped there, leaving forever unsaid something that I knew had to do with love and permanence. And my mind, for a change, overruled my cock and heart, so I had not taken her up on it.

Then, two weeks after the election, Betty Page called me at 2 A.M. She was so controlled and considerate that I knew it was something horrible or exciting, like cancer, or Edwards' death. My first thought was that I was glad Connie had not decided to spend the night. My second was a thrill of anxiety over what Betty Page would say.

"I'm sorry it's so late," she said.

"Where the hell were you?" I asked, the anger bursting out along with the anxiety. "What's up?"

"We're flying in tomorrow. Can we see you?"

"We?"

"Don't worry," she said. "It's done. We tried again. You must have figured as much." My heart pumped, and I felt a giddy moment. She had gone back to him. I'd imagined it, but not seriously. I'd really thought she was trying to throw off the trauma of her long campaign coming to naught, and finding a way to break with her husband.

"My ass, I did!" I burst out. "Goddamnit, Betty Page!" I paused, and in that moment I thought, well, I was putting horns on her with Connie and she on me with Pom. It was a mug's game, both ways. I wanted to cry.

"Well," she repeated softly, "it didn't work."

"Then why 'we'?"

She paused to say it very carefully. "There's something he wants to speak with you about. He doesn't want to talk about it over the phone."

"What the hell is it, Betty Page?" I demanded. "Why all this dramatic bullshit? My God, it's 2 A.M.!" My disappointment over her attempt at reconciliation with Edwards, *without even consulting with me*, had been caustic to my raw vanity.

"Oh, Aubrey, fuck you!" she boiled up. I had seldom heard her so angry since that first night when I brought her husband home bloody and drunk from the robbery attempt. I tried to butt in and bludgeon down her anger, but she had already gotten it under control. "He would have called you himself," but she was on the brink of tears now, too, upset by her own outburst.

"But he's too sick, too damned drunk." That doused my outrage.

"So what's it about?" I said, mollified.

"He's going to tell you about the President."

"About—" I gasped.

"About the President being a thief," she said softly. She said it. It had to be true. The *President!*

"Jesus," I said. "Where can we—?"

"A good dark restaurant, someplace off the Hill, where we can feel relaxed, feel—"

"Cantina d'Italia," I said. "What time? Jesus!"

"Make it twelve-thirty," she said. "In your name."

Virtually sleepless, but in my best dark suit, I showed up at twelve twenty-five in front of the Cantina, a rich, dim restaurant that cared fastidiously about its food. I paced out front for five minutes, then went downstairs and waited for fifteen more.

I was getting to the watery part of my Galliano and soda when I spotted them coming down the stairs and saw her move her lips, pronouncing my name to the maître d'.

The owner's quick eye caught the Speaker as he bowed his head the way tall men do coming down stairs, and then there was that little nod by the owner of recognition that a *personàggio* had arrived. He ushered them efficiently to the alcoved table where I rose to greet them. She looked so beautiful to me in the dim light, and he so caved in, that I bug-eyed first her, then him. But as I stood, waiting for both of them to sit, his practiced ease with people got us past the first hurdle.

"Sit down, Aubrey," he said, quietly, smiling with no trace of warmth, but no enmity, either. "The king is dead." What a flat sound it had. Was it some hideous pun?

Nervously, my hand shot out under the table to touch her, but I withdrew it like a small fish darting back behind its rock.

"You look great," I said to her, instead. And she did, her face smoothed by the flattering light, at rest. She had put her mind in order while we two, the Speaker and I, had treacherous, unfinished business.

We made small talk, and he ordered a double Cutty Sark on the rocks. At least, I thought, there's not going to be any pretense. When it came, along with my second Galliano and soda, and a white wine for her, he took a rattling gulp of it and looked at me straight. Now I would find out how he was going to deliver the President into my hands.

"You know, when he didn't come, it beat me," he said very quietly, so that I pulled up my chair to the table and leaned toward him. I could not avoid glancing quickly at Betty Page, but her replying look was assessing, curious almost.

"It was certainly a factor," I said. His eye went reptilian flat for a moment, a prelude to anger, then refocused on me.

"I know what, and I know who, created the atmosphere in which I was beaten," he said, still almost in a whisper. "We don't have to go into that. For the thing at hand, it's not necessary."

The words cooled me. He meant, of course, that he would as soon destroy me as look at me, but that he had a better use for me. I was afraid of him. The sting of the dying adder.

But it was a time to shut up and listen.

"The President is a liar," he said in a bitter hiss. "He lied to me about supporting me. When I pleaded with him to respect his word, he waffled."

I nodded. I might have said that by the last two weeks of the campaign, Edwards was poison. No politician in his right mind would support him.

I had ordered one of those big, odd antipastos: sliced mushrooms, artichokes, spring onions, pimentos, tomatoes, olives, all to be dipped in a hot bath of anchovy-flavored cream sauce, heated over a candle. I thought it would relax everyone. It came and my mouth watered for it, but I dared not drop my gaze from the blasted face of the Speaker.

"He let you down," I said. "No doubt about it."

"He let me down," the Speaker picked up, and I saw for the first time how programmed he was to tell me what he had to tell me, no matter how Kamikaze it was going to be. "He let me down, Aubrey," he sighed, the Cutty gone and another double in front of him. "I am going to give you the story of your life."

My God, I thought, my palms popping sweat. I wished I could get it out of him a little faster, but he was taking his time, feeding his hate with a little drama.

"Of all reporters, I have least reason to give you anything," he said.

I nodded in agreement, but thought back in the cerebrum far enough for it not to show on my face. "You pigfucker, you almost got me killed for it, too." He slugged the hootch again, suicidally.

"But," he went on, picking up a mushroom, to my relief, "you are also the one reporter whose doing the story will hurt him most."

Again, I could not avoid looking at Betty Page. She gave me a half nod and let out a sigh. She, too, was getting tired of the drama. But the Speaker was determined to do it his way.

"Your stories on Boles give you the background," the Speaker said. "You won't have to learn the case from the ground up. You won't make mistakes."

I was shaken. The President and Boles-Panjunk?

"Oh, the President has good reason to dislike you," he went on with a smile, reflecting all the amusement of a skeleton. "The Secret Service saw you come out of"—he paused, wondering what to call her, as I groaned—"my wife's room."

"I—" I started to interrupt.

"The crazy bastard thinks I planted you there, suspecting that he would . . . would try to come there. He couldn't face the possibility that you were the better. . . . He did not want to—"

"Let it go, Pom," Betty Page stepped in. "We've talked all that out, okay?" She looked at me, still cool. I felt a little frightened that she was taking the whole thing with such sangfroid. "The President found out

you were there that night. The President accused Pom
of planting you there." She reached over and took his
wrist, not his hand. It was a gesture of familiarity, even
accommodation, but not love. I could see now why we
were all in a restaurant. This way, the Goddamned
thing would stay civilized, controlled.

"Wait a minute," I said, the reporter in me giving
away to my own more special interests. "The President
told you," I said to Edwards, "that I had been planted
by you in a closet to compromise him?"

"Right," said Edwards. "I have proof—"

"Proof? Tapes? Tapes?"

"Right," said Edwards.

"You have—"

"Let's do—" we both began at once. I was boggled.
Was this the story? Betty Page chimed into the confusion.

"Let's not—" I waved them both hushed.

"You are saying," I whispered to him, my heart
speeding up, "that the President called you, suspected
you had planted me in a closet to compromise him and
that when he accused you, you tape-recorded him?"

"Yes, but—" he began. Well, it was a hell of a story,
but I wasn't the man to write it. Immediately, I began
to wonder if I could stay on the paper if the thing broke.
But I wanted to get it all out straight before I began
to worry.

"And that's how you found out that Betty Page and
I—"

"No," he said. "I assumed—"

"So you told the President that I had come there on
my own without your knowledge."

"Yes," he said. "And—"

"And so the President sees himself as being turned
down by Betty Page, who in turn—"

"That's some of it." I felt uncomfortable every time
the fact of our affair came up. But if during these two
weeks they had been comparing notes, going through
twenty years of agony until they were anesthetized to
what each had done to the other, then this affair of

Betty Page and me must have been easier than I'd have thought.

"And the rest is Boles-Panjunk?" I said. "Do you have—"

"Tapes?" he said. "Yes."

"Motherfucker," I said softly, then looked over and said, "Excuse me, Betty Page. You are going to give me tapes on the President and Boles?" I asked him.

The horsey face, its bags now sagging under the eyes as I had never seen them before, regarded me acidly. Alcohol and all, his eyes showed the dark flickers of that genius, the knowledge of where every lever was, that almost mechanical pre-eminence in the use of power.

"I hate the President worse than you, Aubrey. You did your job, dirty, spiteful as I thought it was. But you did it with a sort of malicious fairness. You called me for comment."

"He—" Betty Page interrupted him. He looked at her and cut her off, sensing as husbands do with wives what she was going to say and saying it himself.

"You saved my life, perhaps, that night, with the very muggers who might theoretically have killed you in jail. It would have been an irony," he said with quick reflection, and smiled at the idea. "But it didn't happen. You got out to shit on me another day."

"I—" I started again. But now he waved *me* off. I was a mass of questions, and I tried to break in and begin asking them, but his lawyer's mind, his orderliness was working now, ably, before the booze caught hold of it. He raised his skinny, preachery hand.

"Let me do it," he said. "Chronologically." He put the drink aside, nibbling the mushrooms, then with his mouth still slightly full, he went on. "Your stories were accurate up to a point on Boles-Panjunk." To a point? I thought. I started to interrupt again, but my last interjections had led us to snipe flights. I shut up.

"I invested the money in the hundred shares that I own. But Nick Kitticon was not my straw. He was the straw for Harry Frieden."

"Holy God!" I said, but did not push him.

"I got George"—that would be Hedaris—"to get a trustworthy man to act as the straw for the President. The $500,000 that the stock made will not benefit Kitticon a dime, nor me."

Even as I marveled at the story, something critical in me said, "No, not a penny," but it gave Kitticon the power to call on the President, the executive branch for a favor, any favor and any time he wanted, just as it and things like it, I suspected, gave the Speaker the power to call on the President for any favor any time he wanted.

And then the Speaker called for that favor and the President did not deliver. The President never thought the Speaker would do the Samson-at-the-temple thing, but the Speaker decided, contrary to the President's guess, to ruin the President. All of that was what the $500,000 had bought.

I said nothing, although I was sure that the Speaker had sensed my thoughts.

"The Boles-Panjunk deal will only benefit the President," he reiterated. "Now let's go back," he said, anticipating my question about how the thing had worked. "You remember Kitticon got the options as counsel and advisor for Boles-Panjunk. Boles is an old friend of mine, an old friend. I got him to put Kitticon in a position to get those options," and now Edwards' sallow face reddened. "I got him there purposely to help that son-of-a-bitch Harry Frieden get a little money for personal expenses, for the campaign. Did it purposely," he said now, more loudly than he should, angry at the memory.

"Easy, Pom," said Betty Page, quieting him with a touch on his arm again. I looked at her, longingly and a little disturbed, but came back to Edwards.

"The President had asked me to find him a little money and Boles had told me his drill was going to make it, going to make it big, if he could get it accepted by the industry. So I helped Boles with Bounty."

"And—" I couldn't resist.

"And that's all I'm going to talk about, Aubrey," he said sternly, "is Bounty, because that's already published by you. And the other two you've suggested I helped bring around on the drill bit, well, you can find out that on your own. They are friends, and *they* didn't betray me."

"So—"

"So, I told the President about how it would all work, and got Boles to give Kitticon the options, which Kitticon transferred to the President."

"In writing?"

"In writing."

"Then, then Kitticon's got to pay taxes, got to declare—"

The Speaker shook his head.

"No," he said. "No. He transferred the options when they were still worth maybe $14,000 on paper, or maybe, if you stretch a point, before they had any real value. There was no capital gains when he transferred them, and, of course, you can make a one-time gift of $14,000 a year, anyway. So the President doesn't have to pay taxes until he sells them. And that can wait until he's out of office, if he wants to."

"Yes," I said, "but there's a hooker."

"Right," said the Speaker. "Letter stock. The options could not be legally transferred. It's no big thing, but it's illegal. And it's probable that the transfer and the holding should have been declared on a prospectus, so that's the second hooker."

"But all that could have just remained totally unknown, since Boles didn't know."

"Right. And the President figured I wouldn't ever talk about it because I set the whole deal up, and, in that sense—"

"In that sense, you conspired to violate Securities and Exchange regulations. In that sense you are a co-conspirator. So he thought you would shut up."

Now he took a big slug of the scotch and eased back in his chair. The telling of the story had put some life back into him. He could see the way the story was going to unravel, with him as the foolish, gulled victim of the President. And, indeed, it could be told that way, as well as any other way.

"And in that sense," he said, bending his long body forward again and going back to his whispering, "the President is also a conspirator because he got the options."

"But I think it's only a misdemeanor."

"Still, Aubrey—"

The restaurant owner came and we all tried to look casual. After all, we had been plotting the downfall of a President, and it was heady stuff. If the owner noticed our uneasiness, he said nothing; he recited his specials and took our orders for veal sautéed in butter and lemon. Edwards ordered another double.

"Still, Aubrey," the Speaker picked up, "a misdemeanor for a President, if that's what it is. And the willfulness comes in here, makes it possibly a felony. A President pleading guilty to a crime?"

"So he thought since you were in it—" I wanted to hear it again, to cinch it in my mind.

"That he could shit on me at will. That I had both Kitticon to worry about and Georgie Hedaris and my own tail." He shrugged. "But"—and now I could see he was getting down to another level of truth on the thing—"but it was going to come unstuck. You and your Goddamn story about those two-bit $20,000 contributions from Bounty: that's what got the FBI in on it."

And that had been the one story I was ashamed of.

"Quiven wouldn't lie, you see," said the Speaker. "He admitted the contributions. He's going to have to plead to a misdemeanor on it himself. Hedaris got the money. That gets it close to me personally. I don't know how Georgie and I will—"

"You mean you got the $20,000 from Bounty?"

"I'm not saying that, Aubrey," he said. "That area is one I'm not going to get into. What I'm saying is—"

"That the Feebs are breathing down your neck while the Prez is getting off with dorcking you," I said.

"Yes," he said, and mused a bit. I was amazed at how well his mind functioned, despite the hootch. Yet hadn't I seen him put down eleven that night at Warren's Alery, on top of however many he'd had before he got there? "And it could be that now I'm no longer in the seat of power," he said bitterly, "that I'll have to—"

"Plead to a felony. Or several misdemeanors."

"You said it. I didn't."

"And since you would probably *have* to plead to at least one misdemeanor," I said, the reporter glands beginning to shoot juice, "then you figure it might as well absolve you of a multitude of sins, beginning with a full statement on your dealings with the President."

He grimaced, but I knew that was his reasoning.

"So you want to shift the onus of the Boles-Panjunk thing over on the Prez, make him take the rap for that instead of Kitticon and Georgie." Then, I thought how he could save both Kitticon and Hedaris. "Why not destroy the option transfer paper? Kitticon can take the profit on the options, pay the taxes, and they and you are saved on that one. Kitticon even makes a nice profit, after taxes, for his pains."

"No go," said the Speaker. "The state grand jury is looking into the Wichita land deals, thanks to you. They've got a broad subpoena relating to all Kitticon's transactions with my office. That option transfer could count as being under subpoena, and if he destroys it, he's got a felony charge for obstructing justice, instead of just a misdemeanor."

"The old Watergate tangled web," I said.

"Yes," he said, "the old tangled web. If we try to cover it all up, all three of us, Kitticon, Georgie, and I, could be swinging on felonies, obstructing justice, plus the misdemeanors. If we go the other route, we get stung for misdemeanors, and Kitticon and I can still practice law, and Georgie only has a black eye."

"And the President in the soup, to boot."

"And the President in the soup," he agreed.

The food came, and I took a hearty bite, drinking

with it a gulp of cold, white wine. My appetite for the story had whetted my appetite for the veal. My soul was singing.

Something would work out with Connie and Betty Page, I was sure, and, meanwhile, what a helluva story! Betty Page ate, seeming a little nervous now that the gravamen of the deal had been laid out. There was only for me to get the tapes, and I was looking for a means of mentioning that to Edwards. Quickly.

He piddled with the food, assured the concerned owner that it was delicious, and finished off another drink. The booze was beginning to show.

"When can I write this?" I asked him. "I've got to prove it. Can I—"

"I cannot give them to you myself," he said, and the bottom fell out of my stomach. Then how could I . . . But he was going on, "I have to be able to say, 'No, I did not give the tapes to him.' I want to keep at least that much deniability."

"But—"

"But, I will make arrangements for you to play them."

Ah, I thought. That old bit. I had once been working with a lawyer on a story about his client, who was a very wealthy, very crooked businessman, but one not crooked in the way that he was charged. The key evidence for my story was some grand jury transcripts that cleared the client. I knew the lawyer had the transcripts but would be disbarred if he released them.

When I reached his office, the transcripts were on his otherwise completely clean desk, two neat plastic folders of stenographic "blues." We made some small talk, and he said pointedly, "I have to go to the bathroom. You'll probably be gone when I get back."

When he left the room, I walked up to the transcripts, picked them up, using pieces of paper from my notebook in order not to touch them. At the office, wearing rubber gloves, I Xeroxed them. An hour later I called and asked if I might see him. He agreed. I went again to his office where he discreetly turned his back, and I plopped the transcripts out of an envelope and onto his desk. He could honestly testify that he had not given me any transcripts. We wrote a dynamite series on the secret transcripts, and his client was freed.

Now that I knew where Edwards stood, there was only the problem of the means.

"May I have the tapes?" I asked him.

"You can hear the tapes, but only for reference." No, I thought, that was only half a story. The real story would be page after page of transcripts of those tapes, even if they would put me naked in the closet of his suite, listening to the President.

"Why not burn him good?" I said. "The tapes will do the job."

"The story will do the job," he retorted.

"There's not anything illegal in taping him," I wheedled. "Considering what a snake he proved to be, it's a good thing you did tape him. Besides, he can still try to lie out of it. If he knows I've got the tapes, he can't lie. I need some proof."

In his heart, now that he'd committed himself to Götterdämmerung, he wanted to see a hot fire. But he was reluctant to show himself up as such a sneak that he would tape the President.

"I need a reason for taping him," said Edwards, uncannily hitting on my thoughts again.

"You've had reasons to distrust him in the past on legislation, haven't you?"

"Yes," he said. "Hell, yes, I have. Four years ago—"

"So for that reason—"

"Is that heavy enough?" he turned to Betty Page.

"Yes," she said.

Soon, he'd be gassed, and that I didn't want. He was just about right now for me to put the arm on him for the tapes.

"Let's go hear them, Mr. Speaker," I said. He fixed me with the serpent's look he had used earlier, but now it was unfocused by the booze.

"In good time," he said. "One more for the road. Okay?" Then he pulled himself up, and the eyes came back cleanly on me. "You can take notes, but I am not promising you you can *have* those tapes. There is considerably more negotiating to do on them, you understand."

"Absolutely," I said. Taking notes was seven-eighths of the battle won. I could see he was the kind of lush who, short of unconsciousness, can pull back from the brink and still do a little damage. I didn't want a renege on note-taking, so when he ordered his next drink, I said, "And the check" at the same time.

Once more I was in that house, and again he was drunk, but this time enough canniness remained for him to set up his dramatic pantomime. He led us unsteadily to his study, unlocked his safe in which I caught a glimpse of rows of tapes, pulled out two which he had readied, and relocked the safe. He put the two cassettes on his desk, beside a Sony recorder.

Then, with a single searching look at me, he left and lay down on the couch in the adjoining living room. I glanced at Betty Page, who shrugged and spread her hands apart, as if saying, "Go ahead." So I went.

On some of the dialogue I paraphrased, but much of it I went over time after time, to make sure I had an exact transcript in case he decided finally that he wouldn't let me have the tapes themselves to copy.

Betty Page brought me a cup of coffee, and I worked an hour before I took a brief break. In the next room, I saw him on the sofa, his mouth slightly parted. He was drunk, at peace in sleep.

"It's been a bad time," she said very quietly to me, as I began fooling with the machine again. "A bad, bad time."

"Can you come over tonight?" I whispered to her, fearing his besotted slumber might be a pose. I hoped I hadn't invited Connie, too, and the mere thought of it awakened me more than the coffee.

"No," she said. "Maybe tomorrow." I looked at that intelligent, serious face with its courage and concern and love. It made it easier to put Connie out of my mind.

"The big thing is that you're back in town," I said, standing to kiss her quickly on the lips, with one eye on the doorway. Then I got back to the tapes.

The important conversation came after Pom had set up the Boles-Panjunk deal and was explaining it to the President. I imagined Pom in his office, wetting that little suction cup with spit to make the connection tight and switching on the recorder as the President came on the line.

"Well, the thing is set," Pom said to him.

"All set, hunh?"

"Right. No hitch. Our friend is, uh, getting the paper—"

"Better hand-deliver, better had do that," said the President.

"Roger. It'll work. It'll be set up this way—"

"Pom"—a note of vague ill ease in the President's voice—"uh, do you think—?"

"No problem, no problem. Not at this end, anyway."

"Yeah, but the fucking FBI. I mean, not just them. I got some zappos in the Pentagon that would tape-record their own grandmother."

"If you give in to that kind of paranoia, then they've won the ball game." God, I thought, how often I had said the same thing.

"Why don't you come down? Lay it out down here?" the President was asking.

"My God," Pom said, feigning annoyance. The rat trying to make sure he gets this blackmail stuff on the record, never learning, just as they never learn on anything crooked, from Watergate. "I mean, I've got the supplemental, the Whip's conference, I mean. Look, I can—"

"No, go ahead, go ahead."

"Our friend will give you a paper transferring all seven thousand options, his rights in all seven thousand options. But he can exercise them, you know, do all the paper work in buying the stock when the time comes."

"Like an agent, right? Is that the way—"

"Yes, exactly. The alternative—"

"Would be to wait until he buys the stock, at twelve."

"Eleven, I think."

"Right, eleven. Then I'd have his interest in the stock, one step further down the line. Little less paper work, wouldn't it—"

"Little more tax problem. The maximum gift is—"

"Oh yeah. Well whoa, then, whoa. Let's do it this way. I don't need any IRS son-of-a-bitch, I mean, you know what I mean on that score, if it's not necessary. They did audit me a quick one because I popped out of the computer two years ago. The dum-dum, I mean, Pom, can you believe that I'd have a dumb mother-fucker of a tax lawyer that couldn't fill out the tax forms of the President of the United States so that—I mean, is that chicken-shit, or isn't it?"

"Roger," said the Speaker, getting it back on the track. "So at eleven, and it is eleven, not twelve, he will buy the stock for you, that is in his name, if you want, or you can hold the option and just let it go up, and he can buy at eleven anytime you want, like a call."

"It's a lovely deal, just lovely. I can't tell you how much—I mean, you're a lovely guy."

My mouth was almost literally watering to get this stuff in the paper. I had to get the Speaker to let me use it as direct quotes. He had looked like a corpse. The way he was drinking he'd soon be, so what did it matter to him?

"It's nothing," Pom was saying on tape to the un-suspecting President.

"We know it's going up?" There was a veiled ques-tion in it.

"Absolutely. Old Boles."

"He doesn't know," the President broke in sharply.

"No. Just you and me and our friend."

"And he's—"

"One hundred per cent." Even then, of course, George Hedaris knew, but he was so much Edwards' alter ego. Yet, even alter egos change. "One hundred per cent," the Speaker cooed.

"Now, you're sure there's no way—?"

"None. It's a steel bit cinch."

The President's chuckle came over the tape.

"A steel bit cinch. Sounds like a— Are you sure about calling your friends in the industry? No problem there? None?"

"None. I'm doing them a favor. It's a good bit. The best. Boles knows that kind of thing like you know the hairs in the palm of your hand." The Speaker laughed and was joined by the President.

"Whacking off has never been a problem with me," he guffawed. "Quite the—" Then, he paused. Was he thinking of how he had made it with the Speaker's wife, one of that long refugee line of more or less prominent mistresses? "No, sir; no sir," the President satisfied himself by neutrally saying. Then, "No, sir," again.

"No, sir," echoed Iago Edwards.

"Well, Pom, I won't forget it. No, sir. The paper—"

"That's something I will pass personally," said Pom. "No copies?"

"No, sir, certainly not." But Kitticon, probably on the instructions of Edwards, had kept one. I wondered why, since they were willing to go this far, they'd drawn up any paper at all. But, of course, that made it legal, almost legal, if improper. To claim a verbal contract was an admission of hokum.

"This is money in the bank," the President was saying, now coming around to his real concern—how to get the cash.

"You can have Kitticon exercise the option at such and such a point, say fifty-sixty"—obviously then not even they had dreamed it would go as high as it did— "and the money can be held in escrow by Kitticon as trustee. I think that can be done. Sure it can, as long as he doesn't assert it as a capital gain. Payable when you want, just—"

"Just have a check made out to him, as trustee, and he gives me the cash—"

"No problem. And you pay tax on it as a capital gain, a long-term capital."

"Of course, of course." The tone of his voice made me laugh. I wondered if the President meant to pay any taxes on it at all when he got it.

Now, I thought, he'll never get it. He'll have to back down on the whole dirty deal. And be branded a crook in the bargain and damned well smelly as a skunk when he runs again. "So, that's about it, huh? Pom, I want to . . . and when did you say?"

"I'll have the paper down there by the leadership conference on—"

"Tuesday next. Tuesday."

Then they said good-by. I heard them hang up with loud clicks, and the clever Little Major read into the tape the date and the time, and thus sealed the fate of the President of the United States.

Over Edwards' shoulder, when he pulled out the two tapes, I had seen that safe full of cassettes. I wondered what all the others were: What other Presidential deals? What compromised fellow legislators and businessmen? Was there somewhere even a tape in which he procured my stay in prison?

Time enough for that. The second tape in hand could cost me my ass. I put it on the little Sony. When Betty Page heard the silence, she came in from wherever she had been puttering around.

"The maid?" I thought all of a sudden.

"I gave her the afternoon off."

"Have you heard the next one?"

"No," she said, "but he told me about it."

"What were those two weeks all about?" I said softly to her, not wanting to wake up the cadaver on the divan.

"Big soul search," she said. "I don't want to talk about it when he's here, even—"

"When?"

"Soon," she smiled, rubbing my neck quickly and a little roughly as I bent over the machine on the desk. "The campaign's over. Tomorrow, okay?"

"Thank God," I said, both in relief and with apprehension about Connie. How would I tell Connie? I knew I had to, and soon, so if it were going to start all over again with Betty Page, it could start clean, well, almost clean.

But not now. I put on the tape. Edwards was calling the President. This time the tones were far different from the scheming camaraderie of the first tape. Even in the President's greeting there was the desire to get off the phone fast.

"How are you doing?" he said, the jocularity as thin as the silver on the new sandwich dollars he was having minted as an experiment.

"Shitty," said the Speaker, obviously a little crenelated with booze. "What's this rumory stuff I hear about you not coming? I need you."

Brief pause.

"Look, I want to get something straightened out first."

"What's that?" The Speaker cautious as a snake.

"You know, that Goddamned reporter. Water."

My feelings were slightly hurt by the President's ignorance of my name.

"Warder," the Speaker corrected him. "That son-of-a—"

"Well, did you know he and— Look, I don't want to be the one, but he and your—"

"I don't want to talk about it. What the hell has—"

"The son-of-a-bitch was in her room!"

"In her room? In her room? What—"

"Now, Pom, I'm just going to lay it out, along with my fears. I want to lay this out. I think I can just lay it out on the phone because I have had the line checked out, and I assume you've had your suite and all, I mean, swept, right?"

"Right. But—"

"All right, I'm just going to lay it out. The agents, the Secret Service, checked out this guy coming from your wife's suite."

"Goddamn her!" Edwards voice barked out insensately angry. "Goddamn her. In my own—"

"Wait a minute. Wait a minute. I'm going to level with you, Pom. I came down there, to drop in, see how

you were, and got the wrong room—" Well, I knew
that was a lousy lie. I looked up at Betty Page who
was listening with fascination.

"The bitch!" Edwards was still fuming. But the President
went on.

"I went in and talked to her. She said you were
asleep, and so I left, but with the whole hotel under
scrutiny, the agents told me—"

"That fucking liar," marveled Betty Page to me.

"That non-fucking liar," I grunted, touching her leg
where she stood beside the chair.

"Pom," the President was going on. And I had a
sense now that he was speaking for the record, too, as
if he might be tape-recording Edwards, even as Edwards
tape-recorded him. "Pom, I know this is going to sound
paranoid. But you didn't put that son-of-a-bitch in
there to—"

"Are you crazy, out of your cotton-picking mind?"
gasped out Edwards. "Are you stark, California mad?"
Then lightning struck him, and he sounded almost
awed. "Wrong room, hell," he said quietly. "Wrong
room, my ass. You were down there trying to do the
old Frieden thing, the old fuckola."

"No, sir!" said the President. "Nossir! Would I have
brought it up if that were it? *No, sir.*"

"You Goddamned fool," said the Speaker. "Don't
you know things are so far gone with me and Betty
Page that she wouldn't even lie about it if I asked her?
Didn't you find that out?"

The President was assessing that in silence. There
was nothing on the line for so long that I thought the
recorder might have failed at that crucial moment.
Then the President said, all control now:

"Then isn't that all the more reason for me to worry
about you, about some kind of—" The Speaker was
cool now, too, the embryo drunkenness lifted, a cruel
beam of sunlight coming through the haze.

"The reporter was in there to screw Betty Page, just
like you were." I looked up at her. I did not want her
to hear this. They were making her out to be some kind

of whore. And I hurt for her. We were both embarrassed now, not touching each other. The tape was dirtying up everyone, Betty Page and me, as well as the two soiled politicians.

"It's not—" I started, but stopped. What explanation did we owe each other for what these men said?

I missed a gap of dialogue and rewound to get it. The President was talking:

"Okay, I believe. I believe. You couldn't have feigned. Okay."

"You better believe. Because you may think you can handle *me*, but you can't handle that prick. If he decided to commit suicide with his paper and say he's been banging my wife, then they'll fire him because they'll think he got his stories by balling her. They couldn't stand that kind of scandal. But *if, if* he ever printed what he heard in that closet—I mean what the hell did you say?"

"I can't remember. I can't remember. Jesus. Good lord."

Edwards laughed cruelly. Now his tone was totally mocking.

"What you can't stand is that a story might come out saying you got turned down by a woman who had her lover, a cheap ragpicking reporter, hidden in the closet. That would ruin your image."

"Screw that," said the President defensively. If he were taping Pom, I'd bet he'd turned the machine off now. "He won't do it. No, he's not crazy enough to write that."

"I don't think so, either. Confession night, hunh?" said Pom, controlling the conversation. He sighed into the mouthpiece. "Okay, now that's done. Okay, no more to be said about it. Now, listen, I really need you, need you out here. It's close, bad."

"I can't really believe that you'd have—"

"Can't believe? I've had this district polled practically down to the shithouse interview level. I'm telling you, I'm in trouble."

"Pom, it's not your press problems," said the President, deciding now to blunt it out. "No, no. I simply can't—I can't juggle it. Now that's the—" He'd thought he could bull it through.

"You can't?" bellowed Edwards. "You can't?"

The President's voice was suddenly mollifying. He realized now the direct approach, the time-saving direct statement had been wrong.

"They've got me scheduled up to here," he said. "My people tell me you're not in that kind of trouble. I'm like the damned fireman. I got to go where the fires are worst. The party wants me here, there, Jesus, everywhere. And the work, I mean the office work is just stacking up. My God, I got bill ceremonies that I just have—"

"I'm telling you your people are full of shit. I have spent $203,000 on polls out here. Do you know what $203,000 will do on polls in this district? I can damned near tell you how every voter in this—"

"My people," said the President, and there was a whine in his voice, "they insist—"

"Your peo-ple drink horse-piss," said the Speaker enunciating each syllable separately. "I know Goddamned well what it is. My—it—the financial stuff about me, would—"

"No, Pom. You know—" But the Speaker cut through, imploring, and I felt sorry for him in spite of myself.

"I need you," he said. "I've got to have you!"

"Pom—"

"Look, I've got to." I now felt shamed for the man.

"I'm sorry," said the President, at last meaning what he said, that, in some way, he was sorry. He was ditching an old political ally, and that was the way it was done, but he was sorry, sorry as a man is when he ditches a mistress, or a wife, or a friend. Again, there was a pause.

"You lied to me," said Edwards coldly, and I knew that in his mind he already felt the frozen dagger of defeat which he would pull from himself and, as he perished from its stab, plunge into the President. "You promised me you'd come out. You're welshing."

"Pom," said the President, "I said I'd come if I could. The exigencies—"

"The exigencies, my Kansas ass." He was sober now, and the thought was in his head that he would sell out the President at whatever cost. I could hear it in his tone. How could the President not hear it. "You fucking lied," said Edwards. "That's it."

"I'm sorry you feel that way," Frieden said. "Damned sorry. And it's not true. We've never lied to each other. Every deal we've had, every talk has been on the basis of mutual trust."

There it was, the reference to the Boles-Panjunk deal. And the key word was "mutual." What the President was saying, knowing the subtleties would reach Pom, was that they had a "mutual" deal in which if one went down, the other would, too. The President was counting on the politician's sense of survival, which was so strong in him, being equally strong in Pom, stronger than revenge.

Edwards, now that he was decided, was not signaling a thing.

"Okay. What's to say? I'm poison for you. You'd rather welsh on a promise than take a little political chance." That speech, I knew, was for the recorder.

"It would be no 'little' chance," said the President, honest at last, now that the decision had been recognized. "It's a tail that could be hung on my donkey next time. I don't need it, Pom. I can't."

"See you around," said Edwards. Now there was in him only bile and hatred, but it was tired, dried out. "Unless you rot first."

Again, there was the click of the sign off, and Edwards read in the time and date, stammering slightly over the date. I listened for a while to see whether any other goody was on the tape, then finding none, popped it out of the Sony.

"It may be the biggest story I ever had," I said wonderingly to Betty Page. "Can I get the tapes?" I asked. But she was gloomed over in thought.

"Can you keep the stuff out about—?"

"I don't know." My mind was working on how I

could get Edwards to approve giving me the tapes, giving me the transfer paper. I'd worry about whether I was going to be fired later. At worst, I thought, if they heard that section of the tape, March would send me back to cityside. And, I could always quit, take my retirement, marry Betty Page. For an old man, my options were wide open. Inside I was singing at what a fantastic story I had.

"We can probably get it knocked out on the basis that it's just sex for sex's sake with very little political implication," I said. I was thinking of Frieden's gauzed-over threat that night in Betty Page's room, not to campaign for Edwards if she didn't come across. But I knew her refusal had been a minor factor, in the President's decision. "I think I can argue that it's just straight scandal and that we ought to stick to the issue. They go for that moral horseshit," I said. "Maybe I can just keep quiet about that part of the tape."

"He'll let you have them," she said, her eyes still reflecting concentration. "If you want, he'll let you have only the parts of the second tape that don't involve—" she looked for a euphemism that would cover it all, gave up, and said, "our affair."

My heart bounded. My God, that would do it. Edwards refuses to give me the stuff about him being cuckolded. How can I write what I can't prove, particularly something like that?

"Saved by suppression of the news," I chortled. I stood up happily and pulled her to me, despite the low snoring sounds from the living room couch. I was too excited about the story to be excited by her, but I grabbed her tail, feeling its full shape in both hands, an anticipation of love soon to be.

"Betty Page," I said, "the campaign is over."

While the Speaker slept I expanded my notes to make a full transcript of both tapes. With Betty Page doing the reversing and restarting, it wasn't all that slow. When I finished, I played both tapes through again, looking at my notes to make sure they were absolutely accurate, or as accurate as we could get them.

That done, I could turn to her with lust again. It had been a hell of a long campaign. Now we were back together. Her marriage with the Speaker was resolved, at least resolved to be dissolved. I had done my twenty-five years at the *Eagle*. And I could see being with her for the next twenty-five.

But, even as I led Betty Page to a corner of the study, out of sight of the living room, so I could really hug her, even then, damnit, I thought of that liquid, metallic, slithering quality of Connie's body. To make an extreme image, it was the difference between a single brilliant clarinet and a marvelous oompah band. But the oompah band was at hand.

"I love you, Betty Page Rawlinson Edwards," I said, looking at her. "I love you, and once again you have given me a lovely, fat, juicy story. I love you."

"I love you, Aubrey Reporter Pig," she said.

From the other room we heard a grunt, and we went back. Edwards was struggling to come to, his angled knees, his elbows twisting on the couch like slow-moving construction cranes. From the bathroom she brought a wet, cool washrag.

"Jesus," he said, coming to, still drunk, from the sound of his slurring. She pressed the dampened rag into his hand, and he wiped his face and mouth, murmured, "Thanks," and cast his eyes around.

They stopped on me, popped open with shock, then narrowed to understanding. "You listened to 'em, hunh?" he said. "Any good?" He laughed, then answered himself, "Not bad, good stuff."

"May I make copies?" I asked.

"Not that one part," he said. "Never." Christ, I thought happily, he was going to do my work for me. "No, sir."

"You mean about Betty Page," I said.

"Not that part, no, sir."

"But the rest?"

He looked at Betty Page, warily, then at me. I could see him trying to ratiocinate. Amazingly, he seemed to be succeeding.

"How would you attribute the source, I mean in the story?" he asked.

"Just say we have 'tapes,'" I said. "Not saying where—"

"Oh, bullcrap, Aubrey!" the Speaker interjected. "There's not going to be any doubt where you got them. Even after what you did to me. It's 'tapes' that worry me. How about saying 'a transcript of tapes'?" He put his head in his hands and gave his head a big shake.

"Betty, baby, get me an Alka-Seltzer." It was astonishing how well he was doing. Maybe that's how it is with drunks. The ones whose hangovers aren't like terminal cancer and who sober fairly fast are the ones most damned. In them, sobriety has fewer allies.

"Saying we have the tapes would be better. Nail it down harder," I suggested gently.

We bargained back and forth gingerly.

Betty Page brought him the Alka-Seltzer. I almost never touched it and so was fascinated by the way it fizzed up. He swilled it down, and his Adam's apple rose and fell as if it were a mechanical pump of some sort summoning up the soul-felt burp that followed.

"Sorry," he said. "In the story, just say 'according to transcripts,' okay? That way, it could at least sound like I made a transcript, right, and gave it to my lawyers, or something. I could hint you got it from the lawyers, or a staffer or someone. Gives me that little deniability. Not much, but a little, little room to maneuver—"

"Maneuver? You can already say you didn't *give* them to me."

"I need just a little more room," he said.

A horrible thought hit me. Could he be setting us up, me and Betty Page?

"What are you going to say when the press comes to you after I break the damned thing? I mean—"

"I'll say we don't know where you got the transcript, swear I didn't give it to you, but that I had made some recordings for both historical and protective reasons, and it sounds like what you have is—is accurate. Some such."

That was pretty good, but I was still worried.

"How about letting me have the tapes, I mean the part that we've agreed on, as back-up? Just to have in the paper's safe. Something that the editors will know is solid. You know, so Mr. March can get word to Harry Frieden that the transcripts are authentic."

"That gets complicated," the Speaker said. He was getting tired again, his mind wanting to lapse back into its druggery.

"Mr. March will not say we have the tapes," I pressed him, "just that we are going with the story and that if the White House denies it, you have assured him that you will have to affirm the accuracy, that you will tell the truth, and have your lawyers back you up with a copy of the tape. Something like that."

The Speaker steadied himself again, and I could hear those superb wheels turning in his head, the good Swiss works fighting to do the diamond thing despite the years of gunk.

"No," he said, at last. "There is no way I can be sure March or you won't screw it up. Tell him that, that I worry about him screwing it up, but that I'll back up the story."

"Great," I said, a little sarcastically. The story was as much in the can as it was going to be. All I had to do was the mop-up reporting. Try to get Kitticon (who wouldn't talk), get Boles, who'd say honestly he knew nothing about the deal, and the President who would say God knows what to me, but who would check through someone with Pom and then would know that we had him by his Chief Executive ballocks. "Okay," I said. I almost forgot. "How about a copy of the transfer paper?"

"Unnn-uh," said the Speaker emphatically. "It's under subpoena out there, and Kitticon could get his ass fried for cutting it loose. Unnn-uh. I don't want to bring any trouble on him, just when you're going to bail him out."

"You must have a copy of it," I said, ignoring what he said, though it was true. I would be bailing out both the Speaker and Kitticon on the Boles-Panjunk deal by removing the implication that they got the $500,000, even though I still implied they ought to get nailed up for a criminal misdemeanor or for coconspiring. "Why can't *you* slip me *your* copy?"

The Speaker smiled.

"Why don't I slip you a copy," he repeated. And then he looked at me, as sober as the lord high executioner and with eyes as hard. "Why don't I? Because that's the jagged end of the beer bottle I'm going to cut Frieden's balls off with if he tries to explain away that damned tape. That's why." Then, surprised at the violence of his hyperbole, he amended it. "That's the other shoe."

20

Trophies

The White House reacted as we expected. First, I called up the Press Office and talked to Frieden's chief flack, saying I wanted an interview with the President. The flack wanted to know what for, and I said, "About something of an intimate nature." That and my name would signal to Frieden that it involved his attempted seduction of Betty Page, which, in a way, it did. But that, of course, was only a ruse to get him to see me. I would not write about it.

In fact, I had said nothing about the closet scene to Cubbins or Mr. March. If I got caught, I would simply confess to them that it was the weakness of the moment that led me into Betty Page's room. I would hope that Mr. March would not fire me for, one, screwing a source, two, involving the paper in a Presidential scandal, and three, cheating on his daughter.

Predictably, the President's chief hatchet man called Mr. March and asked him what was going on. Mr. March was smart enough to say we had a story that was solid as a rock indicating the President had profited mightily from the Boles-Panjunk deal, without saying what made it so solid.

The hatchet man got a promise from Mr. March that we would hold it up for at least one day. We, in turn, got a promise that they would not leak it in its kindliest form to some other media in the hope of getting gentler play.

The request for a delay meant that some intermediary, probably old McFadden, would be approached by the President to find out whether the Little Major planned to back up our story and whether, if he did, Edwards could be talked, bribed, or bullied out of doing so.

Later that same day, the Speaker got me on the phone. He was sober and in good spirits for a man who'd just been kicked out of Congress by the voters after twenty-six years of service, was about to be divorced, and was going to have to plead guilty to a criminal charge, or at best, be named as an unindicted criminal coconspirator.

"They had McFadden call me," he said. "Just got off the phone with him. I told him to tell Frieden that if I was asked honest questions by the press, I'd have to give honest answers."

"That'll sweat him," I observed.

"Is that okay?"

"Perfect."

"How you doing on the story?" I was always amazed at how politicians could slip in and out of acquaintanceships. Here was a man whom I'd helped destroy, whom I'd cuckolded, and who had me jailed and maybe tried to have me killed, as friendly as a good neighbor.

"Got it blocked out," I said. "We should get somebody over at the White House calling us in tonight or tomorrow morning."

"They'll have something hoked up," he said.

"Kitticon won't talk to me," I said.

"I don't want him to," said the Speaker. I still worried that I was being set up somehow. But the voice on the tape was the President's, and Betty Page was too sure the Speaker was playing straight for me to be really worried.

"I called Boles for comment, just asking if he knew whether Kitticon had transferred any options. He said 'No,' which let me clear him in print."

"I talked to him, too. I told him what we've"—I

liked that collective pronoun—"got. He won't talk to
anyone else, but I wanted him to know."

"He stuck by you," I said consolingly, allying myself
with the skunks to get the fox.

The Speaker wanted to know when I was going to
break it, and I said I thought on Sunday, when we'd
get our biggest play and thereby bomb the *Post*, the
Star, the New York *Times*, et al. All that was needed
was the White House comment. Then I could start
writing.

The story was so big that even Cubbins had shut up
after telling Mihalik about it. Most of the time, a story
was the chatter of the city-room well before it broke.
But we were actually maintaining security on this one.

To lose it now, even a piece of it, would have been
a heartbreaker. I knew the paper was thinking Pulitzer
on it, but as happy as that possibility was, I didn't let
myself consider it. It was a fickle prize, not to be
counted on.

As I wrote the story, I felt the anxiety building in me.
I was glad when Connie March, her hair down her
back as it used to be, came over to my desk late in the
day. I had not seen her for two nights, and I was hopeful that I would be with Betty Page the next morning.
I was nervous and elated by the story, but I felt traitor-
ous now toward Connie.

"Got a big one?" she asked. Damn, I thought, those
cherry nipples through the blouse.

"Yeah," I said, realizing the truth of what Freud
said about puns being unrecognized modes of giving
depths to clichés. "Keep quiet about it, okay?"

She nodded, and I was on the brink of spilling it
when I perceived that telling her would reveal something about me and Betty Page. The mere fact I had
the story implied a return to Betty Page. How else
would I have gotten such a story?

I looked into those flattish eyes. Near-sighted women
have a look of penetrating attention, which is only a
result of their disability. The reverse, in a way, was
true of Connie, I thought. The lack of depth in her eyes

was physiological. It did not mean there was any shallowness, any lack of profundity in her. Fixing me with her gaze as she did, I saw the plunge of her concentration, of her seriousness.

"I am a very superficial person," I said softly. "I am not a man to be taken seriously."

She looked querulous a moment, then caught it up.

"You're back with her," she said, holding it in, self-protective.

"It's a piss-ant's way of telling you," I said.

She didn't blanch. She had her old man's toughness, and I was almost afraid of her, afraid of what she would try to do now through Mr. March, or what she would do to me if she ever got to be boss.

"No," she finally said, still softly so no one would hear. "It's not so bad. You could have taken me out to lunch at some fancy place and poked it at me over the wine bottle." She started to turn away, but came back and put her hands on my desk, leaning her weight on them.

"You know," she said, "you're all shits. The cop, you, even Mark. Every one of you used me in one way or another. What the hell would I have been to you if—"

But I broke in.

"No, it would have been the same. I'd have had the hots for you if you'd been a schoolmarm."

She stared still into my eyes, and I wanted to flinch. Instead, I went on talking.

"So don't slobber around in that 'poor little rich girl' shit."

"Okay, then why?" she said, and now she was vulnerable.

"Ask yourself," I said. "You picked us. You know, it's still a game where the man wants to go to bed with the woman, but the screw or non-screw is still her choice. You could have refused to come over for the champagne—"

"Why doesn't it work for me?"

I wondered how to give it to her straight, her defenses down. But we were, at this moment, as distant as if we had never touched each other.

"The cop and Mark can speak for themselves. I was too old, among other things."

"Other things?"

"Okay, her, for one. I should have told you about that when you began liking me, but then you were a big magnet and you were pulling me away, and like I said, I began to dream about you. On the other side I did have to *think* how much of it was liking you or whether part was fantasizing weekends at Eaglesmere and becoming a graying eccentric like your old man, and having a rich, beautiful, young wife."

Talking about it had made me tense, so tense I was beginning to slur. I looked to her to say something to relieve me. But she said nothing, waiting on me, again.

Then all of a sudden I was so tired, so terribly tired. I had this great story, half done now, and I was going back to Betty Page. But I had seen in Betty Page some strengths, or did I dare call it willfulness, even meanness, that I knew I feared? My tooth was kicking up again.

The vision of Connie and wealth and maybe even a family for us had simply wearied me. I felt an embryonic tear of self-pity forming behind my right eye.

What I wanted, more than anything else in the world, was to be home drinking a cup of chocolate with my wife before we crawled into the warmth of night, snuggled up together.

Or, since I could not be with her, I wanted to be drinking with my copy-desk crony at the threadbare Detroit Lounge, making nasty mild cracks, two newspapermen who in their hearts knew they hadn't quite made it and who didn't care that it was too late for fate to reverse itself.

"And ultimately, I am sick of myself, maybe always have been. But I'm too shallow to let it get me down," I said to Connie. I had not wanted it to turn into a creed, but she was still listening, knowing that she would at least get a clue to what I really was, what she might conceivably have been bound up to for the years of a marriage.

"So, I stay cheerful, and reasonably brave, and work

hard and retain a lot in my head which now, after the years, lets me compete with those who are more real, the real newspapermen. No, I don't quite mean that. I am a real newspaperman, but I imagine that I might have been a poet. A poet is something. And a newspaperman is a winding-sheet around yesterday's events. No, the newspaper is the shroud, and the newspaperman is the shadow of a shroud."

The talk was making me very anxious, and I rubbed my forehead, pretending I was pushing up my hair. She was studying me to see how much honesty there had been in my long speech.

"You really see yourself that way, don't you?" she said. "It's not just the you're-better-off-without-me speech." Half of it was a question.

The weariness just wouldn't lift. Now I was getting some tingles in my chest, and I knew from the last time what it was, another heart thing. I couldn't tell her. And it wasn't the kind of fainting that had hit me at Betty Page's so long ago, and in the jail. I had this coming, I thought. I have it coming. But I had read enough after my last one to know that if I nursed it, husbanded myself for a day, I could get away with a minimum of hurt.

The thought of my heart giving out on me, right here, upset me, and I knew the upset could do me more damage than anything else, so I just said to her, all selfish now:

"I see myself as not the guy you need and you as something I couldn't handle. And I'm all wrapped up in guilt because I see myself as your wily seducer." I smiled at her, forgetting the tingle for a moment. "I'm not sufficiently liberated to see it, I mean to feel it, as a two-way street."

"Jesus," she said, depressed, maybe even sorry that it had just petered out without any fireworks. She'd have wanted fireworks, being her old man's daughter. Then selling off her losers—oh God, how often had I seen women do it, how differently from ours their minds work—she said, "Well, I learned from it, Aubrey." Then, as if that were too harsh a judgment on me, perhaps thinking of the fire, when even I felt I'd done the right thing, she added, "Anybody who gets you won't be all unlucky."

I reached out, took her hand, feeling the tingle down under my arm a bit now, and squeezed it. She squeezed back and walked back to her desk.

Now, I thought, easy does it, easy truly does it. Just put this story together, and get it through Cubbins and don't worry about the White House comment. Somebody else can piss around with that. Just write the story and get it in to Cubbins and extract a big promise from him not to let it get screwed over too much, for him personally to keep it as much my way as he can, since as bad as he is, he's the best they've got. And then a trip to the old doctor-o.

I finished putting the story together mechanically, feeling that tingle under my arm and in my left chest. Now and then it was punctuated by sharp little pains, but nothing serious yet. I thought about the pain as I wrote, thinking how funny it was that it had started in my tooth.

Next would be the slightly upset feeling in my stomach, and sure enough, as I thought of it, it began. But I couldn't be sure whether the queasiness was part of the real McCoy or just nervousness over the repulsive mystery that soon would be controlling my body.

I whacked up the story. The Goddamned thing was endless: twelve takes—short pages—and I could have written more. Plus, I'd talked them into running the full texts of the two tapes, or at least what Edwards had agreed to let me have. Thank God, for the omissions. That scandal was all I needed. And the heart thing: I wondered what Connie would think: that she had caused it? No time to tell her different now.

I began copyreading it, feeling a little sag in my arm.

It didn't read well, not the way I had hoped. But Cubbins could do that. I had rough-hewn the damned thing, and he was a good enough editor to shape it.

The story read:

"President Frieden took an active role in an illegal stock deal that has guaranteed him some $500,000. His partner in the enterprise was House Speaker Pommery Edwards, who did most of the work but came out with paper profits of only about $7,000.

"The devious transactions in an oil drill firm's securities were revealed in part by the *Eagle* over the past few months. The revelations helped bring about the defeat of Edwards in this month's elections after 26 years in the House.

"But the President's $500,000 bonanza was unknown until the *Eagle* obtained transcripts of remarkable tapes that show Edwards and the President actually shaping the illegal deal."

Then I wrote, "(Cubbins: insert two grafs, no more Goddamnit, of WhHse comment. *Please* save rest for deeper down in story.)"

"The transcriptions of a telephone call between Edwards and the President show the President at one point calling the transaction, which violates Securities and Exchange Commission rules, 'a lovely deal, just lovely.' At another point he says, 'This is money in the bank.' "

Then, I used the old time-tested chronological device to tell a complicated story.

"The deal was set up this way:"

From there on the story wrote itself. The business of Kitticon getting the options, the drill being pushed by Edwards to the oil companies, the stock soaring. Then:

"But unknown to Boles-Panjunk, the distinguished beneficiary of the $500,000 increase in profits on the 7,000 options was not their counsel, Nicholas Kitticon, but the President of the United States.

"By written agreement, Kitticon was to serve merely as the 'straw' or 'front' for the true owner, President Frieden. Under the scheme, after Frieden left office, or sooner if the cash was needed, Kitticon would exercise the options.

"At that time, Mr. Frieden would get the money with no record of it unless he reported it on his income tax. Under certain circumstances even this could be avoided by paying it into a trust from which money could then be dispensed for at least some of the President's needs.

"As the President and Speaker excitedly discussed the sure-fire money-making scheme, the President paused at one point to question whether the call might be tapped by the 'f— FBI' or 'some zappos in the Pentagon that would tape-record their own grandmothers.'

" 'If you give in to that kind of paranoia, then they've won the ball game,' commented the Speaker."

Then, I quoted another batch of stuff from that taped conversation and got on into our breaking the story of the Speaker and Boles-Panjunk.

I ate some crow about implying the Speaker was to be the big profiteer. My draft then summarized the campaign and got to that crucial phone conversation when the President said he wouldn't go to Kansas to give the Speaker his eleventh-hour help.

"The two men exchanged hot words over the President's refusal to make a last-ditch effort to save the Speaker from defeat, the transcripts show."

And I detailed that transcript since it was really more colorful than the first one. I wrapped up the story with a few historical notes about how the "Nixon Tapes" had finished him in Watergate, and about how it wasn't illegal to record a telephone conversation if you were one of those taking part in the talk.

I walked slowly up to Cubbins' office with the copy, listening to myself for anything that would mean I was worsening. Along with the fear, I felt relief. The story was done, shed like a snake's skin.

"Handle this yourself," I said to him.

"Of course, of course," he said, reaching out to grab it.

"No, I mean all the way," I said. "Copyread it and do whatever rewriting it needs, and it's not written all that good, and make sure no fucking bum head gets hung on it." He looked up irritated at me, this added burden. By now I was sweating from my forehead.

"What's the matter with you?" he asked, standing.

"I'm having a fucking heart attack," I said, and began to cry, knowing I was being overdramatic, a ham, and all that; and, for some reason, precarious as I felt, I loved Cubbins, because in this cruel, scheming business, my old friend and enemy, Michael Cubbins, was, finally, all I had to love.

How many times had I heard those ambulance sirens. And how many times, more lately than before, had I thought about the way it would be riding to the hospital in one of them.

Please, God, I thought, as we headed north toward the Hospital Center, please, no ironies, no cross-street crash, no death spasm to come out of this mild pain and grip me on the way to the hospital. I did not want some old rewrite friend to put in those hackneyed lines . . . "wrote 'thirty' to his life as he had to so many millions of words of copy" . . . or "died, as he had lived, in front of a typewriter on a hard-breaking story."

I resolved when I got out of this, I would write my own obituary with the theme that an honest pol named Fred Harris had once used on his election campaign, "No More Bullshit!"

Next morning, flat on my back, I mused that maybe at a certain age, reporters should have a shuttle service between the cityroom and a hospital. The joke used to be that the White House was running a shuttle for its personnel between their offices and the criminal courts.

I timed it pretty well, the doctor had said. A little more time, and I'd have had a Richter Scale-four coronary. This was just a little fellow. There must be no more booze, jut a bit of watered wine and, okay, Galliano and water. He was one of these guys who also believed in bicycle riding and non-acrobatic screwing.

Was there anything else I could do for a living besides reporting, he wanted to know. I told him I didn't think so. He said, then try to do more feature and less hard-news investigation. I said I didn't think that would work. He sighed and said to try to stay in a more settled state of mind when I got out.

"Maybe get married again?" I asked.

"Maybe," he said, "but not to a French cook."

He'd kept me sedated the first day so I didn't see the paper until the day after we broke it. Cubbins had weakened it, putting in his usual "allegedly illegal" for my "illegal." But that was par. He'd done it up so that, while I might not be enthusiastic, I was relieved that it was accurate and adequately written.

I looked at the big streamer across the front page and thought, well, I'll never beat that one. And at the end, on the jump page, Cubbins had put a small mutt box headed, "Reporter Stricken." It said I had a mild heart seizure "within minutes after writing the last words" of the story. Pulitzer bait, but a nice touch.

The White House comment had been that the President had considered a business transaction involving Boles-Panjunk, but it had never been consummated. That was half-true. But the press would never let the son-of-a-bitch go until the story had smoked out just the way I had it.

Besides, the Speaker still had his *coup de grâce* in the form of that written transfer. In a way, I sort of hated to see Frieden get it. The Speaker had tried to kill me, and I felt no compunction, even now, about what I had done to him.

But the President had never done anything to me except show a flattering interest in my mistress, or fiancée, or whatever Betty Page was. He'd been a good President, and the fact that he needed the $500,000 so bad showed that he hadn't been a terribly big thief up to then and that his wife's money wasn't even at his disposal.

This was a story that was going to run a long, long time and could wind up polishing him off for a second term. And no matter what the rest of the press did, I was going to get credit for busting the thing.

I lay back and slept, still under more drugging than I liked.

When the doctor let the calls start, late the second full day, Connie called and said she hadn't tried to get into the coronary room because she'd thought it would upset me.

"You're a good person, Aubrey," she said. I guess that was what I mainly wanted to hear from her.

Cubbins, March, and a batch of others called. Brent, my FBI friend, didn't give his name over the phone; I had to guess his voice.

Mrs. Murtry came by early on the third day. They let her in. She said she'd checked with the doctor and that she had some good news which the doctor said might brighten me, if it didn't kill me. He was a funny man, and I assumed he was making a joke.

"It's not sure," she said, "not sure, but we are making some progress with Quiven." Oh boy, I thought. When Murtry's "not sure," that means it's damned *near* sure. "I called up his counsel," she said, "after your story, and he's in trouble on the contributions."

"Yeah, I know. I was going to work on that next if . . ."

She looked irritated that I had scooped her, so to speak.

"Who told you? Oh yes, the Speaker's wife," she said. "Well, it is true, and he isn't going to want to have to testify in the case, and this is giving the D.A. out there problems on the safecracking."

"So?"

"So, I talked to the D.A., too, and he's thinking of letting you plead to a misdemeanor and getting probation, if it can all be set up."

"Sounds good," I said.

"If he's starting out with plea-bargaining on a serious misdemeanor, say illegal entry, then he may be willing to settle for even less, maybe nothing."

"Disorderly conduct?" I said with a wan smile.

"Maybe destruction of private property."

"Hell, Mrs. Murtry," I said, "tell 'em yes. That's the charge for busting out a neighbor's window in a softball game."

At last, she smiled.

"We'll shoot for nothing." But something in that troubled me. I thought of the frantic night, of my partner in crime, Buddy Drosnahan, drinker of morning Guinness. I sort of wanted a Guinness at the moment.

"Drosnahan?"

"He's got his own lawyer."

"I got him into it."

She looked puckery all over again.

"Look," I went on, "I really can't let him do a worse rap than me. How the hell does that look?"

"I'll try," she said. I felt she was secretly pleased.

Betty Page called to explain why she wasn't coming. She'd told the doctor we were "fond" of each other, she said, a bit embarrassed, and he'd said wait twenty-four hours and see how he takes a day of telephone calls. Mrs. Murtry, I assumed, had been looked on by the doctor as a therapeutic agent rather than a friend.

The next day, Betty Page got in before visiting hours.

"You need a shave," she said, to mask the worry.

I took her hand.

"It scared the hell out of me," I said. "What's happening?"

She sat beside me, still holding my hand, and I watched her lips, thin and supple and young-looking as she talked quietly. Drugged still, I just let my mind rove over what I knew she had under her fall suit jacket and her skirt, and wished I could see her legs. But her hand was lovely, graceful, still as some small, furry, shapely animal in mine.

"We're separating. The children know now. Jay"—the young one—"wants to stay with me, at least until college a year from now. He'll spend summers with Pom." That meant no living together until summer, unless we got married.

"How soon are you breaking it up?"

"A month, two months, when Congress goes home. He's going back to Kansas. He isn't going to get well here, he knows that. And I don't think he'll get well there. But there're enough firms who'll take him on in a minute, lush or not."

"How about money?"

"College and support for Jay." She shrugged. "Enough for me until I can get doing something that will make me something. That was never the problem. He's being okay. Too dependent really."

"He's not letting up any?"

"No, it's every day just after noon," she said. "He had this idea he was going to leave a big legislative record, but it was fantasy. The transcripts killed him with his friends, ex-friends. Everyone up there thinks he must have taped them, too." I laughed as much as I dared to, recalling that safe full of tapes.

"He did, too, didn't he?"

"Yes," she said. She dropped her head and kissed my hand. "No, I'm not going to help you get any more of the damned things. I'm going to try to get him to destroy them."

"Even that's not a bad story," I said. "Speaker destroying tapes of his friends so they'll love him again." But my heart, figuratively and literally, wasn't in any more newspaper stories right now.

"I'll be able to screw when I get out of here," I said.

"When's that?" She stood and brushed my hair up from my forehead while I patted her on the tail.

"Two weeks." I was feeling woozy. "Two weeks," I said.

"That's nice," she said, then repeated it, throatily, "that's nice."

The little item on the heart attack must have gotten picked up on the wires. I got a call from Renardi. He and Drosnahan had a consulting company going. They had some foreign accounts, guys who didn't worry about the criminal investigation, but did care about technical developments in the oil industry.

"We just got a bank draft for $75,000 from Indonesia," Renardi told me. "That's for openers." He laughed in that good, reckless way he had. "They want to buy some drills. Would you believe that I talked to old man Boles and butter wouldn't melt in his mouth?"

"Trade heals the world's wounds," I said. "Does he want you to come back to work for him?" I joked.

"No, baby," said Renardi, "but he says he'll be glad to give my client a special rate on the drills if that would help get word about them to the North Vietnamese and China."

"Tell Drosnahan to push hard right now for a quick

plea," I said. I told him what Mrs. Murtry had told me and what I'd told her to try to do for Drosnahan.

"He already knows. She talked to his lawyers. He says 'thanks' and that he'd have called you, but his lawyers say the potential defendants should be sanitized. Makes the two of you sound like urinals." I told him my mouth felt like one from the drugs.

The time in the hospital went fast. I got a lot of reading done. The visits tapered off, except for Betty Page. When I left, the pills and "do and don't" food lists made me feel like an old man. But my body felt great.

I did the exercises. I stuck to the diet.

Betty Page spent a lot of time with me, cleaning up the house, and later, taking walks with me as the winter began to come on hard. Our love-making was cautious but warm. I knew if I really let go, I could die in the sack. Something told me that, and when my heart thudded, I was scared. Still, it was good loving. And for her, I rationalized, it was a helluva lot better than what she'd gotten at home for years.

In late December, Betty Page came in from a snowy day with a *Star* and a bag of groceries in her arms. The paper said the FBI had nailed the fire bombers of Eaglesmere. They were, as the earlier threats suggested, anti-Semites, one of whom had worked as a construction man on the mansion's addition four years ago. He had confessed with a colorful, if slightly tilted, sequent:

"I built it. I burned it down."

"Scooped again," I called to Betty Page in the kitchen.

Reading the story, I thought of that night with Connie. I supposed that was as close as I would ever come to falling in love with a young chick and marrying money and being an editor.

For a moment, I lusted for her younger body, even as I looked at Betty Page, efficiently laying out the two settings and soup dishes. Ah no, I mused, it was better now for me.

Should I have told her about Connie? I had been

tempted to, and was now, wrong as I knew it to be. It would get me a cleaner start toward our life together, one freer of deceit. It would shrive me.

But it would enforce on her a feeling that I was as untrustworthy sexually as I had been journalistically—morally—in the Renardi affair. Easier for me to carry it than unload it, and maybe more honorable. And in my acceptance of concealment, I felt relieved.

In January, when the new Congress came, Pom went home. For the last months he had been routinely smashed by five or six, escorted around by faithful Georgie, like Antigone leading Oedipus. Betty Page actually went out to help him get settled, along with Hedaris. But they both came back, Hedaris to a job with a veteran member who needed an administrative assistant, and Betty Page fuming.

"He's got himself some damned trollop," she said, fresh off the plane at National and dropping by my apartment on the way to Wesley Heights.

"Already?" I asked.

"Still!" she said, getting a little more amused about it, seeing the ridiculousness of criticizing him while we sat over coffee and Sanka in my apartment. "He'd known her before."

"Who—" But she was already answering.

"Damnit, one of my assistants in the campaign. I'm out stumping for Pom, and he's—"

"Stumping your assistant," I laughed.

"When she should have been stapling press releases—" she fed me the next line.

"Pom was stapling her."

We whooped with laughter at our wretched jokes.

By February, I was back in the office on a half-day schedule. This time I was doing just what the doctor said. Everything. I was in love with Betty Page, and I wanted a long time with her.

He told me the heart had healed, was scarring over much better than last time. I'd be better than before, if I kept up the healthy foods and the rest of this proto-human life. I didn't believe him, but I ate veal at

Cantina with more lemon than butter, mixed my Almadén with water, and had grapes for dessert.

The paper put the Pulitzer nomination in for me. Cubbins and Mr. March entered it in my name, rather than in the paper's as some papers did when too many reporters or editors had worked on a story.

They had photoduplicated the big scrapbook with the entry in it, and put a duplicate cover on it for me. What with its leather front, glassine on black innards, its ringing endorsements from all the political good-doing organizations, the various liberal professors, and the editorials from around the country, the thing cost a cool $450, I'd bet. It looked like the good-by testimonial book for a board chairman of ITT.

Connie was cool to me. They were thinking of moving her over to national side, the next progression. And it made me uncomfortable. I succeeded in controlling my thoughts of what a great screw she had been by convincing myself such recollections would be suicidal. She was too young to forgive me yet for being happy with another woman.

It wasn't long before my affair with Betty Page became known and I got a lot of long-nosed looks from prudes on and off the paper. With some justice, they felt it was unethical to pick up stories on someone while sleeping with his wife. But I wasn't going to rent a public forum to explain. And both of us were generally well enough liked, or sufficiently ignorable, so that gradually what talk there was died down.

The Frieden story, meanwhile, had proliferated. First, he was pressed to make a public accounting of all his holdings. When he demurred, some Democratic Congressmen threatened bills to require Presidential accountings of all their finances.

The Securities and Exchange prosecution quickly bogged down. But the vengeful Speaker, still anesthetizing himself daily in Wichita, cut the Kitticon transfer paper loose through a friend at the New York *Times*. Cubbins was heartsick that we hadn't gotten that goodie, too. The SEC cranked up for real.

Meanwhile, a state grand jury was hearing the Wichita land case where, it was clear, several county tax assessors had been bribed. The two trusts were in violation of some law in neighboring Oklahoma where the land trust had also done business, and the Speaker, now an ex-Congressman and his power dissipated, was called before an Oklahoma grand jury. He was fighting it under an out-of-state witness law.

Quiven was plea-bargaining on the political contribution. The sort of frankness he had shown to Mr. March and me on the telephone had been his downfall. A true schemer would have tried to pawn off the $20,000 as part of an employee fund, or simply his own personal contribution. But Quiven had acknowledged it was company funds, which put him in the way of a felony count. The prosecutor wanted to find a way to get him off with a misdemeanor.

The President, as we expected, gave up all thought of getting the $500,000, but not until the Speaker produced the document. That threw it back to Kitticon. The money was dirty now, and to put the best construction on it, particularly with the SEC breathing down his neck, Kitticon tried to give the stock to a band of deterritorialized Sioux. The Sioux council advised the band against it, and Kitticon was now looking for a more accepting charity.

All in all, it was going to be a bad time for Harry Frieden when election time came next year. The Democrats were already looking to regain control of the White House, and even of the House, what with the passing of the Speaker's mace to an honest, but weak, man from Illinois.

I worked the periphery of the story. My illness had gotten me behind, and I didn't want to kill myself, to be literal about it. Since the last stories entered for the Pulitzer were from before my illness (they cutely printed the heart-attack story as the last page of the nomination scrapbook), nothing I did or didn't do would matter now on the prize.

Mr. March and Cubbins figured that keeping me out

of trouble, thus in a state of apparent respectability, would serve them best. They were dying for the damned prize. For the *Eagle*, it had been a long, arid season. And the wanting had spread to me, too.

Anybody with any pull on the paper was pushing the Pulitzer bunch to hint at who was winning the thing. As it turned out, Cubbins got the first news, and the two of us went to Mr. March's office.

As we waited for him, I looked at the two helmets and thought of the fire and Connie, as we had been just before the fire bombs went through. I had my own helm in the apartment in the middle of the bookcase, with space around it so it stood out. Betty Page had been even less enthusiastic than Connie about my mounting her with the heaume on.

"You can put it on and go screw a horse," she'd said. "But I am not making love to a tin can."

Old March was proper toward me, but no more. Although I had cast off his daughter as he'd asked, and even had a heart attack at the same time to prove the daughter's worth, still . . .

Just then, Mr. March arrived and quickly asked Cubbins for the news.

"It looks like it'll go through the selection committee," Cubbins told him.

He explained that an ex-*Eagle* reporter, who'd edited a crusading chain of weeklies, gotten a Pulitzer ten years ago, and was now teaching at Ohio State, had been on the selection committee two years ago. Such judges had their own "old boys" network, and he'd heard some solid rumors.

"They got Aubrey through the first reading," Cubbins explained, "but there's going to be trouble on the board." The selection committee was made up of editors, most of whom would overlook a simple theft or even the rumors of adultery. Safecracking was something else, but still imaginable under the right circumstances.

The board was less permissive. A more academic group with the conservative view that newspapering was a profession rather than a craft, they had turned down Pearson and Anderson years ago when their exposé of a corrupt Senator was the obvious choice. They had not liked the smell of the muck the two men assiduously raked. Clearly, they would be even less taken with my safecracking.

"Who the Christ do we know on the board?" Mr. March said frantically. "Can your Ohio State man do anything for us? Is there any Senator . . . ?" He was thinking that we had gotten this far, and that if it took a little leverage from a Senator, a banker, or anybody else, he'd exert it. I knew that he wanted it so badly he wasn't above a bribe.

"We just have to hope," said Cubbins.

"We need ideas, not hope," he sneered. I wondered if the years would ever turn Connie into something like this, by turns an idealist and an ogre. "I want it. It's ours."

"Maybe we could blackmail them," I said dourly. I was disgusted.

Unflatteringly, Mr. March looked at me to see whether I was serious. He had his own crime in mind, however.

"If we could get the minutes of the selection committee, it would give us a strategy. Give us some modus for influencing these guys. Christ, I know everybody. If I can find out where the buttons are, I can check off these guys and get somebody whispering in their ears at a party. We're so Goddamned close."

"I can bust the safe and get the minutes," I volunteered sarcastically.

"You're going to get too damned smart, Aubrey," Mr. March attacked me. And maybe he was right. "I could have put the *paper* in for this thing, and it would have taken the curse off the safecracking, you know. It was me, I, who made the decision to put *you* in."

We ended by leaving the list of board members with Mr. March. I was sure he'd find some way of lobbying for it, and I didn't want to know.

A few weeks later, we found out. There was a beautiful irony in the way we learned. The news came from a cop, Knowles Irvin, my old friend in the Secret Service. He got me at home, calling from a bar.

"I ain't saying who this is," he said chipperly when I answered the phone. I racked my brains for his voice. It had been a long time. Since the President's Cuba trip. After I became poison with the FBI, Knowles had not even returned my calls.

"Okay," I said, "I make you for a cop."

"You know which one?"

"Yep."

"Then you know who this came from"—he would mean the President, overheard by an agent and passed on to Knowles. "You gonna get the Pulitzer."

"How hard?" I asked, gasping.

"Hard. Very hard."

"Oh, baby," I squealed. "Oh, baby. Thanks"—I started to say his name in my excitement. "Thanks, thanks, thanks. I owe you endless drinks in our old safe age."

"Congrats, shithead," he said. "You have it coming. Don't even *hint* where it came from, okay?"

"Thanks," I said again, and we hung up, and I said aloud, "My God, I got the Goddamn Pultizer Prize."

I called up Betty Page and swore her to secrecy and then March at home, and Cubbins, and Connie. I also called up Dinan Blathe, my Episcopal priest friend, because I saw God's hand in it and wanted to get some thanks up that way besides my own alien prayers of joy. Of them all, March was the most excited. Semi-hysterical with self-justification, pride in his paper, and delight at the honor I had brought it, he gave me a $2,000 raise on the spot.

Despite it all, I felt a pang, knowing how my wife would have been pleased by it. God, I said, get word to her, okay? Fuck it, I thought immediately, it's so maudlin. So let it be. "God," I said aloud, "thank you for the Pulitzer Prize and for so many good people in my life."

In a few days, it would leak out of the Pulitzer bunch

at Columbia, the way it always did when a controversial winner had been chosen. But, and I took a special pride in this, I had nailed the news up first—with a leak.

After the prize was formally announced, I became a very fashionable Aubrey Reporter. Three lecture bureaus took me on and began booking me on the college circuit and even to some trade groups, although not the American Petroleum Institute.

I got $1,500 per speech, but found out that the lecture bureaus charged 30 per cent off the top, and one even took the 30 per cent off before travel costs were deducted. I resolved to investigate the bastards as soon as my fad ended.

I also began getting invitations to Georgetown parties, a feeler from a newspaper syndicate to do a column five times a week, and numerous pleas from people around the country to help investigate their plights.

The painfully written letters about how the Veterans Administration, Social Security, lawyers, courts, and so on were screwing them weren't all that new. It was the flood of them that depressed me. I could not help the writers. The newspapers could not help them. And nobody else could, either. It gave me a Miss Lonelyhearts feeling, made me think of my inundated desk as a sort of Wailing Wall.

The Georgetown parties were enormous fun at first. Everyone oohed and ahhed at me, and the charm of these people was seductive. Money that isn't constantly being turned over sometimes puts a patina of niceness on its owners, and sometimes the niceness filters inward.

Some were cultured, amusing people. I found that the music I listened to at home was what they listened to, the books they read were the books I read, and the poetry I liked were poems about which they, unlike my newspaper friends, could talk familiarly. It was easy to fall into this siren world, and I wound up at the parties two, even three, times a week.

It was also damned flattering to have the Secretary of the Interior ask you whether you planned to write a book about it all, or to get a come-hither look from a Senate committee chairman's new wife.

Once, over caviar, not lumpfish, but fresh caviar, and some kind of special black-bread cracker, all served up on silver and good china, I looked up to see Betty Page watching me.

"Glut that sagging belly while you can," she said, coming to me. "Didn't the doctor tell you about all the salt in caviar?" I popped the caviar in my mouth and took her hand.

"Ummyummm," I answered her, then with the thing swallowed. "They're really nice people, liberal, all that. You're just a cynical old lady who's seen it all."

"I sure did," she said. "What happens when one of them starts feeding you stuff about somebody else in this bunch, the way they do when they trust you?"

"So what's so bad about that? I blow the guilty one out of the water. These are good sources. . . ."

"You become the servant to their vendettas."

"Oh, they're not that bad, Betty Page," I said, but I knew what she meant.

Predictably, Georgetown dropped me before I could drop them. My rival lion was a conservative Supreme Court Justice who had sided with the liberals to reverse a recent repressive decision against the press.

I respected the guy because the ruling made it easier for me to avoid testifying about sources, but he was a pompous horse's ass. A good-looking British gossip reporter he'd been making had gotten enough inside dope while on her back with him, or knees, to do a vixenish piece on the vagaries of her Justice-lover's fellows on the bench. ("Justice Bennoit keeps himself from nodding in the court's secret sessions by industriously and expertly picking his nose.") Even by Fleet Street standards, it was sleazy stuff.

Her own Justice came out as a supersachem. I knew of the liaison because the male reporter she'd been balling at the same time was an old friend, and he put me under no strictures about the Justice. It was a Georgetown mess, sick and squirmy.

At a party, I had nastily whispered about the Justice and the British girl to my hostess. I'm not sure why I did it, maybe to curry favor in order to look better-informed than anyone else. It was one of those compulsive things I did sometimes, like talking about cancer with a man whose wife had just died of it. When I turned, I saw the Justice right behind me.

"Many happy returns on the First Amendment, Aubrey," he said, showing all the class I lacked. "Next time," he laughed with a tuned chill, "remind me to vote the other way."

The invitations tapered off. Then, too, my Pulitzer was now two months old. I didn't belong up there in Georgetown, and it wasn't all their fault. My feelings were hurt, but Betty Page thought it was funny.

Summer came, and Jay, the Edwards' son, went to stay with his father, after much promising of reform from Pom. He'd gotten the drinking down to no worse than in his regular Washington days, and besides there wasn't much she could do to block Jay, short of taking Pom to court. It gave Betty Page and me an easy freedom.

I'd banked most of the Pulitzer money, but splurged some of it on having the Morgan repaired, and repainted, into perfect condition. Early on a Saturday, we took off for Spruce Run, the old country inn I'd gone to with my wife years ago.

I picked up Betty Page at her new, smaller house near Kalorama Circle. Tennis had browned her face, and the wrinkles showed whitely. Her hair, where it showed from under the bandana, was bleached from the sun.

The trees were full, heavy with the heat. At her temples, there was a glistening of sweat on the cosmetic-less skin. I peered at her intently, pleased as I always was that she looked younger than her years, and that she always would. With a little pang I thought of Connie. I might be starting off on a week's trip with her. But when all was said and done, it was the years that had ended our affair—that formula I had run over so often.

Betty Page caught my stare and looked both quizzical

and flustered, reaching to her hair as if that is what I had been gazing at.

"You think I'm getting old," she said.

"No," I said, grateful to her for being slightly wrong in a way that my correcting her would give her pleasure. "I was thinking that when I turn fifty-nine you will be fifty-five and that you will still be beautiful."

"And—?" she asked, pleased, walking the one step to where I stood by the shining fender of the Morgan.

"And that I am glad that is the way the formula works instead of—"

"You keeping company with somebody nineteen."

"Well, nineteen would be *too* young." That was as close as I would ever come to telling her about Connie.

"Onward, onward," she said, now nudging me to get into the car. It started with the roar of a good, aging sports car newly tuned.

We crept through the sulphur and carbon streets of the city to Rhode Island Avenue, where the long, double street at last let me get the car moving. The hot wind felt less gritty on our faces.

It was still mostly fields, ugly road signs, and ugly cities until we were north of Harrisburg. Then, to our right, the Susquehanna spread out eastward, and we dreamed of taking a canoe trip all the way down from Jersey Shore. I said, "Well, look, why don't we plan it now. Maybe . . ."

It didn't really matter whether we ever did or not, because seeing the smooth water and the riffles, we could imagine it. Farther north was Lewisburg, and way off to westward I saw the blunt tower of the federal penitentiary. Once, disguised as a lawyer's assistant, I had visited there to interview a prisoner. With bad luck, I mused, I could have wound up there, framed by the Speaker. Except he was no longer the Speaker.

"Over there's the penitentiary," I said to her. Shorter than I, and the car low anyway, she craned her neck, but that one view of it was now obscured by the woods between us and the tower. I knew she was thinking somewhat the same thought I had thought, for a little farther along, she said:

"The case?"

It was down to a solid offer for me to plead to destruction of private property. My agreement to plead to something had wangled Drosnahan off entirely. Besides the prosecutor was reluctant to push the case now that it had produced the Speaker's defeat and its corollary prosecution of the prosecutor's star witness, Quiven.

For me to plead to the misdemeanor, it only remained for Mrs. Murtry to get some assurance from the judge that he would not jail me or fine me more than $500.

"In the old days," I told Betty Page, "you could just buy a judge. Now, you don't pay him, you just negotiate with him. It's damn near as demeaning as buying him."

"Pom could still find you the right judge in any state in the union," she said with a sort of pride.

The hills had begun. We turned off toward Jersey Shore, into the mountains, following the narrower roads until we got into the valley of Pine Creek, more river than creek. Now the coolness came, and the pines and deciduous trees marched steeply upward from the road. The cool woods smelled of wet ferns, freshened with springs from up the mountainside.

"Away," she said, reaching over and gripping my leg lightly. "We're away. Aubrey Reporter and his girlfriend, Doggrelist." Away, but where to?

"Maybe, now," I said, "I'll really quit. I mean quit my kind of reporting." She never nagged me about it any more, did not, I guess, see it as so much of a threat, particularly now that she was thinking more of her own independence. And I also suspected that her lack of discomfort was partly because the Pulitzer had made me a bit more respectable, not so respectable as a Speaker's wife, even a Speaker's betrayed wife, but still, a heavier person than a mere gumshoe.

"Suit yourself," she said mildly.

"Buying a little paper would just be more work than now," I said. "But writing editorials, or if they'd let me do just a couple of columns a week. Of course, I don't write all that well, but—"

"You know," she speculated without suggesting, "if

we did get married, decide to, we've got enough put by between us so we could live on damned little work at all. I could pick up a few thousand a year lobbying for some cause or running some little trade group, and you could pull in ten, fifteen thousand in articles or on a book."

We'd been over it before. It never stopped being inviting, and now outside of the city, it all seemed so logical.

"Catch up on reading, screwing, traveling—"

"Funny order of priorities," she said.

"It seems so possible, doesn't it?"

The land was now depopulated. Beside the narrow woods were hunting lodges all locked up. There were a few upland farms, laid out neatly on odd-shaped fields that caught the sun.

Once all this country had been great spruce and hemlock and pine, and it had been timbered right down to the raw earth, the raped logs floated downcreek to Jersey Shore. The state had bought the naked land and let it grow back, and so it was a thick forest of second growth now, not majestic, its mountains low and rounded, but remote.

Spruce Inn was in a town of fourteen people winter population which swelled to sixty during the summer and was engorged with a hundred and fifty hunters in the winter deer season.

Since the time I had been there, the proprietor had handsomely repainted the plankings of the three-story building with its long veranda, all settling slightly. Inside were the big and little parlors, each with relics from the timber days when the town had been a significant rail stop.

There was a fine Chickering piano, and antique cabinets, a polished-brass oilman's can with a plaque, the inscription long rubbed off. In a glass-front cupboard was a set of china plates with "Reading Railroad" on flags unfurled among the faint, dancing bergers and bergères.

I had made reservations for us as man and wife. A moderate Pennsylvania Dutch streak seemed to permeate both the employees and guests, nothing so strict as the Amish, yet still illiberal about such things as grown-ups screwing out of wedlock.

That evening, the energetic proprietor lent us his old pickup equipped with a hand spotlight, and we drove up the dirt roads "spotting deer." My Morgan would never have gotten over the ruts, but the pickup bobbed and bounced along the mountain roads.

From time to time, Betty Page spotted the shining eyes of a deer. Then we saw its shadowy, stately form return to its grazing or, striated by the dark trunks of trees, tread off deeper into the woods. I could not see how a man could shoot a deer. Easier shoot a man.

How good I felt the next morning. There was neither soot in the air, nor newspaper to report to, nor worry about whether my story had been profaned by some slopjar typographer.

"Hey," I said softly to Betty Page's sleeping face, itself so innocent and beautiful beside me. "Hey, wake-up time in the mountains. Time for the bird walk."

We'd brought the fat *National Geographic* bird book her older son had left at home, and walked diligently up a trail the state men had hewn to a mountain look-out. I stopped every few yards, getting winded rapidly, and careful, careful.

After lunch, slightly drowsy with the walk and the food, we went upstairs and took a shower, soaping each other with bay rum soap on a string—my small splurge for our trip.

Thinking now so often of marriage, I looked assessingly at her body. And I could tell from the way she squeezed my stomach, which had softened from the lack of exercise after the heart attack, that she was thinking something similar.

"It's like a couple of horse traders looking at teeth, and under the tail and into the ears, isn't it?" she said, smiling at me from under the shower. Her damp hair, cut long, clung to her head, making her look shorter, different, but oddly no less attractive. I squeezed the flesh of her arm.

"Yes," I said. "Only better. You're a very sexy mare."

I reached down and soaped her labia, knowing it was just an excuse to feel them. I thought of that wild day in the bathroom where I had gone crawling across the floor after her. With my finger, I felt the groove of her outer lips.

"A slot machine that always comes up cherries," I said.

"Oh God," she laughed in mock horror. "What an awful thing to say. What a thoroughly piggish thing to say."

We dried each other, and I raised the window, feeling a rush as the cool from the creek and the mountainside enveloped my warm body. In that light breeze was the smell of herbs, slate in the sunshine, the faintest touch of something dead by the creek or in the woods, lilac and the renewing pines.

"Ah, Betty Page," I sighed, caught up in the perfection of it, perfection of everything this one time. Her face was still damp from the shower when I reached to touch her cheek.

I kissed her, moving my hands to touch her shoulders and her back, feeling down her backbone, each nubby bone.

I let it wash over me, so happy to be away where there were no demands but what I put on myself or what she put on me. We turned from the window, and she pulled on over her head a short cotton gown.

There was the swell of her breasts below the ruffled yolk, and her legs seemed stubby sticking from the bottom of the frilled hem. Yet, how young she seemed, her hair towel-dried and then the towel turbaned on her head.

"What's all this clothes?" I said. "Eve in the fig leaf?"

Naked as I was, and with her feeling so sleek, I passioned quickly, gently lifting the cotton gown. The oval mirror of the old dressing table reflected us, our heads cut off by the tilt of it.

Her legs were brown, shapely, and mine were hairy and pale. At my waist the meat rubbered out. I was bending slightly, pressing my cheek to hers, both of us staring now in the mirror, and I saw how my chest had slipped to my gut.

Yet, it was unutterably sexy, there in this clean, silent room. I pulled slightly apart from her, ran my hand along her inner leg. In the mirror, she watched its path, my hand on the tanned leg, then across the border to the pure whiteness where the sun had not reached.

I cupped her mount for a moment in my hand, then broke our embrace and slipped my index finger gently into her, looking up briefly to see her fascination. I had never watched anything like this before, and it was making my heart throb.

She had a light grip on me, and I felt overheated. The gentle half-moon of her belly began to move back and forth to force my finger. Of a sudden, she slicked up.

I glanced in the mirror at my stupid, tensed face, thinking how silly it looked all aglow with lust, and her face, too, had the wooden look of old German wood carvings, stylized and thus unnatural, yet reflecting perfectly the one expression the artist was attempting to portray: in this case, not spiritual but physical passion.

"Oh, Betty Page," I said, looking now at her instead of the mirror. "It's so good, so good." She swung in hard against me, fiercely kissing my lips, and I thought, this is more than any oompah band. I crouched so she could slip me into her, but it was too awkward this way, although it also looked marvelously sexy in the old mirror.

"It's so much better than a dirty movie," she gasped, without meaning it to be funny. I laughed, limpened a moment at that thought, but I was too heavy into the passion now to reflect.

We stumbled to the bed, fell into it, and I moved fully on top of her. She pushed me off for the moment it took to grab the pillow from the top of the bed and slip it under her.

I lifted the clean cotton nightie above her breasts, noting again happily how they still rounded up from her chest though she was on her back. Firm tits, I thought. They'll stand the gaff. Trading horses, I thought. The idea got me slightly back from the brink of orgasm.

To keep from coming, I dropped down on her body. I kissed her breasts slowly, tonguing the nipples into hardness, as she rubbed her labia against me.

For a moment, I thought, maybe I shouldn't be doing this, maybe I shouldn't let go this way with my heart the way it is. But there rattled through my mind the familiar folk wisdom that the only time men die in the sack from screwing is when the sex is illicit. And I did not regard this as anything but honorable.

I moved off her for a moment, slipping my arm all the way under her body between her legs, so I could feel her rubbing her quiff on my forearm. She had stopped touching me except gently on the shoulders.

"You there?" I panted.

"Almost," she said.

She veed out her legs, and I crouched between her. There was a fumble of hands, momentary panic as I missed the first try, then slipped into her body. We were kissing each other frantically, knowing it was going to be just right, and wanting everything there was that we could get out of it.

Our lips together, I heard her throat noises. Then, bam, I started pulsing. I had to break from her lips to free my gasp of release. I held hard into her, and she arched her body up from the pillows to keep the tension.

When it was done, she swiveled, still tensed slightly, to get what pleasure there was left in the friction. I kissed her gently, feeling her soft breath still coming briskly.

"We are a pair of very passionate senior citizens," I said.

"Are you okay?" she asked, worried now about my heart.

"God, yes," I said.

Then, in each other's arms, we slipped toward dozing.

One day, I thought, we might marry, but meanwhile

how good this was. Maybe, she would simply stay independent, and why not? We loved each other, and at this stage of our lives it was easier for her, and not all that hard for me, to do without being married. Her younger son would be away at school in the fall, and we could stay with each other or not, as we chose.

But whatever, whatever, how good it was now.

I opened one eye a crack and saw the curtains rustling. The sunlight hit their whiteness with a glare, then, as they stirred, there were ripplings of brightness and shadow in the curtains.

As if it moved purposefully across the room, the wind then touched my body. I had not realized how sweaty we were until I felt the light breeze on my skin and ran my finger along Betty Page's moist back.

Soon the sun would dip down behind the mountains, and the room would become genuinely chilly, and if we had not already done so, we might get up and go to supper, or we might just stay.

And in the morning there would be a breakfast of scrambled eggs and breaded fallfish—silver chub we called them when I was a boy—and toast with butter and brown ceramic mugs of steaming milk flavored with strong coffee and sugar.

Then, *gli enigmi sono tre:* we could hike up the trail, slowly, to the Algerines marsh, then back in time for a late lunch; or we could borrow gear and try, as I had so many years ago, for the bass that I knew lay deep under the riffles where Spruce Run fanned out into Pine Creek; or our bodies luxurious with food, we could go upstairs and brush our teeth and go back to bed, sleeping away the morning, our window open on the mountain and its heavy green furze of second growth.

"*Gli enigmi sono tre,*" I whispered to her dozing face, remembering with pride now where the phrase came from: Turandot. She stirred, raising her lips slightly toward mine.

The room's only concession to modernism was its dialless telephone. Now, it rang. I wanted to think it was the proprietor questioning us about supper, but I knew it was not.

It was Cubbins.

"Aubrey," he said, "I swear to God I hate to bother you. The fucking Speaker has conned Emerson Quiven" —my God, this is going to be about Bounty Oil, I thought—"into talking with you about an even sleazier deal the President pulled. I mean, you know, this could be the one. . . . Could you call Quiven, and if he agrees . . . ?"

I put down the telephone. I felt the old tightening in my stomach over a new, big story, another real pisser. If I didn't get to it first, then the *Times*, or Mintz at the *Post* . . .

I sat on the bed and leaned to kiss her.

"Christ!" she said.

"How do you like night driving?" I replied.

WE DELIVER!
And So Do These Bestsellers.

RELAX!
SIT DOWN
and Catch Up On Your Reading!

Bantam Book Catalog

Here's your up-to-the-minute listing of every book currently available from Bantam.

This easy-to-use catalog is divided into categories and contains over 1400 titles by your favorite authors.

So don't delay—take advantage of this special opportunity to increase your reading pleasure.

Just send us your name and address and 25¢ (to help defray postage and handling costs).